# Celluloid & Tinsel

A Thornton King Adventure

# By The Same Author

Books:

Angel
The Museum Mysteries and Other Short Stories
The Journeys We Make
Dead On Time: A Thornton King Adventure
Just In Case: Another Thornton King Adventure
Dead On Target: A Further Thornton King Adventure
The Cinelli Vases: A Thornton King Adventure
No Official Umbrella: An Autobiography
Doctor Who & The Space Museum
The Double Deckers
Hildegarde H. And Her Friends
–Illustrated By Arnold Taraborrelli

Plays Published:

Beautiful For Ever
Champagne Charlie: A Music Hall Entertainment
Generations
Oh Brother!
Peter Pan: A Musical Fantasy
Red In The Morning
Rosemary
The 88
Third Drawer From The Top
Thriller Of The Year
Women Around

# Celluloid & Tinsel

## Glyn Idris Jones

Published by
Douglas Foote

ISBN 978-1-909381-00-1

www.douglasfoote.com

# Prologue

The plan, as all plans are, was perfect and she had it down to a T, knowing exactly what she was going to do. Just as Max the day gate keeper's shift was ending she'd give him a hoot on the horn and a cheery wave to make sure she was seen. She would then drive to the village, giving him enough time to get well out of the way, and then drive back and park close to the studio. By that time sleepyhead Ted would already be on the gate and away with the fairies, especially if he had been a while in the boozer before clocking in. The only time sleepyhead Ted woke up during the late night shift was if a car hooted, night security clocked on or, at two in the morning his rumbling stomach told him it was time to open his lunch tin. She would be able to walk passed him unnoticed and leave the same way. She had checked that there would be no night shooting and so the studio would be empty; she could take her time.

Not wanting to draw attention to herself, and rather than waiting in her car she decided to have a cup of coffee at the local café, which would give Max plenty of time to leave and Ted enough time to doze off but the minutes seemed to drag as she nursed her drink. And the more that the minutes dragged the tetchier her nerves became.

Mavis hovered by the serving hatch waiting to pounce on the young woman sitting in the bay window of the teatime café and clear away the coffee cup and plate before she left for the evening, but the young woman gave no indication that she wanted to leave. Mavis looked at her watch. Ten minutes to six. Officially the café closed at six thirty, but Mavis hoped to leave a bit earlier and this young woman was spoiling her plans. Mavis busied herself with stacking the clean cups ready for the morning, banging as loudly as she could to alert the young woman that the café was about to close.

Finally the young woman placed the cup onto the saucer, stood up and started to put on her coat. Mavis not wanting to let an opportunity go by or anything stop her from leaving, dashed to the table and grabbed the cup and saucer and, dropping a curtsy, she scurried back to the kitchen to wash up the offending articles and put on her outside coat ready for the off.

The young woman smiled and said thank you before she made her way out of the café and back to her car. It was only a 5 min drive back to Breconfield Studios. She stopped at one of the side roads just a short walk from the main gate. Better that she could slip passed sleepyhead Ted in case the car woke him up.

Wrapping her mac around herself she quickly crossed back to the main road and headed for the front gates of the studios. As she had planned Ted was slumped in a comfy chair in the corner of the gate house. Through the window the glow from the electric fire was enough light to show that he was asleep. She slipped passed the barrier and the closed door of the gatehouse and made her way across the open parking lot to the main building.

She fumbled in her pocket for the key she had been given. What if it didn't work, what would she do then? In her haste she nearly dropped the key but eventually her trembling fingers turned the key in the lock and the large heavy oak doors of the Breconfield Studios building slowly opened. Once inside she knew where she was going, her own office was off in the east wing, down one of the long corridors which ran the length of the building. But tonight she was headed in a different direction. There was no need for her to turn on any lights, there was enough light from the emergency exit signs and from the lights outside the windows to guide her to the executive offices.

Crossing the large lobby area she reached the bottom of the stairs when a noise caught her attention. She stopped to listen. Maybe somebody had followed her. But why? Only one person knew that she would be here and he wouldn't have said anything, in fact he was the reason she *was* here. That and the money of course. No she thought, her nerves were playing tricks.

At the head of the stairs was a large window which cast light virtually to where she was standing. One step would take her out of the shadows and into the light. She hesitated. Finally, not hearing anything more, she pressed herself against the wall and slowly started to climb the stairs. As she neared the landing the view from the window would give her a clear view of the car park below and the main entrance gate. If anybody had followed her she would see them from here.

Stopping in front of the window she looked out. Nothing. Nada. Nicth. She laughed nervously to herself and took three large breathes in an effort to calm down. Just then something touched the back of her legs.

Her scream could be heard on the other side of the paint and plaster workshop. She ran the remaining steps to the first floor her heart pounding before turning around to look at her assailant. Samson the studio cat sat in front of the window looking up at her.

She slumped against the wall and dropped to sit on the top step laughing at herself, a nervous laugh to relieve the tension.

Mel Preston that genius of the film world (or so he liked to think) was pouring over the accounts of his latest film *The*

*Return to Batani*, not to be confused with the 1954 masterpiece *The Guns at Batasi* starring Richard Attenbourgh. His office was dark except for a pool of light over his large oak desk. Figures swam before his eyes as he took a swig of his bourbon. Why had he become a producer? He should have stayed a director. He could do a better job than the prick who he had hired. He was already doing most of the directing anyway. But producing was where the money was, and Mel needed money.

So he sweated over the three sets of books that he kept. One in the office for official reasons, showing a loss, the second for the Tax Office also showing a loss and the third, the real set, for himself. He took another swig of bourbon. Then he heard a scream. So unexpected he knocked over his glass spilling its contents over the books.

'Shit!' he yelled as he tried to mop up the liquid from the page. 'Shit. Shit shit shit shit!' He managed to dry most of what was spilled with his hankie. No real harm done. But what was that scream? There should be no one here tonight. There was no scheduled shooting. Maybe someone was rehearsing a scene. Maybe that prick of a director was trying to lay one of the millions of young hopefuls that always hang around movie studios. Even so they shouldn't be here and he shouldn't be here, although technically he was working late and no one would question him, though they might find the other sets of books. He quickly closed the ledgers and stuffed them into the top drawer of his desk. He had better find out just who was in the studio.

After waiting a couple of minutes to ascertain if she had been caught out and having, more or less  recovered enough from her fright, the young woman made her way along the corridor. Her footsteps silent on the thick heavy carpet. Luckily it would seem no one had heard her scream. She stopped at a large panelled door with the words *Courtney Burrows II* embossed on a brass plate. She again fumbled through the keys she had been given. This also worked beautifully. The door opened into a large expensively furnished and decorated office, all oak panelling and heavy dark furniture. She knew exactly where she was meant to be. Making her way across the room to a large portrait of a strikingly beautiful woman wearing a diamond necklace, tiara, earrings and bracelet, she slide her hand behind the picture and found the clasp which released with a small click a catch and the picture swung forward.

Everything was as he had explained. She didn't need the piece of paper with the combination on it but not trusting herself she read the numbers once more by the light filtering through the large bay window.

'6 right, 24 left, 14 left, 23 right, 16 left,' she mouthed as she rotated the dial in front of her.

Click. The safe door sprung open.

Her heart started to beat faster once again. What would she find? There was the usual documents and contracts etc, nothing of great interest, at least not for her. A small amount of cash, but not enough to warrant taking and alerting those in the know that there had been a break in. She was looking for a set of ledgers. Nothing.

She went through the pile of papers and files again. Nothing. Then she noticed that one of the brown card files contained some old black and white photos. She knew who these people were. They all worked or had worked here at the studio. At the bottom of the stack was a piece of paper on which somebody had been doodling a hangman and written across the page was a name. Mel Preston.

She thought for a moment. Mel Preston. What could he have in common with all these pictures most of which had been taken while he was a young boy? And why the hanged man? Maybe she should check his office.

She quickly returned all the files into the safe except the one with the photos, and closed the safe door and closed the picture. Leaving the office she locked the door and made her way to the east wing of the building and her own office and that of Mel Preston.

Quietly she opened the door. It wasn't locked. "Strange," she thought.

Although she had already searched Mel's office and found nothing, that piece of paper had intrigued her. What did it mean? She made her way around to the front of Mel's desk and tried various drawers. In the top drawer she saw the accounts ledgers.

He heart started thumping again. How did they come to be here? She carefully removed them from the drawer as if they were fragile porcelain figures and placed them on the desk in front of her.

She was so engrossed in what she was doing she didn't hear the door open or someone enter the room.

Max alighted from the number 17 bus at the corner of Hazelhurst and Mapleton road. A two minute walk took him up Mapleton and across the main road to the gates and another days work at the studio. Three quarters of the way up Mapleton he walked passed her car. He was a couple of feet away before he realized whose car it was.

Max wondered why her car was parked outside the studio. He hadn't noticed it the night before and it seemed weird to say the least. Was she in the studio at this hour? If so, why? And why hadn't she parked inside at her usual spot? Maybe Sleepyhead Ted was dead to the world and she had decided to leave it here instead. He retraced his steps and made a closer inspection of the car, noting the key was still in the ignition. Maybe she had car trouble and couldn't get it to start. But then if that were the case all she had to do was call rescue. It was all very strange, but Max was not one to mentally ponder too long on a problem and decided he had better investigate further so he opened her car door, slipped into the driving seat and turned on the ignition. There was no problem. The car immediately purred into life. He slipped it into gear and drove for the studio gate. He could see Sleepyhead Ted fast asleep at his post and gave him a blast on the horn. Ted didn't move. He gave him another blast. Still Ted didn't move. A thoroughly irate Max got out of the car and went to lift the barrier, leaving it up as he drove through and parked in her allotted space. There was something very odd going on so just to make sure he wouldn't be connected with it in any way he took out his hankie and gave the steering wheel a good wipe and, for good measure, both door handles when he got out. There was no reason for him not at some point to have driven her car but better safe than sorry.

# Chapter One

Friday, and it would be the thirteenth wouldn't it? The end of another totally barren week: arid you might even call it. Summer was officially over but it was unseasonably warm for the time of year and the office of Thornton King, private investigator, might just as well have been in the middle of the Sahara, the Kalahari, or the Gobi Desert; any desert for that matter, for all the business that came its way.

The telephone lay silent on his desk and had been like that all day. He thought for a moment of calling *TIM*, not to find out the time, he already knew that, but just to hear a voice, even a recorded one. *At the third stroke it will be five thirty five exactly, Pip Pip Pip. At the third stroke…* Or maybe he would call Holly only, as sure as God made little green apples as his mother always said, it was bound to be a bad time to phone. He had a serious knack of always calling her at inopportune moments, like when she was engrossed in her favourite television programme.

He looked around the office for the umpteenth time as though he didn't know in detail every aspect of it, every spot on the wall, every cobweb, every crack, every bit of peeling paint, and there really wasn't much else to see: his battered old grey metal filing cabinet surplus to government requirements, that looked for all the world as if it had been dropped from a tall building. There wasn't much in it, just some empty folders at the ready in the top drawer waiting to be used and in the next one down half a bottle of his favourite whisky, *Famous Grouse*. The others were jammed fast and unusable. On top there sat a kettle on a metal tray that had once displayed the *Guinness* toucan but most of the illustration had been worn away though you could still see the beak if you looked hard enough. There was of course also milk and sugar for brewing up coffee and tea, all under a damp tea cloth in case there were any flies about.

Then there was the desk at which he sat, also ex-government surplus, not much in its drawers either apart from stationery; and a chair opposite for any clients who might just happen to pop in. There was also an old electric heater inherited from his parents' house when they had central heating installed. The summer of '74, had been a hot one for a change so there had been no need to use it but in winter, even though it would go through power like there was no tomorrow, probably because of the damp that caused running condensation on the windows, it did very little to actually heat the room, and the electricity bill seemed to get bigger and bigger every time it was shoved into his mailbox. Had it landed on a mat it would have landed, he thought, with a mighty thud. He eventually got around to paying it when the reminder arrived in red. Thornton thought it financially prudent not to pay bills until the very last moment. If he had been an eighteenth century member of the aristocracy his tailor would have died destitute and starving.

If ever he got seriously rich he would make sure his next office was *en suite* as well so that he didn't have to walk a mile down a dark chilly corridor in winter to an even chillier loo, lavatory, toilet, john, bathroom, whatever you want to call it, every time he was in need of a pee. It was always a wonder Percy could be found let alone be encouraged to point at the porcelain. He would be prepared to give his extremities, an arm and a leg, for a warm loo.

He really ought to get some pictures for the bare walls he decided, that might brighten the place up a little, a couple of those cheap mass produced oils you could get at *Woolworths* for next to nothing, highly colourful landscapes but hardly what one thinks of as works of art. He had previously contemplated that idea when visiting the unfortunate deceased drug dealer's shop in Westbourne Grove but had immediately forgotten it; not abandoned the idea, just forgot about it or never got around to it which amounts to the same thing.

He didn't really know why he kept an expensive, for what it was, office in the centre of London, a stone's throw from Tottenham Court Road and Oxford Street. He could just as well carry on business, if there was any, from his flat in Victoria Park, his landlady being Her gracious Maj, the Queen of England as he never tired of telling people, but maybe it would be too difficult for punters to find and would more than likely be forbidden by the terms of his lease, so the office it had to be, only his world seemed devoid of punters.

Right now, having finished once more the survey of his almost bare domain, for Thornton King, ex-secret service, now private eye, the day was over and he was about to put up the shutters, metaphorically speaking, and make his way home to Hackney.

Having attempted on and off all day to do *The Times* crossword puzzle and having solved no more than three clues which, you have to admit wasn't saying much for a private detective but was around his daily average, he had given up; but then he always maintained you needed a special weird kind of mind to do crossword puzzles, the kind of mind that solved ciphers and unravelled codes. Holly was an absolute wiz at them: could get through one in ten minutes flat; seven letter words, nine letter words, eleven letters, answers in three parts, see twelve across, see seventeen down, no matter how obscure and arcane the answer she was sure to get it. She also invariably won by a handsome margin when playing scrabble. Maybe women were just better at that sort of thing or maybe it was part of her training as a valued member of Her Maj's secret service. But then he had also been a member for a number of years, obviously not so valued, and a fat lot of good the experience had done him when it came to crossword puzzles or games of any kind for that matter. He couldn't even win at Cluedo. Spies would have been a different matter had he ever come across any.

He looked at his watch. Almost time to call it a day, almost the rush hour. There was a discreet knock on the office door. He was looking forward to a pint in his favourite pub that kept on changing its Irish barmen: they came; they went, never to be seen or heard of again. Maybe it was a case of the mountains of Mourn that roll invitingly down to the sea, and when they discovered London's streets weren't paved with gold after all, back to the mountains they went; but he couldn't afford to turn away a potential client so he called out to whoever it was to enter, the door wasn't locked. He didn't add that the door couldn't lock anyway and wouldn't lock until he felt secure enough financially to call in a locksmith. He wasn't what you might call a dab-hand at do-it-yourself and these days call-outs of any kind be they electrician, plumber, or locksmith could prove very costly indeed.

True he had solved two cases for well paying clients but that was over a period of time and bill bills bills; they kept coming in. It was seemingly a never ending tide. The bank balance was forever being depleted and there were those minuscule matters like income tax to pay and, unless something happened soon to alleviate the position, he would once more be in the red to the satisfied smirk of his vulpine bank manager who always wore the expression of "I see you are overdrawn again, Mister King," or words to that effect with an upward inflexion on the Mister King if he actually said it. He was terrified of his bank manager and always hoped when he went to the bank that the man would be out to lunch or busy elsewhere or preferably locked in a vault on a time switch. Even when he gave that look from a fair distance it put the wind up Thornton King and it always took him by surprise when he received his monthly bank balance just how much money he had gone through. Where does it go? It wasn't because he was a spendthrift, far from it. Certainly he liked the occasional comfort, the occasional small indulgence, but it was only occasional.

Though he enjoyed his food he simply wasn't the oysters, caviar and champagne type. Nightclubbing held no fascination for him, he felt they were the next best thing to Dante's inferno, and his philosophy was you can only sleep in one bed at a time so what's the point of owning half a dozen homes scattered across the globe together with the enormous expense of their upkeep? The world is well supplied with more than adequate hotels. But his finances were like the Indian rope trick. The magician plays the pipes; the boy scrambles up the rope and disappears, so it was with his money. He kept on meaning to jot down a daily account but, like a diet or a New Year's resolution, the endeavour was still-born or died shortly after.

He was in the act of tossing the day's folded newspaper into the waste bin beneath his desk to join the unsolicited mail and the boxed bony remains of a takeaway chicken dinner when there was a firmer knock on the door. "Don't tell me," he thought, "that a camel is about to cross my desert." Whoever it was had obviously not heard his previous invitation to enter so he repeated it rather loudly.

The door opened and somewhat to his surprise his visitor turned out to be a blue rinse granny; whole flocks of which are to be found in retirement enjoying their deceased husbands' pensions and insurances in the Florida sunshine.

She was wearing a very smart and expensive looking, which in fact was what it was, light wool two piece suit in a powder blue, possibly to match her hair, sensible brown shoes, obviously also expensive, her figure as slim as a young girl's, no trace of a widow's stoop, arthritis, liver spots or any other infirmity that afflicts the elderly and, to complete the picture he would find she had something else he found rather attractive, just a hint of an alluring trans-Atlantic accent. The only jarring item was the large bag she carried, rather like a carrier bag and looking as if it were made from a brown rexine much creased by age and constant use. Obviously she could carry it with the straps over a shoulder but what kind of an excuse was that?

'Mister King I presume?' The voice was full, resonant, and fruity.

"Who else?" Thornton thought, being the only person in view. It was hardly likely that Doctor Livingstone would be discovered in his office but, being the gentleman he was, he got to his feet to answer her.

'Good evening, madam,' he said. He had a very pleasing voice as well when he chose to use it. It had been remarked on more than once. He felt sometimes he must have had some Welsh in his ancestry. 'Please do come in,' which wasn't exactly the right thing to say either as the good lady, he presumed she was a good lady or she wouldn't be visiting him, bringing with her just the faintest hint of a delicate perfume, was already well into the room, in fact virtually at his desk, 'and take a seat,' he added, indicating with an open hand the visitor's chair on the far side of the desk.

His old chair that had always been in that position since he started up in practice had finally given up its woody ghost. Perhaps that was due to the size and avoirdupois of his previous client, one Aurora Pemberton known affectionately as Rory who, together with woodworm, had been the cause of it becoming somewhat dangerously loose and wobbly at its joints and no amount of glue was going to remedy the situation. Rory did have a tendency when stressed to need a sugar high and gorged herself on doughnuts, the stickier the better. No, the chair had definitely passed its usefulness and was a danger to limb if not life and he was quite pleased with his new one. Well, to be accurate, it wasn't new exactly, it was second hand and he had bought it for three pounds from an enormous furniture depository just behind the Euston Road that had stacks of everything a household might need and more.

The chair was rather solid with a high back and arm rests.

Rory certainly wouldn't have been able to get into it, the arm rests would ensure that but then, having solved the murder of her very rich uncle; Thornton was hardly likely to see Rory again so it really didn't matter. If she did put in an appearance for whatever purpose they could always adjourn to his favourite pub. He had tested a few chairs before deciding on this one and he had purchased an inexpensive cushion from an Indian fabric shop down Whitechapel way to place on the seat. It had an appropriate design of camels on it, well what could pass for camels; you could tell that from the hump.

After dusting off the cushion with a handkerchief, removed from her sleeve and replaced there, his visitor sat down. Thornton, taking his own seat, was slightly put out by this. It was a brand new cushion and he thought it rather rude but maybe she had a bad experience once and was now rather eccentric when it came to cushions and chairs.

'Now, what is it I can do for you?' He asked. He had narrowed his eyes slightly to indicate his disapproval but she didn't seem to notice.

'Spring van Clef,' the lady said, staring him full in the face with eyes that once must have been of a startlingly vivid blue but now seemed to have lost a little of their glitter, as though spring, or van, or clef or all three together should mean something to him. Her stare, despite the diminishing in colour, was still quite fierce and a little disconcerting.

'I beg your pardon?'

'That is my name, my stage name that is. You obviously haven't heard of me. I am an actress.'

'Ah, yes, I might have known, from the carriage, from the voice.' He made a rather floppy circular gesture with one hand.

'Yes, I am known as Spring van Clef. My real name, not that it matters is Esther Huntington nee Fartfooker.'

Thornton swallowed hard, averted his gaze, bit his cheek and did his best not to look startled. He was hoping against hope the phone would ring to divert attention. It remained stubbornly silent.

'Yes I know,' the lady said, having watched the movement of his Adam's apple and not being taken in by the assumed urbanity. He refocused on her with some difficulty. 'It doesn't sound too good in English I agree but it is in fact a very ancient and honourable German Yiddish name and one I should be proud of but can you imagine for one moment that name on a marquee or in lights? People in the film industry, though so many of them are Jewish themselves, just look down a list of credits and you will see what I mean, do not accept names like that no matter what one personally feels about them. You would be surprised at the number of actors and actresses who you would never dream for a moment of being Jewish who, like me, have changed their names. Would you, for example, think that Tony Curtis is Jewish? Jerry Lewis? Ethel Merman? No, you wouldn't. Danny Kaye? Well maybe not Danny Kaye.' She dismissed Danny Kaye with a flick of the hand. 'Michael Caine? Kirk Douglas? Lauren Bacall? Shelley Winters? Dustin Hoffman? Oh, the list of wonderful talent is simply endless, especially if you add producers, directors, writers, composers, musicians.'

He felt he was expected to say something here but she had rabbited on so he had actually forgotten what her real name was.

So what is it you feel I can do for you, Mrs… er Mrs van…?'

'Clef.'

'Clef.'

'*Miss* van Clef to be exact. Mrs Huntington yes, Mrs van Clef no.'

Thornton nodded: van Clef, Huntington, Fartfooker, what difference did it make whatever she called herself? It was what she wanted of him that mattered. He studied her carefully. Even in old age she still showed what a beauty she must have been as a young girl, a young woman even. Some women, and some men if it comes to that, do grow old gracefully, accepting the inevitable with the passing of the years, whereas others hate the whole process and somehow it is reflected in their faces. The neck and hands which are usually the first give away when it comes to age in this case didn't seem to follow the pattern. The hands did not sport protuberant blue veins, knotty knuckles or blemishes of any kind and the neck was hardly creased at all. The result of cosmetic surgery? Thornton wondered. If it was it was certainly seamless and obviously Hollywood's expensive best.

'Have you heard of a girl by the name of Charmaine Carmichael?' She asked.

Thornton thought for a second or two. Had he heard of a girl called Charmaine Carmichael? He didn't think so. 'Actually no,' he said after a suitable studied pause, 'I don't recall ever hearing that name. Should I have done?'

She looked him up and down, that is up and down the part of him she could see seated behind his desk. He wondered if she approved. Thankfully that day, it wasn't the case every day, but that day he was wearing his best summer suit with quite a natty if slightly gaudy tie that had taken his fancy and bought on an impulse in Carnaby Street. It was tat and wouldn't last long he knew and was definitely not worth what he had paid for it. You gets what you pays for and Carnaby Street was not exactly known for quality.

'You read the newspapers don't you?' The tone of her voice suggested it would be dangerous for him to deny it.

'Not all of them, no. They're getting more and more expensive. Do you know I used to get five or six papers to see me through a Sunday and now I have rationed myself to only one? I do get *The Times* every morning. I like to do the crossword. It's a real brain teaser. Keeps the old mind in trim don't you know? And the *Evening Standard*. Do you do crosswords Miss…?'

'So you must have seen her name in at least one.' She wasn't exactly getting snappy but obviously wanted to come to the point rather than waffle on about crossword puzzles.

Thornton remained silent which meant no, he hadn't seen it. 'Very well.'

She dipped into the bag and brought out a newspaper which she unfolded and laid facing him on the desk. Thornton picked it up and saw it was headed the *Breconfield Courier. Founded 1897 and incorporating The County Citizen* and it was a week or so old.

The front page was devoted to a local beauty contest the winner of which had been disqualified as she had lied about her age and everyone was taken in until a jealous rival put the record straight. Thornton thought that a great shame as, judging by the photograph, she was by far the best looker in the bunch which on the whole consisted not exactly the *crème de la crème* of bucolic beauty, and quite naturally why she had won the title and for one joyful moment was draped in that coveted blue synthetic silk sash and had that jewelled tiara perched on her blonde curls. It might be nothing more than paste but it was a tiara after all, perhaps the only time in her life she would wear one. However, rules were rules he supposed and had to be abided by no matter how many tears might be shed, accompanied by consoling hugs from the other girls, including the now smug faced newly crowned queen who had really resented being placed second and was seething inside until the announcement of the disqualification was made.

Now, as the flashbulbs popped and the teeth gleamed white behind those scarlet lips and the tears of joy ran down her cheeks regardless of the damage done to her make-up, Thornton felt sure next year the newly crowned queen would enter the Miss Great Britain contest and, who knows, maybe even Miss World, Miss Universe? He could visualise it all so clearly. She would be eliminated fairly early of course. The world was well supplied with ravishing young females and he couldn't remember when last a British girl had won a major title in the beauty stakes.

'Page two,' Esther Fartfooker said, this time snappily and thinking – "Men! Most of them are all the same. Show them a pair of tits or a derriere and everything else goes by the wayside. That's the nature of things."

Thornton picked up the paper and turned to page two where a headline immediately, as she had intended it to, grabbed his attention – *"Murders at Breconfield Film Studios"* it read and went on to detail the few known facts. The victims were a secretary aged twenty four by the name of Charmaine Carmichael, *"whose lifeless body was discovered in her office when personnel turned up for work the following morning. Edward Brown, aged sixty four and a widower was also discovered dead at the gate having been brutally slain by a vicious blow, or repeated blows, to the back of the head. Mrs Ida Chapman, a cleaning lady and a widow residing in a neat eight thousand pound bungalow on Riverside Drive who has worked at the studios for more years than she could remember as had her husband before her, found the body of Miss Carmichael and alerted the police. She was working late that night, but evidently she has informed the police she neither heard nor saw anything suspicious. The young secretary, who had herself worked at the studios for a number of years, was discovered slumped over her desk having evidently been strangled. A post mortem revealed that to be the case. There were no other injuries. The police are following a number of possibilities in endeavouring to solve the puzzle of these two tragic deaths."*

"That means Mister Plod hasn't a clue," Thornton thought.

Reading further he learned that Charmaine Carmichael was descended from a long line of cinematic names going all the way back to the legendary D.W.Griffiths of *Intolerance* and *Birth of a Nation* fame, as her great grandmother, Greta Garnet, actually Greta Fartfooker who, 'though not in the same class as Clara Bow or Lillian Gish, did feature in a number of old silent movies,' Esther, taking over from the paper, went on to inform him. To make the truly big time she didn't have *it* but, like Jean Harlow or Dolores del Rio, she certainly had *that* and plenty of it. She didn't add that Greta liked to spread it around a little but then that was Hollywood of the time; think of the Fatty Arbuckle scandal.

'She used to go into hysterics whenever she watched the Keystone Cops,' Esther said, carrying on with the family history, 'and of course she simply adored Charlie Chaplin, thought him an absolute genius which, in a way, I suppose he was; *Modern Times, The Gold Rush, The Great Dictator,* wonderful old movies. He was Jewish too you know. He lives in Switzerland now with his wife Oona. She is the daughter of that famous American playwright and Pulitzer Prize winner Eugene O'Neill.'

'Jewish?'

'I believe not. Irish I would think with a name like that. I've lost count of how many children they have, the Chaplins I mean. He was actually English you know. Yes, born right here in London, but America was the land of opportunity and that's where he ended up, before moving to Switzerland, in later life of course. Greta was enraptured by Buster Keaton as well, thought *The General* a little masterpiece of comedy. Also she had this big romantic feeling for the handsome Douglas Fairbanks though that of course never came to anything. After all, millions of women all over the world felt the same so he had a pretty wide choice. German film at the time, after the First World War we're talking about, was booming but was all expressionism and just too depressing for words, all crime and horror. How many times would one want to sit through films like *The Cabinet of Doctor Caligari* or *Metropolis? Nosferatu?* Good films though they were. Consider Fritz Lang's film '*M*' made a bit later, 1931 if I remember correctly, all about a serial killer, very nasty, starring Peter Lorre. The Nazis, when they came to power, made great play over that movie, that Jew actor, Peter Lorre he was called in an anti-Semitic film. But anyway, to move on, also there was the spectre of inflation in Germany where eventually a million marks would buy a loaf of bread. And Greta craved gaiety so, soon after my father, Helmut Fartfooker, who was a lighting cameraman at UFA, the German studios, arrived in England, Greta was dragging him off to Hollywood where she felt all the action was and she might just get a chance to meet her hero, Douglas Fairbanks or, second best, Valentino, as well as make it big time in the industry.'

Thornton wondered if, as a mine of information, she was going to feed him anymore nuggets of cinematic history and soon had his answer.

'I naturally followed in her footsteps by becoming an actress as well and married Jerome Huntington who fortunately had nothing to do with films. We had three children one of whom, Elsie, married a Dennis Carmichael and their only child was Charmaine. I did not approve of the marriage I'm afraid. I don't wish to appear like the clichéd interfering mother in law or at all snobbish but the man was as common as muck. No class, no class at all. No interest in anything but football, he was a Tottenham fan evidently, though I don't think he was a football hooligan, no, he didn't go as far as that, and of course, not being Jewish, he could haunt the pub on a Saturday night.'

"*Charmaine herself,*" he went back to reading, "*once had ambitions to follow in her grandmother's footsteps in the entertainment business but an unfortunate speech impediment about which it seemed nothing could be done put paid to those hopes.*"

She could have been a star in old silent movies, Thornton decided, scanning her picture, as she was an extremely beautiful girl and he could certainly see the family resemblance to the woman sitting opposite him, with her high cheekbones and the large eyes, but evidently once the budding actress opened her mouth all thoughts of romance ran screaming into the night. That's not exactly how the newspaper article put it, it was a bit more subtle than that, but Thornton got the gist. The article continued,

"*According to her grandmother, the famous film actress Spring van Clef, who had a starring role in Guns of Batani, its successor currently in production at Breconfield Studios, and not to be confused with Guns at Batasi as so many people do, a film made in nineteen fifty four and starring that wonderful British actor David Attenborough. In the new film Spring plays the part of a kind of aging Mata Hari though fortunately she doesn't suffer that lady's end. It was during the previous Guns of Batani filming that, coincidently, the male lead, Cord Wainer was accidentally electrocuted while being made up ready to go on the set. Being denied her ambition to be an actress, Charmaine made up for her big disappointment with the next best thing, actually working in a film studio. She was personal secretary to the director of the* remake, one Mel Preston, *now a producer, and it was her grand-mother, Esther van Clef, through her contacts in the business, who procured her the job."*

'She was an adorable girl,' her grandmother said, interrupting his reading, 'and loved her work. I simply can't think what beast would possibly want to do this dreadful thing, especially as there was no evidence of you know what, interference, if you know what I mean, and I feel so responsible.'

He wasn't quite sure yet what she expected him to call her. As it was a first acquaintance Miss Fartfooker would have been the most polite he supposed but was more he felt than he could manage without a smile which would have been extremely rude. He had already forgotten the husband's name.

'The reason why I am here is I want you to investigate my granddaughter's death and bring her killer to justice.'

It must have been obvious from the start that it was what she wanted but nevertheless it still came as something of a shock. It was his turn to stare.

'Investigate?'

'You're an investigator aren't you? It says on your plaque down-stairs, *Private Investigator.*'

'Yes, but…'

'But?'

'Surely the investigation into a murder is in the hands of the police? They have the expertise and lawful duty for that. It's simply not up to private individuals, whatever their occupation.'

Spring made a very rude noise at the mention of the police which had Thornton wondering if she had had dealings with Reg Venables, that is if Reg hadn't retired by now to that pristine little house beneath the Heathrow fly path. But no, that couldn't be because the murder was way out of his manor and would be investigated by Scotland Yard anyway, wouldn't it? He was a bit vague about police protocol. Sometime or other he should really take the trouble to look it up, who does what exactly. He made a mental note. In his line of work it could be useful information.

'Well, are you or aren't you?' She insisted. 'And you have been very highly recommended.'

Thornton frowned. He didn't like the sound of that. The last couple of times he had been highly recommended nearly saw the end of him, the first time drugged and floating unconscious down the Thames to be fished out with a boathook by a very strong young woman, the second almost coming to a sticky end via the Italian Mafia and saved in the nick of time by the photographer Adrian Spangle who just happened to be in Milan at the time busy with his camera at a fashion show. That was after the Americans, the Russians, the Japanese Yakusa, the Chinese Triads and some shady East Europeans of unknown origin had all had a go. It was quite an adventurous caper and he was truly lucky to survive. In fact the odds of his not surviving were such that, if he had taken a bet on it, he would now be an extremely rich man.

'Might I enquire as to who it was recommended me?'

'Certainly. The Countess Cinelli.'

'Ah yes, the Countess.' Charming lady, if a little on the ripe side. He thought back on the countess, the pickle she was in at the time and which he got her out of; her love of *Romeo et Juliet* cigars, recommended to her by none other than Winston Churchill himself, or so she said. He had Holly Day to thank for that recommendation. 'You know her well?' He asked.

'We're not exactly bosom friends', she answered, 'if I may use that expression without these days having to put up with the accompanying innuendo and sniggers but, yes, I do know her fairly well, and have done so for a while. We met when I was filming in Rome since then we take tea together whenever we're both in London.'

'Yes, that seems to be the done thing with the countess. If you're not in London and available she takes tea with Holly. And how is she?' Thornton added wondering why the countess had never boasted of her connection with a film star no matter how minor, or maybe it was because Esther wasn't exactly in the top bracket and not worth boasting about.

'Thriving.'

'I'm sure she is.' He nodded, smiling as he pictured her.

'When she told me how you saved her life I knew at once you were the person to come to.'

'Saved her life? She told you that?' The smile broadened. 'Well, if I may be allowed to contradict you, Mrs van Clef...'

'Miss. Actresses are a miss. In the old days actresses were billed as Mrs if that was their status. Modern actresses are always a miss.'

'Miss van Clef, saving her life isn't quite correct.'

'Whatever it was you did it was tantamount to that so here I am hiring you to find the monster that killed my granddaughter and, just as important, the reason why he would commit such a ghastly crime.'

'How do you know it was a man who committed this ghastly crime?'

'I would have thought it a natural assumption to make.'

'Really? Women are incapable of murder?'

'No, of course not, but...'

'Mrs van Clef... Miss... man or woman as the case might be, the attempted solving of a murder as I have tried to explain is not something a private investigator undertakes. It just isn't the done thing. Every day run of the mill human failings is what he deals with, not murder.'

'You've not done it before?'

'Well...' He thought about this for a moment, but not for long, the answer was so obvious. 'Yes, as a matter of fact I have but that was purely by accident while investigating a supposed suicide before it turned out it was in fact murder. But even that isn't entirely correct as the actual death *was* accidental no matter the intention which was evidently just to put the frighteners on the victim. So, as I said, murder really is out of our brief.'

He had no intention of mentioning the Princess Spitskaya, an adventure which involved a series of the most bizarre killings imaginable.

'Please don't shilly-shally Mister King. It may not be every day of the week, I quite see that, but I don't see why not, on the odd occasion if the police are unable to solve it.'

'You don't know that the police are unable to solve it. They must be working on it...' he looked down at the paper as though it would tell him something about the police and looked up again... 'right this minute and these things sometimes take time. It is not for outsiders to interfere. It's how long since this happened? No more than a few days really and it's been known for cases to be kept open and solved in twenty years or more after the crime had been committed.'

'Is that so?'

'It is indeed.'

'Look at me, Mister King.'

'I am looking at you Mrs... Miss van Clef.'

'What do you see?'

'A remarkable, if I may be as bold as to say so, very beautiful and charming lady.'

She shook her head. 'Don't flatter me, Mr King. I've lived with flattery all my life and I can do without it. What you see is someone who is hardly likely to be around in twenty years time thank you very much and I would like to go to my grave or the crematorium, whichever, knowing the mystery has been solved and my granddaughter's killer brought to justice.'

'Mrs van...'

'If it's your fee you're worried about, no matter how outrageous it might be...'

Thornton bridled a little at this. Had the countess been telling porkies about what she had paid him, inflating them somewhat? He could just imagine it. "Oh, yes, my dear, it cost a positive fortune, an arm and a leg as they say, but he was well worth it in the end. He saved my life you know."

He supposed his expenses might have been a mite excessive what with the swish car hire, the wonderful but expensive Italian restaurants and all but, if she believed he saved her life, what are a few extra lira between friends?

'... you may rest assured I have ample funds with which to pay you,' she continued. 'Apart from my earnings as an actress, not that the film studios are all that generous if they can possibly avoid it, actors are the cheapest things on the set you know. Studio heads believe actors are two a penny which alas happens to be true, always has been unless you're a universal mega star and can command the earth and get away with the most outrageous demands. At least we're not rogues and vagabonds any more, that's something to be thankful for I suppose. And although it's true I do happen to be resting at the moment, my husband, Jerome, was a realtor in California and to put it vulgarly, simply loaded. So...'

'Miss van Clef...' He held up a hand to stop the torrent of words and was about to say there was no way he could possibly help her, loaded husband or not, when he suffered a vision of his bank manager and the thought that he was turning away a client sent waves of apprehension tingling right down to his toes and his fingertips so instead he said, 'Thirty pounds a day plus expenses.' He didn't know where it had come from but it was out before he could have second thoughts.

'Good,' Esther Fartfooker said, and took a fistful of bank notes from her rexine bag. 'How much would you like on account, would three hundred do?'

"I'll telephone the locksmith first thing in the morning," Thornton thought.

# Chapter Two

U nfortunately Spring van Clef or Mrs Huntington or Esther Fartfooker's acting contribution to the multi-million dollar epic *The Return to Batani* currently in the making at Breconfield Studios was over, unless she was called back to do some post production work which she didn't think very likely. For one thing it would be costly as by some oversight it wasn't in her contract so she was in a position to make demands and, as is only too often the case in the film business, the picture was already running way over budget. It was naturally being funded by that American giant *Centurion Film Corporation*, the British film industry, with the exception of commercials with enormous budgets paid for by big business, being in its usual dire state; that is flat on its insolvent back and unable to sit up and produce a full length film of any quality. The *Carry On* series was made on the cheap and there was always *Hammer* of course, founded in 1934 whose movies were very popular. Maybe people had subconscious desires of being bitten by the undead, but there was very little else coming out of British studios. It seemed more than likely Esther's scenes would end up on the cutting room floor anyway. After all she was hardly a major star and her role wouldn't be missed so he could not, with her help, be able to gain access to the studios. If she did decide to pay them a visit, everyone knew Charmaine was her grandchild, they had all offered their sincerest and in some cases insincere condolences for what it was worth and they would be highly suspicious of her return. They wouldn't particularly want to see her again anyway; would just want to forget it and get on with their lives.

But of course it would never be forgotten. "At some time in the far distant future," Thornton thought, "there was bound to be gossip and reminiscences around any number of dinner tables."

Esther couldn't very well make the excuse that she left something in her dressing room or she just came back to see old friends and be sociable. Her granddaughter's body still hadn't been released but lay in the mortuary for post mortem and forensics to thoroughly examine though why they should go to a whole heap of trouble when the marks on her neck were a dead giveaway wasn't certain. How long does it take to discover if there's any strange flesh under the fingernails to determine a struggle or whether she was sexually assaulted?

'Charmaine's parents then,' Thornton asked, 'I would like to talk to them first.

'Good gracious! Whatever for?'

'Because in many cases of murder it is often someone very close to the deceased who is the killer.' He said this as though he personally authenticated the theory though he couldn't actually recall where or when he had heard it. Maybe it was on one of those TV programmes involving crime, criminals, detectives and police of which there were many on both sides of the Atlantic.

'Well you can forget Charmaine's parents; neither of them would have hurt a fly and both of them have been dead a number of years which is why Charmaine lived with me.'

'Oh. A dead end you might say. Sorry. You say she has an uncle and an aunt, what about them?'

'What about them? David is a ship's captain and is away at

27

sea and Mary married a fat Greek who I do not approve of and who for her sins lives in that smoky hellhole, Athens. Not that I have visited that city to find out personally I hasten to add but I am led to believe it is terribly terribly polluted, even worse than Los Angeles so I am informed and that is saying something.'

'Well, unless there is a prodigal son or some scallywag hidden away somewhere that certainly rules out any member of the family.'

Esther was beginning to seriously wonder if she had made the right choice.

One piece of information she did give Thornton when he questioned her further about her granddaughter was that she believed the girl had been having an affaire, well, was in love anyway even if it wasn't an actual affaire, with the same screen writer, Joachim Caswell who was also working on the current film, the original writers having been fired and someone needed for daily rewrites of which there seemed to be many. There were a few of the original white pages left interspersed with blue pages, yellow pages, pink pages, green pages. The script had become a veritable rainbow and more rewrites would no doubt be forthcoming and, even so, any number of scenes would end up on the cutting room floor.

Again it was a name that rang no bells with Thornton. Writers are in themselves virtually ephemeral. The credits come up on screen and are immediately forgotten while some talentless director like Mel Preston claims the film to be solely his own creation; *A Mel Preston Film* as though nobody else had anything to do with it. He was the kind of man who would even have liked a credit for the ice cream, popcorn, and soda sales.

Ten years previously *Full Throttle Film Company* produced seventeen episodes of that wonderful children's serial *The Limey Gang are Here* on which, currently unknown to Thornton, a certain Joachim Caswell was employed as script editor and writer of a number of scripts.

"And do you know where I can locate this Joachim Caswell?"

"Of course. At the studios. Where else? A little acid seemed to drip with the voice."

Thornton thought about this and decided it might be better and probably save a lot of time if he were to beard the lion in his den rather than out in the jungle. After all, if he had in fact been Charmaine's paramour, Thornton was a great one for sometimes using old-fashioned language, he would be suspect numero uno. Unfortunately Esther, who wanted as little to do with him as possible, did not know the man's address and the telephone directory did not list a Joachim Caswell, not even a J. Caswell who might have been he. He would naturally be ex-directory. It stood to reason, Thornton supposed, that someone quasi-famous, after all he had evidently won a couple of Baftas in his time though he hadn't graduated to Oscar level, not even a nomination which was hardly surprising as his credits consisted mainly of television, a couple of documentaries for theatre release and some public information films, would not want to be bothered by the hoi-polloi. Fans can be so demanding and it was not unknown for some VIPs to be diligently harassed by a stalker, a most unpleasant experience. He had written a couple of full length screenplays but trying to interest a producer in an original required a convocation, a gathering behind the Pearly Gates, of the Almighty together with his angels, archangels, innumerable saints, cherubim and seraphim, and a few Bronze Age prophets thrown in for good measure, the most likely result being a rejection, as had happened more times than he cared to think about. The problem was that film producers wanted another *Gone with the Wind* or *Wizard of Oz*, both big money spinners, the biggest, and both rejected a number of times (Who's interested in the Civil War? As one was reputed to have said) before finally making it, and the producer not knowing whether he was buying a turkey, a lame duck or a pig in a poke.

Of course Joachim Caswell could always be a pen name. Strange choice but then maybe it was in deference to a well loved aunt or some such. Maybe when he was a poor struggling young writer trying to break into show biz he had high hopes this favourite aunt would peg it and leave him a small fortune to ease his way but unfortunately for him she left it all to a cat's home. On the other hand it could be his real name.

The phone book was cast aside and the next step would be to call the *Writers' Guild* and find out if they could help. They couldn't. The girl he spoke to via the telephone was quite charming and very sorry but adamant they could not give out personal details of any members. If Thornton would like to write care of the Guild they would pass the message on and it would then be up to Mister Caswell to reply or not to reply. To be or not to be, thought Thornton as he put down the phone.

Writing would take far too long. He needed to see this Joachim Caswell as soon as possible so the next step would be to try and see him in the studios. The sixty four thousand dollar question here, was how to get into the studios. He was quite sure they would not welcome a visit from a private eye, especially as they were more than likely fed up with the police prowling the precincts, lording it over everybody and interfering with everything. Having never stepped foot inside a film studio the police would no doubt be full of curiosity and irritating questions.

But first he needed to delve a little deeper into the murder itself and that necessitated a visit to the Newspaper Library in Colindale and, if they couldn't help, a visit to Breconfield itself and the offices of the *Courier*. On second thoughts maybe he would skip Colindale. It was a bit of a schlep out there and he might as well go straight to the local paper.

With the exception of the film studios and a well kept not too unattractive nineteen fifties council estate of semi-detacheds on its outskirts, Breconfield was a quiet pretty little town, various aspects of which could be admired in the yearly calendar produced by the local newspaper every Christmas, with or without a festive sprinkling of artificial snow.

It was a stone's throw from the bustling hurly-burly of the big city, in a world all of its own with an old fashioned atmosphere of yellow London brick, oak studded doors and mullioned windows.

The *Courier* offices were situated in the High Street together with a card, souvenir, and nick-knack shop smelling faintly of pot pourri, an antique dealer smelling of furniture polish, a book shop smelling of nothing in particular, an old fashioned butcher who still used a wooden block on which to chop his meat and who believed it should then be laid out in the most artistic and aesthetic a way as possible decorated with sprigs of parsley.

There was a fishmonger whose fruits of the sea: cod, haddock, bream, Dover sole, halibut, tuna, mackerel, salmon, lobster, clams and fresh water trout from a nearby farm lay on sloping marble slabs, kept cool with occasional jets of water. There was also an old-fashioned tobacconist who stocked pipes and accessories and who still sold snuff and tobaccos with an all-uring scent out of large jars and you could decide on your own favourite mix which he weighed out on old-fashioned highly polished brass scales. Thornton stopped by the window for a moment and thought pipe-smoking Reg Venables, if he was aware of its existence, would be in a second heaven. The elderly tobacconist, a small man in a grey woolly cardigan, looked as though years of dealing with and handling tobacco had stained his complexion a dark brown.

Oxfam was there next to a long established (a photograph, the staff posing in long white aprons, showed the facade circa 1900) greengrocer come grocery store; its merchandise a little on the expensive side but specialising in exotic fruits and vegetables not usually found in run of the mill English greengrocers; lychees for example, mangoes, pawpaw, Kiwi fruit, pomegranates, Jerusalem artichokes, dates, olives, Hubbard squash. It also specialised in various herbs and spices, condiments, virgin olive oil, genuine feta cheese and sheep's yoghurt so there were inviting mixed smells emanating from this establishment. The upper middle classes on the whole kept a good table as well as Labradors, green Wellington boots, four wheel drives and ponies for their Jodhpur clad young daughters.

With the exception of paved sidewalks, macadam roads and electric light it was possible to imagine Breconfield as a location for *Cranford*, a Bronte novel, or a Charles Dickens and it had in fact been used as such a number of times by both film and television companies, and commercials for products that relied on the nostalgic make-believe that there were good old days that were the best but alas were no longer, except for the advertised product of course that took one immediately down memory lane.

Some of the large shop windows, the bottom edges of which were only a foot or so above the pavement, were bowed with leaded panes, and the ancient stone water trough for the refreshment of horses was still in situ only now, rather than water, it contained a colourful flower bed of pansies, lobelia both white and purple, and marigolds. There were also colourful hanging baskets outside some of the shops. Breconfield was indeed what is known as a picture postcard town.

The High Street was quite short so it didn't take Thornton long to find the newspaper office behind its double bowed windows. A discreet highly polished brass plaque assured him he was at the right place, the bell hanging on its metal spring jangled merrily as he opened the door and he was immediately greeted by a charming young middle-aged lady who, despite the Indian summer, wore a sea green woollen suit and who wanted to know how she could help him.

Within seconds he was ensconced in front of a large much scratched wooden lectern on which was placed a pile of *Breconfield Couriers* of recent date, safely fastened with cord at their centres to keep them in position.

As he surmised there were a number of reports and articles relating to the murders, more than would have been found in the nationals which, having reported it, possibly published a follow up and that would have been that as other more important, scandalous, national, or universal news stories broke.

If the scandal of the moment put a member of parliament in the frame that would be good for quite a few overlarge front page headlines. Horny misbehaving vicars were old hat and hardly worth mentioning anymore. Not even the *News of the World* bothered with them anymore unless the behaviour was truly sensational and not merely a run of the mill peccadillo. The papers could always come back to the murder if the guilty party was arrested, indicted and brought to trial. Murder trials are always good for a few column inches.

Interviews with studio personnel was what interested him most. First, on the same page as the results of the recent agricultural show with a photograph of the prize bull, ring through his nose and showing a truly magnificent pair of balls, and a fund appeal by the Reverend Giles Hebblethwaite for the restoration of the sixteenth century church, from the roof of which thieves, at risk to life and limb, had stolen the lead, was one by Mrs Ida Chapman, a resident for many years of Riverside Drive. She had little more to say than that she had told the police she had not heard or seen anything suspicious. When questioned about Mister Brown who she must have passed when she left the studio she said she thought he was asleep. He was known by everyone as Sleepyhead Ted.

Thornton decided if he wanted to question her further she was bound to be found demolishing a milk stout in the nearest pub to Riverside Drive which naturally would be *The Fisherman's Arms* complete with oak beams, oak tables, oak chairs, oak stools, oak settles in the inglenook, barley twist legs and prize trout in glass cases on the walls, each one with its little label giving weight, date caught and the name of the angler. English country living, even so close to London and even with its council estate nearby, has always been unique.

There was nothing else of interest in that edition so he went back one and found an interview that could lead to something. It was given by an Ernest J. Bloomberg, aged twenty, who described himself as a production assistant. He didn't actually give out what number assistant he was and the question was never asked so he could have been a first assistant for all Thornton knew but somehow doubted. Never mind, first, second, third or fourth, Bloomberg sounded interesting and should be followed up. A photograph revealed a skinny, narrow shouldered young man in glasses and *Save The Whales* T-shirt who in fact could have passed for fifteen or so rather than his given age and he evidently, according to the article, had ambitions to be not only a screenwriter but eventually a director as well. He had worked at the studio since he was a sixteen year old runner and was now engaged in working on the film *Return to Batani* produced by Mel Preston the sequel to *Guns of Batani* and which was a remake of an earlier film of the same name. The remake was being co-produced by Courtney Burrows II, son of the studio's founder, Courtney Burrows I, and the original was written by one Jimmy Harrowfield. This really aroused Thornton's interest and he decided he would delve further back to the rather bizarre death of the film star Cord Wainer. Could there possibly be a connection with the recent murder? At this stage of the game who rightly knew?

Obviously the next step was to gain admittance to the studio and a couple of days later a mini-bus drew up at the studio gates and Thornton, together with a dozen assorted film buffs of various ages, sizes, and sexes, alighted after the young lady who was their official guide and who had given strict instructions that they were to follow her and were not allowed to stray from the group under any circumstances whatsoever. It's a wonder she didn't waggle a finger at them like recalcitrant schoolchildren whilst giving this instruction.

'After all,' she then cooed with a cheesy smile, 'your tour of the studios is a rare privilege and you wouldn't like to interrupt any shooting in progress and completely spoil a take, now would you?'

They all shook their heads in agreement.

On the way out from London the guide, clipboard in hand, pointed out various landmarks that had been the site of film locations and the cameras in the bus duly clicked away. The locations for the most part were pretty dreary and the last one of course was the village of Breconfield itself. The reason for the clipboard was that the guide, whose name according to the metal badge pinned to the lapel of her jacket was Marguerite, was fairly new to the job and not all that au fait with the films she had to mention so did a quick downward glance to check before each one. Even so at one point she had felt rather foolish and blushed furiously when she misread her notes and was roundly contradicted by a know it all. There's always one in every group just as there is inevitably the ultimate bore who everyone, not always successfully, tries to ignore or get away from.

Thornton wondered as they moved on whether he should get into conversation with this middle-aged, pale, mousey looking creature in a tweed jacket and corduroy trousers and sporting a rather fierce twitchy moustache in case, as a know it all, he could give Thornton any information on the writer Joachim Caswell.

During the journey this had not been possible as Thornton was seated next to a bosom heaving lady in a low cut flimsy chiffon dress decorated with some species of plant no botanist had ever seen but could no doubt soon be discovered as a new species in some tropical jungle.

Her necklace of highly coloured plastic beads was enormous and her camera seemed to click away even when a movie wasn't being mentioned and she gave off a mixed message of sweat and Californian Poppy. This together with her ample size that overflowed her seat made her a little too close for comfort and she had informed Thornton her name was Cynthia. Thornton returned the compliment by telling her his name was Charlie, Charlie Thorpe.

Thornton's smile made Cynthia feel she had scored a definite hit here and, let's face it, Thornton was far from unattractive with his melting dark brown eyes and sensuous tempting mouth, eyelashes that needed no mascara and that any girl would give her eye-teeth for, and his companion's heaving bosom gave every appearance of imitating waves in a storm tossed sea.

'Oh, isn't this so exciting?' she twittered girlishly. 'This is the studio where *Guns of Batani* was filmed you know with that gorgeous actor Cord Wainer. Wasn't it such a shame his having to die so young?'

'Live hard, die young, and be a good-looking corpse,' Thornton said with a grin.

She would have rapped him on the arm in admonishment with a bunch of knuckles if she had had a hand free but her handbag in one hand and her camera in the other saved him from that so she did the admonishing verbally instead.

'Oh, how awful! You horrid horrid man to say something like that.'

'And I do believe that was the case with Cord Wainer,' he added. 'He was without doubt a no-talent big head who couldn't act for toffee but women adored him and I reckon he probably looked pretty good dead, once the undertakers had done their stuff.'

This did the trick; stopping her in mid-flow, the bosoms subsiding like pricked soufflés.

'Now please remember to stay close to me,' Marguerite ordered sternly as, having led the way, she watched the last visitor leave the bus and she mentally counted the number in her charge. 'This way please.' All being present she stood aside to usher them through the turnstile; 'Wait for me on the other side,' she called in sing-song fashion.

Max in his little wooden hut couldn't be bothered to even lift his eyes from his copy of *The Sun*, no doubt he was ogling page three or studying form and it wasn't until Thornton, last in line, reached the turnstile that he glanced up.

For the briefest of moments their eyes met and Thornton felt he had seen this man before but the gate man gave no hint of any recognition and went back to his newspaper and Thornton shrugged it off.

'Right, are we all here?' This was a rather needless question from Marguerite as they had all, as requested, dutifully gathered on the other side of the gate. One of them would have to be caught in the turnstile of course and that one had to be Cynthia who for a moment or two had a little difficulty squeezing through. She managed it eventually, a little breathlessly and with a little more sweat and they set off on their tour, Thornton lagging behind, making sure he was the last of the group and waiting for his opportunity to slip away.

They hadn't gone very far when Max raised the barrier for a chauffeur driven Rolls Royce Silver Cloud to sweep in and disappear behind a far building.

'Are we all here?' Marguerite repeated as though she didn't believe it the first time. 'The gentleman you saw in the Rolls Royce a moment ago,' she waved vaguely in the direction it had gone, 'was Mister Courtney Burrows II, head of these Breconfield Studios that were founded by his father of the same name, Burrows that is, not Breconfield.' She giggled. 'Right then, as we're all here let us continue our visit to this famous studio founded in nineteen thirty four, incidentally and as a matter of interest for those of you who enjoy horror pictures, the same year as *Hammer Films* came into being. As I told you, this studio was founded by Courtney Burrows I and currently they are under the management of his son of the same name which is why he is called number two to differentiate him from his father.' She paused for a moment, frowning, wondering if she was repeating herself or had made that quite clear. She obviously had because no one asked any questions and all were gazing at her with rapt attention. It made her slightly uneasy. 'During the war,' she continued, 'a number of propaganda films were made here. Older members of the group might remember "Careless talk costs lives" or the one about food; "Nutritious meals from your allotment."'

No one seemed to remember or even show an interest but Marguerite carried on regardless. She had been instructed as to what to say and she was keeping strictly to her script; not even Mister Know-it-all was going to stop her.

'Some of these early black and white films have become classics in the eyes of cinema lovers everywhere. After the war the studio fell on quite hard times, so much so that it was almost ready to be declared bankrupt when the most wonderful thing happened.' Marguerite looked almost awestruck over what she was about to tell them. It was in her opinion virtually an epiphany, a cinematic moment almost equal to *The Ten Commandments*. 'As Mister Burrows sat in his office weeping and distraught at the possible loss of his life's work and wondering how he was going to carry on, there landed on his desk a simply brilliant script that would turn out to be their salvation in the nick of time. That script was of course the original…' pause for effect… '*Guns of Batani!* Mister Burrows knew even before he had finished reading it that he had a sure fire winner on his hands and so it proved. He mortgaged his lovely house with its lawns sweeping down to the Thames. His wife, Marlene nee Barclay, to get the ball rolling, pawned all her jewellery, of which if I may digress for a moment, there was a quite substantial amount, Mister Burrows having always been generous to a fault. They eventually found other investors who got news of this most likely hit. News, both good and bad, travels fast in the film world, and soon the studio was once again on an even keel.'

By the end of this amazing spiel that had all the women, when they thought of their home life and, even if at times they were grateful for small mercies, wishing they had been fortunate enough to marry a man like Mister Burrows. Handsome is as handsome does but above all filthy rich is even better. Instead they had to cope in their semi's with a very ordinary selfish layabout of a husband with absolutely no get up and go, with a mortgage to worry about and being behind with the rates, and a brace of truculent rowdy ravenous kids forever hungry but who wouldn't dream of eating anything that was good for them. All the men meanwhile dismissed every word as self-promotion and aggrandisement.

C ourtney Burrows II, born with the proverbial silver spoon in his mouth, and quite a large one it should be said, was ridiculously spoilt from the very beginning to grow up suave, sophisticated, self-centred and rotten to the core. On the death of his father he had inherited a mini-empire, his to do with as he pleased, the only condition being that he had to see to his mother's welfare as long as she lived which turned out to be not very long, succumbing as she did to a drastic attack of pneumonia. He wept over her grave, to be accurate, their graves as she was buried next to her husband, and immediately after set out to be the playboy and philanderer he was by nature.

At his public school he hadn't exactly been a dunce but neither was he ever top of the class, knowing full well what was in store for him on the death of his father and the fact that he would never have financial worries, or so he thought at the time. His pocket money had been generous to a fault and whatever he asked for he got. It was more than likely this fact that set him on the downward path.

He had a beautiful home filled with priceless antiques and works of art and, although physically not all that prepossessing, he sported a trophy wife who he loved to show off even if he didn't actually love her, for most of the time hardly noticed her in fact.

The fact that he was married didn't stop him playing the field and his money and position in life spoke volumes. The casting couch was too enticing, too easy. It was the casting couch in fact that led him to his wife in the first place; Evelyn, generally known as Eve, a minor film actress of absolutely no talent but extremely beautiful. She had one small part in a *Full Throttle* production that quickly disappeared and she was the worst thing in a film that was in itself bad enough, to get the bird. The critics had a field day trying to conjure up suitable adjectives to describe it and the more pseudo-intellectual members if the fraternity came up with bad puns that were the lowest form of wit, but that is the way with critics. She was so dull and so boring, her beauty didn't even excite the mackintosh brigade but she did land that very rich husband and wasn't the least bothered that he fooled around as she was, to tell the truth, a little on the frigid side, usually referring to it if and when it happened as *this messy business*. If it eventually worried her too much she could always sue for divorce and live off the alimony. In the meantime she enjoyed playing lady of the manor, was rude to her servants who came and went with regularity, entertained lavishly and had a string of fair weather friends who would have deserted her the minute her hospitality was no longer available and couldn't give a fig that she was never to appear on the silver screen again.

For Courtney himself perhaps the biggest disappointment in life was not having children. He would have loved to present to the world a Courtney Burrows III but after two early miscarriages it was out of the question. Of his son, his love-child, the world was not supposed to know anything about, he could do nothing. He hadn't in fact seen him since he was a child and that only briefly and from a distance, and he had no idea what he might look like now that he was a young man.

Unfortunately, Courtney Burrows II had a fault even worse than his infidelity. He had become an inveterate gambler and when his losses mounted to a point where he was no longer able to honour them, rather than possibly losing his beautiful house, his beautiful belongings and his supposed status in the world, he was forced to look for financial help elsewhere. What else could he do? So, though he was still ostensibly in charge, he lost control of the studios and became no more than a figurehead.

T he little party of tourists arrived first at a large shed that was open to the elements at both ends and with a very high glass roof covered with years of dirt and pigeon shit. 'This is the plasterer's shop,' Marguerite informed them, stating the obvious and forced to raise her voice in order to be heard over a pop number blaring from a portable radio, 'where they put together anything made of plaster.' She giggled again. She seemed to have a habit of giggling. It was probably due to nerves being so new to the job and hoping not to make too big a hash of it. 'They can make mouldings for rooms in period houses for example, like… like this piece here.' With her free hand she waved vaguely in the direction of a number of pieces hoping there was at least one that would prove she knew what she was talking about, 'Statues, as you can see if you look around, oh so many things necessary for filming, garden ornaments, … things like that… in plaster,' she lamely dribbled off.

A few of the workmen both old and young in splattered overalls gave the group the once over but, finding nothing to their tastes apart from Marguerite who they had seen before and who they had already decided amongst themselves in a heated discussion during a tea break was the ultimate virgin, decided it would be too much of an effort to break the ice and went back to their work without a second glance. There never seemed to appear anyone half decent on these walkabouts; no one to go ooh and aah and perve over that is.

'The plaster is mixed in these huge tubs, baths or vats, whatever you want to call them, that you see here,' Marguerite continued at the top of her voice, not realising the music had momentarily come to an end and there was no longer any need to shout. 'And if I were you,' she said with a smile, 'I wouldn't like to fall into one and come out looking like a mummy.' This was met by a dozen blank faces so she dropped the smile and hurried on. 'The next part of the studios we will visit will be the carpenter's shop where they build the sets amongst other things.' She didn't stipulate what the other things were. 'It will probably be quite noisy in there with hammering and drilling and that. Oh, by the way, if any of you have any questions you would like to ask please don't hesitate.' She looked around, not in expectation it needs to be said, in case she couldn't come up with the answer to a question put to her. No one had a question to ask. It would seem rather that they had lost confidence in Marguerite's expertise when it came to the practicalities of film making and wanted to get on with the tour in the hopes that they might catch a glimpse of some of the stars, perhaps even get some autographs. Most of them were clutching their books at the ready just in case.

They moved on to what looked like a main block; large, with a fairly modern extension, square, bare concrete and ugly, and entered one by one through a single glass door, gathering in the corridor on the other side, gazing around with curiosity until their attention was once more focused on their guide. In truth there was nothing to see but a corridor the length of the building with the door through which they had entered and similar doors at either end, all painted a dreary institutional green and desperately in need of a new coat.

'Now in this building, on this floor first of all...' clipboard still in hand she opened her arms in the manner of a flight attendant indicating a plane's emergency exits or oxygen masks, '...we have actor's dressing rooms.'

This was more like it. A frisson ran around the ladies in the company. Maybe now they would get a glimpse of some famous actor.

'These are not star dressing rooms of course. Stars have their own dressing rooms on or close to the set.'

The frisson was dead in the water.

'When are we going to see an actual studio?' This was from the moustachioed Mister Know-It-All, his moustache twitching in overtime before it settled down after a soothing stroke or two. Thornton wondered it didn't start purring. His name was actually Kevin Macintosh and it sounded as though he hailed from somewhere north of the border, Glasgow more than likely. Marguerite found it difficult to understand him but his attitude gave her sufficient information.

'All in good time, sir.' Marguerite was a little terse with the gentleman in question. After all he had already made a fool of her once and she wasn't going to risk it again.

As for Thornton he hadn't been able to get near the guy. Cynthia had interposed her ample self between him and the rest of the company. The moustachioed creature appeared to like it.

'On the floor above,' Marguerite continued, 'we have offices for various members of the staff, like for example, writers who might be working on current or future productions.'

Thornton's ears pricked up immediately and he glanced at the dingy ceiling as if he could already see Joachim Caswell's office above and his quarry sitting there oblivious of the hunt as he typed away on yet another amendment.

'Now, if you will kindly follow me please, from here we will go downstairs so that you can get a glimpse of make-up.'

'Oh!' the frisson was back again. 'Isn't that where the film star Cord Wainer died?' This was from a lady who, with the exception of the moustache, was a dead ringer to play twin sister of Mister Mackintosh. To add to it her voice sounded like the creaking of a door the rusty hinges of which badly needed oiling.

'That's correct, yes. Please be careful on the stairs. Stairs can be so treacherous as we all know and we wouldn't want anyone twisting an ankle now would we?'

No, we definitely would not.

Marguerite was so busy ushering her charges carefully down the stairs, no doubt keeping a sharp eye open for possible torn tendons and twisted ankles, she failed to notice one of her party was missing. Thornton wasn't going downstairs; he was silently on his way up.

He found himself in a corridor exactly the same as the one he had just left. He moved slowly along looking at each door as he passed hoping to find a name but, except for being numbered, they were all blank. Each door sported a small brass fitting into which a name card could be inserted but they were all empty. Anonymity seemed to be the norm along here. Of course he could always knock on a door and make a polite enquiry but suddenly there was no need because he found one open and the room had an occupant.

Seated at a desk, typewriter clattering away albeit with two index fingers was no other than Ernest J. Bloomberg who looked up and peered through his jam jar bottom spectacles when Thornton gave a discreet knock. As the lenses were for close-up work all he could see was a vague shape until he took them off when the shape came into focus, someone he had never clapped eyes on before, and he said, 'May I help you?'

Ernest was wearing a *Save the Brazilian rain forest* T-shirt and hoping his visitor might be another journalist craving an interview regarding the murder. Ernest would give as many interviews as he could. Fame was just around the corner, the crooked finger of fame in fact was beckoning and the more interviews he gave the better.

'Yes,' Thornton replied, 'I'm looking for Joachim Caswell, can you tell me…? Oh, wait a sec, don't I know you? Yes, I'm sure, you are…' He snapped his fingers as if trying to recollect.

'Ernest J. Bloomberg,' Ernest J. said, quick to introduce himself.

'Yes of course, of course, I recognised the face immediately.'

Ernest J. squirmed with pleasure. Recognised immediately huh?

'Am I interrupting?'

'Not at all! Not at all! Please come in.'

'It's just that I see you typing away there,' Thornton advanced into the room, 'and I would hate to temporarily put a stop to inspiration. I should imagine for a writer that could be extremely irritating to say the least. What, if I may be permitted to ask, are you working on?'

Ernest was now sure this was another reporter and turned on what little charm he possessed which, if truth was to be told, wasn't saying all that much but one had to admit he did try and it wasn't really all his fault.

His physical appearance to begin with wasn't exactly inviting what with his narrow shoulders, slight stoop, and concave chest but, that apart, he put the blame for his lack of the social graces firstly on his mother who seemed to spend most of her life ignoring him while she remained glued to the telly, leaving it usually only to perform the necessary or make herself a cup of tea. Too many meals in the Bloomberg household consisted of baked beans on toast or tinned spaghetti and, if they really wanted to splash out, possibly a Mister Kipling fancy cake or two or a slice of Joe Lyon's jam or chocolate Swiss Roll to follow. Plenty of white bread and margarine of course and the cheapest generic strawberry jam available from the supermarket shelves, containing very little fruit but a lot of sugar and a deadly poison to diabetics.

It might be said of course that Ernest could have improved his physical appearance by judicious and frequent visits to the gym but it was his very appearance that put him off. He just knew that stripped down to vest and shorts would produce sniggers, possibly even snide remarks meant for him to overhear. It had happened at school during what was called physical training so he had avoided it whenever possible. Children might be told that it is the height of rudeness to make personal remarks but they do it all the same.

Then there was this person who passed himself off as his father, addicted to roll up cigarettes in liquorice paper and, like the gate man and possibly everyone working in the plaster shop, riveted every day to page three of *The Sun* and who Ernest J. considered to be a moron; well, to be on the generous side, slightly dim at least.

Whenever they did meet up which wasn't very often, usually on the stairs when one or the other wanted to use the bathroom, they had absolutely nothing to say to each other. In fact it sometimes seemed they lived on different planets let alone in the same house and were never a family. Maybe the father wondered where this strange young creature invading his home had come from, metaphorically speaking. If he had known about such a thing he might have thought his son was a changeling. Ernest J. on his part often wondered if he actually was one. Where *had* he come from he would think that he was imbued with such oodles of genuine talent when his parents were both as thick as two planks?

Both parents had to take a measure of blame then for his shortcomings where the social graces were concerned. Things might have been different if he had had sisters. He often wondered what life would have been like with girls in the house. A constant line

45

of panties dripping over the bath tub and, more than like, hair clogging up the plug hole he would think when in a bad mood.

Whenever he looked in the full length wardrobe mirror in his bedroom, which was often, he almost despaired. It was no wonder from a very early age he wanted nothing more than to work in show business, the world of dreams, fantasy land, the ultimate escape and, though he might not have realised it, writing *Hour of Agony* was therapeutic if nothing else. He had such great ambitions that would more than likely never be fulfilled. But then what made him so different? Didn't millions of others feel the same way? How many preteens were there who desperately wanted to be pop singers as famous as The Beatles?

'Please take a seat,' he said, not getting up but extending his hand to a chair on the other side of the desk and noticing yet again when he turned it over that he had been biting his fingernails: a shame really as he had rather beautiful delicate hands that could have been at least one redeeming physical feature. He had read somewhere once that Rodin on completing a new work was having it admired by visitors to his studio and the general comment was "Oh, the hands! What beautiful hands," everybody gushing enthusiastically over the hands, so the sculptor took up a mallet and chisel and chopped them off. "The whole must be appreciated not merely a part," he was reputed to have said. It could have been an apocryphal story. After all what the great ones do the lesser will prattle of.

'Yes, do take a pew,' Ernest J. said to the still standing Thornton who duly moved to sit down. 'What am I working on?' he continued before Thornton had even settled in the chair. 'I'm working on a full length feature screenplay.'

'Indeed?' Thornton said, 'How fascinating. May I ask what it is about?'

'Certainly. It's about the pains of a young man growing up in today's society.' He could have said in our household but society was better, universal as it were. Weren't writers working on their first project, be it film, teleplay, play or novel, supposed to use what they know, be autobiographical to a certain extent?

Only to a certain extent mind. Some things couldn't possibly be exposed to an unsympathetic world.

Throughout his young life the size of his todger, or his John Thomas as his mother called it, had been a cause of great dismay, if not rage, sometimes leading almost to a primal scream. Why should he have been cursed in this manner? Miniscule would describe it, but he didn't think that bit of biography should be included in *Hour of Agony*, physiologically important as it was. He might change his mind later when the script was finalised and he could discreetly and in good taste slip it in somewhere, in reference to another character maybe. A bit daring he thought. It's all very well people saying size is unimportant; it's what you do with it that matters, but when it was as small as his it mattered a great deal. He could have accepted his other shortcomings more easily if he could have flourished a truly gigantic you know what but it was a black cloud forever on his horizon. When the parts were handed out he was definitely last in the queue. General de Gaulle's wife at a dinner when asked what she wanted out of life replied, "A penis," and that's how Ernest J. felt. The fact that Madam de Gaulle's accent mispronounced happiness was beside the point.

Ernest J. was still a virgin because the thought that if a girl finally wrapped her searching fingers around it and burst into hysterical laughter he would simply curl up and die of shame. His blood ran cold even thinking about it. Was it true what they said about Napoleon, that his wienie was teeny which is why he went warring all over Europe just to confirm his manhood? What did Josephine think of that and how many good men had to die at the gates of Moscow or Waterloo or wherever merely to prove Napoleon's manhood, as well as proclaiming himself emperor of France and putting a few of his relations on various thrones in both the old and the new world?

Ernest wondered if he got straight down to the nitty-gritty with no foreplay would that be a good tactic? Not really. She would probably lie there for a while wondering when he was going to get going.

He would never though write in his play about how he answered an advertisement in a magazine, a periodical he kept under his bedclothes where he thought his mother would never find it. His mother occasionally, when leaving the telly probably to make herself another cup of tea, might spend a few minutes cleaning his room while not missing anything on the box and waiting for the kettle to boil. That is she flicked a duster around merely moving the dust from one place to another unless she was feeling really energetic and there was nothing she particularly wanted to watch at that moment, then she would open a window and give the duster a good shaking outside. She never made his bed. Perhaps the reason for that was because her son, being now of an age when she could be embarrassed by the stains on his sheets, kept her well away from it so the magazine was quite safe. Sheets all crumpled up ready to shove in the washing machine did not reveal those tell tale stains. Of course the magazine would have been even safer if he thought to put it under the mattress, and if she was suspicious that something not quite right was going on, she would refer it to his father and under the mattress was the last place either of them would think of looking. She had warned the lad often enough when he was younger and in the bath not to play with his eggs in case he broke them. The fact that his eggs had hardly put in an appearance the advice was a bit premature and made for a rather bemused boy wondering for a long while what on earth she was talking about. When they finally did drop he got the picture and immediately wanted to play with them to see just how fragile they might be and, in so doing, discovered something else that was much more fun to play with.

So he answered the advertisement by filling in the coupon and sending it off together with his money order for payment, buying himself a vacuum enlarger guaranteed to add circumference and inches in a matter of weeks if used every day, but it turned out to be a total waste of money as far as enlargement was concerned that is. He didn't think he was in a position to return it and ask for a refund and it did excite him somewhat when in use, not every day of course, that would be an indulgence too far and could have painful consequences if one took notice of the warnings in *Eric or Little by Little* or *A Boy at Fifteen* by a Reverend gentleman who probably was over stimulated to a degree and broke out in an agitated sweat when writing it.

He was always fearful that if his mother ever did get around to cleaning his room in a proper manner she would discover his toy so he kept it on top of the wardrobe where he knew she could never reach. It necessitated climbing on a chair whenever he wanted to use it but that wasn't a bad thing. The slight delay and the anticipation caused even greater excitement. He had sent off his order and watched for the postman every day until it arrived in case his mother got there first. Daddy was already at work. He had decided if she should see it on the doorstep and want to know what it was he would say it was something technical to do with film making and she wouldn't understand. With his new acquisition he hurried up to his bedroom, locked the door and indulged in his first attempt at increasing the size of his willy.

'And its title?' Thornton asked… 'in case I happen to see it on the big screen one day.'

'It's called *Hour of Agony*. Of course that is only a working title. It could always be changed.'

'And how far have you got with it?'

'I'm doing a rewrite at the moment.' Ernest J. failed to add that was the umpteenth rewrite so far.

'Oh, I'm sorry; I'm interrupting your concentration. I know how you writers feel about that.'

There it was "writers" again. Ernest J. preened more than a little under the flattery. Fancy a total stranger walking in and referring to him as a writer. If he had been blest with a different set of parents they would more than likely be extremely proud of him but with the ones he was stuck with they probably couldn't care less. Maybe one day *Hour of Agony*, when it had done its theatrical distribution, like *The African Queen* would play on the telly any number of times, especially at Christmas, and his mother would finally sit up and take notice. On the other hand she probably wouldn't even twig that it was written by her son.

'No, please!' He said. 'No problem. No trouble at all. Only too happy to answer any questions you may care to ask,' he added, still under the impression that Thornton was a journalist. It never occurred to him to enquire what paper, magazine, or media area his visitor represented.

He lifted a pack of cigarettes from the desk. Obviously all serious writers and men of genius when working smoked like chimneys. Was it not Mark Twain who said "a woman is a woman but tobacco is a smoke?" And he had seen that in so many Hollywood films, smoking that is. He extended the pack in Thornton's direction and was a little disappointed when his uninvited guest shook his head. Surely all journalists, being writers themselves, working frantically every day to deadlines they had to meet so as not to incur the editor's wrath, must smoke like chimneys? Maybe his visitor had just put one out and didn't fancy another so soon so, before his new friend lost interest, he thought he had better elaborate on the vicissitudes of being a scriptwriter, in particular the loneliness as opposed to easy peasy journalism with its raucous bonhomie in Fleet Street pubs and, having lit his cigarette, blown out a cloud of smoke and coughed long and loud, he said, 'The problem you see is that you have to show your script to people to get their initial reaction and, as everyone reacts in a different way, criticising and coming up with suggestions for improvement, that's why it necessitates so many rewrites.'

His grammar had failed him lamentably. He took another drag of his cigarette, held it over the ashtray and, although there was no ash as yet, tapped it a number of times with a stiff forefinger. He had seen that in the movies as well and wondered for a moment why he had neglected to give a stage direction to that effect somewhere in his script. He must remember to put it in for the sake of authenticity.

'And how many people have you shown it to?'

Ernest J. shrugged and took another drag of his cigarette. The smoke got up his nose and made his eyes water so he stubbed out the hardly smoked butt. Apart from the fact that he couldn't really afford it, he hated smoking. He didn't know why he ever started in the first place. He would have to give it up and boast to all and sundry about what magnificent will power he possessed. He might put a scene like that into *Hour of Agony*. After all the boy only took up smoking behind the bicycle sheds at school because of peer pressure and even though his character would find it hellish attempting to give it up, cold turkey as it were, in the end he would come through.

Then, much to Thornton's surprise, he suddenly started to sing, '*Row row row your boat merrily down the stream, merrily merrily merrily merrily life is but a dream.* That's how the film opens,' he explained, 'solo voice singing sadly, unaccompanied, a capela that is, perhaps with an echo, sort of like from a distance, ghostly, know what I mean? Atmospheric. And then of course the music would be orchestrated and be the theme music right through the film, coming in at appropriate moments. I've written to a very famous composer asking if he would be interested in writing the score but so far he hasn't replied.'

'That's a very...' he paused to find the right words... 'original opening,' he said, 'have you shown your script to Joachim Caswell?'

Did Thornton imagine it or by the look on Ernest J.'s face had the temperature in the room suddenly dropped ten degrees?

'Don't mention that man,' he hissed in a sudden shower of saliva. 'He's a shit, a turd, a horrible great steaming dump!'

'My my,' Thornton said, not knowing what else to say in the face of such vehemence. Ernest J.'s paler than pale complexion had suddenly turned a sort of mottled pink as though he had just broken out in a rash and was in dire need of some antihistamine.

'Of course I showed it to him,' he yelped, 'and do you know what he said? First of all he threw it back at me. Yes, literally threw it across the room and said it was bilge, tommyrot, crap, and go and rewrite it. Then, "no, don't bother", he said. "Stay an assistant, be a road sweeper, be a bus conductor, be a shelf stacker, but whatever you do don't ever fancy yourself as a writer." Yes, I remember every disgusting, every hurtful, painful word. He is without any doubt my bête noir and what did I do to him to create such enmity? It's no wonder van Gogh cut-off his ear and shot himself.'

A slightly startled Thornton wondered what van Gogh had to do with it but let it pass. He was enlightened by the next statement issued with great authority.

'All true artists, and that includes genuine writers as opposed to hacks like Joachim Caswell, have to suffer for their art. That's a known fact. It's what brings out the best in them.'

Ernest J. Bloomberg took off his glasses to give them a good wipe with his handkerchief before putting them on again. Obviously they had misted up alarmingly with the memory of his humiliation.

'I hope you won't write that in your article,' he said, 'about, you know, what Mister Caswell said. I'd simply hate it if people thought he was right. Myself, I think in fact I put it down to jealousy on his part; he hasn't written a single decent word in yonks, take my word for it.'

Article? Thornton raised his risible eyebrow, and then the penny dropped. He also thought he ought to make some kind of an excuse for Joachim's behaviour if it was all Ernest J. had made it out to be.

'Maybe…' Thornton was searching for the right thing to say here. 'Maybe he was being cruel in order to be kind.'

'What!'

'You know, by being slightly disparaging…'

'Slightly!'

'…he was really urging you on in a subtle way to better things.'

'Subtle?'

'Like one day your screen credits…' Thornton moved his hand horizontally from one side of the room to the other as though he was envisaging cinemascope… 'could read "Written and Directed by." That's what you want isn't it? Or even better…' The cinemascope gesture was reversed… '"An Ernest J. Bloomberg Film." That's what they all say these days, isn't it? Total credit, like no one else had anything to do with it.'

Ernest J. nodded, too moved for words and his glasses steamed up again. He was even tempted to take up and light another cigarette but didn't find it too hard to resist.

'And maybe an Oscar or two for best screenplay and best direction,' Thornton added as icing on the cake as he studied his nails. 'On the other hand,' he looked up, 'I admit his criticism could have been less crass, less virulent as you say it was but maybe he was in an extremely bad mood that day.'

'He was always in a bad mood, always going on about how badly the companies had treated him or, as he put it, cheated him. Cheated was the word he mostly used. Robbed was another.'

'Oh?' This was the first interesting piece of news Thornton had received.

'Yes. It seems that crappy filmed kiddies' television series he wrote all those years ago for this very same company and of course *Centurion* who distributed it, has made an absolute fortune: shown all over the world; syndicated seven times in the states, here on television any number of times as well, BBC and Independent television and he has never received a penny in royalties which if he had, as he was always telling anyone who would listen, would have made him very very rich by now. And, according to him, there was a clause in his contract stipulating that royalties should be paid for every showing come hell or high water. The company was supposed, according to contract, to set aside five percent from every sale just for that purpose. He just went on and on and on about it. In a way I suppose I did feel a bit sorry for him even though it got a bit on the boring side. After all we writers should stick together. It's a cruel dog eat dog world out there but the way he carried on you would have thought he had just rewritten the whole of Shakespeare.'

"Did this have anything to do with the murder?" Thornton wondered. "Was this motive enough? But why take it out on an inoffensive little secretary, lover or not as the case might be? It just didn't make any sense."

'This is very interesting,' he said out loud. 'I would like to interview this Joachim Caswell, hear it all from the horse's mouth as it were, which is his office?'

'You're sitting in it.'

'I beg our pardon?'

Ernest J. Bloomberg was suddenly looking very smug.

'You're sitting in it.'

Thornton looked around, frowning.

Ernest was smiling. 'He's done a runner, hit the road, done a bunk, skedaddled, scarpered, buggered off, and nobody seems to know where he is. That is...' he tapped the side of his nose, '...nobody but me. And shall I tell you why he's disappeared? Because I think the shit murdered his girl friend.'

# Chapter Three

'You knew about that? I mean, you knew that she was his girl friend.'

'Of course I did. Didn't the whole studio know about it? They hardly made a secret of it, did they? Making goo-goo eyes and slobbering over each other the whole time, well at every opportunity they could get anyway. If you want my opinion it was quite sick-making. Puke puke puke! If I put a scene like that in *Hour of* Agony it would get the bird. No one would believe it for a minute. Hoot hoot they'd go. You would hear them hooting all over the cinema. Then I think she might have given him the brush-off you know which is why he topped her. But that is only conjecture of course. Did you know Cord Wainer was a homosexual?'

This too came out of the blue but it would seem Thornton's earlier surmise was correct unless the man was AC/DC which was more than likely and he wondered why, like van Gogh's ear, this had suddenly come into the conversation. If it were true it would be a terrible disappointment to his myriad female fans worldwide, and some male ones who never got the chance to know him and now never would. But then he wouldn't be the only heartthrob to hide his true nature.

'Cord Wainer was married,' Thornton said.

'What difference does that make? Oscar Wilde was married and had two kids. Somerset Maugham was married. Cole Porter was married. Noel Coward of course wasn't married but everyone knew about him from the start, I mean, like Ivor Novello, with him there was no hiding it was there? I mean he was so out of the closet marriage would have just been too ridiculous for words.'

'You seem to be very knowledgeable, Mister Bloomberg.'

'Ernest, please.'

'Ernest.'

For a while they sat looking at each other in silence. Thornton finally broke it.

'Well?'

'Well what?'

'Very knowledgeable.'

'I'm a writer.'

'That would explain it.'

'Yes, you would be surprised the number of married men who play the field you know with or without their wives' knowledge. Sometimes it is a marriage of convenience of course, the wife being lesbian or frigid or something like that. Oh, they might be very fond of each other, love each other even, but sex? Definitely not, no, no, not sex, so the hunt for both of them goes on elsewhere. Maybe that's the answer to a happy lasting marriage. Oh yes, Cord…well, he was always touching up the girls all over the place wasn't he? And they loved it of course, stands to reason, famous handsome film star and that, but you could tell that was just a smokescreen and like I said they usually seemed to enjoy it. I thought he was a slug, a sort of greasy lounge lizard, but then I'm not a girl. Still he came on to me in the gent's toilet one day. Don't look so surprised.'

This was because Thornton was thinking Ernest J. Bloomberg was not exactly a great pick-up by any stretch of the imagination, not even in semi-darkness, and it must have shown. Maybe Cord was drunk that day. He did tend to overdo the hard stuff in the lunch break or so rumour had it. Maybe he just liked them skinny and pimply.

'Yes, stood right next to me at the urinal and he didn't have to do that, there were plenty of empty ones all round, and flashed his erection right under my nose, would you credit it?' Ernest J's voice had risen to a higher pitch and Thornton forbore to enquire as to what his nose was doing so low down. 'Obviously thought I would take him up on it and give him a quick hand shandy maybe before anybody came in. Or maybe he thought he could lure me into a closet for something more... more... I refused of course. I mean, I wasn't disgusted or anything like that. I'm not homophobic, anti-gay, no, by no means, but the thought of it just gave me the screaming habdabs. Brrr!' He gave a theatrical shudder for emphasis. 'Interpol will have to be called in you know.'

He'd changed direction once more. It seemed to be a habit.

'For being gay? And anyway, it's a bit late for that wouldn't you say? Considering the man's been dead these last couple of years or however long it's been. Let's see... 1971 wasn't it?'

'I'm not talking about Cord; I'm talking about that shit Caswell. He will have to be extradited of course.'

'From where?'

'From Ro...'

'From where?'

'No, I mustn't say.'

'But you already have. You were going to say Rome and how do you know that's where he is?'

'I've heard him talking, haven't I? He has a friend who works in the studios in Rome. He was always going on about how terrific this guy is, how long they've known each other, would do anything for each other, like brothers they were and he kept on saying he must get around to visiting him one day instead of just keeping up a correspondence. Well, I think that day arrived and I think he felt through his friend he could maybe get work in the industry there. I don't think he speaks any Italian but I suppose he thought he could always come up with visuals for television commercials, ones that didn't require dialogue or, if they did, it would be voice-over anyway and someone else could write the Italian.'

'This isn't all part of your wild writer's imagination is it?'

'Of course not.'

'Do you know the friend's name?'

Ernest J. nodded in the affirmative but wasn't ready to say although he was dying to so he changed the nod to a shake. He hadn't given this information to the police when they were making their enquiries and he was just a wee bit angsty about giving it to Thornton. After all as a newspaperman what would he do with it? Would he have the information and his source splashed all over the front page in lurid headlines? And would that mean jail for withholding evidence? Mind you, it would seem it's quite a good experience for a writer to go to jail. Think of Wilde and Genet, Verlaine and Joe Orton. No, in his opinion you can't trust reporters further than you can throw them and most of them being horribly overweight due to all that bonhomie in pubs that wouldn't be very far.

'Well, if you don't want to give me the name, as you seem to know a great deal of what goes on in this place, maybe you can give me Caswell's address in London.'

For an answer, Ernest J., after a moment's thought, pushed his glasses up onto his forehead, he had seen various directors do that when working, picked up the phone and waited for it to be answered; pursing his mouth a little while he did so. This would show the reporter how important he was in the studio. Unfortunately his bravado was somewhat diminished when the glasses slipped down again so he decided to leave them there. Switchboard, evidently extremely busy as always, eventually came through.

'Oh, yes! Marty...' He cast a glance in Thornton's direction; first name terms you will notice. 'This is Ernest Bloomberg... Bloomberg, you know, working on *Return to Batani*... Yes, that's right. Put me through to accounts will you please? I'll hold.' He smiled at Thornton who he was sure was duly impressed and placed his hand over the mouthpiece. 'They're a pretty dim lot in accounts,' he said with an air of superiority, 'so they won't know much about what's been going on. Only interested in facts and figures.' He returned his attention to the phone. 'Oh, yes, I need some information please… The home address of the writer Joachim Caswell… What for? Oh, information for *Return to Batani,* an expenses claim. Thank you.' He held on a moment longer and then scribbled the address on a piece of company note paper and handed it across the desk to Thornton.

'Thank you,' Thornton said, glancing down and noting the address was in Hampstead before slipping the paper in his jacket pocket. 'I'm much obliged.'

'Don't know what you want it for. You know he's not there.'

'Nevertheless…'

Thornton had a sudden vision of an irate Marguerite storming into the building and, deciding he was going to get nothing more out of Mister Bloomberg for the moment he would politely bring the conversation to an end. As it was he needn't have bothered when the telephone rang and Ernest nearly leapt out of his skin. He picked up the phone and looked at his wrist watch. 'Oh, my God! I'll be right there!' He dropped the phone and got to his feet. 'Sorry, can't chat anymore. Wanted on the floor.' He was already heading for the door. 'Nice to have met you.' He still hadn't thought to ask what paper Thornton was from.

Thornton got up to follow.

Ernest fairly flew down the stairs and along the corridor but, when Thornton caught up with him outside the building he discovered the young man had been brought to a halt, confronted by a sullen looking bunch of tourists and a furious Marguerite with quivering clipboard.

'Ah, so there you are. At last! We've been hu…hu…hu… hunting everywhere for you.' Her agitation almost caused a loss of speech.

The Glaswegian midget's moustache was twitching in what

seemed like a South American rhythm.

'Lost half our tour we have,' an obviously disgruntled Cynthia said, 'thanks to you.'

'I was about to call security,' Marguerite whimpered, 'and that would really have upset the applecart wouldn't it?'

'What applecart,' Cynthia asked.'

'It's an expression,' Marguerite explained. 'I believe it was used by George Bernard Shaw.' Marguerite had obviously been to drama school and was between engagements.

'Who's George Bernard Shaw?' someone else queried. 'Is he here in the studio?'

'Not unless he's been resurrected,' Marguerite snapped, thoroughly discombobulated. She turned back to the escapee. 'When I noticed you were missing we had to think of where we last saw you and someone, I think it was Cynthia, suggested this building.'

Cynthia smirked with self-satisfaction and Mister Know-It-All Kevin smiled with her and gave his moustache another stroke, a little on the suggestive side and soothing at the same time. Cynthia went all coy. They were obviously getting on like a house on fire.

'I'm terribly sorry,' Thornton rolled on his back wagging his tail for forgiveness, 'but I bumped into an old friend here.' He placed a hand on Ernest's shoulder and gave it a little shake. 'Well, not old in years of course as you can see but let me introduce you, this is the famous screenwriter Ernest J. Bloomberg.'

'Oh yes?' This was from Mister Mackintosh again, showing off in front of his newfound friend. 'What might you have written then?'

'Work in progress,' Ernest said.

'He's currently working on *Return to Batani* and mark my words one day he's going to be very famous.'

'Is that so?' Kevin said but before he could continue Cynthia stepped in with, 'May I have your autograph please?'

This was the very first time Ernest J. Bloomberg in all his tender years had ever been asked for his autograph and although he knew it wouldn't be the last he could have gratefully thrown his arms around Thornton and kissed him then and there for setting the wheels in motion. Slightly shaky he duly signed the autograph book but, as another was thrust under his nose, he remembered where he was supposed to be and fled, sprinting across to the studio block at the rate of knots, lickety-split in fact – a little infra dig for someone of such importance and incipient fame.

# Chapter Four

Thornton sat in his office studying the notes on his yellow legal pad; that is he gazed myopically at the page in front of him because the paucity of those notes made itself obvious in less than a minute so he heaved a sigh and made a couple of doodles as an attempt to start him thinking. It didn't work. Only a qualified psychiatrist would have been able to decipher what the doodles meant and even he would have some difficulty with it.

Although he had had a suspicion that Ernest J. was right and a visit to the flat in Hampstead would be a waste of time and, although he loathed tube travel at the best of times, feeling in a somewhat mood for martyrdom and knowing up to now his investigations had been a virtual failure, he undertook the journey nevertheless, just in case.

He did indeed find out it was a waste of time though there were side benefits. After the smell, noise and litter of the tube he enjoyed a bracing walk on the Heath, gently admonished a somewhat startled gentleman for throwing his dog a stick. He also discovered a Kurosawa revival, *Throne of Blood*, Kurosawa's version of *King Lear*, was showing at the local cinema. If he had time he would take that in. He loved Japanese movies; maybe he would invite Holly to share the pleasure.

Loitering in a hallway at Caswell's block of flats, having rung the doorbell a number of times and getting no reply, an adjoining door flew open and he was accosted by an elderly heavily rouged hatchet-faced lady with plucked eyebrows and false ones drawn up in a wide arc, a suspicious neighbour, wanting to know what he was up to before she dialled emergency and called the police. He obviously had no right to be in the building. Although the stance was somewhat aggressive, she remained in a position from which she could retreat and slam the door hurriedly should the stranger prove threatening and advance on her.

Joachim's flat was apparently empty and of Joachim there was no sign. Thornton didn't give the impression of being a putative burglar but she believed you never can tell, especially in London. A burglar didn't necessarily go around wearing a mask, carrying a jemmy and with a bag over his shoulder marked "Swag" but one read so many hair-raising tales in the local newspaper and her locality was not without its fair share of crime. Her glaring at him in somewhat belligerent fashion was something quite unusual for London where, if there was anything suspicious going on, neighbours normally stayed behind locked doors and pretended they were out, even if the telly was going full blast and a dead giveaway.

On hearing the reason for his visit the good lady confirmed the flat was empty because she was a friend and, as Joachim was a bachelor, she looked after things for him when he wasn't around and she would know if he was at home. She hadn't seen him for quite a few days.

'When were you last in there?' Thornton asked. 'For all you know he could be dead. He could be one of those corpses one reads about that lie festering for days before being discovered, sometimes for years even. Sometimes they get desiccated and become mummified.'

"Not a chance," was the answer. She had been in the flat to

check on things that very morning, only an hour or so before Thornton's arrival, and it was completely devoid of corpses, mummified or festering. She would have noticed the smell if nothing else.

Then would she happen to know where Joachim had gone to?

Negative: most definitely negative. It would seem he had departed in something of a hurry, leaving no message.

So to date how far had Thornton got in his enquiries? Not very far it had to be said.

His visit to Caswell's flat having turned out to be a dead end he took the journey out to Breconfield once more, this time to pay a visit to the pub nearest to Riverside Drive only to find it wasn't *The Fisherman's Arms* of his imagining but *The Drover's Arms* and, although it boasted the requisite number of old black beams in between which the ceiling was a grubby brown from years of tobacco smoke; pipe, cigar and cigarette, and although it had diamond window panes and boasted its requisite pieces of oak, it did not sport prize trout in glass cases but old cracked oil paintings of prize bulls.

The pub was virtually empty when Thornton entered. Obviously it was too early in the day except for a couple of regulars, two local workmen in the building trade by the looks of it. Thornton was doing his Sherlock Holmes bit. Elementary my dear Watson, elementary, they wore overalls and looked as though they were grimy with cement dust. They were no doubt seated in their usual place, washing the dust from their throats, and regarded the stranger with deep suspicion as he waltzed up to the bar with a breezy, 'Good morning, landlord.'

'And a top of the morning to you, sir,' the landlord growled, obviously not in too good a mood for some reason or other, 'and what can I get you?' Thinking what can I get you apart from a drink because he had a shrewd suspicion the young stranger who he had never clapped eyes on before was bound to want something more from him? After a lifetime of working with booze and bottles and listening to maudlin drunks telling him their life stories, troubles and woes, he was something of an amateur psychologist. He wondered for a moment if this was a travelling salesman though he carried nothing obvious like a sample case for instance. He could though have an order book nestling in a pocket.

'A lager and lime please.' Thornton put on his most engaging smile.

Ah, there it was. He might have known. 'A lager and lime it is,' he said, thinking another city gent ordering poofy drinks: correction, a single poofy drink, ruining a good glass of beer and he wasn't likely to have more than one. Surprised he hadn't asked for a lemonade shandy.

'And what might you be doing in this neck of the woods?' The landlord asked as he pulled the beer, 'Just visiting are you?'

If you keep a pub long enough you are not only curious as to possible motives where strangers are concerned but your amateur psychiatric instincts come galloping to the fore.

The regulars, their pint mugs on the table in front of them, craned forwards all the better to listen in.

'Actually I'm looking for someone.'

'Oh, yes?' His suspicions were duly confirmed. 'And who might that someone be then?'

Thornton was a little put out by the man's decided squint. He wasn't too sure he was being looked at or whether the look was directed elsewhere, like on the ceiling for example. Which eye should he concentrate on was the question. He decided on the right one as being a little more stable. The left appeared to flutter alarmingly and he didn't want to be accused of staring at an affliction.

'You wouldn't by any chance I suppose be acquainted with a lady by the name of Ida Chapman, would you? I know she lives on Riverside Drive but I don't have a number.'

'Ida? Of course I know Ida.' He scratched and rubbed an itch on his nose and then pulled at his dewlap between finger and thumb and stared at Thornton. The squint apart his eyes were a pale grey that telegraphed a warning not to mess with him. Even though well into middle age and carrying quite a gut he was obviously his own bouncer and kept an orderly house. 'Everybody knows Ida. Don't they, lads?' This was in the direction of the regulars who nodded their heads in unison. 'In here every Saturday night without fail for her drop of milk stout, that's our Ida. I suppose you're another one wanting to talk about the murder. I'm surprised she puts up with it. However, if you must know…'

And this was why, when he had finished his lager and lime and indulged in a small handful of salted peanuts from a bowl on the counter, Thornton thanked the landlord, nodded to the regulars who nodded unsmilingly in return, and set off on the short walk for number 73 Riverside Drive where he found himself face to face with Ida Chapman. The good lady was quite happy to welcome her visitor over a nice cup of tea served in a delicate Victorian china cup ("they were my grandmother's"), strong enough to melt the spoon and accompanied by chocolate digestive biscuits on a plate from the same service. It was almost as if she knew that Thornton would be coming and that he was particularly partial to chocolate digestive biscuits. Next to chocolate digestives *Garibaldis* were his other favourite. His mother always referred to them as fly cemeteries.

He sat in the dimity parlour redolent of furniture polish while she went off to the kitchen to wash her hands, put on the kettle, brew up, remove her pinny and make sure her hair was respectable. She didn't want to appear a frump in front of her visitor. Thornton worried that she had opened her door and without any introduction welcomed in a complete stranger, but obviously Ida Chapman was a trusting soul. He hoped that trust would never be misplaced. He just knew she was the type of person to be too easily conned. If the boys had some of the black stuff left over from a previous and offered to macadam her drive for a couple of hundred quid she would most likely agree to it and then be squeezed for more to finish the job, unless she was cannier than Thornton imagined.

Despite the furniture being obviously old and rather shabby and just a hint of rising damp staining the wallpaper it was a well-kept and comfortable room, very snug in winter he thought with its gas fire, at the moment the surround adorned with burnished Benares brass ornaments, a couple of egrets carved out of horn, two large World War I shell cases holding obvious artificial flowers and three ebony elephants in a row; large, medium and small. There were even antimacassars over the chairs. Thornton wondered if maybe there were flying ducks anywhere in this house and when last did men plaster their hair with macassar oil? There were modern equivalents he supposed, like Brylcream for example.

When she had returned with the tea things, all bar the pot, he thought he would ease into his enquiries by making polite conversation.

'It's very good of you to see me, Mrs Chapman,' he said. 'I hope it's not inconvenient.'

'Not at all, not at all. I don't get many visitors so it makes ever such a nice change.'

'Your husband was in Africa?' he asked.

'Goodness gracious no,' she said with a smile, 'whatever could have given you such an idea?'

'The elephants.' He inclined his head in their direction.

'Oh! No. No. Eric never left England, but his younger sister Kathy emigrated to South Africa a good many years ago now and she sent them to us, together with those bird things, I believe they're meant to be egrets, and we have a set of table mats with Zulu designs on them; maybe not Zulu but some native ones anyway. They live in Johannesburg now, in one of the suburbs, can't bring the name to mind for the moment but it'll come to me. Oh, yes, Hillbrow I think it's called. We don't hear from them all that often. He's in the business of selling farm machinery which means he's away from home a great deal travelling the country. I think the company he works for is called *John Deere*. Kathy, that's my sister in law, sent us a brochure once as though we would be interested in farm machinery but I suppose she just wanted to show us what her hubby does for a living. I've often thought I'd like to make a visit but somehow just haven't got around to it and I feel it is too late now and she's not been back to the old country. They don't have children which I think is a big disappointment.' She sniffed.

Thornton thought he had better cut her off before she gave a whole family history possibly starting with her own siblings, nephews and nieces. There was only so much polite small talk needed before getting down to the nitty gritty.

'You've lived here a long time?'

'Oh yes, a good many years, forty or more. It was the best investment Eric ever made, getting a mortgage and that, you know. I'm glad it's a bungalow because as one grows older stairs do become just that bit too much of a climb, don't you agree?'

Thornton, in the prime of life, had never given old age much thought but he agreed nevertheless.

'Did your husband work at the studios?'

'He did. That is, until his unfortunate accident.'

'Accident?'

Accidents happen every day but, snatching at straws Thornton wondered if it could have anything to do with the murders.

'He fell from a gantry you see, broke both legs, truly terrible it was. In hospital ever such a long time with his legs in plaster and held up by pulleys and that, traction I believe it's called, in such pain and he always hated sleeping on his back but thank goodness for the National Health and the nurses were so kind. He was an electrician, you know, a grip, a gaffer in fact, and he was up there focusing some lights or something of that nature, this is what he said anyway, and he lost his balance and fell. Never got over it.' She shook her head at the memory. 'Was on disability allowance from then on. Made life hard which is why I went to work at the studios myself. If you want something done properly you best do it yourself he always used to say but it didn't apply in this case, did it? No. So dangerous it was, messing about so high up when there was no need I'm sure, but that is what he was like, and stubborn as a mule.'

She produced a handkerchief from her sleeve with which to wipe her nose.

'There seems to be a bit of a jinx at that place,' Thornton said.

'Oh, accidents will happen anywhere won't they?' She replied philosophically, 'and a person has to accept that. They do say that ninety percent of accidents happen in the home and we did get a little from the studio in compensation. Only a little because they completely denied responsibility and of course the insurance company made a tremendous fuss trying to get out of paying anything at all. Insurance companies tend to do that I suppose. Mind you, they do have to protect themselves from fraud don't they? But how can two broken legs in traction possibly be fraud? Did they believe he did it on purpose? Very upsetting it was, most upsetting.'

'And where may your husband be now?'

'Eric passed away two years ago.'

'Oh, I am sorry.'

Ida shrugged, 'One gets over it but it is hard. I still miss him you know, the way he would sit here by the fire of an evening reading his newspaper.' Hands clasped between her knees she sat gazing at the empty hearth. 'His spectacles in their case are still up there on the mantelpiece.' She pointed to where they lay. 'That's where he used to get them from before he sat down. Or I sometimes think of him out in the garden at the back pottering about. He couldn't do very much in the end, of course, not with his legs. I do a bit out there myself these days though I do need assistance now and again. I'll have to give up the job soon I suppose. The arthritis is beginning to creep up on me. I feel it first thing in the morning mostly, especially if it's cold and there's dampness in the air, you know. Fortunately one of my neighbours is a keen gardener himself and he comes round to help out. We have a quince tree out back that gives simply masses of fruit every year, a positive abundance and I always give him some as a thank you.'

"Abundance?" Ida has been reading a how to improve your English or increase your vocabulary type of book, he thought. Or she heard the vicar use the word in his sermon at harvest festival time. "Thank you God for an abundance of riches,' that sort of thing. He wondered if some of her quinces went towards decorating the church.

This having seemingly brought the small talk to an end, at least as far as Thornton was concerned, he thought it time to move on to Charmaine's murder. It was at this moment that the kettle started to whistle in the kitchen and Ida got to her feet.

'Ah, there's the kettle. If you will excuse me for a moment, I'll just pop into the kitchen and make the tea.'

Thornton had to abide in patience until her return and that is how he came to nibble on chocolate digestives. Well he did more than nibble. Apart from the peanuts he hadn't eaten since breakfast, he was ravenous and the chocolate digestives rapidly disappeared.

When they finally got around to it Ida seemed only too happy eager in fact, to repeat what she had told the police and Thornton learnt little of anything new except, and this he thought could be of some importance, Charmaine, Ida informed him, was not discovered in her own office as reported. 'Oh, no, she was in Mel Preston's office when she was killed and that was late at night too. They was not shooting night scenes for *Return of Batani* and, apart from security, the studio was empty. What could she have been doing there?'

'Thank you,' Thornton said, as he got up to leave.

'I haven't been of much help I'm afraid.'

'Oh, I don't know.' He was wondering how she knew about the position of the body and decided it was more than likely down to studio gossip. 'Anyway, if you think of anything else, if anything else comes to mind, will you let me know? Anything at all no matter how insignificant you might think it is.' Thornton wished he didn't sound quite like a cop from a television series. He handed her one of the brand new cards he'd had printed. 'You know where to find me.'

'Yes,' she said, inspecting the card, and showed him to the door.

N ow looking at his legal pad Thornton had to admit he was not getting very far with his investigation and it would appear he had reached a dead end when Esther Fartfooker paid him a second visit. This time she was all in pink which was hardly her colour and certainly didn't match her hair. She didn't bother to knock but entered the office as if she owned it which of course at the moment she more or less did.

'Good morning, Mister King.' Her tone was businesslike and that was obviously her mood.

Thornton half rose and sat down again, without a word extending an arm towards the visitor's chair. He winced visibly as once again Esther took out her handkerchief and dusted the cushion before sitting down. He wouldn't have been surprised if she'd picked it up and plumped it. She was still carrying her large rexine type bag and Thornton was intrigued. Surely a lady of her means could afford a much more expensive handbag, a *Vuitton* maybe? He noticed she wore no jewellery, not even a string of pearls to set off her pink outfit and she didn't even sport a watch. She was obviously no Imelda Marcos though as she was still wearing the same pair of shoes. She brought his musings to a halt.

'Well?' She barked.

'Well?'

'What news, man? What news? Or don't you have any?' If she had carried a walking stick or a brolly she would probably have banged it on the floor in a display of impatience. There was definitely a note of exasperation if not accusation in that question.

'I'm afraid I've no news for you yet, Mrs… Mrs…'

'Van Clef.'

'Van Clef.'

'I see. You're not going to take twenty years over this I hope.'

'I most certainly do hope that as well, Mrs van Clef.'

'Look, for goodness sake why don't you just call me Esther? That is so much easier. Van Clef is a stupid name anyway. Can't think why on earth I chose it in the first place. I thought it sounded romantic but then I was very young and the young do such stupid things at times. It's quite true what they say, that youth is wasted on the young. And, if I may, I will call you Thornton.'

'Of course.'

'So Thornton, exactly where are you, if anywhere, in your investigation and don't prevaricate?'

'To be quite truthful, Esther...' somehow it seemed slightly awkward using her first name... 'nowhere.'

There was no obvious reaction so he continued. 'Someone somewhere must have inside knowledge that could lead me to the killer but who? At the moment I believe that someone could be Joachim Caswell but that is only surmise.'

'Well, for goodness sake, haven't you spoken to him?'

'Not yet.'

'Why on earth not?' She sounded more than just a little irritable at this point. The walking stick or umbrella would have banged on the desktop let alone on the floor.

'Because he's fled the country. I believe, or so I have been reliably informed, he is hiding out in Rome.'

'Then follow him there. Lord have mercy on us, Thornton, get on with it, what are you waiting for?' This obviously meant what am I paying you for?

'Easier said than done, Esther. Rome is a big city, how do I find him when I get there?'

'You're the detective aren't you?' Her eyes opened very wide as though this was a question that she simply should not have needed to ask.

He pulled a wry face. 'You make it all sound so simple.'

'You make it all sound so complicated.' The *you* was heavily accented.

'It *is* complicated, Mrs van Esther,' he was slightly rattled. 'Murderers have no wish to be found out, not usually anyway, and do tend to cover their tracks to the best of their ability though I believe they often unconsciously leave a clue behind.

In this case whoever it was hasn't.'

'Hasn't what?'

'Hasn't left a clue behind, not that we are aware of, and a murder without witnesses can be almost impossible to solve. I believe whoever killed Charmaine also killed Teddy Brown.'

'Why?'

'Why?'

'Yes, why?'

'So that there would be no witnesses; because Brown could easily have seen him leave.'

He was beginning to sound as if he was the one losing patience. 'If Joachim Caswell is our killer…. and I'm not, mind you, saying he is… in fact I believe just the opposite, but he is at the top of the suspect list and he must know it which is why, innocent though he may be, he has fled the country. I still believe though that he could impart valuable information that would lead me to whoever perpetrated this ghastly crime.' Sometimes Thornton sounded as though he had been reading not a how to improve your English or extend your vocabulary type book but too many crime novels of the cheaper sensational kind. Either that or he had listened too often to policemen like Reg Venables on a soapbox sounding off.

'Then for goodness sake stop beating about the bush, waste no more time. Go to Rome and find him. I take it you are free to do that? No other commitments? The Italian police or immigration officials should be able tell you where he is because of his passport. He would have had to give an address where he would be staying.'

'I frankly doubt the Italian police or immigration authorities would cooperate. I'm sure they've got more important things to occupy them.'

'Slip them a bung.'

This took Thornton somewhat by surprise but recovering he said, 'If only I knew the name of his friend there, the one who works in the film studios.'

'Is that all you need? For goodness sake why didn't you say

so in the first place? The friend's name is, let me see…Luca… Luca… yes, that's it… Luca Biancchi.'

This really did take Thornton by surprise. Was this the piece of miniscule information he had been waiting for? 'How do you know that?' He asked.

'My granddaughter, as I told you, was infatuated with this man Caswell. I didn't approve of course; not that I had anything against him personally you understand, but writing is such a hazardous profession, busy one moment, penniless the next,' "just like being a private eye," Thornton thought, 'and love on the dole wouldn't have suited Charmaine one bit. I'm afraid if she had a weakness it was having too fond a love of the good things in life. If Charmaine had been offered the gift of a Mini she would have demanded nothing less than a Rolls Royce. She was that kind of girl. Anyway, more than once the devious Mister Caswell evidently tried to lure her to Rome, telling her what a wonderful city it is, what a wonderful time they would have there and his friend Luca Biancchi would make sure they did. Yes, indeed I remember the name and what kind of good time would it have been, that's what I would like to know? Fortunately, not that it matters any longer, she resisted his blandishments. He never mentioned he already had a wife. Put it down to the seven year itch I suppose. I hope that answers your question. Now, I suppose you are running somewhat short of funds and need an injection of cash in order to pay your fare to Rome and your keep while staying there so will another five hundred do?' She was already dipping into the bag to produce the requisite number of notes which she laid neatly stacked on the desk.

'Excuse me for asking this, Esther,' he said, 'I hope I'm not being too impolite but my curiosity is piqued, I can't help but notice that you wear no jewellery and why do you carry around that rather, if I may say so, ugly old bag when you could be carrying a really expensive fashionable designer handbag for example?'

'In answer to both your questions, Mister Detective, I would have thought it pretty obvious. First of all I am not one of those people who waste money on expensive trash simply because it happens to be fashionable or has a fashionable name attached to it and it is in reality a complete rip-off. If there is one thing I object to in life it's being ripped off. That is the expression isn't it?'

Thornton wondered if this was a warning shot in his direction.

'I always think people like that must have very little in the way of brains. Secondly, London, like Rome, is also a big city and its streets are not paved with gold but they do harbour any number of pickpockets, thieves and muggers looking for that crock one way or another, and whereas an old lady with a fancy handbag would be an obvious target, none of those pickpockets, thieves or muggers would look twice at this shabby old thing, I hope, or attempt to snatch it.' She lifted up the bag and waved it about. 'Were they to be aware of what it contains they certainly would have tried to rip me off by now. So does that satisfy your curiosity? It's called being cautious or playing safe.' She got to her feet and he followed suit. 'So, Thornton, I will see you on your return from Rome and I hope you have more positive news for me. This...' she patted the bag ... 'is not as deep as you may think, not a never ending source of wealth you know, not the goose that laid the golden eggs and you know what happened to her. Good day to you.' With which she swept out.

Thornton looked at the money lying on his desk, shook his head and thought he had better book that flight to Rome pronto. He didn't actually know what happened to the goose that laid the golden eggs, it wasn't one of the tales his parents told him when young and he wasn't interested enough to want to find out.

# Chapter Five

'Where's that god damn son of a bitch?' Wagner yelled through the soggy half chewed end of a cigar as he stormed passed Shirley Dorland's desk heading straight for Courtney Burrows office. Shirley placed a trembling finger on the intercom in front of her and said somewhat belatedly, 'Mr Wagner for you Mr Burrows.'

Courtney Burrows looked up as Wagner stormed into his office and slammed the door.

'Why the hell can't you look after your own people?' he screamed. I've got some fag ponce accountant from LA telling me Preston's asking for more, in fact a lot more. Now we both know that's not going to happen. So if you can't keep him in line then I'll do it for you.'

Courtney shuffled his feet and rapped his fingers on his desk top. He hated being told what to do. All his life he had got what he wanted without question and now here he was with some fat, balding, sweating American crook who was also not used to being gainsaid, ordering him about. He really hated this man.

'What do you expect me to do?'

'I expect you to take some responsibility for your mistakes. Daddy's not around to help you anymore. You dipped your wick in the honey pot, now the bees are stinging.'

Courtney looked at the repulsive man standing in front of him. "How had his life come to this?" He thought to himself?

'I said I would sort out Preston and I will. But it's difficult with the police around asking question's about that stupid girl. It's all the fault of that Caswell; he's been a flaming nuisance from the beginning.'

'Forget Caswell. He's being dealt with.'

'What do you mean?'

'I mean forget Caswell. He's no longer a problem. Our man in Rome is keeping a close eye on him so he is no longer a problem to the studio.'

Burrows sighed. 'What do you want me to do about Preston?'

'Advise him that it's not wise to bite the hand that feeds him.'

'What if Preston doesn't take my advice.'

'Then the hand that feeds him will strike back. Nobody is indispensable.'

'Is that wise? To threaten him I mean?'

'That is not a threat Burrows. It's a guarantee. We go back a long way, you and I. You should know me by now.'

So it was not too long after Esther's visit and that dastardly terrorist attack on *Pan Am 110* bound for Iran but still on the tarmac at Leonardo da Vinci International Airport, and the IRA's attempt at planting a bomb in the number one car park at Heathrow, that Thornton found himself disembarking safely at Rome after his comfortable flight on the Lockheed Trident of newly formed British Airways and, having claimed his luggage and passed through immigration and customs, taking a taxi to the Holiday Inn.

Following Esther's prudent example he had invented for himself a special money belt to hold his wallet of traveller's cheques, bank card, and large lira notes, leaving only the small change to be possibly pick pocketed. If anyone tried to get at anything more they would have to be very intimate indeed.

He had for one mad moment thought of putting up at the *Palazzo Cinelli* but decided maybe that was not such a good idea. Knowing what the Countess charged for her rooms, even in the low season and even with a possible discount as a favour both to him and to Esther, the brown rexine bag would be empty in a week and anyway not all the memories of that place were happy ones.

He would of course, out of courtesy if nothing else, pay a visit to the palazzo before leaving Rome. The countess was bound to have been informed that he was in the city and would be most put out if he did not; or so he flattered himself. Anyway, he felt he ought to thank her in person for the magnificent and unexpected gift of the Cinelli Vases which, despite his occasional penchant for bumping into things and being slightly accident prone, were still safe and sound in his Hackney apartment, half filled with sand to stop them toppling over, a trick he had learned from that so-called art dealer in the Westbourne Grove who came to that extremely sticky and painful end that didn't bear thinking about.

Once ensconced in the hotel, the next thing was to try and locate this Luca Biancchi and through him hopefully the fugitive Joachim Caswell. The telephone directory listed no fewer than four L. Biancchis and any number of others with different initials which, as Thornton didn't speak the lingo and didn't think he would make himself understood over the telephone, was not of much use. Was Biancchi the Italian equivalent of Jones, Smith or Brown he wondered?

Obviously a visit to *Cinecitta*, the famous studios founded in 1937 by that fascist dictator Benito Mussolini for the purposes of propaganda, (*Il cinema è lamas più forte*) was the next step.

Nine kilometres from the centre of Rome, getting to the studios necessitated another taxi ride, this time with an un-shaven loquacious driver beneath a sweat stained cap who had a tendency to gesticulate wildly as he talked which meant temporarily taking his hands off the wheel with the result that there were a couple of near misses. They were, of course, never his fault as he screamed profanities at what or whoever he considered to be the offending party, and gave them the finger. If he stayed alive, presumably the rosary and a number of religious postcards that decorated his windscreen and dashboard would make sure of that, he evidently wanted to get into films in a big way as he started off by scratching his unshaven chin, showing his bad teeth and saying, 'I am extra.'

For a moment Thornton wasn't too sure what this might mean. Did he mean it was an extra fare to go out to Cinecitta? He could have taken the bus but a taxi had seemed the most obvious choice. The next remark clarified things.

'Tree filum I bin in.'

'Oh yes?'

'Oh, yes. Tree filum I am one extra.' He named the films, none of which Thornton had ever heard of or was ever likely to hear of, not being for example in the same league as *Bicycle Thieves*, *La Strada*, or *La Dolce Vita*.

'Now I must have biggest parts in filum business,' the man continued. Was he fondly imagining himself playing romantic leads? A bit too long in the tooth for that even if he hadn't been quite so plain and the teeth had been good. He could play villains perhaps. He was certainly giving something of a villain like performance as a taxi driver. 'You are an actor?' He asked, glancing in his rear view mirror at his passenger seated behind him and almost knocking a couple of kids off their Vespa but avoiding them at the last second. Little did he know at that moment he was actually a knight in a battered old cab because the kids were about to snatch an old lady's handbag but had to concentrate on regaining balance so lost out on that one as she was given time to step away and clutch the bag protectively to her bosom as Thornton saw when he turned to look back.

'So you are?'

Thornton had lost the thread. 'What?'

'You are actor I am thinking.'

'Afraid not.'

'Producer maybe. Yes. Big time producer.'

'No, again 'fraid not.'

If he's not an actor and not a producer what could he be that he wants to go to *Cinecitta*?

'You can get me inna da filums?'

'For the third and hopefully the last time, afraid not, old chum'

'Maybe you are noble English lord then, yes?'

'No, afraid not.' Thornton wondered what noble English lords had to do with the film industry. Maybe the man imagined them as being all powerful and capable of pulling strings.

But Thornton not being a noble English lord he gave up on that one and started to tell Thornton all about his beautiful wife of twenty odd years and his even more beautiful bambini of which there were many ranging from sixteen to six months, the sixteen year old whose name was Mario would one day play centre-forward for Inter Milan that was for sure and, if he cared to, Thornton could come and see the family for himself, all of which got them to the main entrance to the studios.

Thornton paid the man, stepped out of the cab and for a long moment stood in front of the rather plain peachy pink building looking somewhat in awe at the large lettering over the door that read *Cinecitta*. He never thought he would one day be standing like this, thinking of all those wonderful movies like *Ben Hur*, a particular favourite, that were made there. He brought to mind all those great Italian directors: Pasolini, De Sica, Rossellini, Visconti, Fellini, Francesco Rosy; all sharing the same rather overcrowded pedestal as his Japanese favourites; *Cinecitta*'s boast being it is the only studio in the world where an entire production can be completed in one place: pre-production, production, post production.

Having entered the building and ascertained that the person he was talking to at reception spoke English Thornton stated his business and was met with silence and a blank stare.

'Luca Biancchi?' Thornton repeated. 'I have come all the way from London, you know? London?' The man might never have heard of Timbuktu or even Tokyo but surely he had heard of London. 'And I need to speak with him.'

Having concluded that his correspondent on the other side of the desk perhaps didn't actually speak English quite as well as he had initially supposed he resorted to what most Englishmen do when chatting to Johnny foreigner; he raised his voice a number of decibels and enunciated everything terribly slowly.

'I'... (index finger pointing to his chest)... 'must... see... (index finger pointing to an eye) ... Mister... Biancchi.' (Index finger pointing vaguely in the direction of the studio).

'Importante?' Was the response from features that could have been made of marble.

'Very important,' Thornton said. 'Molto importante!' He felt he did have a few words of Italian at his command, especially ones that were the same or virtually the same as in English. That was the thing about continental languages; they were just English with a different accent.

Without another word but still poker faced the man picked up a telephone and after a few moments gazing steadily at Thornton all the while as though wishing to remember every feature in case the enquirer had some nefarious plan in mind, he eventually turned his attention to the phone which had obviously been answered and gabbled into it at the rate of knots, not one word of which Thornton understood except for the name Luca Biancchi, so at least he knew he was in the right place. The phone was put down and narrow-eyed scrutiny returned to Thornton.

'Sorry. He is not here today. Try again tomorrow.'

Was this a brush off or was it genuine? Under that basilisk stare Thornton stood for a moment thinking.

'I tell you what...'

'What?'

'Why don't I leave a note and get him to call me? I'm staying at the Holiday Inn. Can I do that?'

'Sure,' with the shrug of one shoulder, 'why not?'

So with a borrowed antique fountain pen that leaked a little turning part of his fingertips blue Thornton duly scribbled his note on the slip of paper he was given and handed it over together with his card, hoping it would do the trick rather than be tossed away the moment his back was turned and decided to head back to town for lunch.

Being still more or less a stranger in the city where should he go? Holly had told him of a restaurant in Trestevere called *La Cisterna* that had been going for simply ages and ages, as she put it, in fact she was quite right, ages and ages was going back to 1630, and where the food was totally delicious, including a *rigatoni all'amatriciana* served with red hot peppers which sounded right up his street and so it proved.

His talkative taxi driver, somehow with a sixth sense, surmising Thornton wouldn't be more than a few minutes inside was patiently waiting, leaning against the side of his cab. Ready to take his fare back to town he was in the meanwhile enjoying a cigarette which, on seeing Thornton emerging, he threw down and ground out with his heel before opening the door for the Englishman to get in, and dashing around to the driver's seat in case the Englishman had second thoughts and started to get out again.

'Where you wanna go now?' He asked, looking once more in his rear view mirror.

Did he know this particular restaurant? Did he know it! How could such a question even be asked? His expansive gesture almost knocked the Virgin Mary off her pedestal on his dash-board. Was he not born in this city? Was he not baptised in this city? Did he not grow up in this city? Did he not hope to die and be buried in this city? He raised his eyes to heaven, hastily crossed himself and touched the picture of the Madonna in case he was tempting fate. Didn't he know every watering place for miles around? And if the visiting gentleman was a gourmet and required the most delicious food in all Rome, in the whole of Italy, he should try the restaurant owned by his cousin Giuseppe where the fish soup, with or without the fish, was too delicious for words to describe and a sensation never to be repeated anywhere else and, for emphasis, he kissed his pursed fingers before handing Thornton a card which he was polite enough to look at before he pocketed it. But Thornton had decided on *La Cisterna* and once Thornton King had made up his mind nothing in the world could ever change it. So to *La Cisterna* he was taken and the meal proved to be everything Holly had said. After which, the inner man having been satisfied, he retired to the Holiday Inn for a well-earned siesta.

T he bell seemed to be muffled and ringing from a fair distance away, almost as if it was coming from the far end of a long tunnel. Thornton, still half asleep, stretched out his hand towards the bedside cabinet, lifted the telephone receiver and croaked, 'Yes?'

'Mister King?'

He was immediately wide awake. He sat up, swinging his legs off the bed.

'Yes.'

'My name is Luca Biancchi.'

The English was perfect; no trace of an accent. There would certainly be no need to shout at this Johnny foreigner. 'You left a note at the studio asking me to contact you, may I ask why?'

'Of course. Thank you for calling back. I'm in Rome as I am hoping to find a friend of yours, Joachim Caswell who I am led to believe is staying with you? Is that correct or, if not, do you know where he might be?'

There was a moment's silence on the other end and Thornton wondered if he had already blown it. He never could think straight when woken from a deep sleep.

'Are you there?'

'I am here. May I ask, is Joachim a friend of yours?'

'No.' Sometimes Thornton could be too honest, not a good trait in a private detective. He mentally kicked himself.

'Then why do you want to see him? Is it about the studio murders in England?'

'Well, yes, it is as a matter of fact.'

'Then I'm sorry I cannot help you.'

'No wait!' There was such urgency in Thornton's voice that Luca hung on.

'Let me put you in the picture, Mister Biancchi. First of all let me tell you what I am not. I am not a member of Interpol. I am not even a policeman, but I am a private detective and I have been retained by a woman, you may have heard of, Spring van Clef?'

'The film actress.'

'Yes. She is the grandmother of the murdered girl who I believe was having an affaire with Joachim, the murdered girl I mean, not the grandmother. You probably know about that. I feel sure, as a close friend, which I am led to believe you are, he will have confided in you. Now I feel certain I know why he has come to Rome. He feels for that reason alone, I mean being so close to the dead girl, that he must be a prime suspect for the murder, but I want to reassure him, personally I don't believe that. I believe he is totally innocent but the reason I want to see him is this, he might have knowledge that would help me in my investigation and which would prove his innocence at the same time. That is, if my investigation is successful, I mean when my investigation is successful.'

'You say you are not a policeman so tell me, why would you be investigating this murder? It is not up to you surely.'

'Good question. I tried to explain to Miss van Clef that it should be left to the police to handle but she doesn't think they're getting anywhere, certainly not fast enough for her liking, and being an old lady she would like to see the matter cleared up before she kicks the bucket.'

'Kicks the bucket?'

'Oh, an old English expression, a euphemism for death. I know there is little point if any in my trying to find him if he doesn't want to be found. I am certainly not going to alert authority of any kind to his whereabouts but there is, I hope, the possibility he may come to me. After all, much as he loves Italy he really will have to return to England some time don't you think? And clear his name? It's either that or disappearing into the jungles of South America or somewhere, a plan of action I wouldn't recommend, not with all the mosquitoes, alligators, spiders, coral snakes, anacondas...'

'Mister King!'

'... so would you be so kind as to inform him that I am here at the Holiday Inn and I await his call? ASAP.'

'A.S. what?'

"Aha," Thornton thought, "your English ain't all that perfect, mate." Aloud he said, 'as soon as possible.'

'I will do that for you, Mister King, but there are of course no guarantees.'

'No, of course not. None expected.'

The conversation was over as the phone at the other end was returned to its cradle.

He got dressed and hovered around the hotel for the remainder of that day. He had a meal and spent the rest of the evening in the bar. Of Joachim Caswell there was no sign. Reluctantly gone midnight he went to bed. If Joachim was going to phone him the call would come through to his room.

The next day was the same. He stayed at the hotel in the hope that the fugitive writer would call but there was nothing.

The following day, with nothing to do and to break the monotony, straight after breakfast he went out and bought the European edition of an English newspaper and, about to enjoy a morning cup of coffee back at the hotel, he opened the paper and on page two the headline hit him straight between the eyes,

THIRD MURDER AT BRITISH FILM STUDIOS

The report then went on to inform the reader that "*the famous film director and producer, Mel Preston, aged 52, who had been working at Breconfield Studios producing the film "Return to Batani" was found lying on the floor of his office. A post mortem will be carried out today but police sources state he apparently* died of a single stab wound, possibly to the heart, the perpetrator using a long bladed knife, possibly a flick knife or stiletto. There was no sign of a struggle and the murder weapon has not been recovered.

In 1971 Mister Preston directed the remake of the film that originally saved Breconfield Studios a second time from certain bankruptcy, not because it was an enormous success but because it was well-funded from outside sources. The film was of course "The Guns of Batani" not to be confused, as many people tend to do, with the epic "Gun at Batasi" made in nineteen fifty four and starring that wonderful popular British actor Richard Attenborough. Employed by the studio to produce the new film, a follow up that Mister Preston, when interviewed shortly before his unfortunate death, said with certainty would be a huge success, would rock the film going public and he was really very proud of it and looking forward to it hitting our screens.

The story takes place during The Great War and in the leading role the film stars that charismatic and very talented young American actor, Troy Tyler. This is only his second movie; the first of course film goers will remember was "Swimming With Sharks" in which he played the role of a rookie detective who breaks up a gang of financial swindlers but, with his fair hair and boyish good looks, he already has a worldwide female fan club. On arriving in England he was met at the airport by hundreds of screaming young girls, many of them in tears and, when interviewed, said, yes he was glad to be here. The character he portrays this time is ostensibly a hunter of big game in Central Africa but who is actually a spy investigating what is going on in what was then German East Africa. Troy is a graduate of the famous Actor's Studio, not on the West Coast but in New York where he studied the Stanislavski method.

Also starring is an actress who needs no introduction, the legendary Spring van Clef who has appeared in numerous films over the years and is known and loved all over the world. She is particularly popular in Japan where a Japanese director we believe is thinking of making a film based on her life.

*The movie is apparently virtually in the can and will shortly be ready for release, our reporter being reliably informed by up and coming assistant director and screenwriter, Ernest J. Bloomfield who is hoping the script he is currently working on will be next in line for production at Breconfield Studios. Mister Preston was not married."*

Bloomfield again! Bloomfield! Ernest was absolutely on the ball, you simply cannot rely on reporters getting their facts right. Mister Bloomberg must be mad as a rattlesnake but he was not the first and he certainly wouldn't be the last to continuously have his name misspelt. Thornton was also intrigued by Spring's role in the movie, having leapt it would seem from virtually a bit part player, hardly more than a five liner, to star status once more.

"Not married" is usually a newspaper's euphemism for gay when they didn't want to say it outright in case they were sued for defamation, only these days who really cares? Could it have been a lover's tiff? Could Preston, like Cord with Ernest J. Bloomberg, if the story he told Thornton was true, have tried to come on to someone who resented it enough to kill?

He started to go through the piece once more and was so engrossed that at first he didn't hear his name being called. When he surfaced he turned around to discover a slightly dishevelled, unshaven, long haired thinning on top individual of uncertain age wearing corduroy trousers with some of the nap worn off, leather patches on the elbows of his threadbare jacket and dark rings beneath his eyes, standing close by. So this was the man, almost a legendary figure, he had come all the way to Rome to interview. Thornton thought him rather pathetic though even someone as pathetic looking as that would be capable of strangling a young woman without too much trouble. And what on earth, according to Esther, did the young beautiful fun loving Charmaine see in him? The attraction women have for some men is truly a remarkable mystery. Maybe Esther was fantasizing over the possible romance.

'Mister King?'

'Mister Caswell.'

'That's right.' Without being invited but taking the invite for granted, Caswell took a chair and immediately fumbled in his pocket for his cigarettes. This was one writer Earnest J. would recognise if the yellowness of two fingers on his right hand was anything to go by. Thornton waited for the cigarette to be lit and the coughing to subside as he studied his man.

'Would you care for a coffee?'

Caswell nodded and indulged in another bout of coughing before he was fit enough to continue.

'Thank you for coming,' Thornton said, 'I'm really grateful.'

'I would have come before but I wasn't certain if it was a set up,' Caswell said. 'I watched you until I was pretty certain you were genuine. I presume it was Spring who sent you after me?'

Thornton nodded.

'Well today clinched it.'

'Clinched it?'

'Yes.' He nodded towards the paper. 'I heard the news about Preston so I thought you must be on the level or it was worth a try anyway. After all I certainly can't be blamed for that killing, can I?'

'No,' Thornton said, 'you certainly can't,' and ordered two more coffees.

# Chapter Six

'**G**ood morning!' A cheerful voice hailed Max as a shadow was cast across Rosie's dimpled derriere.

"*Rosie, girl of the day, an economics student from Leeds has a strong belief in saving the trees of Borneo and likes to travel,*" Max had just read, but now he tore his eyes away from Rosie's ample posterior towards the cause of the interruption only to see, not a photograph, but a real life ravishing beauty gazing at him from the open window of a not too impressive car.

'Hello,' she said. 'I have an appointment with Mr Wagner, the agency sent me over.'

Max must have looked a little confused so she continued, 'The Merrill agency for office staff both permanent and temporary. You know, "We can accommodate all your needs and fill any vacancy?" That's their motto.' By the look on Max's face Holly was wondering if the vacancy in his mind was what needed filling. 'I'm a replacement secretary. You know to take the place of that poor girl who was…' She bit her bottom lip to show her distress… 'murdered. I don't normally work for the Merrill agency, it's just that no one else wanted the job…' she trailed off.

Max continued to stare at her.

'Where do I go?' she enquired.

'Oh, main building over there on the right, reception will tell you.' Max had finally come to his senses.

'Thanks,' she said.

He raised the barrier and she drove through. Max looked down at his paper but Rosie saving the trees in Borneo seemed to have lost her allure.

Holly's arrival having been announced on the intercom, the great man himself opened the office door. 'Miss Day isn't it? Please come in.' He extended a hand in greeting. Holly just knew it would be like shaking hands with a cold wet fish, but she held out her hand in turn and tried not to be revolted at his touch.

He held onto her hand a little too long and led Holly into a spacious oak panelled room furnished with a large oak desk and executive swivel chair. There were also two large black leather sofas either side of an open fireplace and with a coffee table in between. A couple of full size posters hung on the panelled walls, *Guns of Batani* of course, and an impressive horse painting that had to be by Stubbs.

'Why don't we sit here?' With an accompanying gesture Anton Wagner indicated a sofa. 'Much more comfortable and less formal, don't you agree?' His slightly brusque manner for the moment indicated that Mister Wagner was used to getting his own way and she had better agree or else.

Somehow his hand just managed to brush her backside ever so slightly. Holly, under any other circumstances, would have considered it sexual harassment and retaliated but instead she simpered coyly, something she was certainly not used to doing, and went along with the game as she took a seat.

'Now, as I understand it, you come to us highly recommended. I'm sure we'll get along like a house on fire.' Wagner tried to make himself comfortable on the sofa next to her but, before he could home in on his quarry, Holly was suddenly at the other side of the couch and he was slightly baffled as to how she had managed to get there. One moment she was within groping distance, the next moment she was gone.

'Yes, well, err… if you have any problems I'm sure one of the other girls will fill you in.' Wagner said, covering an awkward moment,

'Super,' said Holly smiling as if she was totally oblivious as to what he was up to.

'Yes… Mr. Preston being no longer with us I am taking his place… now about your duties…' He got up and reached for a silver cigarette box on the coffee table, opening it in her direction. She shook her head.

'Do you mind if I do?'

'It's your office.'

"Oh," he thought, as he reluctantly returned the box to the table, "this one's no pushover, in fact a tough nut to crack. Still I always did like a feisty woman and a challenge." The very thought had him quivering like a gun dog. 'As personal secretary, I'm sure we'll get to know each other very well.'

He had sat down again as close as he dared, not wishing to hasten matters but, as he did so, Holly got to her feet and was seemingly now admiring a large picture over the fireplace, 'my what a lovely picture.'

"God," she thought, "is it really necessary to gush?"

'Oh, yes, yes indeed,' Wagner said. He seemed to be less and less in control of the interview. The cigarette ploy having failed, deciding to try another tack, he got up and stood close behind her. Any closer and she would have felt his breath on her neck. 'Would you like a drink?'

She let him stand there for a moment before she moved away, surveying the office and talking as she went.

'Shouldn't I really be getting started? The ups and downs, the ins and outs of office life?' She smiled.

"My God!" He thought, clinging eagerly to the sexual innuendo, "is she flirting with me?" His heart was beating loudly and he suddenly wondered if he was due for a coronary. It was quite possible. Had he taken his pills that morning? He couldn't remember. He made his unsteady way to a side board and lifted a crystal decanter full of whisky, pouring himself three fingers or more. He wiggled the glass in Holly's direction as an invitation but she shook her head.

'I'm really looking forward to working with you,' she simpered. 'I've always loved the movies, ever since I was a kid. I even thought at one time I would like to be an actress.'

'And why not?' Wagner prompted, 'a beautiful girl like yourself? Maybe we can arrange a screen test.'

'Really!' Exclaimed Holly. 'Do you really think so? That would be wonderful.'

'Of course,' said Wagner grandly, 'all I have to do is say the word; it's that simple.' Glass in hand he started to make his way across the room to Holly. 'It's like we're all one big happy family. We all help each other. I help you, you help me, simple!'

'It's going to be really super working here,' said Holly, 'I can just feel it.'

Once more she managed to evade his advances making a beeline for the door, 'And the sooner I start the better.' With which she was out of the office and the door closed behind her.

Wagner took a few deep breaths and a slug of whisky. His heart seemed to have gone back to normal and he was wondering what the hell had happened.

Outside Holly also took a few deep breaths to calm her nerves. Talk about swimming with sharks. She was going to have to defend her honour on an hourly let alone a daily basis. He still hadn't actually told her what her duties would be.

'So shoot', Thornton said.

'I beg your pardon?'

'Well let's start with you and Breconfield. I'm led to believe you bear the studio a grudge.'

'Oh, yes? A grudge. Is that what you would call it? And who could have given you that bit of information?'

'A certain up and coming young writer and director told me that.'

'Ernest Jacob Bloomberg. He of the big dreams and minuscule talent.'

'You are unkind but yes, the very same and that's what the J stands for, is it? I was wondering. I imagined it might stand for Jehosaphat.'

'And what exactly does Ernest J. Bloomberg think he knows about it, if anything? What did he tell you exactly?'

'Just that.'

'How would he know?'

'He listens in to conversations, all part of being a writer I'm reliably informed by Mister Bloomberg. Evidently you've been doing a lot of sounding off within hearing distance.'

'Sounding off! Is that what you call it? With every justification I might say.'

'Tell me about it.'

Joachim was trembling slightly and seemed very nervous which was not surprising considering he had so recently lost his girl-friend, lover, partner, whatever you wanted to call her, was himself probably under suspicion for her murder and on re-turning to England was likely to face intensive interrogation.

'Well it's not Breconfield I'm mad at. No, not at all. It's the two film companies I hate, loathe and detest and have every reason to.'

'Oh? Strong words, strong emotions. Why would that be?'

'Because they're each a no good, two-timing, rascally bunch of thieves that's why.'

'Those are indeed pretty harsh words.'

'And well deserved, believe you me.'

'All film companies?'

'No, of course not, but *Full Throttle* and *Centurion*, in cahoots to deny me what is legally mine. They are the only film companies I have worked for, the only ones I have any knowledge of; though I am sure they're probably all tarred with the same brush if it comes down to it. Think of the stories one hears about Hollywood, that new world Babylon. I thank my lucky stars I never went to work there though of course working for *Centurion* amounts to the same thing. My work was in television until *The Limey Gang are Here,* the filmed series made by *Full Throttle.* Before that I was commissioned to write a number of scripts both for the BBC and Independent Television and I wish to God I had stayed with them, instead of getting mixed up with this crowd, but when you're offered work with what looks like a foolproof contract, you take it, don't you?'

'I really wouldn't know. I've never worked to a contract, not in the way you mean.'

'Well don't. Take my word for it; it's a cut throat business and no mistake, everyone for himself and devil take the hindmost. Believe me, if ever you are in that position make sure you have a damn clever lawyer to dissect every word; though sometimes even that may not be enough because they have damn clever lawyers as well who will beat the shit out of your damned clever lawyer and it's the lawyers on both sides who laugh all the way to the bank. Have you ever seen a movie contract? I mean a proper movie contract other than the flimsy four page piece of crap I was fobbed off with that in my eagerness, my naivety, I was only too willing to sign.'

'Can't say I have actually. No.'

'Wade through it if you can. I tell you, Mister King...'

'Thornton.'

'What?'

'My name is Thornton.'

'Yes, well, Thornton, I tell you, a movie contract is the modern equivalent of *The Canterbury Tales, Beowulf, Morte d'Arthur* and *Genesis* all strung together; the thicker, in volume that is, the better. The studios then feel, having paid out a small fortune for it, that they have had their money's worth. Look at this contract, they'll say, it's a hundred pages long, isn't it a beaut? Oh of course it is and the lawyers have earned another fat fee. But, there is bound to be somewhere in the very small print, some pettifogging piece of legal chicanery, that will get you by the short and curlies and in this case so it proved.'

There was silence after this tirade and Thornton waited as

Joachim took a sip of his coffee, the cup trembling slightly in his unsteady fingers. He didn't always show such patience but wasn't going to hurry things and have the man clam up on him. The cup was put down rattling slightly on its saucer and another cigarette was lit.

'I've no doubt you want to know why I'm pissed off with them.'

'I want to know anything you can tell me about the companies, the studios, the personnel and what goes on there. For example who do you suppose would want to kill Mel Preston?'

Joachim laughed and rubbed the side of his nose as though he had developed a sudden itch. 'Who wouldn't want to kill Mel Preston is more like it. I can think of any number starting with Ernest J. Bloomberg.'

'Yes, our budding young genius. He hates your guts too do you know that?'

'Of course I know it and all because I had the temerity to criticise his ridiculous screenplay. If looks could kill every time we passed each other I would have dropped down dead fifty times over. Believe me it needed criticising and I was as gentle as I could be with it.'

'His version is slightly different but let's leave that. Why would he of all people want to kill Mel Preston?'

'I only said Bloomberg to give you a sort of example, because of the way Preston always treated him, rather shabbily, even more than shabbily, quite cruelly in fact, especially in front of everybody on the floor and usually when there was a silence so everyone could hear him playing the big man. It was truly embarrassing, Ernest J. being his whipping boy of the moment and, whatever he may be, the boy certainly didn't deserve to be made to look a complete idiot and, even if he might think of it, he is absolutely incapable of an act of violence. Mind you, Ernest wasn't the only one. Unless he was brown nosing which he was pretty good at, as so many of them are, it comes with the territory as Arthur Miller might have said, Preston was also pretty good at putting down virtually anybody who crossed his path who he disliked or thought of as inferior which was practically everybody within spitting distance and which is why there will be so many suspects.'

'And which doesn't really give me much to go on, does it?'

Caswell shrugged, took another sip, took another draw, and stubbed out his cigarette. A passing waiter replaced the ashtray with a clean one. Caswell looked up and nodded as though thanks were required, then returned his attention back to Thornton.

'It's a big canvas. What can I tell you?'

'Tell me why the grudge then?'

There was now a very long silence as Caswell pursed his lips and sat there thinking but Thornton still wasn't going to push it. Who knew what valuable information might come out of this confession, painful though it may be?

'Well...'

There was another pause. It was like drawing teeth without an anaesthetic Thornton thought but what the hell, he had time and who wants to see the sights of Rome anyway? Come to think of it he would actually like to see the sights of Rome. This journey made it three times that he was in the eternal city and he couldn't remember even seeing the Coliseum though the first time he did throw a coin in the Trevi fountain and it worked: he was back. Maybe next time he could visit on holiday. His tummy though was beginning to rumble a little and he felt if he didn't get anywhere soon he might have to invite Joachim to lunch with him, courtesy of that brown rexine type bag. A good wine might act in lieu of an anaesthetic and loosen him up a bit.

Caswell fished in his inside pocket for his wallet, opened it and passed a small photograph to Thornton who took it and saw it was one of a little girl kneeling in a garden, a very ordinary but well kept suburban garden and laughing she had her arms around a small dog of indiscriminate breed. He raised that eyebrow he was so fond of using as he wondered what this could be about and handed it back with, 'Yes, she's very pretty. Who is she?'

'Her name is Dora. Do you know what that name means,

Mister King? It comes from the Greek and means a gift and she is that. She is my daughter. Yes, I was married, married and divorced. Guess I was never meant to be the domesticated kind. Writers can be very selfish people. I know I am still a bit young to think of death but we are all mortal and who knows when the old bugger will strike? Even if we know it has to come, death can still take one by surprise even though we know we are born to die and we are dying from the moment we are born.' He took a long look at the photograph before slipping it back into his wallet and his wallet into his pocket. 'She does look pretty though, doesn't she? Unfortunately, Mister King...'

'Thornton.'

'Ah, yes, Thornton. Unfortunately she will never be able to look after herself, I never know exactly how to say this but she will never be normal, self-sufficient, never be able to stand on her own two legs as it were. She will need constant care all her life. It isn't obvious in the photograph but when very young she suffered from an attack of meningitis you see.' He dropped his head, stopped talking for a while, obviously to regain some composure, to control the trembling in his hands; then he looked back at Thornton.

'You may or may not know this but, like I said, ten years ago I was script editor and wrote eight or nine of the scripts myself, I don't remember exactly how many, for a filmed children's television series called *The Limey Gang are Here*. Am I repeating myself?'

'It doesn't matter if you are. Not being a kid myself and not having any kids I never watched it but I have heard others talk of it. Seems it was extremely popular.'

'Seems? Was? Still is, is more like it. There are seventeen half hour episodes in all and it has been the most terrific success, being shown all over the world from Argentina to Zululand I shouldn't wonder, twenty seven countries at the last count, syndicated at least three times in the states if not more and shown on British television, both the BBC and Independent stations a number of times. Each episode cost peanuts to make when you think what an expensive business it is making movies. I believe the budget for each one was twenty five thousand pounds. That's small change to a large studio. The money was put up of course by the distributors which, as you no doubt know, was *Centurion,* probably mob money I shouldn't wonder, doing a bit of laundering don't you know, but that's only a guess on my part and of course I could be biased. What am I saying? Of course I'm biased.' He gave a rueful lopsided smile. 'Wouldn't you be?'

'I don't know. You haven't got to the crux of the matter yet.'

'Very well, the nitty-gritty, the nub of the matter is this. I know my contracts state that I gave the copyright in perpetuity to *Full Throttle Films* but the condition here is that there is also a clause which entitles me to royalties on sales. So far in ten years I haven't received a penny; not a single solitary sou and I am raging mad about it. On top of this I have four songs in the series and I have received no royalties from them either except small payments made by the *Performing Rights Society* every time an episode is aired so I know how well the series has been doing. The English producers maintain they went to Hollywood to argue the case with *Centurion,* the Writers' Guild has tried, the Writer's Guild in the West Coast has tried and all have failed. *Centurion* has told everybody quite simply in so many words to fuck off. Yes, I mean that. Terrific diplomatic language from a high ranking executive wouldn't you say? So are you surprised that I am mad? Instead of living from hand to mouth for years and always worrying where the next penny was coming from I should have been a fairly rich man today if they hadn't reneged on the contract. And, Thornton, I wanted that money for my little girl. It would have meant so much for her well-being. So much for the protection of international copyright.'

'But you're working at the studio now, or have been, why is that?'

'A sop to Cerberus. I still have to earn my living don't I? No matter how piddling the reward. Keep body and soul together? Keep the wolf from the door and any other cliché you care to consider.'

'Is that really the reason?'

'Why else? There aren't that many jobs going and some producers believe writers live on ideas and fresh air so are virtually willing to work for free. Also these days they feel old hands like myself are passé and it's the young lions who have taken our place so opportunities aren't that thick on the ground. Courtney, probably in an effort to keep me quiet, offered me work and I accepted it. It would seem though that it's also a bust flush. It's not going to make any difference. They screwed me and I am going to screw them for every penny I can get.'

'How?'

Caswell stayed silent, looking passed Thornton into the middle distance.

'So,' Thornton pressed, 'has *Centurion* told anyone why they haven't paid these royalties?'

Caswell came back to earth. 'They have, and it is impossible to believe. They maintain the show hasn't gone into profit. That's a laugh. They keep three sets of books, one for themselves, one for public consumption, that is for anyone like myself who may be interested, and one for the IRS and, anyway, nowhere in my contract does it state that payments are dependent on profit. Profit and losses aren't even mentioned.'

'So there's no more to it than that?'

There was a long pause as Caswell stubbed out his cigarette in the clean ashtray and thought about lighting another but had second thoughts. He really was smoking far too much. If he carried on at this rate he wouldn't live long enough to enjoy screwing the companies for every penny he could get.

'Well, yes, there is something else but personally I believe it to be irrelevant. You see, when we were making the series we had a crooked accountant who stole some money fiddling the figures. It wasn't very much, probably a little less than two grand in all but *Centurion* have used that as another excuse not to pay out and what can a person like myself do about it? I don't have the money to sue. Lawyers are expensive and the company must feel pretty smug getting away with it all these years. It is possible that *Full Throttle* may have got some remuneration but I wouldn't really know about that. If they did they kept dead shtum about it.'

'Do you think this could have anything to do with Preston's murder?'

'Who knows? I do think the Mafia is involved somehow but again that's simply conjecture on my part.' He shrugged and lit that briefly delayed cigarette.

'Are you going to return to England?'

'Of course.'

'So do you have any idea, any idea at all, who might have killed Charmaine?'

Caswell shook his head. 'None whatsoever. Poor kid.'

Thornton wondered if he was serious or if that was an act.

'What do you suppose she was doing in Preston's office that time of night?'

There was silence for a moment and then Caswell looked directly at Thornton for virtually the first time. Up till now his gaze seemed for the most part to be everywhere else, the arm of his chair as he fiddled with it, the table top on which the coffee cups sat, various aspects of the room, people passing by. He was like a kitten on hot bricks. Now Thornton felt the truth was coming out.'

'She sometimes worked late but that night she was there because I asked her to be.'

This time both Thornton's eyebrows shot up almost reaching his hair line.

'What for?'

'I wanted her to go through facts and figures for me, maybe come up with something I could use to put pressure on the company. She knew all about my situation and, I hate to say this but I feel, if I could have got the company to pay out a substantial amount she would share it. I'm not exactly every girl's idea of a prince charming am I?'

Thornton shrugged. 'Attraction doesn't always depend on

looks and as a writer, you know it. Think of that Greek shipping billionaire, hardly a pretty picture, and the beautiful women who see him as prince charming. 'But why Preston's office? He was a minor cog in the machine; surely facts and figures wouldn't have been in his office?'

'Some would. Don't forget he was sole producer on *Return to Batani* and this would involve a great deal of finance both above and below the line. But Preston's office wasn't the office I asked her to check.'

'Oh,' said Thornton.

'It was Burrows office.'

'Courtney Burrows, the head of the studio?'

Caswell nodded, 'He has a safe in his office, I asked Charmaine to check there. I was sure that he must have some accounts in there that would give me the proof I needed. Maybe she found something about Preston in there. He was probably shitting himself over the fact his film has gone way over budget, nothing unusual there I suppose but the executive producers would be screaming for his blood. Could it be he committed suicide do you think?'

'No I don't think. From what you have told me do you honestly believe he was the kind of person to take his own life?'

'I guess not but you never know with suicides, do you?'

'The weapon used to kill him hasn't been found so it couldn't have been suicide.'

'No, you're bang to rights there. Well, where do you go from here?'

'To be quite frank I have absolutely no idea.'

'Then can I make a suggestion?'

'Please. Be my guest. Any advice is welcome.'

'Why don't you delve a bit deeper into the history of Breconfield Studios? Go back as far as you can and I reckon the person to start with would be Spring van Clef. After all she's been around long enough and more than likely knows an awful lot about a dark and murky past if there is one or at least, more than anyone else she would know what's been going on.'

'I'll do that. Well, thank you for coming to see me.'

'There's one more reason for me to be gutted. The original directors of *Full Throttle* were a man named Ray Timpson and one Larry Grant and they approached me one day saying they had the chance of producing a filmed series for kids but they were totally devoid of ideas, could I come up with something? Now, when I was a kid, my dad bought me an eight millimetre projector and you could buy little cans of film some of which were about a group of American kids, five or six, I don't remember exactly, a real mixture called *Our Gang* and the things they got up to, good comedy rough and tumble keystone cops type stuff. They came immediately to mind and these were my exact words to Messrs Timpson and Grant, *"Why don't you do a British version of Our Gang?"* And, Thornton, do you know what their answer was?'

Thornton shook his head.

'"Who, or what, is our gang?" That's exactly what they said, virtually in unison. "Who was our gang?"' He shook his head. 'I've regretted ever since that I didn't have a tape recorder with me that day because if it hadn't been for me and my childhood memories *The Limeys* wouldn't even have come into existence. So can you understand why I am so mad?'

'And these two directors, where are they now? Apart from what you've just told me this is the first time I've heard them mentioned. As far as I was aware *Full Throttle* is just a part of Breconfield.'

'Yes, it is now and has been for a number of years. James and Larry were bought out. James died some time back and Larry simply disappeared off the face of the earth. Who knows where he is or what doing, if anything? Ponsing around in the antipodes I shouldn't wonder. I'm sorry, apart from giving you a bit of ancient history, I'm afraid I haven't been of any help, have I?'

'Who knows at this stage? I'll mull over what you have told me and see if I can make two and two equal four and not five. Would you fancy some lunch?'

It was at this point that Thornton noticed a gentleman app-roaching their table. He was very tall, handsome, tanned, with piercing blue eyes and didn't look at all the image most Anglos have of Latins. It wasn't that all Italians have brown eyes, there are plenty of blue eyes in the north or even on Sicily thanks to the Normans and you can't get further south than that. The man was immaculately dressed in a light summer suit and an open neck cotton shirt, obviously stylish and expensive.

'Oh!' Caswell got to his feet. 'Oh, Thornton this is my friend Luca... Luca, Thornton King.'

'How do you do?' Thornton got up and offered his hand which was taken and firmly shaken. Luca with those eyes seemed to be looking right through him and Thornton was captivated. This was a man he felt he could really be friends with.

'Please, do sit down,' Thornton said.

'Grazie. Molto gentile.'

'Were you checking up on us?' Thornton asked, smiling.

Luca sat down. 'I suppose you could call it that. Or maybe it was just curiosity.'

'Well I take it you do know what happened to the curious cat.'

'Be that as it may, what would happen to the world if it weren't for curiosity? I'll take my chance.'

'Just curious enough to make sure Joachim was all right.'

Luca nodded and said, 'May I make a suggestion, Mister King, regarding your enquiries?

'Thornton.'

'Thornton.'

'Please do, I'm truly up a cul de sac here and without a paddle.'

Luca frowned slightly. Obviously he wasn't quite sure what this meant.

'Actually,' Thornton decided to enlighten him, 'the saying is "up shit creek without a paddle" but I was being polite.'

'I see.' There was as pause. 'Well, my suggestion in order to give you a paddle to get you out of the shit is this, why don't you ask more questions of your client, Spring van Clef? Get her to give you a run-down, a history of the studio? I'm sure it must be quite fascinating.'

'I'll do that. Thank you. As a matter of fact Joachim here has just this minute suggested the very same thing.' He got to his feet. 'Well, as you can see, I'm strictly on the level, no hanky-panky and your friend is fine. Not about to be clapped in irons and deported under heavy guard. In fact we were just about to go to lunch. Will you join us?'

'If I may, with the greatest pleasure.'

On the way out Luca asked to be excused for a moment as he evidently saw someone at the bar who he knew and wanted to have a few words with. As they talked the man looked across at Thornton and Caswell and smiled before returning his attention to Biancchi who evidently said his adieus and went back to the duo waiting for him by the door.

'Sorry about that', Luca said, 'studio business. Never lets up does it? Well, shall we go?'

They went to *La Cisterna*, Thornton having fallen totally in love with the place. They dined outside and ordered *papatini romana* and from a comprehensive selection chose a white to go with the noodles; a bottle of *Aurente Chardonnay Lungarotti*, the lunch being courtesy of Spring van Clef and, what with the air fare and the hotel, Thornton was going through his five hundred much too fast and would soon be moving on to his credit card.

Spring was not going to be at all happy with the Rome visit when he came away with hardly anything to show for it but still, not to worry about that now, why spoil a most enjoyable lunch. Luca was entertaining and full of high spirits. Caswell on he other hand was a bit on the quiet side but who could blame him? Luca suggested Thornton take a tour of the studios, he would be more than happy to show him around but, as much as he would have liked it, Thornton turned down the offer saying he had to get back to London as soon as possible and report to Miss can Clef.

'Maybe next time,' Luca said as they shook hands. 'Maybe next time. You are taking a plane today?'

'Eighty-thirty,' Thornton said, looking at his watch. 'So,

delightful though this has been, I guess it's necessary to call time. I must make a very quick visit before I leave.' Not being able to resist name dropping, 'The Countess Cinelli,' he added.

Thornton placed his cabin bag on the floor beside him as he leaned forward over the basin and turned on the taps to wash his hands. There was one other man in the men's toilet at the airport, washing his hands a few basins away and Thornton, with a sideway glance, thought he knew the face but couldn't quite place it. He was a stranger in Rome so where could he have seen it before? Was the man there when he came in? Or did he follow? Maybe he was in a cubicle. Was he someone he came across during his previous visit? It wasn't until the man turned to face him and smiled before moving over to the hand dryer that the penny dropped. It was the guy Luca went over to talk to at the Holiday Inn and suddenly Thornton's radar signalled danger in spades, or was it pure coincidence that their paths should cross in a gent's toilet at Leonardo da Vinci Airport?

Having ostensibly dried his hands the man moved closer but stopped when the door opened and someone else came in. The newcomer, obviously in dire need, made a dash for the urinals, hopping from one foot to the other as he hastily unzipped.

Luca's friend gave no indication of leaving but returned to a wash basin and stood looking at himself in the mirror. Now Thornton definitely knew this was no coincidence. He pumped a good portion of liquid soap into the palm of his hand. There was no attendant on duty and until the door opened to admit the new arrival he had been alone with Luca Bianchi's friend, accomplice, whoever or whatever he was, and who definitely meant mischief, of that Thornton was certain; and once the third man left, he would be alone with him again if no one else came in. He couldn't rely on a stream of people needing to use the loo and the would be killer was between him and the exit door. A quick thrust with a stiletto and it would be all over in a matter of seconds. But why? Was Joachim in on this? Or was it just Luca? But again the big question – why?

The third man finished, shook himself off, zipped up, let out a fart and a long sigh of relief and dashed for the door, obviously in a hurry with a plane to catch. No one else entered, and sure enough in a flash the flick knife was in his hand and the man virtually hurled himself in Thornton's direction. Both of them knew this had to be fast before someone else came in to interrupt. The man's momentum was brought to a sudden stop as a cabin bag goal kicked by an ex-scrum half rugby player hit him in the solar plexus and virtually winded him and, as he doubled up gasping for breath, Thornton followed up his attack by rubbing his soap laden hand across the man's eyes and leaping backwards out of harm's way. Winded and blinded, the would be assassin lashed out with the knife but Thornton had picked up his bag and was already on his way out. He was trembling, his heart was beating much too fast and it would take him quite a while to recover.

So that was the reason for Biancchi's appearance at the hotel. It wasn't to make sure his friend Caswell was all right but to see Thornton for himself and point him out to the would-be hit man. There simply was no one in the world you could trust. The hit man must have been keeping tabs on Thornton since his return to the hotel after that lunch, waiting his opportunity and the airport toilet providing the first chance he had.

On his way back to some semblance of normality, Thornton boarded the plane, smiled at a very pretty cabin attendant, received a charming smile in return, took his seat and fastened his safety belt. He hoped it wouldn't be too long before the drinks trolley came around. He could certainly do with one.

# Chapter Seven

Thornton had hardly been in his office five minutes, in fact the furred up old kettle hadn't even had time to boil, when the phone rang. The suddenness of it made him start. He stared at it and let it ring for quite a long time as he thought it could only be from one person – Spring van Clef and he really didn't want to talk to her.

He had spent eight hundred pounds of her money with virtually, if positively nothing, to show for it. Sooner or later he would have to face her but not right now, not this minute. He would have to psych himself up to it, preferably after a couple of bottles of very strong ale or a double *Famous Grouse*.

But the phone kept on ringing. Whoever it was on the other end was not going to give up in a hurry. Eventually he switched off the kettle, plucked up the courage to lift the receiver and put it to his ear.

'Thornton King.'

'Holly Day.'

'Holly!' His relief was palpable, from an almost inaudible "Thornton King" to an extremely loud and excited sounding

"Holly!" It was loud enough in fact to make her wince and remove the receiver from her ear.

'What a lovely surprise', he said, 'great to hear from you.'

'Yes, well you could have got in touch with me you know. You use that thing in front of you called a dial. See it there, do you? You select the numbers you want and, if you can remember them in sequence, insert your index finger and then you turn clockwise engaging each number in turn and hey presto! Guess what? I pick up the telephone this end when I hear it ringing and wonder of wonders it's my old friend Thornton King. Will miracles never cease?'

'Yes, sorry Holly', he apologised. When she was as sarcastic as this it meant she was really pissed off.

'It's been some time, wouldn't you say?' She sounded more than just a wee bit narked and he thought he had better get on with it.

'What can I do for you this fine day, Miss Day?'

'Oh, nothing in particular, thank you. I was just wondering how you are, that's all. Silence might be golden but it can also be worrying, and if anything sticks in my gullet...'

'You have a gullet? Do ladies have gullets?'

'... it's not knowing what is going on. You were a long time answering.'

'Well, fret no more, dear friend and don't sound so suspicious. I am fine thank you. Got myself a client.'

'That's nice. What have you got to do for him or her as the case might be, can you tell?'

'Sure. I'm investigating the Breconfield murders.' He tried to sound nonchalant but there was no mistaking he said it with some pride.

There was a long silence. Thornton's conversations seemed to be forever punctuated by long silences. He was beginning to wonder if she was still there when finally she came back.

'Why are you investigating the Breconfield murders? That's a job for the police I would say.'

'That's what everybody keeps telling me but my client evidently doesn't rate the efficiency of the force very highly. It would appear to her they are dragging their feet.'

'I don't suppose she's been having dealings with that veteran of the thin blue line, one Reg Venables. That could be the cause of it.'

'Shouldn't think so. Breconfield is way outside his manor. And anyway don't you think his retirement is about due?'

'Thornton, it took you an age to answer the phone. Were you down the passage?'

'Well no… I thought it might be from my client and I don't particularly want to talk to her at the moment. My investigation so far has got nowhere. I went to Rome which is why you haven't been able to get hold of me, just got back actually, went to find the writer Joachim Caswell and give him the third degree but didn't learn much, nothing to go on anyway. He's a bit of a mess actually. Quite frankly I don't know where to turn next.'

'Then I'll tell you. You quit.'

Silence was back again before Thornton answered. Holly always had a good reason for voicing her opinion.

'I can't do that, Holly. I've spent a whole heap of her money and if I quit I have no way of paying it back. What would it do to my reputation, what there may be of it, and why should I quit anyway?'

'Because your life is in danger.'

This time it was Thornton who maintained the long silence until he laughed. With memories of his only too recent dustup at Rome airport it wasn't a very convincing laugh, carrying, as it did, overtones of extreme nervousness.

'Come off it, Holly, in danger from what, from whom?'

'I don't want to discuss this over the phone. Let's meet. How about *Valerie's* in Old Compton Street. You do know it, don't you? Of course you do it's so easy enough to find, Old Compton Street isn't that long. Hopefully you'll be able to find Old Compton Street without a map or too much trouble.' She was being sarky again.

'I know it; I've been there quite often with one of my very

favourite people just so long as I don't die from a surfeit of cream. Those bloody cakes are truly delicious and I can never resist temptation.'

'You don't try hard enough. Shall we say tomorrow morning about eleven? How does that suit you? Eleven always seems to be a good time for a morning meeting don't you think? You won't have to drag yourself out of bed too early.'

'Eleven suits me fine.'

'Till tomorrow then and in the meantime be careful. Don't do anything stupid.'

'As if I would. You know me.'

'Yes, Thornton, unfortunately I do.'

He put down the phone and wondered just what he had got himself into.

She was already seated when he arrived. It wasn't an enchanted evening and she wasn't a stranger as he smiled a greeting and waggled his fingers across a crowded room and, taking in the cup on the table in front of her, mimed would she like another. She shook her head. Then he pointed to the assorted confectionary displayed in the glass cabinet on the counter to one side of him. She shook her head again so he ordered a coffee and a giant chocolate éclair and went to join her, giving her a peck on the cheek as he sat on the bench next to her so they could talk sotto voce. She had put up with a great deal of trouble and some angry looks in keeping the seat vacant for him, the place was that busy.

'You look great, a million dollars', he said. It was a quite unnecessary compliment because he had never known Holly look anything other than great and a million dollars. She could be hauled through a hedge backwards and she would still emerge from it looking as if she had just stepped out of a beauty salon. It wasn't just the hair or the face, the figure or the carefully manicured hands; it was also the stylish clothes she wore which came from having a rich banker daddy he supposed

110

who every now and again topped up her government salary, say on birthdays or at Christmas, which enabled her to do her shopping in Bond Street or its environs. What they thought of her at the department where most of the girls looked like frumps and wouldn't know style if it slapped them in the face is anybody's guess.

'So, Thornton,' she said. 'Just exactly where have you been these last few days? I've rung your office a couple of times and got no reply. I also rang the flat. You really ought to get yourself an answering service.'

'As I told you when you called, I've been in Rome.'

'Again? Was it a holiday break or was it something to do with your new client?'

'Second one. There was someone there I wanted to get information from but I've told you that haven't I? And I think it may have turned out to be a waste of time.' Or was it, remembering the attempt on his life? Had he inadvertently stirred up a hornet's nest? Hornets, wasps and kindred insects do not take kindly to their nests being disturbed.

'And did you find time to visit the countess?'

'But of course, a very brief visit I'm afraid. Had a plane to catch.'

'And she was delighted to see you I'm sure. How is she?'

'Sad to say still smoking those filthy cigars but otherwise apparently in top form. She really is in quite remarkable nick for a woman her age. If she were a car she would be a vintage Rolls Royce. I managed to avoid the tongue sandwich which she was only too eager to impress on me.' He grinned as Holly pulled a face. 'I satisfied her with a Serbian kiss, one peck on each cheek and one more for good measure and gave her your best wishes.'

'Life span does get longer and longer, Thornton, or are you unaware of that?'

'I think it's her toy boys who keep her going.'

'So she does have more guests.'

'Naturally. Americans doing Europe can go home and boast of having stayed in a real palazzo with a real living breathing, cigar smoking notwithstanding, member of the Italian aristocracy; good old European family. She more than likely plays up to it neglecting to mention her birth and bare foot Sicilian upbringing and the fact that she is not of royal blood but only a countess, and that only by marriage. Americans, always Americans. I met a couple of couples while I was there and of course they immediately gave me addresses and phone numbers in the states and an invitation to come visit, which was very hospitable of them I admit, but would I really want to go to Pittsburgh or Detroit or Decatur, Illinois? Somehow I very much doubt it.'

His coffee and éclair arrived. He gave the waitress a smile as she put down his order to which she responded by raising an eyebrow and po-faced passed on. Thornton shrugged.

'So, Holly, the warning, what is it all about?'

'Thornton, if I were you I wouldn't be investigating anything at all in Breconfield Studios.' She had looked around before lowering her voice almost to a whisper.

'Oh? And why is that?'

'Because we believe, that is, the department believes...' She looked around again to make sure no one was eavesdropping but the other customers seemed intent on chatting to each other or engrossed in *The Guardian* and none looked in any way suspicious... 'the Mafia are involved.'

'In the studio?' Thornton's voice, when he eventually found it, was almost a squeak.

'Shhh! Yes. I'm serious, Thornton.'

'Oh come off it Holly, you're kidding me surely. What possible interest could the Mafia have in a piddling little British studio, one that relies on handouts to keep it going?'

'Who do you think is doing the handing out? It's called invest-ment, Thornton.'

'Whatever it's called. They might have infiltrated Hollywood and run Las Vegas, but here? I don't believe a word of it.'

'That piddling little British studio as you call it is playing host to a major American corporation, is it not? I'm afraid I am not kidding, Thornton. We've been keeping a close eye on the situation, the goings on if you like, at that place for some time and, although we don't as yet have sufficient solid evidence for an arrest, we will keep on watching it until we do. Needless to say we are wondering if Cord Wainer really was the victim of an accident or a victim of another sort.'

She managed to say this without emotion, after all, the man was dead and, despite the crush she once may have had on him, there was no use crying over spilt milk, or cold corpses either for that matter.

'My thinking exactly. In fact I've always thought that. I have a shrewd suspicion he was a victim of one of Spitskaya's lethal little darlings, remember her?'

'Oh, Thornton! How could I possibly forget? It didn't happen twenty years ago, it happened like yesterday. Fortunately I am not the kind of person who suffers from nightmares or I would be a right basket case with that crazy woman in my dreams.'

'Well that little bunch of vipers and their mentor are no longer with us thank goodness but I still can't see why the Mafia would be interested in Breconfield.'

'Ever heard of money laundering?'

'What's that got to do with it?'

'Film production is an extremely expensive business, right?'

'Right.'

'Supposing they budget seven or eight million to make a picture, that's just a figure plucked out of the air, could be less could be more, could be lots more, and with inflation the way it's going in my opinion it is going to become astronomical. So you budget for that figure. Seven million, but you know the picture will come in at only four million or even less, what happens to the other millions? That's a whole lot of money to put in the bank in somewhere like the Seychelles for purposes other than making films, like stocking up again on drugs from South America for example, which is why, hush-hush, Thornton,' she put a finger to her lips, 'the department is taking a keen interest. The American connection is always interesting don't you think?'

'So you're suggesting Charmaine Carmichael was killed by a

hit man? That's ridiculous, Holly.'

'It would appear so I agree but do you know what Charmaine was up to the night she was killed?'

'As a matter of fact I do.'

'Tell me.'

'She was in Courtney Burrows office looking for material.'

'Why, and just what kind of material?'

'Why? Because the writer Joachim Caswell, the one I've mentioned and who she was having an affair with, asked her to try and find something he could use against the film company which he feels has treated him very badly.'

'In what way?'

'By not paying him what he feels is his due.'

'That's a pretty universal phenomenon. Is there anyone who doesn't feel like that?'

'No, seriously, Holly, it would appear he does have a pretty solid case.'

'So she shouldn't have been in Burrows' office and she may have found that certain something he could use which is why she was killed. Why would she do it for him anyway?'

'I told you, they were or are… sorry other way round, definitely were, past tense, lovers.'

'Then he is suspect number one.'

'Indeed he is and that's the reason I went to Rome because that's where he is at the moment.'

'You mean he skipped town.'

'Yes, he's keeping his head down because he knows he is top of the suspect list and I'm sure if the police knew where he's holed up they would want to extradite and interrogate him. Anyway I wanted to talk to him first which I did. The man is innocent.'

'Are you sure of that?'

'Ninety five percent.'

'The other five percent could prove you wrong. Why did he skip town in the first place? You don't find that just a wee bit suspicious?'

'We'll see. There are perfectly innocent people who take immediate fright and virtually piss their pants, if you'll forgive the vulgarity, at mere sight of a uniform and give every indication of being guilty of something, like people blushing when accused of something they didn't do. He could be one of them. But, as he confessed to me, he asked Charmaine Carmicheal to search Burrows Office. He feels slightly responsible. How she ended up in Preston's office, who knows. Caswell couldn't have had anything to do with Mel Preston's killing, he was in Rome and I can personally vouch for that. But there is something I do have to tell you in light of your warning.'

'Oh, yes?'

'Yes. He has a friend there by the name of Luca Biancchi. Ever heard of him?'

'Afraid not but I could make enquiries.'

'Well, remember the name. Fine upstanding, handsome, straight as they come looking fella who tried to have me eliminated, or in colloquial terms, bumped off. In a public toilet of all places, how infra dig.'

She listened to his story and then took a sip of her coffee grown somewhat cold and Thornton finally got around to biting into his very large chocolate éclair leaving a little bit of cream around his mouth. Holly smiled and with little finger touched the corner of her own mouth to indicate it and he licked the cream away before wiping his lips with his paper napkin.

'I can never resist these things they're so tempting. They're the next best thing to sliced bread and you know what else, custard slices.'

'I seem to recall in the office you were rather partial to chocolate digestives. I really am surprised Thornton that with all that fat and carbohydrate you're so partial to you are still so lean of frame. One day you're going to wake up, look in the mirror, and realise with age and stuffing yourself silly on all the wrong things you have grown somewhat corpulent, if not positively obese and none of your clothes fit anymore and you have to let out your belt half a dozen notches.'

'Don't worry. I'm still young, fit as a fiddle and good for a few more years yet. The lean and hungry look is in fashion.'

'When did you last take exercise?'

'Today?'

'Doing what?'

'Coming here.'

They both laughed and the waitress returning and still carrying her tray gave them a suspicious look. She was on her way to collect empties.

'Nice girl', Thornton said within earshot. 'I really should come here more often.'

Holly frowned in disapproval and the girl walked back and in passing gave Thornton a ravishing smile.

'See?'

'Thornton King, you are a monster who will never change, just grow worse with the passing years,' Holly said laughing.

# Chapter Eight

Thornton had decided to take the bull by the horns as the old saying has it, or in this case, the cow as it were. He picked up the phone and dialled Esther's number. It took a long time for her to answer.

'Yes? Who is this calling?' She snapped, sounding in a really bad mood, but maybe that was just her way. Some people simply hate talking on the telephone like some people hate taking medicine.

'Thornton.'

'Ah, the private investigator.'

He didn't like the sound of that.

'So you're back. Any success?'

'Afraid not so I would like to see you again.'

'Really? Is there any point in that?'

'I believe there is, yes.' He didn't add that he thought it extremely important which was why he was calling in the first place.

'What is it you want, Thornton? Oh, never mind. I don't want to schlep all the way into town to call at your office. Come to the flat.'

'When would be convenient?'

'Right now would be convenient, I've no engagements this afternoon.' She didn't bother to add she had no engagements every afternoon bar Thursdays when she attended her bridge club but it had been cancelled due to a flu epidemic which was why she was in something of a bad mood; slight withdrawal symptoms.

'I'll be as quick as I can. It depends on how quickly I can get a cab.'

'Why don't you take a bus? It's cheaper?' With which she put down the phone.

Thornton got up and moved over to his battered old filing cabinet that most definitely had seen better days. He took out the file marked *Fartfooker*, he was beginning to like that name, much preferred it to van Clef or Huntington, it did have a certain ring about it he thought, closed the drawer and went back to his desk to jot down the address.

Naturally there wasn't a cab in sight and it took a walk down the Charing Cross road almost to the National Portrait Gallery and a rank before he found one.

Esther's flat was in one of those prestigious old redbrick mansion blocks close to the Albert Hall. In fact if you looked out of the front windows when they were clean you could get a partial view of the Albert Memorial.

Thornton took the ancient lift shuddering to the third floor, found the right door and rang the bell. It seemed an interminable time for her to answer it. Maybe she's on the loo, he thought, or deaf, or the bell isn't working, he hadn't actually heard a ring. He looked around. If she didn't answer he decided he would take a stroll down to the *Victoria & Albert,* his favourite museum and spend a happy hour or two there so the journey wouldn't have been entirely wasted: but eventually the door was opened and he was ushered into the flat to follow her down a long dim corridor and into the drawing room; a brown room with a high ceiling, moulded cornice, large windows, and the very slight musty smell of age.

For a woman of her years she looked quite ravishing in the palest grey silk trouser suit with wide flairs that flapped when she walked like a yacht's sails as it tacks in a high wind. On her feet was a pair of soft embroidered Moroccan slippers and Thornton noted she was wearing jewellery: her gold wedding ring; another, possibly an engagement present with a quite impressive diamond surrounded by garnets. She was also wearing a pair of gold pendent ear rings and they weren't the clip-on sort. Her ears were pierced, something he hadn't noticed before. On her breast was a Petra Dura brooch; a white rose and jasmine flowers against a green leaf and dark background.

'Would you care for a cup of tea?'

Thornton didn't care for a cup of tea at all but thought it politic to accept.

'Good. The kettle's on so it won't take a moment. Make yourself comfortable.'

With which she swept out flapping away as she went. Her absence gave Thornton the chance of looking around the room.

The furnishings, including by the look of them, the curtains in a heavy maroon velvet with Napoleon tie-backs, pelmets and net swags, were all circa 1930 or maybe even 1830 and not all that interesting. There was a glass fronted bookshelf and a cabinet with doors to hide what is in many people's eyes that modern monstrosity, the television set.

It would seem as though Esther was not interested in large objects that could be considered antiques, but on a heavy old-fashioned highly polished sideboard there was quite a collection of miniature Staffordshire pieces of glazed pottery; some of it was inscribed *Souvenir of* or *Greetings from* various seaside resorts around Britain, from a time when Britain's seaside resorts welcomed visitors, and the collection included a number of pieces by Goss, much sort after by collectors. There were also, as a sort of token to art deco, a couple of pieces by Clarice Cliff glazed in orange, blue, white, and yellow triangles. Thornton wasn't quite sure by its shape if one of them was a vase or a jug. He plumped first of all for the latter as it looked as though it sported a possible spout but, on second thoughts, it could have been a vase as there was no sign of a handle. Confused he moved on.

The walls were a bit brighter with what appeared to be a hand blocked acanthus design genuine William Morris paper.

The most interesting part of the room were the pictures that covered the walls and here Esther had really chosen wisely if one is taking their value into account which would grow year after year. There were two John Pipers, a Hockney swimming pool scene and a Lucian Freud. There was also a silkscreen portrait by that strange creature Andy Warhol and a couple of sea prints with wild waves and lashings of spray by Hokusai.

The remaining paintings were British Victorian. One seemed to be painted totally in various shades of brown and showed an almost naked seated man, his lower half wrapped in what looked like a leopard skin, and a young smiling boy standing in front of him, their heads almost cheek to cheek. The boy too was naked except for a couple of thongs around his waist, knotted and descending for decencies sake to a strategic place. He was holding an empty drawn bow and on the floor there lay a leather quiver of arrows.

'I see you're admiring my Lord Leighton.'

He was so engrossed with the picture he had not heard her come in. She was carrying a large silver tray with the tea things: milk, sugar, slices of lemon, and the pot under a smart Heal's cosy; no chocolate digestives, no *Garibaldis*, but a Battenberg cake instead which she placed on a coffee table in front of a couch over the back of which was a beautiful throw, a Medieval hunting scene in crewelwork, then she joined him looking at the painting.

'It's called *The Hit*,' she told him, 'by Frederick Lord Leighton and was exhibited at the Grand Paris Exhibition of 1900. It was immediately snatched up of course and has been in the hands of the original owner's family ever since, never to be seen in public again.'

'Then how come you've got it?'

'Oh,' she laughed, 'this is not the original. I wish it were. I fell in love with an illustration of this picture when I was only eleven years old or thereabouts. It was in one of those knowledge of the world encyclopaedia things, you know, in ten or more volumes. I tracked the painting down and was granted permission to go and see it, taking the photographer Adrian Spangle with me. Do you know Adrian?'

'Oh yes. Adrian seems forever to be popping up in my life one way or another.'

She gave him a curious look.

'No, not that way.'

'Hmn… Well, to cut a long story short, I was given permission for Adrian to photograph it which he did. He made two copies of which this is one and the other he kept for himself. Over the years the colour has faded unfortunately which is why it appears to be all sepia now.'

'Well, I'm not in the least surprised that Adrian wanted a copy for himself.'

'You mean because of the homoerotic overtones? I harbour the gravest doubts about Lord Leighton I must say.'

"My goodness," Thornton thought, "she really has been going through the encyclopaedia, all ten volumes more than likely. She will be coming out with some Magnus Hirschfield or some Kinsey next."

'I've been in Adrian's mews cottage,' he said, 'more than once for various reasons that we needn't go into and I don't recollect ever seeing this particular picture.'

'It's possibly in a room you've never been privileged to see.'

'A mews house is hardly a mansion, Esther. I think I must have seen every room. 'Oh, wait, Yes, I do believe I did see it. But where?' He shrugged. 'Not that it matters.'

'Then maybe it's in his country cottage.'

'Adrian has a country cottage?'

'It's in Suffolk. He calls it his love nest.'

'Hmn…'

'I believe he inherited it from an uncle and it has a most unique feature. Next to the box seat in the outside loo there is a handle that you pull upwards and it flushes sawdust, or so I am reliably informed. I've not had the privilege of experiencing it myself. It's Edwardian I do believe.'

'Fascinating.'

'Isn't it? Still practical of course. I don't know how true it is, but it's said that the models for this particular painting,' she had gone back to regarding it, 'were two Jewish brothers from London's East End, the man being in the artist's employ. The child is very pretty, is he not? Now come along, Thornton and have your tea. How do you take it? Milk and sugar or lemon?'

'Just milk please, no sugar.'

'And how do you like it? Strong?'

'Just as it comes, as long as it's hot.'

'It most certainly will be under its lovely cosy. Well sit down there opposite me so we can talk and in the meantime I'll pour the tea.'

'Talking of Adrian, I'm surprised the countess didn't show you her book of photographs by him, photographs of internationally famous people. I'm not in it even though he did take my photograph not so long ago.' Thornton smiled at the memory.

'Was it a commission?'

'You could say that I suppose. Although it was only for a passport the countess insisted Adrian take it.'

'Good gracious!'

'Good gracious indeed. Both Adrian and I argued that there were far cheaper alternatives but she insisted Adrian take the photos. She is firmly of the belief he is the best photographer in the world and being the best photographer in the world he is the only one someone like her should use and he is naturally extremely expensive.'

'The countess Cinelli can be a trifle eccentric at times, don't you think? The photograph was good I take it?'

'Not really. Adrian was having a bad day so his heart wasn't in it and he said if his heart isn't in it he just cannot take a good photograph. I think in reality it was because I am neither famous nor a celebrity and anyway does a passport photo ever look any good? It looks more like a police mug shot. What did he charge you for the photograph of the painting?'

'Not a sou.'

'Very un-Adrian. He's usually a mercenary little beast.'

'He said as long as he could have a copy he was more than happy.'

Esther, who had finally got around to handing Thornton his cup, got up and walked over to the bookcase to remove a large volume in a sparkling white cover protected by a clear plastic sleeve.

'By his book I presume you mean this?'

'Of course! You must be in it. I didn't know that. Is there anyone else connected in any way with Breconfield who would be in it?'

'There is. Jimmy Harrowfield, an elderly gent now. What would he be? Sixty six? Seven? Somewhere around there. Maybe even a little bit older.'

'And what was he famous for? I don't know the name.'

'He was a writer.' Esther returned to her seat and her tea.

'Was?'

'I'm afraid so.'

'Esther, actors never give up acting. Do writers give up writing?'

'Some do, some do it quite dramatically, even successful ones. Hemingway shot himself remember? Virginia Woolf drowned herself in the River Ouse, and there were others of course. Edgar Allan Poe for example. If they didn't actually shoot themselves they drank themselves to death. Anyway Jimmy now keeps a pub, *The Green Man* in Hackney.'

'I know it. It's in my manor.'

'It was Jimmy who saved Breconfield's bacon all those years ago by writing the first *Guns of Batani*. It was an original story. Goodness only knows where he got the inspiration from and original stories don't go down well with studio executives but the studio was really struggling after the war once the government stopped wanting propaganda and information films, and the picture was a huge success all over the world. I'm surprised Jimmy wasn't nominated for an Oscar for best screenplay. Was Oscar around back then? I'm a bit hazy about it. Anyway he should have won an award of some kind. That's Jimmy there, look.' She extended the book in Thornton's direction.

He put down his cup to take it from her and looked at the picture of Jimmy Harrowfield, an elderly gent standing behind the bar of *The Green Man*, the pub reputed to have the longest pewter bar in the country. It was horseshoe shaped so ran halfway up the saloon, across into the public, and down the other side. "Must take a hellava lot of cleaning," Thornton thought. There didn't seem to be anything particularly distinguished about Harrowfield but the photo indicated he must have been an extremely handsome man when young with a dimple in his chin to rival that of Kirk Douglas.

'But if he was such a wonderful writer, why did he give it up to keep a pub? Not quite from the sublime to the ridiculous but pretty close wouldn't you say?' Thornton closed the book and carefully handed it back. It was placed on the table, not too close to the Battenberg cake for fear of an accident and of which Thornton had not as yet been offered a slice. The little square Claris Cliff china plates, serviettes and dinky cake forks remained unused.

'Disillusionment I believe,' Esther said.

'Why?'

She sighed, took a sip of her tea and put down the cup. 'It's a long story, Thornton but quite simply I believe the studio destroyed him. He was badly treated and that is a fact. Well, not by the studio per se but someone connected with it.'

'That seems to be the fate of writers in general and with that studio in particular. And who might that have been who treated him so badly?' Was he imagining it or were Esther's eyes suddenly full of tears?

'You must forgive me, Thornton, I have never spoken of this

to anyone and the memories are still painful, even after all these years. There are some memories that are meant to haunt you all your life, I do believe that, memories that your conscience will not let go.' She took a handkerchief from a pocket, wiped her eyes and blew her nose before putting the hankie back again. Then she picked up her cup to drain her tea before putting it down again and lifting the tea cosy. 'More tea, Thornton?'

'No thank you. One cuppa is enough for me. To tell the truth I'm more of a coffee addict than a tea drinker.'

'For goodness sake, Thornton! Why on earth didn't you say so? There was really no need to stand on ceremony. You could have had coffee. It would have been no trouble, no trouble at all.'

Thornton waved a hand indicating that it really didn't matter in the least. He waited as she poured herself another cup using a serviette to hold the handle so she didn't burn her fingers. She then refilled the pot with water from a jug and the cosy was replaced, being patted a few times as if was a pet. Her eye caught the Battenberg.

'Cake, Thornton.'

'No thank you.'

'Are you on a diet?'

'No.'

She cut herself a slice but before she could put it in her mouth -

'Jimmy Harrowfield,' Thornton said.

'Yes. Jimmy. This goes back a long way, Thornton, back to nineteen forty five or six. I don't remember the year exactly. I think it was six. Yes, must have been six. Anyway, there were the three of us, Jimmy, myself, and Courtney Burrows, founder of Breconfield Studios and what was then *Breconfield Productions*. We were known as The Three Musketeers. It's believed, in order to get the film on the road, Courtney mortgaged his beautiful riverside house at Thames Ditton in Surrey and Marlene, his wife, pawned her jewellery of which there was a fairly substantial amount including a couple of rare pieces I believe.'

'Yes I know.'

'Do you?'

'I did a tour of the studio and learnt it from the young lady acting as guide.'

'Well...' She got up and walked over to look out of the window, standing there quite a while before turning back. 'Forgive me, Thornton I have never told anyone this...' She sat down but remained silent. Thornton was intrigued. Esther wanted desperately to talk but was evidently also extremely reluctant to do so. She took a sip of her tea, put down the cup and sighed.

'Thornton, this will go no further than this room I hope. Can I trust you?'

'Implicitly.'

'Hmn...' There was another silence. This was going to be like pulling teeth without an anaesthetic he thought as now she fiddled for a moment with her Battenberg cake before looking up again. 'It's true the mortgage and hocking Marlene's jewellery, though she resisted that as long as she could I can tell you, raised enough to launch the project, but it was not enough to make the actual film and investors were few and far between despite its promise; so Courtney wondered if he might not have better luck in the states. Both New York and Hollywood proved as barren as England but he met a most persuasive gentleman in Las Vegas, a real smooth talker who hailed originally from Chicago I believe and who assured Courtney the money could be easily raised if he would be prepared to take a chance.'

She stopped again and Thornton wondered if she was going to take another sip of tea, fiddle with her cake or return to the window. There was information to be got here and, as with Caswell, he had to remain patient until she was ready to spill the beans.

She took the cosy off the teapot, lifted the pot, put it down again and gazed at something over Thornton's left shoulder until she was ready to talk.

'In those days, Thornton, recreational drugs were not so universal a problem as they are today but there were still plenty of outlets among the upper classes who enjoyed them at their cocktail parties etcetera, and in the privacy of their own homes of course. Well, the upshot was that Courtney talked both Jimmy and myself into going along with his scheme which was to bring the drugs into the country in sealed cans of unexposed film. Naturally customs officers, even if they were suspicious, wouldn't want to open a can and ruin the film and the paperwork was all in order.'

'Did nobody think to ask any questions?'

'Such as what?'

'Such as why was the studio importing film from the states instead of buying it right here?'

She gave a little shrug. 'I guess nobody did think to ask. Anyway, it wasn't too long before Courtney had enough finance to set the ball rolling and later other investors chipped in when they thought success seemed assured. Courtney, Jimmy, and I were inseparable in those days. Marlene was a stay at home and we hardly ever saw her. We were night clubbers; she preferred to curl up with a good book. To be quite honest, when she was one of the party we found her company rather dull. Jimmy's wife, Emma was a stay at home as well but, while we were out till the early hours, she was in but not alone. Be that as it may, Jimmy didn't ask for up front money for the script or indeed anything at all apart from expenses, enough to keep him solvent I suppose, until the movie was finished, as he knew the pickle the studio had been in and that was very generous of him. Then the situation got very ugly when one day Jimmy, I think slightly the worse for liquor and who could blame him? informed us that his wife Emma had run off with another man. In those days this was bad publicity. Don't ask me who the man was. I don't know. Even though this event had nothing to do with the studio, when he should have been supportive, after all we loved each other each in our own way and we had so much fun together, Courtney behaved very badly, virtually kicked Jimmy in the teeth as it were. Said it was Jimmy's problem, which of course it was, and Courtney refused point blank to have anything to do with it. I don't think he would have actually found Emma or anything like that but problems can be shared by friends can they not? That could have been overcome, faded with time, but things got worse. Courtney in collusion with a shyster lawyer, a typical Uriah Heep with a handshake like a wet fish and who always seemed to have flakes of saliva in the corners of his mouth, I remember that so well and I took an instant dislike to him, found a loophole in Jimmy's contract, genuine or not I never found out but Jimmy was forced to leave the studio he had helped save. Courtney's son took over when Courtney grew tired. In fact we didn't know it then but he was dangerously ill and he died not too long after. Jimmy attended the funeral and of course we talked which is how I know he had taken on the pub.'

'And that's the whole story?'

'No, I'm afraid not.' She took another sip of tea and it was a few moments before she put the cup down to continue. 'Jimmy and Emma had a daughter, Beryl, a sweet unspoilt girl, very pretty, inherited her father's good looks in a way, always chatty and laughing and making you feel she had known you all her life and there wasn't a care in the world. Naturally she was the apple of her father's eye being such a delightful creature and an only child. Edgar Courtney Burrows II, the man who is now in charge of Breconfield Studios visited Jimmy in his pub. I have no idea why he did that, what was said the first time or how they got on, remembering how Courtney's father had behaved, but the result of his visit was disastrous. Perhaps he meant to undo his father's wrong or to thank Jimmy for attending the funeral but, whatever the reason for his visit, he saw Beryl and not long after that, to put it bluntly, he seduced her. Could it have been with that clichéd old line, how would you like to be in pictures? Maybe not. Beryl would have been the last person to fall for that. Well, whatever it was she was soon starry eyed and in love with him. She fell pregnant: he left her, old old story, Thornton. She was never the same. It wasn't quite as bad as in earlier times but not like it is now when an unmarried woman can have a child and not be at all bothered about it and it seems to me that many of them are getting younger and younger. I'm no prude, Thornton. Hollywood shenanigans knock that out of you and you would be more than surprised I'm sure to know what goes on in Tinseltown but it seems such a shame that these young women don't know any better about it and having an illegitimate child in those days, only thirty odd years ago, no time at all in fact, was considered shocking and young girls to whom it happened could often or not be locked away in an institution, out of sight, out of mind. I believe while she was there she gave birth to a son who she named William.'

'And where might William be now?'

'Nobody knows.' She gave another shrug and a little pursing of the mouth, 'He was taken in by an orphanage, or children's home whatever it's called these days and was later fostered. Evidently he wasn't with his first foster parents very long before running back to the orphanage to complain of being badly treated. What kind of abuse it was I really don't know but after a short spell he was sent to another couple, a Warren Peterson and his wife Eileen who were much kinder, very loving in fact so that was some compensation for what he had previously gone through with the first couple. The world unfortunately is full of very nasty specimens. All in all it is not a pretty story.'

'How do you know all this?'

'From his grandfather of course who asked me to try and find out what had happened to his daughter. It was my turn then to play detective.'

Thornton wondered if the word 'play' was a dig but decided not, it was just her manner of speaking.

'He didn't know about his grandson, possibly still doesn't and probably just as well. I've never told him that part of the story. Best, I thought, to keep it quiet. Beryl didn't last long after and died in the institution.'

'So Jimmy Harrowfield had a really bad time all in all, first Courtney number one, then his wife, and finally his daughter. You're quite right, Esther. It's a pretty sordid story. Did Jimmy not want some sort of revenge after all that? He's only human after all.' He was thinking of the murders but what connection there could be was beyond him.

'Jimmy is the gentlest kindest person you could ever hope to know. I shouldn't think revenge is a word in his vocabulary and, as far as the way Courtney raised the money for his film is concerned, I think he has regretted it all his life. In a way I do too but we were young, Thornton, and ambitious and we could see a golden opportunity slipping away for want of any assistance. There, now you know our dark secret. It was so many many years ago '

'How long did you keep up with the drugs scam?'

'Only till the studio and the film were financially secure.'

'And there were no other ramifications?'

'Yes, of course there were.' She paused again. 'Courtney had to take on board the smooth talking gentleman from Las Vegas. He, and no doubt his associates, were not pleased and became most threatening. Courtney managed to calm things down by insisting it had become too dangerous to continue and it couldn't possibly go on for ever anyway. Another cup of tea, Thornton.'

'Thank you, no.' He had hardly touched it and it had grown stone cold anyway. 'Who would want to kill Mel Preston and why?'

'I've no idea.'

'Did he know about the drugs?'

Thornton, you are the only one apart from Jimmy and myself who knows about it. Not unless Courtney in his cups was indiscreet. No, it had nothing to do with that and I can't think he could have found out though, knowing Mel, I would certainly believe he was up to something that had him killed.'

'Tell me about him. How did he come to be working at Breconfield?'

'In those early days the studio had an editor who was a perfect genius, truly a one off. He could tell the rhythm of a scene to a frame, not one frame before or one after. Of course film makers at that time indulged in optical effects like irising, or wipes, cross-fading, etcetera but, whatever the director or producer wanted this man could deliver. He was a real treasure,

Thornton, they are few and far between believe me and his name was Leonard Preston. Leonard had a young son who was a bit of a tearaway, just out of borstal, for petty thieving I think it was, and heading fast down the slippery slope. One more conviction and it wouldn't be borstal it would be prison, so Leonard asked, begged Courtney to take on his son, give him a job in the studio, and Courtney of course agreed. Probably felt pretty good about it, giving a young delinquent a chance to go straight. Mel started off as a runner, then clapper-loader, went on assistant by assistant until he made assistant director, then director and finally as you know producer. Quite frankly as a director he was no great shakes but then it's a case of many being called few chosen. Isn't that the saying?'

Thornton wasn't quite sure whether it was or wasn't but let it pass.

'Anyway,' she said, 'that's the story of Mel Preston.'

'Not quite. We still don't know why he was killed or who killed him.'

'There is someone else connected with the studio who could be of interest, Max Dooley. '

'Max Dooley?'

'Quite a character.' She gave him a quizzical look, 'You haven't heard of Max Dooley? One of the gate men at the studios. He was Cord Wainer's bodyguard.'

'Of course! I thought I knew him from somewhere.'

'I will tell you about Max Dooley. Max was also an ex-borstal boy, more than that he had served at least one term in jail, for G.B.H if that's the correct term'

'It is; grievous bodily harm.'

'Max Dooley is a dangerous man, Thornton; you mess with him at your peril.'

'All well and good but what I really would like to know is how he came to be associated first of all with Cord Wainer and then the studio.'

'The story as I heard it was that Cord, nine sheets to the wind, was making a nuisance of himself in some seedy club or other.

Max was there and, before there could be a nasty incident, if I may put it that way, if nothing else Cord's pretty features wouldn't have been so pretty, he stepped in and, as I said, you mess with Max at your peril. The following night Cord was back in the club but more or less sober this time. Max was also there, they got chatting and that was that.'

'He became Cord's bodyguard.'

'More than that.'

'Oh? What?'

'He became Cord's procurer.'

'Young girls?'

'Boys.'

So Ernest J. had been bang to rights though Thornton still found it a little difficult to believe that Cord could have fancied him.

'Of course,' she continued, 'Cord's death meant the gravy train had come to a stop so what was Max to do? He could have sold the story to the newspapers, it was sensational enough but would the papers buy it even if they believed it? Without the boys to give their side of the story there was no evidence and I can't imagine for a single moment any of those boys coming out of the woodwork to make a full confession. Can you? I also think, I have no proof of this mind, that pressure was put on Max from up above with the promise of dire consequences should he step out of line. So what to do with him? It was obviously decided to keep him where he could be more or less supervised, give him something to do and pay him a salary well above what the job warranted. Max, after all, is not exactly the brightest pebble on the beach and who knows when he might turn out to be useful.'

Thornton wondered if this was a hint but decided not to pursue it and returned to Jimmy Harrowfield's grandson. Here was another story.

'And this couple, what did you say their name was?'

'Who are you talking about?'

'Sorry, gone off at a tangent; the couple who adopted the grandchild.'

'Oh, the Petersons.'

'The Petersons, where are they now? They might know where this son is, what's his name? William?'

'Somehow I doubt it but I'll give you the address anyway.'

She got up and went to an escritoire to check in her address book and write it down before returning to hand it to him.

'By the way, you'll never guess, but you had no sooner left for Rome when I had a quite unexpected visitor.'

'Yes?'

'Yes. Talk of the devil. Courtney Burrows of all people. I hardly saw him at all when I was working at the studio despite the fact that his father and I were so close and I knew him from infancy as it were, so it really was quite a surprise.'

Thornton was immediately busy putting two and two together. A vision of the airport in Rome kept popping into his head.

'Said he hadn't had a chance to commiserate with me over Charmaine's death and that was the purpose of his visit. Very charming he was for a rattlesnake. I told him I had hired you to investigate it and he thought that a marvellous idea. He wanted to know how you were getting on and I informed him you were in Rome though I didn't say exactly why.'

Curioser and curioser thought Thornton.

# Chapter Nine

Colleen at her till was flirting outrageously with Max and the queue of people was building up fast behind him. Their patience wouldn't last forever but Max was not one to be trifled with. Ernest J. didn't mind the skin congealing on his custard but had had enough trials and tribulations that morning and was in no mood for congealed shepherd's pie as well, so against his better judgment, piped up.

'What's the matter with the till can't you get it to ding?'

Suddenly the canteen was silent as all heads turned to look at Ernest J. Even though they all felt the same way none would have dared say anything.

'What did you just say,' Max almost yelled, as he shoved his way down the queue to stand in front of Ernest. The youngster, trapped between the food counter and bodies on one side and a handrail on the other was regretting having opened his big mouth but had to stand his ground. Max who had for a long time been looking for an opportunity to draw this thorn in his side bunched his hands into fists ready to strike.

'I said can't she get the till to ring,' answered Ernest rather limply.

'And just what's that meant to mean?' Ernest J. stared at Max's huge fists opening and closing. He couldn't concentrate. His mind was racing but he had lost the ability to speak. Visions of himself bandaged from head to toe and lying in a hospital bed as nurses standing by giggled and sniggered, commenting on the size of his willy and his family, friends, and well wishes stood around the bed and talked in hushed tones, expecting his death at any minute. He didn't know which was worse, family and friends, or giggling nurses. He looked up at Max and opened his mouth, and closed it again like a fish out of water. Max grabbed him by the front of his ban fox hunting Tee Shirt. Ernest screwed his eyes closed as he expected a blow any minute.

Max raised his hand.

'I think what he meant to say,' a voice interrupted, 'was that there is a problem with the till, and couldn't another solution be found before all our food becomes cold and inedible.' She had placed herself between Max and Ernest J.

There was a shaking and nodding of heads from the others in the queue.

'Oh,' said Max, as he looked at Holly. Holly smiled sweetly.

'I thought he was trying to be funny,' answered Max, 'he being a smart arsed git and all.'

'I'm sure that's not what he meant at all,' said Holly still smiling. 'Now why don't you and I have our lunch together?' She said as she took his arm in one hand and her tray in the other, and turned him towards the till. 'If we stand here for much longer, my tea will be cold and my fruit salad will be warm.'

Max beamed as Holly paid for her lunch. If looks could kill, Colleen would have been tried for first degree murder with a blunt instrument.

Ernest J, finally opened his eyes to see his saviour walking away arm in arm with Max towards a table by the window.

A couple of days later saw Thornton knocking on the door of the pristine little house in Torquay to which the Petersons had retired. He had taken the trouble to call before leaving London to make sure they would see him and giving his time of arrival so that he wouldn't waste any time, any more of Esther's money, and they would be expecting him. He hadn't told Esther where he was going in case more information went the wrong way. The next time he saw Holly he would have to tell her all about Courtney's visit to Miss van Clef. Was there anything suspicious about it or was there not? It certainly appeared to be highly suspicious.

As he stood waiting for an answer to his ring, through the little stained glass square of window in the door he could see two figures approaching and the door was opened by a lady who must have been about the same age as Esther but couldn't have been more different. Where Esther was tall and slender with a pale complexion, Mrs Peterson was short, pink cheeked, and roly-poly. Her husband stood silently behind her but nodded his head as she greeted Thornton. They were both smiling broadly. She stepped to one side and opened the door wide for the visitor to enter.

'This is my husband,' she said, turning to face him and extending a hand to point at the smiling man as if Thornton hadn't already guessed as much. He nodded and would have shaken hands only Mister Peterson, still smiling, was standing too far away and moved aside in his turn in order to let them pass. The couple reminded Thornton for all the world of Jack Spratt and his wife.

'It's Mister King, isn't it? That's right,' she beamed, 'come this way,' and she waddled off to open the door to the best front room.

Warren Peterson brought up the rear, still smiling. Thornton wondered if he ever stopped and if he ever opened his mouth other than to put food in it.

The front room had dimity net curtains, well nylon actually, meant to look like net but beginning to turn slightly yellow with age. The window ledge, on which there was not a speck of dust, boasted what looked like bad copies of Royal Doulton figurines. If the house had been in London he would have guessed they were got in the Shepherds Bush market. The carpet was of a rather garish design in great sweeping slashes of purple and green, very modern, bought through a Littlewood catalogue no doubt with easy monthly payments. Mrs Peterson was dressed in a cotton frock that obviously came from C&A and wore slippers on her feet because of her bunions that could get quite painful. Warren Peterson's clothes came from Marks & Spencer; casual summer shirt beneath a cardigan, slacks and open toe sandals with socks. Thornton could picture him on a beach or paddling at the water's edge with his trousers rolled up to just below the knees and a knotted handkerchief on his head to ward off the sun's rays. These were the people who should have had the seaside souvenirs on display but maybe they went in for something else like sticks of rock or kiss me quick hats and on rainy days sat in a shelter looking out to sea, frequented the tea shops, the chippy, or amusement arcade, amused by the laughing policeman, now and again putting a penny in the slot to play a game but never winning anything.

The furniture in the room was Parker Knoll except for an old worn armchair with a crocheted antimacassar close to the glazed tiled fireplace beneath a quite large nineteen thirties mirror with pink panels. Obviously that particular chair was for the master of the house. There was no sign of a television set but, believe it or not, there actually was a set of flying ducks.

'Please, do sit down, Mister King, while I go to the kitchen to make the tea.'

'Please don't put yourself out for me,' Thornton said, holding up a hand like a policeman on point duty.

'Oh, it's no trouble, no trouble at all, Mister King. You've come all this way.' She made it sound as if London was on another continent and with a dismissive wave of the hand she was gone in a wobble of buttocks which left Thornton facing the husband, still smiling.

There was another of those silences that seemed to haunt the private investigator but then, like any blue-blooded Englishman, he rose magnificently to the occasion in the traditional British manner that had for many years subdued whole continents and held together a world-wide empire.

'Nice weather,' he said.

Mister Peterson nodded in agreement after which there didn't seem much more to say until he volunteered his first remark.

'You had a good journey then I take it?'

'As good as could be expected in an unhygienic piece of rolling stock that must have been at least fifty years old. On my way here it was imperative I wash my hands so I stopped briefly at your local.'

'Oh, that wasn't necessary, not necessary at all; you could have used our bathroom. That's very hygienic.'

With what he had already seen of the house Thornton was quite sure it was but what it couldn't do was supply a noggin or two. He would have to use it before leaving though when the noggins he had imbibed on the way began to make their presence felt.

Mrs Peterson returned, no tray this time but a cup and saucer in each hand, one of which she gave to Thornton and sat down holding the other.

'I do like a nice cup of rosy,' Thornton lied, looking at the dark brown brew in his cup.

'Rosy?'

'Cockney rhyming slang, Mrs Peterson, you know, Rosy Lee, tea.'

'Yes. I've heard of that, rhyming slang,' said Eileen. 'Yes, I've heard of that. I've heard it spoken on the telly.'

'A bit queer is that,' said Warren. 'I don't know why people can't just talk proper English. It's beyond me, that is.'

'The tea's not too strong for you I hope,' said Eileen, nodding towards Thornton's cup.

'No, it's just right,' he lied again. 'But doesn't Mister Peterson get a cup?'

'Oh, no. Warren wouldn't want a cup right now, would you, dear? No, he wouldn't like one just this minute, no. He'll have a cup later with his tea. Won't you, dear?'

Warren nodded.

'By his tea I presume you mean his supper.'

'Supper, dinner, whatever you care to call it.'

Thornton hoped he hadn't given offence.

'We call it tea,' she went on, 'six o'clock on the dot come sunshine or shower. Isn't that right, dear?'

Warren nodded again.

'Now, what is it we can do for you, Mister King? I'm led to believe from your telephone call that you are enquiring about William, would that be correct?'

'It is indeed. Do you know where I can find him?'

'Has he done something naughty then?'

'Not at all, I just want to question him regarding an investigation I'm on. Another matter entirely but he might have helpful information for me.'

'Oh! Oh dear, we could have saved you all the trouble coming here had we known. You see, we haven't seen William... how long has it been, father?'

'Let me see...'

'Oh, a good ten years at least, yes.' She put down her cup and wiped a tear from her eye. 'We took him in, gave him a loving home when he was very young and, I really don't know why, one day he just upped stakes and was gone, just like that, not a single solitary word to anyone.'

'Just like that,' Warren Peterson confirmed it with another nod, 'and we haven't had a word from him since. I don't know, I really can't fathom out where we went wrong.'

'I'm sure you didn't do anything wrong, Mister Peterson. Teenagers take it into their noddle to do the strangest things; sometimes even they don't know why. It's all to do with hormones I suppose, growing up. How old was he when he took off?'

'Fifteen. I will say this for William; he was always an adventurous boy. Never got into any trouble mind, never gave us a problem, not until he went that is. Always up to something he was.'

'Did you call the police?'

'What?'

'Report him as a missing person.'

'We did, but what could the police do? If someone wants to disappear there's very little hope of ever finding them, is there? People go missing every day. The world's a big place, Mister King. Unless something has happened to him, if a person doesn't want to be found he won't be.' She gave her eye another wipe.

'Well, if you don't know where he is, do you have a photograph of him?'

'Of course, of course.' Mister Peterson got up and walked over to a sideboard, opened a cupboard door and came out with a brown embossed mock leather photo album that somehow reminded Thornton of Esther's bag. He crossed back to stand in front of the visitor with the album open at a certain page. It was an old-fashioned album with tabs to stick photographs on the page. Thornton took it and what he saw were photographs of a nine or ten year old boy in short trousers with tousled blonde hair and a cheeky grin as he looked towards the camera.

'Do you not have anything more recent than this?'

'I'm afraid not.'

'He suddenly decided one day he didn't want to have his picture taken anymore. He said it was childish.'

'A strange thing for a child to say.'

'Yes indeed. But we didn't try and force him or anything like that. No, we just let it drop, though we would have liked more photos of him growing up. He was such a handsome lad... Is,' he corrected himself.

And Mrs Peterson couldn't hold back the tears any longer. Warren moved over to her and laid a hand on her shoulder, gave it a gentle squeeze and a rub.

'There, there, love, don't take on. Don't take on.'

Thornton looked at the photographs a moment longer and

waited for Eileen to recover before he spoke again. 'Do you think I could possibly take one of these away with me?'

'Yes. You'll find one at the back of the album we didn't particularly like. You may take it with you.'

'Thank you.'

Thornton turned to the last page and there loose between page and cover was a picture of the boy William, only this time he was obviously not very happy about something because, instead of his usual grin, he was scowling quite heavily and this was no doubt the reason why the Petersons did not like that particular picture. It had not been fixed in.

Thornton slipped the photograph in the inside pocket of his jacket and got up to leave with a thank you for the tea and the photo.

'You don't have to send it back,' Mister Peterson said. 'We don't really want it. Don't know why we kept it all these years.'

Though there seemed nothing more to say, so as not to appear rude, Thornton lingered a while longer making desultory conversation, used the hygienic bathroom and, in case they should want to contact him, left his card which Warren placed carefully on the mantelpiece.

What a very nice couple the Petersons are Thornton thought as he settled down in a window seat in a cleaner slightly more up to date carriage travelling from Exeter to London.

He found himself mentally humming the song *Tea for Two*. He would have sung out loud except that it more than likely would annoy or embarrass the other passengers. Knowing what his singing voice was like he wouldn't have been at all surprised if one of them didn't leap to his feet and pull the emergency handle bringing the train to a grinding halt. Unlike other countries where train journeys are a shared experience, train journeys in England are meant to be taken in a monastic silence. That's one of the unwritten rules strictly adhered to.

Seated opposite him was a couple obeying that rule, obviously long married and with nothing more to say to each other but for exceptional circumstances. The man was engrossed in his newspaper; the woman was reading a book.

Why, he wondered, did the boy William suddenly up stakes and disappear with not so much as a word, much to the bereavement of the Petersons because that's what it amounted to he was so obviously the centre of their world. He took the black and white snapshot from his pocket to study once more. It may have been taken on a Box Brownie or similar, the quality of the print was hardly first class and it was already taking on a brownish tinge. There was definitely something wrong with the boy he was scowling so heavily. Thornton looked out the window for a moment watching the passing scenery. The train flashed through a station at such speed it was impossible to read the signs to know where they were.

He returned to the photograph and turned it over. Written in a spidery hand was "William aged 10." He must be about twenty four or five now and why, Thornton wondered, should he be so interested in the lad anyway? Because, through his grandfather, he was part of the history of the Breconfield studios? Because, albeit born on the wrong side of the blanket, he was the son of Courtney Burrows II. But even if Thornton suspected something he couldn't think for a moment what possible motive the boy could have had for murdering Charmaine, or Mel Preston for that matter no matter how badly the man might have behaved and, anyway, how did he know the boy was even in the studio or within a hundred miles of it when the killings took place? And yet, and yet, something was nagging him. He slipped the photo back into his pocket. The couple opposite still hadn't said a word to each other as they both turned a page in unison. It was like a double act and it lasted the entire journey.

# Chapter Ten

Reg Venables was behind his desk relishing his favourite sandwich, hot salt beef in rye with lashings of good old English mustard. He thanked his God for an establishment almost within spitting distance that went by the name of *Bloom's Deli* and he thanked his God that his dentist, a lovely gentle lass had returned from her Edinburgh trip, ousting the Eastern European butcher who, because of the most excruciating toothache, (nothing else would have got him in that chair,) had been treating him in her absence, if treating is the right word for the extra agony she inflicted. She must have learnt her dentistry in Tibet practising on yaks. He was surprised he even had any gums left.

So the all clear having been given on his ageing molars and with no more toothache to worry about he could indulge in his hot salt beef sandwich knowing it wouldn't touch a raw exposed nerve and send him screaming through the roof. If the toothache hadn't been so severe and he could have held out until Doctor Williams returned he wouldn't have let the butcher within ten yards of his mouth, but he was eventually persuaded to undergo the agony of surgery by his lady wife who was tired of him getting up at all hours of the night to go to the bathroom and with a cotton bud dab tincture on the offending tooth for a brief moment's relief. She wasn't getting her beauty sleep and she resented it. Besides, the smell of cloves in the middle of the night upset her. In fact a mixture of stale pipe tobacco smoke and caries, added to the cloves was not conducive to sweet breath no matter how vigorously you brushed your teeth and, if it was lying dormant for a while, he had, against all reason, got into the habit of poking the tip of his tongue into the cavity to tease a quiescent nerve. Perhaps it was a challenge for it to do its worst.

His chewing was interrupted by the appearance of young Roper who stood grinning at the door; always a bad sign. If it was good news Roper wouldn't be grinning. There was something truly perverse about that lad. Reg's half eaten sandwich was momentarily suspended mid way to his mouth.

'Well, what is it?' He growled through the mouthful that was already in place.

'You have a visitor, sir.'

'Oh, yes, and who might that be?'

Roper's grin could have been a false alarm. It could be the Chief Constable come to congratulate him over something or other though for the life of him he couldn't think what. Reg was forever dreaming of mounting the ladder of preferment, or retiring. He couldn't make up his mind which alternative was the more alluring. He imagined it would be the first. One can only potter so much in a potting shed before going slightly potty oneself.

'One guess guess who?'

'Don't play childish games, Roper, can't you see I'm having my lunch? Indigestion's the last thing I need. Just tell me who it is and mayhap (good word that, Reg thought; he would definitely use it in his memoirs when he eventually got around to putting pen to paper.) My visitor whoever he or she may be can wait till I've finished.'

'It's Thornton King.'

'Oh, God!' Reg groaned. His God and Hymie Silberstein might keep him well supplied with salt beef sandwiches but why wasn't he left in peace to enjoy them? He could sense an incipient attack of indigestion. 'What does he want now?' That man was forever spelling trouble with a capital T. 'I'm not here. No. Wait! On second thoughts all right, usher him in, Roper.'

Roper stepped outside and could be seen making a rather suggestive, albeit unconscious, come hither gesture with his forefinger and Thornton appeared in the doorway, breezy as ever.

'Good morning, Reg!'

'Is it?' Reg put on his fiercest scowl which meant whatever Thornton might have in mind he was in no mood to be trifled with. 'Thank you, Roper that will be all.'

Constable Roper, who was dying to find out the reason for Thornton's visit, plodded away crestfallen like a deep sea diver with a weighty helmet and lead in his boots.

Reg in his most regal manner indicated, sandwich still in hand, that Thornton could take a seat opposite which he did.

'Right Thornton, lad, what can I do for you this time?'

Although by now Reg Venables had a grudging admiration, even a sort of affection you might say for Thornton King, he sometimes wished he'd never arrested him in the first place, especially as it turned out to be a false arrest.

'What is it you want?'

'Are you still noshing on that salt beef, Reg? You'll O.D. on it one of these fine days.'

'Come to the point, Thornton, I haven't got all day you know. There's work to be done.'

'Criminals to nick.'

'Exactly.'

'Forms to full in.'

'Unfortunately.'

'Motorists to harass.'

'Now now Thornton, we'll have none of that sort of uncalled for remark, not if it's my assistance you're after. Any more of that kind of talk, there's the door right behind you. Leave that sort of thing to those who fancy themselves as comedians.'

'Only a joke, Reg.'

'That's what I have just intimated, and in very poor taste if I may say so. By the way, talking of motorists, how's your friend and mine, Mister Norris getting along?'

'Haven't seen him for a while, Reg.'

'So it's not him you've come about then? Thought maybe he'd overstepped the mark once too often. We've had our beady eye on him for quite a while you know.'

'I'm sure he's well aware of it, Reg. And I'm sure he's keeping a beady eye out for your lads. No, it's something totally different.'

'Well let's be having it then.' Reg took the penultimate bite of the sandwich that had finally reached his mouth.

Thornton took the photograph from his pocket and slid it across the desk. Reg looked down at it, stopped chewing for a second, raised an eyebrow and looked up. 'What's this when it's at home then?' And, having made that enquiry and swallowed took the last bite and started chewing again.

'It's a photograph isn't it? What does it look like?'

The chewing stopped.

'One more crack like that, Thornton and you'll be out of that door so fast you won't know what hit you. Lightning or jet propulsion will have nothing on your rate of exit.'

'Sorry Reg. Sometimes my tongue runs away from me, like it's got a life all of its own, can't seem to control it somehow.'

'It'll do more than run away if you're not careful. I'd bite it if I were you. What is that old saying? Keep a civil tongue in your head, is that it?'

'Or in somebody else's.'

'That is disgusting, Thornton. I can do without that sort of gross humour if you don't mind, what passes for humour I mean and being sarky with me gets you nowhere. Why are you in such a jolly mood anyway? Won the pools or something?'

'I should be so lucky. And when that happens I'll be on the next plane to the Bahamas or some such hotspot for a spot of luxurious self gratifying living.'

'Well you're certainly not here for the sight of my pretty face. All right then…' Having finished his sandwich Reg wiped his fingers on a paper napkin so as not to get grease on it and picked up the photograph, '…so what's all this about? This little bugger been up to mischief has he? Looks like a right little villain to me.'

'Everyone looks a right little villain to you, Reg. It's in your nature to suspect the whole world of misdemeanours which is why you're such a good cop.'

Reg looked up and almost snarled. 'From sarcasm to flattery, whatever next?'

'No, it's about a missing person.'

'Relative of yours is he?'

'No, I'm pursuing the matter for a client.'

'How long has he been missing?'

'About ten years.'

There was a long silence before Reg looked up from the photograph. Was this another example of Thornton's misplaced warped sense of humour? If it was, like Queen Victoria, Reg was most definitely not amused. A Victorian novelist in fact might have noticed his voice taking on a dark and sinister tone as if there was already a damp and dreary cell just waiting for this smirking shyster private eye who sat there wasting valuable police time. As a matter of fact Thornton wasn't smirking but Reg liked to think he was.

'And just what, Thornton, do you expect me to do about it? Have you lost the last of your marbles? We have difficulty tracing people missing for ten days let alone ten years.'

'I'm fully aware of that, Reg,' Thornton said, immediately hating his stilted prose, but Reg Venables invariably seemed to have that sort of effect on him. Why couldn't he have just said "I know that"? Simple and straightforward. 'I don't expect you to instigate a search or anything like that. No, the favour I'm asking Reg is, would it be at all possible for one of your police artist wallahs to do me a decent size sketch of what he thinks that lad would look like now, age twenty four or thereabouts?'

Reg pursed his lips and rubbed his nose between finger and thumb as he gazed at the photograph then he sniffed and looked up.

'Very well. I'll scratch your back. Who knows when I'll want you to scratch mine? Leave it with me, old lad. Give me a couple of days, all right?'

'Very grateful, Reg. I owe you one even if it's only a hot salt beef sandwich if ever you're skint. How's the lady wife by the way?'

'Fine, she's fine, thank you for asking.'

'Give her my best.'

Reg nodded.

Thornton pushed back his chair and got up to leave but before turning away he dipped into his jacket pocket and dropped a small package on the desk. Reg eyed it warily.

'What's this, lad? What's this? A bribe is it? That's a criminal offence of which I am positive you are well aware.' Was it that sort of syntax that invariably had Thornton responding the way he did. In the mouths of the semi-literate an effort to appear well informed and superior, modern jargon was destroying the English language.

'No, Reg, it's a present. I found this quite incredible old-fashioned tobacconist, shop I mean though, come to think of it, the tobacconist himself was pretty ancient, and I thought this could be something you would appreciate.'

'Oh, yes? Sarcasm, flattery, and now bribery.'

Reg picked up, opened the packet and put his nose close to it. A look of pure rapture spread across his face.

T hornton's next port of call was an orphanage in north London, an impressive if slightly decaying Edwardian house the developers hadn't yet managed to get their Philistine hands on to replace it with a modern monstrosity such as would set Adrian Spangle climbing up a wall and which could be leased out at enormous cost.

Set in a beautiful garden close to Highbury Fields Thornton

was greeted at the front door by what everyone usually thinks of as a motherly lady with a beaming smile that turned into a frown when, on being the recipient of his card, she lifted her lorgnette and read his details. She was now Miss Iceberg 1974 and if he wasn't careful before any more time passed he could suffer the same fate as the Titanic.

'And just how may we help you...' she looked down at the card, looked up again... 'Mister King? Are you by any chance related to any of our charges?'

'No.'

'Then if it is information you are seeking about any of them I'm afraid we cannot help you. Everything here is strictly confidential and has to stay that way; you do understand of course.'

'Of course. I wouldn't dream of compromising you, er... Do I call you matron?'

'You may call me Mrs Amory.'

'Mrs Amory. I was in the secret service for many years and I am fully aware of how leaks of any kind are frowned upon.' That didn't come out quite the way he meant it so he hurried on. 'No, all I want...'

He was interrupted in mid-flow when a nearby door opened and a second lady put in an appearance, obviously curious as to who the visitor was and what he could want. This one looked even more matronly than Mrs Amory if that were possible.

'Good afternoon,' Thornton said with a smile.

She nodded but didn't return the smile.

'Hilda...' and then to Thornton... 'This is my assistant Miss Phillips. Hilda this gentleman is asking for information that we cannot possibly give him and...'

'Excuse me, Mrs Amory, one moment if you please, but you haven't heard what it is I want.'

Mrs Amory and Hilda Phillips silently waited for him to explain his mission.

'On behalf of his foster parents I am trying to trace a missing person. He is no longer, and hasn't for a long while, been someone in your charge so I shouldn't think secrecy is the order of the day and I desperately need some information, good news I hope, that I can pass on to his adopted family to ease their grief.'

He thought that sounded rather good. Maybe a little on the melodramatic side but a genuine altruistic plea for help on behalf of a third party, especially with heavy frown that accompanied it.

Mrs Amory looked at Miss Phillips who looked at Mrs Amory and they both turned with serious faces to look at Thornton.

'You had better come into the office,' Mrs Amory said at last, and he was ushered through the door from which the previously smiling Miss Philips had emerged only a few moments before to find himself in a cosy parlour come office; a comfy old sofa and easy chairs but also the usual desk, typewriter and an old filing cabinet, rather similar to Thornton's only this one in sturdy oak rather than dull battered metal.

'Do take a seat, Mister King.' A gesture indicated which chair he was to use. 'May I offer you some tea?'

'Thank you, no.'

'Very well. Please state your business and if, mind you I only say if, we can be of any assistance we will naturally endeavour to do our best.'

Thornton wondered if everybody in a position of some authority spoke the Queen's English in such a convoluted manner or was it a result of drinking too much tea? He opened his document case and took out a ten by four, handing it across the desk to Mrs Amory seated there with Hilda standing beside her.

'Does that mean anything to you?' He asked.

'Is this the person you are looking for?'

'It is.'

'Hmn.' She raised her lorgnette once more, looked at the sketch, and lowered the glasses.

'Well?'

'It's not a bad likeness, not bad at all. How did you come by this if one may ask?'

'I had an artist draw it for me from an earlier photograph.'

'You have that photograph?'

'I do.' He produced it from his case and passed it over. She looked at it a long while.

'Yes. This young man is William Harrowfield. Fancy someone being able to do this,' indicating the sketch, 'from that,' the photograph. 'The drawing is a good likeness is it not, Hilda?'

'It certainly is. He was here just…'

Mrs Amory coughed very loudly.

'Oh. I am sorry! Was I not supposed to…?'

'Well, you've really let the cat out of the bag, now haven't you?'

'And set it among the pigeons,' Thornton said with a grin.

Mrs Amory didn't find that in the least amusing. 'Well I might as well finish Hilda's sentence for her despite least said, soonest mended. What she was going to say was yes, William did pay us a visit, only a few days ago as a matter of fact, but I must say he gave no indication whatsoever that he was a missing person or in any kind of hot water so what gives you that idea, Mister King and, more importantly, what is your interest? Be honest with me please. From long experience I can always tell, and so can Hilda,' she nodded in her companion's direction, 'it's from being with so many children for such a long time of course, but I can always tell when a little someone is telling fibs. Children are forever telling little fibs and hoping to get away with it.'

'Be assured, Mrs Amory, I wouldn't dream of telling little fibs, nor would I even dream of telling big ones. But where, if I may ask, are these children you talk about? I fully expected to have to raise my voice in order to make myself heard above the clatter of children playing, of childish bickering, screams, and chatter.' Thornton could be as rhapsodic as anybody at times.

Mrs Amory looked up at Hilda Phillips and smiled and Hilda smiled back before they both turned to smile their matronly smiles at Thornton.

'It's their rest hour, Mister King. They're all in bed and asleep, I hope. Children do need plenty of rest you know.'

'So do some adults, Mrs Amory, I never feel I've ever had enough sleep. I wake up tired.'

'What you need then is a good tonic, iron possibly if you're at all anaemic, or a holiday, that's what you need: the seaside maybe; go for long brisk healthy walks along the cliff tops, stride out, breathe in that bracing sea air. Get a lungful of it. Now, you were going to tell us about William. We are all ears, aren't we, Hilda?'

'We certainly are.'

'He looks such a sad little boy in that photograph,' Hilda said.

'I would say he looks more angry than sad.'

'But why should that be? He seemed so settled and happy at the… Who was it took him in, Hilda?'

'I'll have to look it up.' She moved over to the filing cabinet. 'So many poor little waifs over the years,' she said by explanation, 'it's difficult sometimes to remember and it was ever such a long time ago. Now I come to think of it,' she paused, leaning her arms horizontally on top of the cabinet, 'he never did mention them when he was visiting. I didn't think anything of it at the time but now, well it does seem rather strange, my memory…'

'Yes, yes, just look it up.'

'There's no need,' Thornton said. 'They are a Mister and Mrs Peterson and they live in Torquay.'

'Oh yes, of course, the Petersons. I remember. Such nice people. They were the second couple to take him in or maybe you are aware of that. The first pair turned out to be entirely unsuitable to look after a child. I don't know why they wanted to foster in the first place. They seemed so right when vetted; good steady income, nice home, long established couple, churchgoers, no record of any kind, healthy, non-smokers, quite charming when interviewed but childless. Who would have thought for a moment they would be so cruel? Unfortunately it happens too much, that and the abuse of old people, bullied, victimised, belittled and frightened, unable to help themselves, and this from those supposedly there to take care of them. Animals too are treated quite abominably and this in a country of supposed animal lovers. I don't know, I really don't. Why does there have to be so much cruelty in the world?'

'We found the poor boy on our doorstep one night,' Hilda chipped in, 'when he couldn't stand it any longer. Shivering with the cold, almost blue he was. He had walked all the way from…where was it from? Well it was miles anyway.'

'It's a wonder he didn't go down with pneumonia. When the couple came to enquire after him, which they did of course, a couple of days later, we informed them he had gone down with it, was in bed, the doctor was extremely worried and he might have to be hospitalised, William that is, not the doctor, and no way could they see him and, if the worst came to the worst they would be held entirely responsible. That was one time I was happy to tell a fib. You could see it got them really worried.'

'And so they should have been. The bruises!' Hilda squealed.

'The brutes!' Mrs Amory added.

'Did you not inform the police?' Thornton asked.

'Maybe we should have,' Mrs Amory agreed, 'but the boy had been through so much. If the couple had been prosecuted he would have been required to give evidence in court and we didn't want to put him through that. But we did inform social services who said they would look into the matter.'

'Why people like that want to adopt a helpless child in the first place I really cannot understand,' Hilda said and, getting a frown from Mrs Amory who had already remarked on that, left her side to seat herself in an easy chair. 'The experience will stay with him for life I'm sure.' She smiled, having got the last word in.

'I'm afraid the world can be very cruel to the helpless,' Thornton said and both women nodded in agreement and thought him a really sensitive young man. 'But why did William come to visit you recently?' He continued.

'Oh, sometimes in later life some of our orphans, how I do so hate that word, some of our children, visit us for old time's sake. I hate the word orphanage as well. Prefer to call it a children's home which of course it is until they find another description for it.'

'They call to say thank you,' Hilda added.

'Just to see us. Maybe to tell us how they're getting on.'

'And did William tell you how he's getting on?'

'Oh, yes, indeed. He's done jolly well, hasn't he, Hilda?'

Hilda nodded and her smiled broadened. 'Jolly well,' she said. 'He's an electrician.'

'Did his apprenticeship and is now fully qualified.'

'That's good.'

'Isn't it? Yes, we're very proud of him.'

'If that is the case there's just one question I have to ask though.'

'And that is?'

'Apprentices are not all that well paid, really no more than a gesture, a pittance, and apprenticeships are lengthy. He would not have been able to keep himself. Somebody took him under their wing. Have you any idea who that somebody could have been?'

Both ladies shook their heads.

'He didn't venture any information of that sort?'

The heads shook again. 'And we wouldn't have thought to ask, would we, Hilda? As something like that never occurred to us.'

'I take it the home is funded by the local council, possibly with government help?'

'Oh, no, Mister King, we are a private charity.'

'Is that so? You get donations from the public at large? Do you advertise like the R.S.P.C.A. for example?'

'There's no need. We have a number of rich sponsors.'

'Big business you mean. Do you never run short of funds?'

'We haven't as yet. Our contributors are very generous.'

'Who might they include?'

'Breconfield…'

A swift turn of the head and an angry glance from Mrs Amory brought a blushing Hilda up short. It looked as though she was about to burst into tears as she realised she had possibly made yet another faux pas.

'You mean the film studio?'

Mrs Amory shook her head. She never could get Hilda to keep her mouth shut and she really would have to have words with her once more.

'Or do you mean Mister Courtney Burrows personally?'

'Oh! You know Mister Burrows?'

'In a way, yes.' No little porkies here.

'We would love to meet him personally. We write inviting him to visit us but the reply is always in the negative, a polite letter from a secretary to say how busy he is. We send him a card every Christmas but he doesn't respond. I would dearly like to meet him personally, shake his hand and thank him for his generosity.'

'Yes, well one last question and I shan't bother you any further. I'm sure I am taking up a great deal of your valuable time.' He favoured them with one of his most beguiling smiles and both women went a littler weak at the knees. Do you know if at any time whilst he was here, William that is and I don't mean when he visited you recently, I mean when he was a child in your care, did William have any visitors or did anyone ever come enquiring after him?'

'There was yet a further shaking of heads.

'You must understand, Mister King that we both can't be here twenty four hours a day seven days a week. We do have staff who share the responsibilities.'

'Are any of them here at the moment?'

'Yes, there is cook who is probably preparing dinner and Miss Austin who is upstairs looking after the children.'

'Making sure they're asleep.'

'That's right. Or at least pretending to be.'

Now there were smiles all round.

'Could I have a word with her do you think?'

'Better not. We don't want to disturb the children do we? I will question her later and if she can tell us anything, anything at all, I will let you know.'

'Please do that,' and Thornton got up to retrieve the images of William Harrowfield and hand Mrs Amory his card.

He gave them a cheery wave as they stood by the open front door. They would be talking about him for quite a while after he had gone. When Thornton turned on the charm he delivered it in spades.

# Chapter Eleven

Though Thornton pondered on what Burrow's connection with the children's home could mean he was no further on with his enquiries than before his meeting with Mrs Amory and Hilda Philips and beginning to feel more than just a little frustrated. His next port of call was obviously *The Green Man* in Hackney, a very pleasant establishment in a wide street lined with lime trees at which owners of parked cars swore and figuratively clenched their fists as they endeavoured to get rid of the sticky goo that dropped on shiny bonnets. It was not at all what one thinks of as London's East End and *The Green Man* was almost a country style pub and within walking distance of his block of flats.

He wondered if he shouldn't have brought Holly along with him. He might be quite a dab hand at turning on the charm when questioning the ladies but she was definitely better with the men, virtually had them eating out of her hand every time. Even Adrian Spangle was charmed by her and that really was saying something considering he spent so much of his time surrounded by the beauties of the fashion world and wasn't in the least impressed by any of them, or interested, not in that way. Even Reg Venables mellowed slightly and became something of a positively purring pussy cat in her presence.

Carrying a copy of the *Evening Standard* early edition, Thornton pushed open the door and entered the pub and there she was in all her glory, the barmaid at the "Follies de Green Man," a statuesque blonde, like Cynthia, of ample bosom and made even taller by having her hair piled up almost as high as was once the fashion with the ladies of Versailles and lacquered firmly in place. She wore a plain skirt but a frilly silk blouse that showed just enough cleavage without being vulgar, a crucifix on a gold chain nestling neatly there. Bangles adorned her wrists, her mouth was a cupid's bow of scarlet and her fingernails were painted a glossy pink. Rosy were her cheeks. Her eyebrows had been plucked and redrawn in a thin higher arc, almost a semi-circle, and there was so much mascara on her lashes they had become beaded and it was a wonder with the weight that she could keep her eyes open. But nothing escaped her minces which is what Thornton would have called them when in slang mood which was fairly frequent – mince pies – eyes. She could sense trouble fifteen minutes before it even started. She eyed Thornton as he walked up to the bar, decided he was definitely a bit of all right and gave him a big cheesy smile, showing a trace of lipstick on her slightly crooked front teeth, and assuring him that she was there to be of service.

'Good evening,' he said, ever the gentleman. 'A pint of half and half if you please.'

'Certainly, sir.'

She reached up for a pint mug, one of a number hanging from hooks beneath the wooden rack above the bar. She was tall enough to do it even without her stilettos, the shoes she wore coming to work but which she immediately changed into slippers for comfort. In a long session stilettos could cripple you and no one sees your feet behind the bar. She started to pull up the first half.

'Nice evening,' she said, 'come far have you?'

'About a quarter of a mile, if that.'

'Really? Haven't seen you here before though.'

'No, this is my first time as the actress said to the bishop.'

She gave a squeak of laughter and a look that said; oh you are naughty, though of course she had heard a whole lot worse than that many times. She put down a coaster advertising *Babycham* and placed his drink in front of him. He laid a note on the counter.

'Have one yourself,' he said.

'Ta, I will. Gin and tonic if that's all right.'

'Be my guest.'

It was invariably a gin and tonic when barmaids were offered a drink.

He looked around. From the public bar could be heard the click of billiard balls and occasional masculine laughter though in the saloon where he stood there wasn't much sign of life, just one old codger sitting at a table and mumbling to himself, now and again adding a trembling somewhat theatrical gesture. Thornton had chosen opening time as, if he wanted a word or two with the Guv'nor, there was no point in arriving when the place was heaving as no doubt later it would be.

The barmaid lit a cigarette with a Zippo and took a long draw before turning her attention back to Thornton and giving him another smile. She noticed him looking at the old codger.

'That's old Kev,' she said. 'Don't take no notice of him. He's quite harmless. You wouldn't think it but I am led to believe he was once a right tearaway. Could even have been…' she lowered her voice to a whisper '… part of the Kray gang, you know. Been coming to *The Green Man* since the year dot following in the footsteps of his dear old dad, or so I've been told who used to leave him outside in the cold in the dead of winter with an arrowroot biscuit while he was in here nice and warm and drinking himself silly. Lots of people used to do it in those days, leave their kids out on the pavement I mean come rain, hail or snow. Kids today don't know how good they've got it and that's a fact. Excuse me.' She moved away to serve a new customer but was soon back.

'Have you worked here long?' He asked, purely to open the conversation.

'A fair while.' She was giving nothing away.

'What do they call you?'

'They call me a lot of things but, if you really want to know, my name's Irene, Reen for short.'

'Interesting pictures,' he volunteered, looking around as though seeing them for the first time although he had clocked them the moment he walked in. The pub did not boast prize trout in glass cases or paintings of prize bulls but there were a number of black and white blow-ups of Breconfield Studios in earlier times and photographs of stars of yesteryear including one of a young radiant Spring van Clef.

'Film studios,' Reen said, nodding in one's direction. 'Breconfield. The Guv used to be part of it.' She said it with pride. 'A writer he was. Wrote the very first *Guns of Batani*, did you ever see it?'

'Not the first one, no, a bit before my time.'

'Yes, it would be, wouldn't it? I would have thought they would at least be showing it on the telly one of these days. I mean, they show *The African Queen* often enough, every Christmas like, you know.' Obviously she was on Ernest J.'s wavelength with this one. 'Not that it isn't a very good picture but I mean you can overdo things can't you? That one's all about East Africa and the Germans in World War I and I am led to believe this new *Batani* they're shooting at the mo is set the same. Cheers!' She lifted her glass to take a sip of what was supposed to be a gin and tonic followed by another draw on the cigarette and moved away to serve a customer who had just walked in, placing the butt in an ashtray advertising *Bass* before turning to give the newcomer a big smile of welcome. Thornton glanced down the bar to ascertain if there was any threat but the wizened elderly man who had just come in looked harmless enough, a pensioner, Thornton thought, and with not too long to go by the looks of it. Kev was still shivering, mumbling, and gesticulating in his corner.

Having served the newcomer his rum and orange, no ice, and dropped his money in the cash register, closing it again with a loud ting, she returned to Thornton to continue her lecture on *The Guns of Batani*. She made it sound as though there were at least half a dozen films of the same name and, 'That there's a poster for it,' she ended, pointing to a large framed somewhat faded two-tone bill depicting a man with a rifle holding a woman in open shirt and jodhpurs and with heaving bosom obviously scared to death surrounded by jungle and wildly grimacing savages wielding shields and spears. They didn't actually have bones through their noses but Thornton wouldn't have been surprised if they had. Authenticity didn't necessarily go hand in hand with film making.

'Interesting,' Thornton said, totally unimpressed, 'very interesting. The Guv'nor must have lots of fascinating stories to tell. Could I have a word with him do you think?'

'Well I don't know.' She frowned, suddenly suspicious of Thornton's motives and quite rightly. 'He's having his supper right now, you know, whilst there's time, before we get busy like, but I'll see how he's doing. Who shall I say's calling?'

'Tell him a friend of Spring van Clef's.'

'Rightyho. You're not a journalist then.'

'I'm not a journalist.'

'Because we've had a few of those in you know.'

'Recently?'

'Oh, yes. All because of the goings on at the studios, as through the Guv' would know anything about that. He hasn't been there for donkey's years.'

She disappeared behind the bar and Thornton heard her loudly delivering the message, presumably up the stairs. He didn't hear the reply but after a moment she returned.

'He says he won't be a mo, he's just finishing,' and she moved down the bar to serve another arrival. Thornton took his drink and his newspaper to a little round table in front of a settle and sat down to wait. It wasn't too long before Jimmy Harrowfield appeared. Reen, busy pulling a pint, nodded in Thornton's direction and the man crossed over to him. Thornton stood up and introduced himself. They shook hands before both sitting down.

'Can I get you a drink?' Thornton asked.

Jimmy shook his head. 'I don't take a drink till closing time. It spells ruin otherwise.' He smiled. Thornton thought it a rather sad smile. Jimmy must once have been a handsome man as his photograph in Adrian's book had indicated and Thornton could see in his face something of the young William. Of that there was little if any doubt.

'Not like Reen then,' he whispered.

'I beg your pardon?'

'Gin and tonic? Without the gin? Money put aside for collection later?'

'Oh, yes.' He glanced across to the bar and laughed. Reen, not knowing what they were talking about, returned it with a smile. He turned back to Thornton. 'You know that old trick then. I'm afraid it's something they all get up to. Bar staff aren't that particularly well paid I'm afraid and every little extra helps. So, Mister King, you're a friend of Spring's. Haven't seen her in a while. How is the old girl?'

'As feisty as ever. Though I feel I must correct you, we're not exactly what you would call friends.'

'Oh?' With a subtle but noticeable change of expression. 'What would you call yourself then?'

'I'm a private investigator, Mister Harrowfield, who she has hired to try and solve the mystery of her grand-daughter's death.'

Yet once again a long silence ensued and Thornton was about to break it when Harrowfield beat him to it.

'Yes. Tragic. Funny, I was always led to believe it was the police who were supposed to solve murders.'

'So everybody keeps telling me but Miss van Clef doesn't seem to have much confidence, if any in fact, in the ability of the police to do it, which is why she has hired me.'

'And do you think you should have taken the job on?'

'To tell the truth,' Thornton pulled a wry face, 'I'm beginning to doubt it.'

'And why would that be?'

'Because I'm getting absolutely nowhere. Every road I take turns out to be a cul de sac. I constantly come up against that mythical brick wall and I'm tired of banging my head. Besides which it's also painful.'

'And so you've come to me. Why? What gives you any idea that I can possibly help you? Because in the old days I was once part of Breconfield? That was a long time ago, Mister King, a long long time ago. I must presume Spring has filled you in as far as that ancient story is concerned.'

'She has.'

'Naturally, but...' he sighed... 'it's water under the bridge, as the saying has it. If I had stayed in that business I would more than likely have ended up a complete nutter. This suits me much better.' He waved a hand around the pub and smiled at the watching mug polishing Reen who smiled back before hanging the mug on its hook and serving another customer who had just entered. 'It's mighty hard work running a pub and of course like everything it has its own problems. Sometimes you do wonder if it's worth it.'

'So you can't even hazard a guess as to who might have killed Charmaine.'

Harrowfield shook his head.

'What about Mel Preston? Any ideas there?'

Harrowfield laughed. 'Do you know something, Mister King? I am going to break my own strict rule and have that drink. Will you join me?'

'Thank you, no. A pint is enough for me. I can never understand beer drinkers who can put away three, four or more of an evening. Where do they put it all?'

'It's a knack, Mister King, a knack that eventually reveals itself in a much extended stomach.' He turned to look over his shoulder towards the bar. 'Reen, do me a favour please, love, and bring me a noggin.'

Reen raised her eyebrows in surprise but went over to the optics to deliver a shot of rum, obviously the Guv's tipple, added ice and a dash of blackcurrant syrup rather than orange and brought it over to the table, the occupants of which had remained silent while this operation was in progress.

She put down the glass and returned to her bar. The saloon was now beginning to fill up and the Guv' would shortly have to be on his feet giving her a helping hand. There wasn't much time. Thornton decided he had better take the bull by the horns once more. Thornton could come up with an apt cliché every time one was needed. He opened the newspaper, took from it the sketch of William Harrowfield and laid it on the table facing Jimmy who looked at it for a long while, his face expressionless, and then he looked up at Thornton.

'Yes?' was all he said.

This rocked Thornton back a bit. He had expected much more of a reaction, if only because the likeness was so obvious.

'Do you not recognise this face?' He eventually managed to ask.

'No. Should I?' Harrowfield's own face remained without expression. He was obviously not going to give anything away.

'Is this yet another brick wall I'm about to bang my head against, Mister Harrowfield? I'm getting a mighty big headache here. This is William, this is your grandson.'

'You don't say.' He took a mouthful of rum and hiccupped.

'I do say! Look at this face, Mister Harrowfield. Look at it! It's your face! How can you deny it?'

'Please, Mister King, keep your voice down or I will have to ask you to leave.'

'Sorry. Sorry.' He looked around and sure enough faces were turned with curiosity in their direction but were hurriedly turned away again when he saw them.

'Well what about Mel Preston then?'

'What about Mel Preston?'

'You haven't answered my question. Any ideas as to who would want to bump him off?'

163

'Dozens.'

'Yes, I've already been told that as well.'

'Mister King...'

For once Thornton hadn't invited the use of his first name, feeling in the circumstances that it was somehow inappropriate.

'... let me tell you something about the film business. Mel Preston was a shit but he was hardly unique. The film world attracts egotistical bastards like flies to a cowpat. How can they be anything else but shits when in too many cases their egos are out of all proportion to their miserable minuscule talents?'

'Doesn't that apply to all big business?'

'Maybe so, but a word of advice, if you value your skin, Mister King, stay away from the film world. It seethes with sharks, they are all hungry and they have extremely sharp teeth and a great many of them. I'm sorry I can't help you.'

Harrowfield drained his glass and got up to leave.

'Good luck,' he said and headed back to the bar, taking his glass with him and ready to give Reen a helping hand.

# Chapter Twelve

Once more back in the office, as Thornton stood in front of his filing cabinet and poured himself a finger of *Famous Grouse,* he was seriously thinking of calling Esther Fartfooker and informing her that he was on the point of giving up. It was hopeless. Unless he had a stroke of unexpected luck he might as well throw in the towel. He felt bad about all the money he had spent, extracted from the rexine type bag but, hell, he did try and he had tried very hard. In Rome he had almost been killed and Holly had warned him in no uncertain terms to quit before he was. He didn't feel there were any more avenues open to him. What more could he do? He believed he had done his best, inadequate though it might seem.

The telephone rang. A short while back he would have welcomed its ring but now it was with reluctance that he lifted the receiver. It couldn't be anything other than bad news or an earful from Esther Harrington nee Fartfooker.

'Thornton King.' It came out in a mumble as though he didn't want the other party to actually hear it and might assume they'd got the wrong number.

'Oh, yes, Mister King. This is Mrs Amory here.'

Thornton brightened up.

'Yes, Mrs Amory. How are you?'

'I'm very well thank you and so is Hilda. She's standing right here beside me.'

'I'm glad to hear it.'

Though he hadn't asked for a report on Hilda's health he could imagine Mrs Amory looking up to smile at her associate and Hilda smiling in return. Could they be the feminine equivalent of Tweedledum and Tweedledee? Pinkie and Perky? Morecombe and Wise?

'You said if I had anything to tell you I should call and that is what I am doing. You know you asked me if William had any visitors when he was with us or if anyone called to make enquiries about him? Well, I have questioned every member of staff and it was in fact Miss Austin who volunteered the information that someone did in fact call. I could elicit no more information from her other than that because his visit took place some time ago, Miss Austin couldn't remember exactly when. Obviously neither Hilda nor I were here at the time and Miss Austin can't even give a description of the man because she had no sooner allowed him in when she was called away to an emergency leaving him standing in the hall and before she really had the chance of getting a good look at him, I mean enough to recognise him in any future event. You know what children can be like, Mister King. Emergencies arise all the time. Evidently this particular emergency took some time to resolve and when Miss Austin returned to the hall the man had gone. But, Mister King, the thing is, during her lengthy absence upstairs he had plenty of time to sneak into our office and go through the files. He would have found the one marked Harrowfield and got all the information he wanted, if that was indeed what he wanted. It would only have taken a few moments because Hilda keeps the files in strict alphabetical order and is very fussy about them, aren't you, dear? I'm so sorry not to be able to help you further.'

He thought he heard her drawing a deep breath.

'Mrs Amory, thank you so much. You have actually been a great help. Now that I know there was someone who knew all about William I think I can take my investigation a step further. If Miss Austin does recall anything else, please don't hesitate to give me another call.'

'I will do that, Mister King. Good day to you.'

'And good day to you, Mrs Amory. Have a good one.'

"Right," he thought, "there were only two possibilities as to who the mysterious visitor could have been; William's natural father, Courtney Burrows II, or his grandfather, Jimmy Harrowfield."

But where to go next? That was still the question. He had already seen Harrowfield who was in denial and he very much doubted if he would be allowed to get within a mile of Burrows. And if he did manage to see him what would his reaction be when questioned about his son? Thornton knew exactly what his reaction would be. The heavies would be summoned and he'd be thrown out on his ear, possibly suffering some nasty physical damage on the way.

He heaved a weary sigh and looked at the page on his legal pad, still virgin except for his doodles. Funds were running low and he didn't feel he could touch Esther for a top up, not without something concrete to show for it. Well, it was almost the weekend, maybe he should give it a rest, do something completely different and clear the cobwebs. Maybe Holly would like to do something. He still hadn't taken in the Kurasawa movie up Hampstead way and if he didn't do it soon it would be off and he would have missed it. He decided to call her.

'Sorry, Miss Day has already left the office, sir. May I take a message?'

'No, that's all right. I'll try calling her at home.'

'She won't be there, sir. She left word, if she was needed, she would be at her parent's house all weekend.'

'Oh. Oh, right. Thank you.'

'Would you still like to leave a message?'

'No, thank you. Have a good weekend.'

'And you, sir.'

Such a polite lot they were in the civil service; except for the tax wallahs of course. Their bite could be pretty vicious if occasion warranted, or sometimes even if it didn't, and a bandage in the form of an apology didn't always stop the bleeding. Thornton had had two or three brushes at close quarters and although he always came away victorious, it wasn't without some severe emotional bruising.

He looked at his watch. Gosh, it was almost a quarter to six. He wasn't surprised Holly had left. They might be a polite lot in the civil service, their pensions might be large and perfectly safe, but they weren't going to work a minute longer than was necessary and that was a fact. World War III could break out and they would still be home in time for dinner.

He might as well shut up shop and go home himself; stopping at his favourite watering hole on the way.

He hadn't looked in his letter box today. He would do it on the way out, see if there was any post. There wasn't, except for junk mail including a flyer for a recently opened pizza parlour not too far distant offering half price bargains. What a good idea. He would get one for his supper. Now what should it be? He rather fancied Hawaiian but eventually plumped for Four Seasons.

It wasn't until the Sunday morning that he had his brainwave. The weekend must have been restful, no struggling with the whys and wherefores of murder. The pizza had been very tasty, more importantly very filling, and had lasted for three meals.

Of course, why hadn't he thought of it before? The immediate answer lay with Ernest J. Bloomberg. That young nosey parker was his only in as to what was going on in the studio. Being Sunday he would have to be called at home. Studios don't work Sundays no matter how far behind schedule they might be; double and triple time is expensive and the unions are hard task masters, but where was home? And being Sunday he didn't want to call too early. People might be wanting a lie-in so he would take a stroll around Victoria Park and call later. Seeing it was Sunday there was no great hurry after all.

When he finally stopped procrastinating and got around to it he settled down with the telephone directory and looked up the name Bloomberg. There appeared to be a number of them mostly residing in Golders Green and Stoke Newington. He didn't think any of those would be Ernest's family so he made a mark against the ones residing elsewhere he thought possible and set to dialling the first.

'Yes?'

'Good morning. Could I speak to Ernest please?'

'To who?'

'Ernest?'

'There's no Ernest here. You've got the wrong number.'

'Sorry.'

It wasn't until the fifth number he called, a Bloomberg in Gunnersbury, and he was already thinking of giving up, that he struck gold.

'Hold on. I'll fetch him for you.'

He held on as he heard an ear-splitting screech at the other end.

'Ernest!'

A moment's silence and then again,

'Ernest!'

She came back to the phone.

'I don't know what's wrong with that boy. He's not answering. I'll have to go and fetch him. Hold on.' The phone at the other end was dropped. Thornton held on. It was going to take a while as she lumbered up the stairs. They seemed to get longer and steeper with each passing day.

Ernest J. was facing his wardrobe mirror exercising with his vacuum pump, excited to knee trembling stage at viewing his reflection and was almost at ejaculation point, he could feel it surging up, ready to explode when there was a loud rapping on his door and he went ice-cold and nearly died of fright.

'Ernest, are you in there? What are you doing? Didn't you hear me call you? You're wanted on the phone.'

Oh, God! Had he remembered to lock the door? He had. The handle was jiggled a few times quite violently but the door remained firmly closed. In the meantime he hastily withdrew the pump (it didn't take more than a nanosecond as it didn't have too far to go) and discarded it by tossing it up on top of the wardrobe before hastily getting into his pants.

'You're up to something in there,' she said accusingly, rattling the door handle once more.

'I was asleep,' he said.

'You couldn't have been. You were down to breakfast not half an hour ago; a very big breakfast if you don't mind me saying so. You'll eat us out of house and home one of these fine days, my lad.'

'Well I went back to bed didn't I? And I need a big breakfast. I'm a growing boy.'

'Huh! Lazy little sod, got me traipsing all the way up these stairs, and why have you got the door locked if I may ask?'

Having made himself respectable, he hoped, there hadn't really been time to check, and resenting his unfulfilled orgasm he unlocked and opened the door and faced his mother who was regarding him with deep suspicion.

'Why was the door locked?' She scowled. 'What were you doing in there?'

'It was locked so I wouldn't be disturbed by the likes of you. Didn't work though, did it?' Attack was obviously the best method of defence.

He padded off down the stairs. She followed and, as he picked up the phone, she did a ninety degree turn into the living room and went back to the telly, the programme coming from a small church in Bedfordshire where a small congregation with even smaller voices and all looking rather embarrassed was pitifully rendering *Fight the Good Fight*. Meanwhile Ernest, making sure she was fully engaged and wouldn't be eavesdropping, picked up the phone.

'Ernest speaking. Who is this please?'

'Hello Ernest. It's Thornton King.'

'Who?'

Making sure she was still engrossed in the telly he pulled his trousers away from his crotch just in case there had been some serious seepage.

'Thornton King. You remember, we talked in your office, that is in Joachim Caswell's office, the other day. I am speaking to Ernest J. I presume. The writer?'

'Oh, yes. Of course I remember you. You got me into a lot of hot water I can tell you, chatting away like that when I should have been on the set.'

'Sorry.'

'Not to worry. It blew over. I knew it would. Got a right bollocking and threatened with my cards and then it was all forgotten. Mister Indispensable, that's who I am. Well, Mister King, what can I do for you this time? Fancy you calling me at home. How did you get my number?'

'Trial and error and a lot of patience. Private Investigators need a lot of patience.'

'I suppose. Private Investigator?'

'Listen, Ernest, I need information.'

'Private Investigator! I thought…'

'Would it be possible for us to meet sometime?'

'What's it about? About the murders is it?'

'Indirectly, yes.'

'What do you mean indirectly? Murder is murder; you can't get more direct than that can you, unless it's attempted murder that goes horribly wrong?'

Ernest J. Bloomberg, as he would be the first to tell you, simply could not help being a writer and coming up with half a dozen or more plots a day. Noel Coward and Agatha Christie had nothing on him when it came to invention and he had read E.M. Forster on how to write a novel. He presumed the advice could also apply to screenplays. He wondered if he turned his screenplay into a novel whether *Penguin* would be interested.

Anyway he was being snappy because he was still in resentful mood over his recent dissatisfaction. He knew he wouldn't be able to do it again for a while and then he would be terrified his suspicious nosey-parker mother might come knocking on the door once more or rattling the handle and that would be completely off-putting. It was one of the problems of living at home and having no privacy. He couldn't wait until he could afford to get his own pad. Maybe he could squat and write another best seller like Orwell's *Down and out in London and Paris.*

He glanced in the direction of the television sound. He would just have to wait until the parents were asleep, though that might be too late as he had to be up at sparrowfart to go to the studio, so he doubted he would do it even then. He hoped he hadn't damaged his toy by throwing it with such abandon on top of the wardrobe. He didn't think so as it was manufactured in plastic and rubber and guaranteed but you never know, plastic can crack, rubber can perish. He would check on it later. His thoughts on sexual satisfaction were interrupted by the voice on the phone.

'Whatever. Will you meet me? You tell me when and where.'

'What?'

'Will you meet me tomorrow sometime?'

'All right. I will be in Wardour Street tomorrow evening about seven.'

'Excellent. Do you know the *White Horse?*'

'Pass it every day don't I? Coming up from the Circus.'

'Meet you there then? How long will your business take you in Wardour Street?'

'Not long. I've just got to drop stuff off for the labs.'

'Say seven-thirty?'

'Suits me fine.'

'See you there then.'

'See you there.' They put down their respective phones.

"How," Ernest wondered, "was he going to spend the rest of a dreary Sunday?"

Thornton whistled his way merrily into his office, regarding with satisfaction the key in the brand new solid brass lock. He dropped *The Times* on the desk, peeped inside the kettle to make sure there was sufficient water therein and switched it on to make a cup of coffee. He had brought a fresh bottle of milk in with him and once his coffee was ready he settled down behind his desk and turned to the crossword puzzle but he hardly had time to look at it when the phone rang. This time it was bound to be a fuming Esther and he still had nothing to tell her. Reluctantly he lifted the receiver.

'Thornton King.'

'Oh! Good morning, Mister King. This is Mrs Ida Chapman here of Riverside Drive, Breconfield. You came to visit me the other day. I don't suppose you remember me.'

'Of course I remember you, Mrs Chapman, how are you?'

'I'm very well thank you and hope you are likewise. Mister King.' There was a long pause. 'You said if I thought of anything that might be important I should call and tell you?'

'Yes?'

Thornton's heart didn't actually miss a beat or kick in at double speed but suddenly he felt something was going to break for him. He was almost holding his breath.

'Well, there is something I've remembered. Can't think why I didn't remember it before but I am getting so absentminded. Comes with old age I suppose.' She was nervously turning his card over and over in her hand.

'What is it you want to tell me, Mrs Chapman? Whatever it is it will just be between the two of us.'

'Well, just a short while before I found, you know, the girl, like that, I thought I heard a scream. I didn't think of it at the time, you hear all sorts of things at the studios, and one tends to turn a blind eye, if you know what I mean. But then I remembered that there was nobody working that night. There was no shooting going on so there shouldn't have been a scream.'

'Indeed.' Said Thornton, his disappointment almost audible.

'Well thank you for the information Mrs Chapman.'

'Oh, but that's not all,'

'Oh?'

'Yes, I think I saw, well actually I did see, someone leaving the building and he did seem to be in ever such a hurry.'

'Yes?'

'I couldn't be absolutely certain, it was dark, but I think the person I saw was Mister Preston. Are you still there, Mister King?'

'I'm still here, Mrs Chapman.'

'I mentioned it to Dick.'

'The neighbour to whom you give quinces because he helps out in the garden.'

'No no, Dick is the landlord at *The Drover's*.'

'Oh, yes.'

'I asked him for his opinion and he said I should tell you. He was most definite about it.'

'And he was quite right, Mrs Chapman. Thank you. I'm most grateful.'

'That's all right then?'

'Certainly.'

'Well… good bye then, Mister King.'

'Good bye Mrs Chapman. If you remember anything else don't hesitate to call me.'

'Yes.'

Thornton put down the phone and took a deep breath before lifting the receiver again. His coffee was stone cold. She had lied to the police. She had found the body but omitted to say that she had seen Preston leave his office just minutes before. Why? Fear no doubt, but then why come forward with the information now?

'Come in, Thornton, come in. You have news for me you say.'

'I have but I'm not sure you will like it.'

'Oh? And why is that?'

She turned away before he could answer and once again, after closing the door, he followed her down the passage and into the drawing room. It was almost as if she didn't want, or wasn't ready, to listen to his news. It wasn't until they reached the room and before they even had time to sit down that she turned to face him.

'Well? And what is it you have to tell me?'

'I believe I know who killed your granddaughter.'

'You believe you know or you know?'

'I believe, and there is nothing you can do about it because someone else has beaten you to the punch.'

'Don't talk in riddles, Thornton, it's irritating to say the least, just get to the point. Here, let us sit down.'

Once settled, she picked up the thread.

'So, what is this news? Explain yourself please.'

'Charmaine was killed by Mel Preston.'

Esther stared at him as though he had suddenly developed a second head. It was a long moment before she spoke.

'Mel? Mel killed her? But why? What on earth…? That's preposterous. What possible reason could he have had? You can't be sure about this?'

'Ninety percent.'

'But why ninety percent, what about the other ten?'

'I don't have any definite proof. I only have conjecture but I have been informed by Mrs Chapman…'

'Mrs who?'

'Chapman, the cleaning lady who discovered Charmaine.'

'Oh, yes. That one. She told the police she neither saw nor heard anything suspicious.'

'That's right but now she tells me she saw Preston leaving the building in a hurry shortly before she went into his office and found Charmaine.'

'And that is it? This is ridiculous Thornton, the man works in the studio. He was working late. There's nothing suspicious about that.'

'No, that's not quite all. Don't forget Charmaine wasn't found in her own office as the newspapers reported but found in Preston's office going through some papers...'

'Of course. And why not? She was his secretary.'

'...and she was doing this at the behest of Joachim Caswell.'

He paused for a second to give Esther time to take this in.

'What if Preston came across her while she was at it and had found something incriminating or dangerous and he felt he had to silence her?'

'No...no no no... It's still not enough. I simply can't believe it'

She shook her head and sat down but now got up again and walked over to the window to gaze out at the busy world, the buses passing by, or to take a look at Prince Albert.

'Believe me, I really do find this hard to believe, Thornton.'

'I know, I know, it does seem pretty flimsy and probably wouldn't stand up in a court of law. Its insubstantial evidence and I can't prove that is what happened and of course there isn't any way now to get something like a confession. Forensics would find traces of Mel all over the place but then why not, it was his office after all? But I am convinced that is what happened. Who else was in the studio at that time apart from Mrs Chapman?'

She turned back to look at him. 'Why did this Mrs Chapman wait so long before telling you this?'

Thornton lifted a shoulder in a shrug. 'I believe because at first she was frightened. While Mel was still around she probably felt it was prudent to keep her mouth shut but once he was disposed of she felt she could come out with it.'

'Then why didn't she tell the police? Why come to you?'

'Maybe she felt that not having told the police in the first place she would be wrong-footed and land up in a lot of trouble, withholding evidence. And I had specifically asked her to tell me anything she remembered about that night.'

'Yes, that is logical I suppose.' She sat for a while, thinking.

'Esther, Mrs Chapman thought she heard a scream. A short while later she saw Preston hurrying away and not much later she discovered Charmaine, wouldn't you put two and two together?'.

'Well, there's nothing more to be said then, is there? You will no doubt be wanting to get on with other things so please let me know to what extent I am in your debt and I will settle up with you. Now, last time I offered you tea, this time in expectation of your visit I have brewed coffee. I think we could both do with a cup and talk of more pleasant things.'

'Cabbages and kings?'

'Whatever.' And for the first time Esther Huntington nee Fartfooker gave the hint of a smile but if the truth would be told it was rather a sad one.

Thornton arrived at *The White Horse* half an hour early with a copy of the *Standard* and ordered a *Famous Grouse*. The pub was already heaving with bodies almost shoulder to shoulder relaxing after work and before going home, talking business or going over the day's events and rushing the barmen off their feet. The rexine type bag would be in evidence no more but he felt the time had come to treat himself once more to his favourite whisky.

It could be that Preston had murdered Charmaine and he felt he had done his duty by Esther and earned his fee but something was still niggling. The problem was he had no definite proof it was Mel and a man is innocent until proved guilty. There were loose ends to tie up. Just as important, he wanted to know who had killed Preston, and why? Being told it could have been any one of a dozen or more disgruntled persons simply wasn't good enough. The man might have been extremely unpopular but could that be a cause for murder? Somehow he doubted it very much. There was more to it than that and his curiosity had got the better of him.

If Mel had been beaten to death say by someone in a rage or had been knocked to the floor and cracked his skull, something like that, obviously an accident, it would have been different but he was stabbed. His own close call with death in Rome came to mind and that meant the killing was deliberate. There was something else underlying it all and he would dearly love to know what it was.

Ernest J. was late. He came in all breathless, struggling through the melee and the cigarette smoke and full of apologies, but Thornton put him at his ease saying it really didn't matter a few minutes here or there. The fact that it was almost an hour hardly constituted a few minutes.

'What would the lad like to drink?'

'It's okay,' Ernest said. 'I'll do it. Let me get you one.'

'No, I'm fine thank you.' Thornton didn't think Ernest would relish stumping up for a whisky. He watched as the young writer swaggered up to the bar there being, for a few moments, no bodies to hinder his progress, and ordered a lemonade shandy. The barman looked at him for a long while and shook his head. Ernest turned to look at Thornton, shrugged, and turned back to the bar. He fished in his jacket pocket and produced his driving licence, holding it virtually under the barman's nose.

'What is that?' He said.

'A driving licence.'

'And whose photograph is that?'

The barman remained silent.

'And what date of birth does it give?'

Without a word the barman served Ernest his lemonade shandy, took his money and Ernest swaggered back to Thornton's table and sat down. He made it just in time as his path to the bar suddenly closed like the Red Sea behind the Israelites. 'That's the way to treat mere hirelings, act superior, show a bit of disdain.'

'I have this problem all the time, Mister King. They simply won't believe I'm of an age. Take me for a fifteen year old. That's why I carry my licence around wherever I go. Cheers!'

'Bottoms up.'

'Well then, Mister King, Thornton, what is all this about?' He lifted his glass to take a mouthful of shandy.

'What is happening with *Return to Batani?*'

'How do you mean?'

'Well the film has lost its producer.'

'That's no problem; they just brought in someone else, a loudmouthed American git flew in. Thinks he knows it all, the little shit. He's already put half the cast's backs up throwing his weight around. That other American shit, Vlad the Impaler is still directing if you can call it that. If you want my opinion he's actually incapable of directing traffic in a one horse town let alone a film of supposedly epic proportions; ponsing around in his jeans and sneakers like he's a teenage heartthrob, wearing a tight T-shirt so that his man-boobs are showing. Some people just never grow up, do they? Maybe it's wishful thinking or they just don't know how to. And he really ought to have a haircut. Long hair definitely does not suit him even if it is the current fashion.' Ernest gave his own lengthy locks a toss.

'Maybe he finds jeans comfortable, workmanlike, and long hair as you say is the fashion at the moment. Is everyone who works in the studio a shit, Ernest J?'

'No of course not. The crew are terrific, most of them, really down to earth, no side, and some of the actors too, those whose heads aren't too swollen, but as for the rest of them, the so-called big shots!' Ernest blew a loud raspberry and gave twos up to an imaginary big shot.

'Who do you think killed Mel Preston?'

'No idea.'

'Really?'

'Really. I'll tell you one thing though, it wasn't me, much as I would have liked to.' And he took another mouthful of shandy. 'I'm starving. Think I'll get some crisps. Want some?'

'No thank you.'

'How about pork scratchings? Peanuts?'

'No, really, I'm fine, thank you.'

'Okay, won't be a sec.' Ernest J. looked around saw that his path was once more clear and hurried back to the bar to return a few moments later with two large packets of crisps, one salt and vinegar, the other bacon flavoured. The pub was all out of his favourite prawn. He ripped open the first bag and held it out to Thornton who declined by shaking his head. Ernest J.

took a large handful and started to crunch. Loud as it was, at least he crunched with his mouth closed. A couple of giggling Essex girls in mini-skirts and badly applied make-up entered the bar. The males made room for them and Ernest gave a low, appreciative, masculine whistle before turning back to face Thornton and take another handful of crisps.

'Is that all you wanted to know? How the film was coming on?' More crisps disappeared into his mouth and the crunching was renewed.

'Not exactly. I want you to look at this.' And he produced the ten by eight from the folded newspaper. Ernest J., index and middle fingers back in the crisp packet, cocked his head sideways to look at it then looked back at Thornton. More crisps disappeared.

'Do you recognise this guy?' Thornton asked.

'Nope. Never seen him before.'

'His name is William Harrowfield; does that mean anything to you?'

Ernest J. frowned and then his face lit up. 'Of course, Harrowfield, the writer of the original *Guns of Batani*. Terrific film. Whatever happened to him? Must be dead by now I shouldn't wonder.'

'Not at all. I spoke to him only recently.'

'Really? Really?' Ernest's excitement knew no bounds. It was such that he lost control of the packet in his hand and crisps flew in all directions. 'You actually spoke to him? Well he was certainly a better writer than that bastard Caswell. Have you ever seen that movie?'

'As I think I said to someone else, before my time.' Thornton removed a couple of crisps from his lap and put them in the ashtray.

'There are lots of movies before your time but that's no excuse not to have seen them. You can view it at the *British Film Institute* if you're interested. They've got a tremendous archive going way back.' He looked again at the photograph, scooped up a handful of crisps from the table and took another mouthful followed by another sip of his shandy to wash it down. This produced a loud hiccup. 'Amazing really, what's in those archives,' he continued. 'Anyway, sorry I can't help.' He eyed the photo once more. 'Can't help feeling there's a story there somewhere worth writing, don't you think?'

'I do indeed. So, as the writer that you are, do you want to follow it up and discover the denouement?'

'For real you mean?' Ernest J. frowned, leant back, and his chin went into his chest. He discovered a couple of crisps on his shirtfront, picked them up quite delicately and transferred them to his mouth.

'How would I do that?'

'Do you think you could remember the face?'

'Yes, I think so.'

'You sound dubious.'

'Hmn…'

'The lad is an electrician. He could be working at the studios. Do you think you could maybe find out if that is the case? You know, make a few discreet enquiries? I believe he could be Mel Preston's killer.'

'Really?' Ernest J's eyes almost popped out of his head and it was just as well he hadn't got around to opening the second packet.

'Although his real name is Harrowfield…'

'Harrowfield? *The* Harrowfield?'

'That's right. He's Jimmy's grandson but…' Thornton put a finger to his mouth '…you don't know that. Understood?'

Ernest J. nodded. He was now almost speechless but a screenplay was taking place before his very eyes, as Mister Askey might say.

'He might be employed under the name of Peterson.'

'Peterson.'

'Now Ernest J. If I may call you that…'

Ernest nodded again, screwed up the now empty first crisp packet, dropped it in the oversized ashtray advertising *Bulmer's Cider* and opened the second bag with trembling fingers.

181

'… I hope, as a writer, you don't let your imagination run away with you and, by jumping the gun, you ruin your investigation. The Greeks have a saying, *Sigà sigà*. It means slowly slowly. It seems to particularly apply to waiters in restaurants when you're trying to order a meal but in your case it applies to your investigation. Got it?'

Ernest J. nodded and managed to whisper. 'Got it.'

'Just remember, if this lad is a killer, you could put yourself in grave danger by letting on that you suspect him or know his true identity.'

This time Ernest shook his head. He had now been rendered totally speechless by the excitement of it all and felt in dire need of stretching his screwed up tight as a drum scrotum between forefinger and thumb only it wouldn't do to perform such an act in public even through his trousers and seated on a bar stool. He was sure his next orgasm was going to be a right humdinger, with or without assistance from the pump. He found his voice and looked at his watch.

'Got to get moving I'm afraid. Trust me, Mister King, Thornton. If there's anything there I'll ferret it out.' He got up to leave.

'Here.' Thornton handed him a card. 'So you know where to get me.'

'Righto.' He glanced at the card before slipping it in his breast pocket. 'Oh, by the way, merely as a matter of interest, they've found a new secretary to take Miss Carmichael's place and boy is she a cracker!' His attempt at a wolf-whistle was a total failure.

'Oh, yes? What's her name? Do you know?' He lifted his glass to his mouth.

'Yes, she's called Holly Day.'

Thornton almost choked on his drink.

'Funny name isn't it.'

'Isn't it?' Thornton said.

# Chapter Thirteen

H olly had decided that she would work late that evening. So far her investigations at the studio had drawn a blank. Fortunately the cast and crew for the *Return to Batani* were on location in Epping Forest so, apart from some hands doing overtime in the workshops and a few assorted office staff already beginning to pack up and go, the studio was relatively quiet; a perfect chance for Holly to do a spot of snooping. She hadn't been in the field for a while and found the challenge exciting. She had managed to evade the groping hands of both Anton Wagner and Vlad the Impaler, who had also tried it on, but she had repulsed his advances in no uncertain terms and he had retreated with a dent in his pride to hunt easier game. The other girls in the office secretary pool had long gone and Holly had a small window of opportunity before night cleaners came on duty. Shirley Dorland, Mr Burrows secretary, usually left at five but in case she was working late Holly carried a stack of files with her, as an excuse. The executive offices were deserted. She placed the files on Shirley's desk and tried the door to Mr Burrows' office. As she expected it was locked but it proved no problem to open it. Once inside she closed the door behind her, locked it and headed for the desk. A cursory glance through the drawers told her that nothing confidential would be kept there and she started to look for a safe. Working her way around the walls she came across a large portrait of a woman, a portrait of a strikingly beautiful woman wearing a diamond necklace, tiara, earrings and bracelet, she slide her hand behind the picture and found the clasp which released with a small click a catch and the picture swung forward to reveal an old fashioned safe.

Holly flexed her fingers and put her ear to the door. She slowly turned the dial. Click, and again, click. Slowly she worked her way through the sequence of numbers and finally the door of the safe gave on a final click and swung forward. She looked at her watch. Time was getting short. It had taken her some time to crack the numbers. Quickly she looked through the stack of documents lying there but there seemed to be nothing out of the ordinary, except for a folder full of old photographs. Holly was now getting nervous as she had already exceeded the amount of time she thought it would take, so rather than risk detection she replaced the file and closed the door of the safe, making sure everything was as she had found it. Quietly she made her way out of the office and locked the door behind her. Checking that she hadn't been seen she took the files she had left and made her way back to her office. Unfortunately, Holly had made one big mistake, and as she quickly made her way down the corridor, the figure of a well dressed man silently followed her until she had returned to her office.

Ernest J. Bloomberg, having collected his shepherd's pie, wrinkled grey/green peas, soggy chips and thick brown gravy, proceeded to shove his tray along the stainless steel rails hoping the cashier would get on with it before his lunch grew stone cold and greasy and even more unappetising than it already was. She seemed to be flirting with every second man in the queue. Hoping for a pick-up, he thought. With a complexion that blemished and one that no amount of make-up could disguise she should be so lucky.

He pushed his tray further along to lift the glass front of a display cabinet and helped himself to a jam roly-poly and custard. Fruit salad, even from a can, would have been a healthier and more summery option but summer was officially over and he was particularly addicted to heavy puddings any time of the year. It was really quite surprising he remained as skinny as he was. All down to metabolism he supposed. Maybe he would put on weight in his middle years, hopefully not a beer belly. Beer bellies on skinny frames were really quite revolting. There was already a skin on top of the cooling custard but he happened to like skin on his custard so that was no turn-off. In fact, he didn't know why, but he found it on the contrary rather a turn on.

Maybe he wouldn't live that long; to put on weight and develop a beer belly. Artists of every kind are too frequently known to die young, even though TB was no longer a popular option, and every now and again he had visions of his early death; the obituaries–*the film industry has suffered a grievous loss with the unexpected demise of Ernest J. Bloomberg OBE the celebrated screenwriter and director. He will be particularly remembered as a double Oscar winner for his film, "Hour of Agony," his very first screenplay written at such a tender age. He leaves a wife and four children.* And then there would be the mourning multitudes. He was so lost in thought he nearly spilt gravy over his *Save The Gorillas* T-shirt. The food in the commissary might not be cordon bleu but at least it knocked his mother's cooking into a cocked hat. I mean what does it take to heat a can of baked beans or spaghetti hoops without burning the bottom of the pan, something she did too frequently? The executive dining room upstairs with its damask tablecloths and napkins, its Queen's pattern cutlery, its sparkling glasses, its scurrying servile smiling to order waiters, its food fit for a king and a wine list that would have done credit to a five star Michelin restaurant was not for the likes of him. Oh, no, he must perforce dine with the hoi polloi but he didn't resent it. Not really. It was probably a lot friendlier and more fun than sitting with the stuffed shirts upstairs.

One day though he would be there, when he was famous enough and rich enough to hold his own in any company and, what is more important, choose the company he wanted to be with. His table would be reserved for the select few.

Colleen was a fan of West Ham United football club and though still very young dreamt of one day walking down the aisle, all in white, the bride of a famous and hopefully rich footballer. When Ernest finally arrived at her desk she didn't flirt with him, in fact didn't even look at him, just took his money, rang it up, gave him his change and smiled at the man following before he had even reached her. Ernest didn't mind. In his opinion she wasn't exactly the bee's knees as far as femininity went. As a matter of fact he found her rather obnoxious. If she wanted a date with him he would have to think up all sorts of excuses to put her off. He found the thought of her expecting him to kiss her so repulsive he almost lost his shepherd's pie. Some men, he thought, simply had no taste though, poor girl, it was hardly her fault.

By this time he had stood long enough looking around for a sight of his quarry. Six times since his meeting with Thornton he had eaten in this dining room in the hope of seeing him and there had been no sign but today, eureka! He struck lucky. There he was, sitting by himself, and Ernest J., his heart a flutter with the excitement of it all, made a beeline for his table before anyone else could get there.

'Mind if I sit here?' he asked.

The somewhat surprised young man looked up from his bangers, mash, and dark brown glutinous onion gravy and, after a second's pause as he sized up Ernest J., inclined his head slightly. Ernest taking this to mean acquiescence, placed his plastic tray on the blue Formica topped table, pulled out a chair and duly seated himself.

'How are the sausages?' He asked to open proceedings.

His newfound companion gave a slight one shouldered shrug. 'Better than some,' he said, 'which isn't saying much. Fifteen percent meat which is five percent more than usual.'

Ernest laughed, which he thought he was meant to do, but the face opposite him returned a solemn, almost expressionless gaze so he immediately stopped. Maybe it wasn't the right thing to do and he really should be stepping on eggshells here if he was going to get anywhere information wise.

The face was certainly the one Thornton had shown him with the sketch, there was absolutely no doubt about that, but Ernest wasn't too sure how to proceed from here without arousing suspicions if Mister Harrowfield, or Mister Peterson, whichever one he was, turned out to be a double dyed killer. Looking at him it was hard to believe but you never could tell. He took a mouthful of pie which gave him a moment to think while he was chewing, chewing being the operative word. The lamb might have been minced but it wasn't exactly tender. It had either toughened up or turned into leather in the cooking or had come from an ancient ewe, maybe even a ram: most definitely scrag end.

'Are you new here?' He asked, having finally managed to swallow his mouthful. 'At the studios I mean?'

'Not really. Why do you ask?' Was he already suspicious of his motives Ernest wondered? Couldn't be surely. The conversation had hardly just got started.

'Just wondered. Don't recollect seeing you before, that's all.'

'You've seen everybody who works here I take it.'

'No.' He laughed. 'I suppose not. My name is Bloomberg by the way, Ernest Bloomberg.'

He thought, had Harrowfield been a few years younger he was perfect for the boy in *Hour of Agony*. He would have been Ernest's first major discovery as a film maker.

'And how long have *you* worked here, Mister Bloomberg?'

'Four years... about'

'Hmn. That's long enough I suppose.'

Long enough for what, Ernest wondered but no elucidation

was forthcoming. Instead, 'What is it you do exactly?' The quarry took a forkful of sliced sausage. His eyes, which had an attractive slightly Oriental shape to them, never left Ernest's face except for a moment with a nod to acknowledge someone passing by. Ernest hoped no one else would want to sit at their table before he got the information he was after which so far was precisely nothing, not even the guy's name.

'I'm an assistant,' he said.

'Assistant? That covers a multitude of sins. Assistant what exactly?'

'Assistant director.'

Was there for the first time the merest hint of a smile on the man's face? Ernest felt himself blushing and hurried on before he could ask more.

'I'm also a writer.'

'Oh yes?' He pushed out his lips and nodded a few times as though taking this in. 'Writer of what? Essays? Short stories? Articles? Books? Poetry? Plays? Maybe I've read something though I don't recall the name.' As he spoke his knife cut another portion of sausage to be smothered in mashed potato and gravy and eventually lifted to his mouth.

Ernest had an uneasy feeling that he was being sent up. Working in a film studio wasn't it perfectly obvious that he would be writing for the silver screen? Okay, maybe as yet he was an unknown but everyone had to start somewhere and there would come a time, oh, yes, there would definitely come a time. He didn't want to be a Woody Allen whose work he couldn't abide. Not up his street at all. No. He usually found the first ten minutes of a Woody Allen film quite hilarious after which the rot and boredom set in. He couldn't for the life of him understand how the man had earned himself such a reputation. And as for being an actor! Oh, come on! He had one gesture and one gesture only, a simultaneous thrust with both arms that he repeated over and over again while the voice took on the same monotonous cadence until it made one want to scream. No, he, Ernest J. Bloomberg, might not yet be a Dalton Trumbo or a

William Goldman, a King Vidor, an Otto Preminger or a Billy Wilder, but one day...

'I'm currently working on a major screenplay,' he said, trying to keep a balance between not sounding too boastful or too piqued.

'Is there such a thing as a minor screenplay?' The sausage had been consumed but the last mouthful of potato and gravy was scooped up to disappear, the knife and fork placed neatly side by side on the plate and he wiped his mouth with a paper napkin. Harrowfield, or Peterson, whichever, had obviously been well brought up.

'I don't know really. I suppose a documentary say, or a short comedy, something like that, could be considered as being minor.'

'And what is your major screenplay about?'

Ernest now knew for definite that he was not being taken at all seriously. In fact there was a distinct possibility that Peterson or Harrowfield or whatever his name was could be thinking something truly terrible like Ernest was trying to pick him up and now the blush, at the very thought of it, came to full scarlet fruition. Was the object of his questioning suddenly smiling? He had no doubt that Harrowfield, youthful and handsome as he was had been around and was well acquainted with those who found him attractive so he would be invariably on his guard. Should he say something? Should he deny it? Bring it up as a joke? Maybe he should say outright, "*look I'm not trying to pick you up, I'm simply making conversation. We can't sit here in silence can we?*" Harrowfield from the beginning must have been wondering why Ernest had chosen to sit at his table when there were plenty of others with empty chairs.

'It's about... about... about the pain of growing up in the world today.'

'Hmn.' He seemed to think about this for a moment. 'Hardly original,' he said, having given it that moment's thought. 'Did you ever see a French film called *The Four Hundred Blows*? The French are very good at making that type of film. There's a marvellous ending when you're led to believe the boy is going to wade out to sea and kill himself but he stops and turns back just in time; looks at the camera, fade. I can empathise with that movie. The Italians can do it too. Think of *Domani i Troppo Tardi,* which I will translate for you. It means *Tomorrow Is Too Late.* That was the very first film Pierangeli made.

'You like movies, don't you? I mean you seem to know a lot about them.'

'I like continental movies best of all.'

'I wouldn't have known about that picture. I'll have to look out for it.'

'Yes.' He nodded and went on with, 'Did you never see, not a movie this time but a play, called *Spring Awakening?*'

Ernest shook his head. 'I'm afraid I don't do theatre much.' What he should have said was he hadn't seen anything since a school production of *Charlie's Aunt* that he didn't think much of.

'A nineteenth century play on the subject, a German writer by the name of Frank Wedekind, or was he Austrian? I forget. Never mind his play is all about the painful journey from adolescence to adulthood. I read about these things. You should too. Couldn't you think of something better?'

That, Ernest thought, was downright rude. He almost choked on the last of his now cold shepherd's pie. Harrowfield pushed his own plate away and got up to leave.

'What's you name?' Ernest blurted it out.

'Jock. Well, nice to have met you Mister Bloomfield.'

'Berg, Berg, Bloomberg!'

'Yes, whatever.'

'See you around,' Ernest said, looking down at his pudding, but there was no answer.

After a while he looked up and around to notice Harrowfield, before he left the room, stop to talk to someone by the door and had a feeling it was him they were talking about. He pretended not to notice but it made him cringe and almost put him off his jam roly-poly but the custard, having had plenty of time to cool even further had grown a skin so thick it was irresistible.

'It's him. It's definitely him.' He couldn't keep the excitement out of his voice.

'You're quite sure.'

'Oh, absolutely, there's no doubt about it. That's a very good sketch you had done. He could almost have sat for it.'

'What's his name?'

'Oh, I'm sorry, he wouldn't tell me that. I did ask him to but he refused to tell me. Do you think he's hiding something?'

'Maybe you could find out by other means?'

'Like what?'

'Like the payroll?'

'No chance, Thornton, sorry, but no chance.'

'Well, did he tell you what he does? Work wise.'

'No.' Ernest was feeling a total failure. 'I'm sorry. I feel I've let you down.'

'Not to worry, Ernest. Well thank you anyway. At least I know where he is. I guess I had better pay another visit to Breconfield Studios. Any news of Miss Day?'

'Haven't seen her again worse luck.'

'Fancy your chances there do you?'

'I wish. Okay, I'm off. Just wanted to tell you you're on the right track.'

'So it would seem. Thanks, Ernest. Keep on with the writing. How's it going by the way?'

'Good, good, though I'm not too sure now it's such an original idea. I might have to do another rewrite, maybe scrap it altogether.'

'No, don't do that Ernest, not after all the work you've put into it. Nothing is original, Ernest, everything has been said before, many times. There's nothing new under the sun. It's up to you to say it in a different way, in your own way, that's all.'

'Yes, you're right there. I'll keep it in mind. Thanks, Thornton.'

Thornton put down the phone and wondered where he went to from here. Out of it if he took Holly's advice. He had done his job and that was that. Or had he? He still had no positive proof it was Preston who killed Charmaine and it nagged him.

All right, Esther seemed satisfied; he had been paid and well paid. There were no outstanding bills and the bank balance was healthy and would be for a while. The manager was virtually kow-towing but the kow-towing would grow less as the bank balance dwindled. He should be looking for his next client but he knew, until either he or the police solved Charmaine's murder without any shadow of doubt, he would never be satisfied. There was nothing for it but to make a return journey to Breconfield.

Thornton was never much of a gambling man but there was a horse he fancied in the two–twenty at Cheltenham, a mare, a handsome looking animal named *Grey of Fallodin* and he had a soft spot for greys. According to the morning paper she was more or less an outsider, should start off at sixteen to one or thereabouts and, in a field of eight, was definitely worth a two-way bet. He looked at his watch. There was time to put his money on her. He would toddle around the corner to his local betting shop and put on a couple of quid each way. After all he could at the moment afford that little outlay for what could be a very good return. There was time while he was about it to grab a quick sandwich and a pint at his local.

He was halfway to the betting shop when an *Evening Standard* bill board at a newspaper stand brought him up short. It was the first edition of the day and on the board in large letters he read

FAMOUS ENGLISH WRITER FOUND DEAD IN ROME.

There was no doubt who the famous English writer could be. He bought a paper. It was front page news which was probably just as well as his hands were trembling so much he probably wouldn't have been able to open it. He stopped to scan it where he stood. Beneath large headlines he read...

*According to our Rome correspondent, in the early hours of this morning, the body of the writer Joachim Caswell, 46, notable for his work on children's television, in particular the ever popular series "The Limey Gang are Here" but*

*also the author of numerous other programmes and the
recipient of awards was recovered from the Tiber. Although
an autopsy has not yet been performed it would appear his
death was the result of drowning and the Italian police do
not suspect foul play. Their theory at the moment is that
he was on his way home after a night out, had possibly
consumed too much alcohol, lost his balance and fell into
the river. A cursory examination of the body revealed no
apparent injury. While in Rome he had been residing at
the home of his friend Luca Biancchi who is devastated
by the news. Recently Mister Caswell had been working
on the film "Return to Batani" being made at Breconfield
Studios, the scene of three recent murders still unsolved. It
is believed Mister Caswell leaves a wife and daughter. The
British Embassy has been informed.*

Thornton lowered the paper and looked around as though
seeing the street for the very first time, everything coming
suddenly into the sharpest focus like that split second before
losing consciousness under an anaesthetic. Mister Biancchi was
devastated at the news? Thornton brought to mind that smiling
urbane Italian face and remembered how he felt this was a man
with whom he could be friends. How wrong can a person be?
Whatever Romeo might have said on the subject, love at first
sight was definitely not to be trusted. In fact was more than
likely to be totally misleading and possibly end in disaster.

So he had been attacked in Rome and almost killed but he
never for a moment thought to warn Caswell about his friend
Biancchi and now in a way he felt guilty, almost a feeling of
responsibility for what had happened. Would Caswell have
believed him anyway? And could it be he was himself still in
the firing line?

Something very odd was happening at Breconfield Studios.
Why else would Holly have taken a job there? It's possible
Charmaine did discover something untoward and had to be
disposed of but then who killed Mel and why?

Once again he remembered Holly's warning. Maybe he had better talk to her as soon as possible, that is before he was the next subject of an unfortunate accident.

He folded the newspaper and moved on to the pub for his sandwich and a stiff drink. He had forgotten all about *Grey of Fallodin* and she romped home by three lengths at twelve to one.

# Chapter Fourteen

'M r King?'

'Yes.'

'It's Ada Chapman.'

'How are you Mrs Chapman? All's well I hope?'

'Yes, thank you. Very well.' There was a long pause. Thornton filled it.

'Was there something else you wanted to tell me? Something you may have thought wise not to tell the police?'

'As a matter of fact there is. As you know, I mentioned that Mel Preston had been in his office the night that the poor girl was murdered.'

'Yes...' there was another long silence, '... and,' Thornton encouraged her.

'Well, a couple of days later, after the murder I mean, when I got to the studio to start work, I found... in my cupboard... a letter.'

'From?'

'That's it, Mister King, I don't know, there was no name with it.'

'How interesting. And just what did this letter contain?'

'Some money and a note.'

There was another long silence.

'And... ?' He encouraged again. 'What was in the note?'

'It said that my service to the studios had not gone unnoticed.'

'May I ask Mrs Chapman, how much money was in the envelope?'

'Oh, an awful lot of money, Mr King.' There was another long pause. 'There was a hundred pounds.'

'May I ask...'

'I wasn't going to keep it Mr. King,' Ada interrupted, 'but Dick at the The Drover's Arms, he said that I deserved it. After all the insurance people, well, they didn't treat Eric very well, did they? But oh Mr King, I'm worried now that I might be sent to jail. One reads all sorts of funny things these days, I mean I had nothing to do with that poor girl's death, and as for Mr Preston, well everybody here is talking about it.'

'Mrs Chapman, I'm quite sure that you won't go to prison, even if the police did find out about the money. Do you still have the note?'

'Oh, Mr King, I'm sorry. I don't. It said that the money was a tax free gift, and so it would be better if I destroyed the note, then there would be no way for the tax office to trace the money.'

"And no way to trace who had left the note," he thought.

'One more thing Mrs Chapman; apart from you and the Landlord at the Drover's Arms, does anybody else know about the money?'

'No, I don't think so. I haven't told anybody except Dick.'

'Good, then I suggest that we keep it that way.'

That was a disturbing call for Thornton. Although Ada Chapman seemed totally unaware she was being paid to keep quiet and one wrong word to the police or the press would mark her as the next to be disposed of, somebody was desperate to keep Charmaine's murderer, and Preston's for that matter, as secret as possible. But who? By everybody's admission no one liked Mel Preston, in fact a lot of people were glad that he seemed to get what he deserved, but there still remained the original reason for the death of Charmaine. What did she find in Preston's office that night, which meant she had to be killed to keep her silent? Thornton felt he now needed to find a way to gain access to Preston's office.

**H**olly was snuggled down on her comfy sofa, legs curled beneath her, watching her, and for that matter the whole nation's, favourite soap, *Coronation Street* when the phone rang. Damn it! It just had to be Thornton. How many times had she told him not to call during her favourite bit of television? She might have known. As far as Holly was concerned, with the exception of this favourite programme, for the most part television might not even have been invented she took so little interest in it. Now and again a BBC period drama of quality caught her eye or the evening news but very little else. The waffle of talking heads programmes, when she was tempted to tune into them, either bored her silly or got her dander up to a dangerous extent. Why didn't she think to leave the phone off the hook until the end of the episode? She glanced at her watch. Five minutes to go. The phone could go on ringing for five minutes except that would be slightly nerve-wracking and she wouldn't be able to concentrate on what was happening in *The Rover's Return*. Unable to stand it any longer, she went over to the phone and answered it, eyes still glued to the screen.

'Yes?'

'Hello Holly, its Thornton.'

'I know damn well who it is, Thornton. Guess what's on the telly at the moment.'

'Oops! I'll call you back.'

She heard him cut off, put down her own receiver and went back to watch the last few minutes. He was cautious enough to give plenty of time for the end music and credits to roll before the phone rang again. She switched off the telly before picking up the phone.

'What is it now, Thornton?'

'Are you mad at me?'

'Now what in the world could have given you such a preposterous idea?'

'The tone of your voice is what gives me that idea.'

'No, I'm not mad at you but I would appreciate it if you wrote in your diary or put up a very large notice somewhere, office or flat or preferably both saying must not phone Holly during *Coronation Street*.'

'I will do that.'

'So is this just a social call or is it more important?'

'I hear you've got a new job. Does that mean you've left the old one?'

'No, Thornton the new job is all part of the old one.'

'I thought maybe it was.'

'I presume it was the budding genius who let the cat out of the bag?'

'It was, and he's dying for love of you.'

'Thanks a lot. I'm highly flattered but I'm not a child snatcher. If I felt inclined towards chickens that little Sicilian monster Luigi would have been a better proposition.'

'I thought you `ad the `ots for `is beautiful young Sicilian body.'

'Thornton, do me a favour, pu-lease. And anyway, in the purported words of Oscar Wilde, this one's much too ugly. So come on, Thornton, there was a reason for this call other than idle chit-chat so let's have it.'

'I need to get into Breconfield Studios again.'

'What for?'

'Something is nagging me.'

'Scratch it.'

'No, seriously, Holly.'

'And you imagine I am to be your way in I suppose.'

'Yes.'

'How do you make that out?'

'What's the name and position of your new boss?'

'Thornton you had better come around. I don't want to discuss this over the phone.'

'I'm in the box just around the corner. I'll be with you in five minutes or less.'

Holly put down the phone and went to take the front door off the latch. Then she retired to the kitchen to turn up the flame beneath the coffee sitting on the stove, a full pot, still almost at boiling point. She heard the front door close, very quietly, and stood stock still. It was not like Thornton King to be that considerate. Normally it would have closed with a not inconsiderable bang. She turned off the cooker.

'Good evening, Miss Day.'

It was a voice she had never heard before, soft and seductive, but it prickled her scalp, sent shivers down her spine and she felt the goose flesh rise. She turned to face her visitor and almost had conniptions when she was faced with a total but beautiful stranger who virtually turned her knees to jelly. It was every fortune teller's prediction come true, "you'll meet a tall dark handsome stranger!" He might not have been dark but he was certainly tall and, beneath his immaculate *Armani* suit, launched for the first time that very year, she pictured an immaculate body to match. Control yourself, Holly, she said to herself. You are either hallucinating or this is an extremely dangerous situation. Here was a perfect stranger who had let himself into her flat and addressed her by her name and that did not foretell a happy outcome. She eventually found her voice though it was no more than a squeak in a high register.

'Yes?' was all she managed to say.

He smiled. Obviously, or so he thought, he had made her extremely nervous which, as far as he was concerned, could only be a good thing. It made what he had come to do so much easier.

'So,' he purred, 'at last I get to meet the fabulous Miss Holly Day who I have heard so much about.'

He looked around and then returned his attention to her still standing beside the cooker and he performed a small old-fashioned bow. If he had come to do her harm, which seemed likely, he was certainly going to do it with panache.

'Allow me to introduce myself, not that you will know me for long but I would like you to know who I am. My name is Luca Biancchi and, as you can guess by that, I am Italian.'

'How did you get my address and what do you want?' She had fully recovered her voice even though she had a horrid feeling that what he wanted was not what she was prepared to give, not easily anyhow.

'How I got your address is immaterial and as for what I want I think this will answer for me.' A flick knife had suddenly opened in his right hand. 'It's a great pity we could not get to know each other better, Miss Day, do you not think so? I would have liked that. But there comes a time, as your friend Mister King would say, when we all have to kick the bucket.'

He was still smiling, his eyes never left her face, and she did not like it. If there was one thing above all else that got Holly blazing mad it was being threatened in any shape or form. She waited for him to make his first move which naturally was to get within striking distance. There was the sound of the front door bell ringing followed up by a loud rat-a-tat-tat and it was enough to distract him for a split second. She lifted the cona of now boiling coffee from the cooker and hurled it at him. He gasped, screamed, and dropped the knife, raised both hands to his face and, as she ran past, she gave him a karate chop that brought him to his knees. Then she ran for the front door, flung it open, grabbed a bewildered Thornton by the hand, slammed the door and ran for the stairs going up.

She put her finger to her lips and they flattened themselves against the wall as the door to the flat was yanked open and Luca staggered out. His beautiful clothes were horribly coffee stained which was nothing compared to his face that had received almost a litre of boiling liquid and would forever show the damage. It seemed his eyes, closed however probably from an instant automatic reaction, had escaped the damage somewhat as he could still see enough to note the lift indicator somewhat out of focus reaching the ground floor and assumed, wrongly, that Holly had taken it. He took the stairs; staggering, stumbling, supporting his balance with a hand against the wall.

Holly waited a good few minutes before she believed it safe to show herself. Of Luca there was now no sign and fortunately he had left the door ajar. She hustled Thornton inside and closed it behind them.

'Well!' Thornton said, 'and what was all that about?'

'Would you like a drink?'

'Not particularly, but you obviously want one.'

'You can say that again.'

'Not particularly, but you…'

'THORNTON!'

'Sorry.'

'So you jolly well should be. After what I have just been through I am in no mood for frivolity thank you very much.'

Having been well and truly ticked off he silently watched as she headed for her little cocktail bar and unsteadily poured herself a large gin, not her usual tipple. She topped it up with tonic and took a long hard swallow, then she lowered the glass and looked at Thornton. She was visibly trembling and suddenly her knees buckled and she sat with a plop in the nearest chair and burst into tears, something he had never seen before and he waited for her to recover. When she had got slightly over the shock and more or less pulled herself together and had taken another swig at the gin, she laughed. It was a slightly hysterical laugh, a laugh to relieve the remaining tension and it didn't last long.

'Phew!' she said, eyes narrowed.

'Feel better?'

She nodded.

'Want to tell me about it?'

She nodded again but didn't say anything, just took another generous mouthful of gin and tonic before putting the glass down, getting up and walking over to Thornton to throw her arms around him, almost winding him with the strength of her embrace. In all the years of their friendship this was something that had never happened before. Meeting and parting invariably involved nothing more than a peck on the cheek.

Taken completely by surprise he didn't know whether he was supposed to return the bear hug or just wait for it to come to an end. The latter happened. She unlooped her arms, stood back, wiped away a tear and smiled at him. He gently thumbed another tear from her cheek.

'Whatever it was, Miss Holly Day, it had to be pretty dramatic.'

'I'll say.' She wandered towards the kitchen, stood at the door and turned back. 'Can't go in there,' she said, 'not yet; broken glass all over the floor.'

He still said nothing; was leaving it all up to her.

'My lovely reliable old cona coffee maker I've had for a thousand years or more is no more; shattered into a hundred pieces, coffee and glass all over the floor.'

'I'll have that drink now,' Thornton said.

'You know where it is. Help yourself.'

He crossed over to the bar, selected a glass and poured himself two fingers of *Famous Grouse*.

'Can't have ice,' she said, 'it's in the fridge. Too much broken glass in the way.'

'I do have shoes on.' He lifted his foot and waggled his toecap to prove it.

'Yes, but you'll cause a lot of damage by treading shards into the linoleum and it's brand new and a very expensive linoleum; not your ordinary everyday kind but cushioned, know what I mean?'

'Okay. No ice. No problem.' He smiled.

'Oh, Thornton you will never ever know how pleased I am to see you. From now on you can interrupt *Coronation Street* any time you like.'

He raised his customary eyebrow.

'No, seriously, I mean it. And if you do I promise not to shout or be mad at you.'

'Okay, Holly. I think you've settled down enough now to tell me what all this is about. What happened in here?'

She sat down again and he did likewise on the couch he had once nearly destroyed with a portion of sweet and sour something or other when it was brand new, hardly out of its plastic wrappings even and he would always be reminded of it.

'You know that Italian by the name of Lucky…? Lucky…'

'Luca.'

'What?'

'Luca… Luca Biancchi.'

'That's him.'

'Luca was here?'

'Here? Are you kidding?' She pointed dramatically towards the kitchen. 'He damn near killed me in there. Thornton, if you hadn't rung the doorbell at that precise moment he would have knifed me with a bloody great switchblade ten inches long. I was that much…' she held up a hand, index finger and thumb pressed together… 'that much away from death. God damn it! Who did he think he was messing around with? Tell me again how you know him?' Her tone had changed. She suddenly sounded very suspicious.

'I met him in Rome. He was supposed to be a friend of the writer, Joachim Caswell.'

'The one found in the river?'

'That's right and it would seem we know now who put him there. Friend?' He shrugged. 'Some friend. As the saying has it, if you have friends like that who needs enemies? Have I got that right? Anyway, maybe he had orders.'

'More than likely.'

'So what happened?'

'What happened?'

'What was the outcome of your little contretemps with our friend Luca? A bit of the old unarmed combat was it?' He made a few karate type chops for emphasis, not exactly convincing.

'I threw the cona at him. The coffee had just boiled.'

The play acting stropped. 'Bloody hell, Holly!'

'I know, I know. So right now I would think he's either on his way to a friendly doctor he knows or accident and emergency at the nearest hospital. They were really severe burns, Thornton.' She sat thinking for a moment. 'I shouldn't think there's much

203

skin left on his face. A shame really. He was so handsome.'

'Holly! He tried to kill you!'

'Yes, and I would like to know who put him on to me. Someone at the studio has realised I'm not quite kosher. That's the only place he could have got my address. So who would that someone be do you suppose?'

'How did he manage to get in?'

'I left the door off the latch for you.'

Thornton shook his head.

'Well you said you were only going to be five minutes and it's just as well you were.'

'Okay.' He got up. 'Well, let me help you clean up the mess.'

'No, leave it for now. You said you wanted to gain admittance to the studios, possibly through me. How do you expect to do it?'

'Who's your boss?'

'The new producer of *Return to Batani*.'

'An American?'

'Yes. His name is Anton Wagner and he's a hideously ugly, bigheaded, hands everywhere, why are you resisting me when you know you really want it? puffed up, self-important sprout who is surely due for a fall from grace, pretty soon I hope.'

'That's a pretty comprehensive description.'

'Till then I have to put up with him best I can. He's most certainly someone I wouldn't trust further than you could throw him. Why is it that some males firmly believe they're God's gift to women when in actual fact even their mothers can't stand the sight of them and their dogs leave home?'

'Right then, if he's as egotistical as you say, that's perfect. I am a world renowned freelance journalist about to do a big story that will be syndicated worldwide and would he be so kind as to give me a few minutes of his precious time to grant me the honour of an interview?'

'And then?'

'Then you give me a piece of paper I can waggle under the gate-man's nose to gain admittance.'

'Why are you doing this, Thornton?'

'I told you why. I really need to satisfy my curiosity as to what is going on, especially now that Caswell has been murdered.'

'We don't know that.'

'Oh yes we do, believe me, Holly, we know it all right and we know who did it. The big question is why and for whom? So will you do this for me please?'

'You make it sound so simple.'

'I've heard that one before as well. It might sound that way but I know the truth is it is far from simple. Will you do it?'

'Yes, on one condition.'

'Name it.'

'I don't know you from Adam. I've never seen you or heard from you before. From hereon in there is absolutely no contact whatsoever. Is that quite clear? The last thing I want is to have you queering my pitch. It took a lot of string pulling and favours repaid to get this job and if I lose it without a result the department is not going to be too happy about it. I might have to join you in the private eye business.'

'Scouts honour.' He held up his hand in the scout salute.

'Your pimply protégé can't give the game away I hope.'

'I am a total stranger. Now, will you let me help you clean up?'

'No. I would much rather do it myself thank you. My kitchen is out of bounds to all and sundry, you being sundry.'

'As you wish. Don't say I didn't offer.'

'Why don't you say good-night and dib dib dib and dob dob dob off? Go polish your toggle.'

He finished off his drink in one gulp, handed her the glass and headed for the door.

'Never leave your door off the latch again,' he admonished her, 'and keep that knife for possible future evidence. Don't put your dabs all over it.'

'I'm not a novice, Thornton.'

'I know that. You're a veteran and the most consummate professional I know and I love you for it. Good night.' He reached the door.

'Thornton!'

He stopped, turned back.

'I don't think he will still be around. He's too damaged. But please be careful.'

Thornton winked, blew her a kiss, and left.

# Chapter Fifteen

T he second unit were on location in Epping Forest which was standing in for a small area of dense African jungle. Epping Forest, sixty-four square miles of it, was a handy location for any scene that demanded trees; trees of any and every description even if they weren't tropical, sub-tropical, or pines typical of the northern hemisphere if doing say a remake of *Nanook of the North*. They were starting to lose their leaves and in this case were adorned with a number of artificial *Jack and the Beanstalk* pantomime type vines from the prop department as a rather vain attempt at authenticity.

Apart from the company there wasn't an animal wild or tame to be seen but once jungle noises like lions roaring, elephants trumpeting, parrots squawking, women ululating and various other tropical type shrieks were added to the sound track, with possibly a bit of primitive drumming or a Karl Reiner type score such as he wrote for *King Kong* and a couple of visuals intercut, library sequences of real jungle, Vlad the Impaler felt he had a pretty good mock up. He had never actually seen an African jungle, though he had tried to find some in *National Geographic* and did East Africa sport any jungle at all he wondered or was it what is called bush with wide open spaces, red earth, thorny trees, giant ant heaps and that, and possibly with Kilimanjaro in the background? If it was the latter there was not a location in the United Kingdom that could stand in for it, not even near Snowdon or Ben Nevis so who knew and who cared? The punters munching their popcorn or smooching in the back row, well most of them anyway, wouldn't know any difference and if it didn't look right and the critics picked up on it he could shift the blame onto his second unit director and location manager and give them a right bawling out, preferably in public.

There was fortunately plenty of library stock of jungle be it Brazil or Borneo it didn't really matter. He remembered the Johnny Weissmuller *Tarzan* films he had seen as a child where the African elephant out on the African plain was transmogrified into an Indian one in the jungle, the former with huge ears and enormous tusks being untrainable, the latter with small ears a more docile beast.

Cord Wainer, not too long deceased, had simply basked in the screaming adoration of fans who greeted him hysterically whenever he appeared in public. He loved seeing himself time and time again in various newspapers and magazines. He loved knowing he was a recognisable figure, a VIP who would receive the red carpet treatment from Argentina to Zululand.

He loved premieres, film festivals, the best hotels, easy and frequent sex. He loved the money. But the one thing Cord Wainer detested and had always complained about when filming was having to get up in the middle of the night for a shivering pre-dawn start to pay for it all, and Ernest J. Bloomberg felt exactly the same way. It was true even on an English summer's day until the sun came up, if it was going to appear at all that is and it wasn't pissing with rain when, if that were the case and it evidently had no intention of clearing up, it would be weather cover back at the studio. The forecasts were followed like Druids studying the runes, hoping the weather would allow outside filming as per schedule.

This particular day started off extremely chilly, especially under the trees and Ernest was well wrapped up in his duffle coat and thick scarf, holding a mug of steaming hot coffee in one woolly gloved hand and fiddling with a toggle with the other as he waited either for orders or for something to happen. It might be chilly but he was glad it was autumn and not winter. Producers never seemed to take into account that there is a season called winter and brass monkeys would lose their balls had they any to start with. Nothing seemed to be happening right at that moment or gave any indication of happening in the near future so he wandered back to the caterer's van to help himself to another bacon sandwich before idling off in the direction of some brutes that were being set up. So much time when filming is taken up just hanging around and Ernest was wishing he could be anywhere other than where he was at that moment.

It was all right for the stars of course, nice and cosy in their heated trailers. Sooner or later they would have to emerge to face the day but in the meantime they had an opportunity to stay warm, be mollycoddled, go over the script once more if unsure of their lines, do the morning's crossword puzzles or maybe carry on reading a good book. If any extras were needed for the scene it wasn't so comfortable for them of course. The bus in which they were delivered had long since had its engine turned off and was no longer heated but, having collected their sausage or bacon sandwiches and hot drinks, they scuttled back to it as being the warmest place they could find and the windows were soon steamed up. For this upcoming scene most of them of course would have to be in skimpy loincloths and wielding shields and spears and they weren't looking forward to it. It meant goose bumps for sure, possibly violent shivering and constantly erect nipples, possibly followed by a bad bout of pneumonia if nothing else. It was just as well they didn't require body makeup, that would have been the last straw.

The youthful American star, who knew the success of the picture rested on his own broad shoulders, was admiring himself, torso naked, in the caravan's full length mirror. He flicked back his blonde quiff and smiled engagingly at his reflection, as lovingly as Narcissus gazing into his pool. He was grateful to his parents back in Minnesota for denying themselves so much so that they could afford the dental work needed to make his smile so dazzling. He rippled first his six pack then his pecs and flexed his biceps before turning sideways to take a Mister Universe type pose as seen in *Health and Fitness* magazines; one knee bent, left hand holding the right wrist and then vice versa, tensing the pecs to see how he looked from there. His waist was slender, his thighs muscular, he was well shaped and well satisfied. It was little wonder the girls screamed and some even fainted (or pretended to faint) whenever he appeared.

Meanwhile Ernest, making his way simply out of curiosity towards where the lighting being set up, to his delight saw William Harrowfield standing near one of the lamps. He wasn't quite so muffled up, obviously made of sterner stuff, but he was wearing gloves. Rather than against the chill of the dewy morning they would sometime, when things actually started to move, be for protection from accidental contact with the heat of the lamp.

Heart slightly aflutter, Ernest approached the young man who, gazing into the middle distance, seemed to be lost in a dream world and hadn't as yet seen him.

'Good morning,' Ernest greeted the other's back. He couldn't help but notice how William's hair curled like baby hair on the nape of his neck. Writers have to notice small details like that.

William came too and turned around. It took a moment for him to register who had addressed him, then he smiled, the eyes took on an even more Oriental look and now Ernest noticed for the first time how blue they were and his heart really did flutter. Ernest J. realised that, if ever curiosity got the better of him, and at some time it ought to if he was going to be a fully rounded writer who experienced everything in life, well as much as was possible, he would stop short at something like murder, it was William Harrowfield he would like to satisfy his curiosity with.

'Didn't expect to see you here,' he said, breathing out steam in the chilly air. 'You going to be regular crew now?'

'No. Too many off sick. Flu epidemic. I'm a stand-in.'

'Oh.'

He realised he still had half a bacon sandwich in his hand and he waved it about as he asked, 'Have you had a bacon sarney?'

'Not yet, been too busy.'

'Shall I fetch you one?'

'Thank you. I'd like that.'

'And a coffee?'

'Black, lots of sugar.'

Ernest resisted the temptation to say he thought William sweet enough. That would have been much too forward at this stage of the game.

'Black, lots of sugar,' he said and tottered back to the caterer's van on somewhat shaky legs.

How was it possible he could feel this way? It had never happened before, not even when he was at school. He never wanted to play around with other boys, there was never a "you show me yours, I'll show you mine" moment though at that age he wasn't yet all that conscious and worried about the size of his diminutive todger. No, the fact was he just wasn't interested which was a bit unusual to say the least. Most boys like to know what other boys possess in the way of equipment even if only by a furtive, sometimes not so furtive, sideways glance at the pissoire. The photographic magazines he secreted in his bed were all of nude girls. Was this just a one off buddy buddy male bonding thing? He knew perfectly well he didn't stand a chance in hell that William would ever reciprocate his feelings but his imagination was running riot with romantic scenarios and next time he used his enlarger he was already anticipating what he would be dreaming of; and he would write it all down in *Hour of Agony*. In the whole history of worldwide cinema, never was there a title better chosen. He didn't realise it at that moment but, as far as Thornton's admonishments were concerned, during the course of that fateful day in Epping Forest, if he hadn't already, Ernest J. Bloomberg was going to lose his heart and be thoroughly indiscreet.

L o and behold, for once there was something in his mailbox other than bills and flyers for various businesses around Tottenham Court Road. There was a slightly bulky envelope bearing Italian stamps. He sat at his desk a long while looking at it and wondering if it was prudent to open it. Various terror groups, in particular the IRA had made letter bombs pretty commonplace and even the smallest could cause a great deal of damage. Should he call the bomb squad and report a suspicious package? He would have his coffee first and think about it. He made the coffee and sat down with his mug, then had the idea that he would with great care steam open the package and inspect the contents without actually disturbing it. He would stop at the slightest suspicion of anything irregular so, leaving his mug on the desk, he switched on the kettle once more and proceeded to do just that, a couple of times hastily withdrawing his fingers when they inadvertently got too close to the spout and were in danger of being scalded.

He went back to the desk, took a sip of coffee and cautiously withdrew from the envelope what simply looked like a few pages of foolscap which, in fact, was what they were and which turned out on reading to be: *AN AGREEMENT between FULL THROTTLE FILM PRODUCTIONS LTD and JAOCHIM CASWELL.* It was dated a good ten years earlier. There was also a letter which Thornton read first.

*Dear Thornton King, You wanted to know why I am so pissed off with Full Throttle so I am sending you here a copy of my contract and you will notice a couple of things which make me believe they are in breach of copyright and therefore that it would be possible for me to sue the bastards for whatever I can get out of them. Firstly clause 4 – "The writer as beneficial owner HEREBY ASSIGNS the entire copyright (both existing and future) in the works to the Producers to hold the same unto the Producers* absolutely throughout the world for the full period of copyright therein and all renewals and extensions thereof." Which is a fairly long-winded way of saying I have signed my life away and that would indeed seem to be the case if it weren't for clause 5 which reads "The writer hereby acknowledges that the payment by the Producers to the Guild of any monies on account of or by way of the Writer's share of the Royalty Account (arising from the distribution and exhibitions of the series and as calculated and defined by the Guild Agreement) shall be a complete discharge to the producers of its liability to the writer in respect thereof to make any payment out of the Royalty Fund to which he may be entitled under the provisions of the Guild Agreement." Please note bene the words: "arising from the distribution and exhibition of the series" and "complete discharge".

Also a bit long winded but I did tell you about film contracts. Basically all it says is that every time the series is exhibited anywhere in the world I should receive a certain percentage of my original fee. Over the years this has amounted to a quite substantial sum, especially if you were to add compound interest, but not a brass farthing have I seen so there has definitely been no "complete discharge", by the producers ie: Full Throttle, in fact no discharge whatsoever. Now Centurion, who are the distributors, maintain they can't pay out any money because the show is not in profit. Firstly I simply do not believe this considering the number of times I know for a fact it has been shown all over the world but that is really besides the point; the point being that my contract is not with Centurion but with Full Throttle and there is – this is what really matters – no such words as profit or loss in my contract. It straightforwardly states I am to be paid a certain amount with each and every showing and that amount has never been forthcoming. Because of this I sincerely believe Full Throttle has reneged on the contract and in view of this the copyright reverts to me. I believe that any distribution of the show now by Centurion is an infringement of my copyright and is therefore illegal. The reason for my approaching you like this is to ask if you know any good copyright lawyer who would be willing to take on *my case. If you do, here is my Italian address. It is of course Luca's.*

The address was appended.

Thornton sighed, put down the contract, leaned back and picked up his coffee, took a sip and put the mug down again. He shook his head. It was too late for Joachim. No copyright lawyer, no lawyer of any description was going to do him any good now, but the whole thing was beginning to make a bit more sense.

If he were to start legal action again the film companies a whole lot of worms could start crawling out of the woodwork so it wasn't necessarily the fact that they didn't want to pay out a few thousand quid in compensation, it was those worms possibly seeing the light of day that really worried them and Joachim had to be disposed of as damage limitation. What should Thornton do next? He ought to have a word with Reg Venables, that's what he ought to do next. He might be a penny short of a pound but he did have some nous and it could be he would have some serious advice to give.

For once Reg was not noshing on his favourite sandwich and when Thornton entered his office he noticed a sweet pleasant aroma as Reg puffed away on his pipe, a look of utter contentment on his face. Thornton was beginning to wonder if Reg these days ever got out from behind his desk or if his buttocks were glued to his chair. He was beginning to spread out a little in that area of his anatomy no doubt for want of exercise. He took the pipe out of his mouth and pointed the stem at his visitor.

'Excellent tobacco, lad; reet gradely as they might say in Yorkshire. You couldn't have come up with a better choice. Thank you. Even the lady wife approves the smell which is saying a great deal I can tell you. It's made life a lot easier in our little household. Normally she hints at her displeasure by throwing open every window in the house in the dead of winter or banishing me to the potting shed. You'll have to tell me the blend for future use.'

'Glad you and she both approve.'

'Any news of your missing lad?' The pipe stem was lowered and now pointed at the chair in front of the desk, the gesture inviting Thornton in friendly fashion to sit and Thornton duly accepted it.

Reg's pipe had evidently gone out as pipes tend to do if not smoked continuously. He thumbed down the tobacco and relit it with a Swan Vesta, taking extra quick puffs to get it really going again.

'Yes. Thank you,' Thornton said in answer to his query. 'Your artist did a really first rate job. The lad's been traced... more or less,' he added.

'What does more or less mean then?' Reg applied the match to his pipe once more before shaking it and dropping it in his ashtray. 'You've either found him or you haven't.'

'I've found him and I haven't.'

'My God, Thornton but you do talk in riddles sometimes. It's beyond me it really is.'

'Life *is* a riddle, Reg.'

'And don't go all philosophical on me, I couldn't bear it. All right, let's leave out the missing person you've found but haven't found and move on to why you're here. Two visits in so short a time? I'm highly honoured. I take it you're looking for another favour?'

'Not really...'

'Another riddle coming up is it?'

'Not exactly.'

'Good morning, Thornton.' He directed his attention to a pile of forms in front of him. 'I've had enough of your shilly-shallying for today. I've got better things to do than listen to your nonsense. You know the way out. It's the same as the way you came in. Oh, and if you should by any chance see Roper on the way, in the canteen as usual more than likely, kindly inform him I want to see him in here, pronto.'

'Not so hasty, Reg, not so hasty. I think you'll be pleased to hear what I've got to tell you.'

'Then spit it out quick, boy, and stop beating around the bloody bush.'

'Right. Now how do you feel about doing yourself a bit of good with the Italian police or Interpol even?'

'Oh yes? I'm listening.' And in fact, suspicious though he might have been, he *was* listening, despite his previous one and only fiasco with Interpol. If he had been a dog his ears would have pricked up. If he was a cat they would have swivelled.

'There is a man in London at the moment; he's an Italian by the name of Luca Biancchi. Last night he tried to kill Holly.'

'Good God!' Reg nearly bit through his pipe stem before he removed it from his mouth and ran his tongue over his teeth to make sure there had been no damage there. 'Is the lass all right?'

'A bit shocked of course, only natural, but otherwise fine.'

'Glad to hear it, yes, indeed. What reason did this bastard have for wanting to kill her? You're quite sure he did?'

'Quite sure and she's holding a six inch flick-knife for evidence.'

'So tell me, what happened?'

'He didn't know what he was taking on when he messed with Miss Holly Day. She threw a pot of boiling coffee at him; karate chopped him here,' he indicated the side of his neck, 'and fled. I just happened to arrive at the scene at the right time and we waited on the stairs for the man to leave which he shortly afterwards did. So, what I have to say is this, did you ever hear of a writer by the name of Joachim Caswell?'

'Boiling coffee? What? Who?'

'Joachim, Caswell.'

'Can't say I have, no.' His pipe had gone out again.

'He was recently working at Breconfield Studios on their latest movie but has been found in Rome; fled there after the murder of his girlfriend and I am led to believe he has now been murdered himself, and murdered by this man Biancchi.'

'So where is he now?'

'In a morgue I would presume.'

'Don't play silly buggers, Thornton, this Bia... Bia...'

'Biancchi.'

'Biancchi, yes.'

'I would presume he's in a hospital or holed up somewhere.'

'And on what grounds do you presume that?'

'Because, like the invisible man, do you remember that old TV series, Reg?'

'Get on with it!'

'And there was the 1933 movie starring Claude Raines? Luca will be lying flat on his back with his head completely swathed in bandages though I shouldn't think he'll be wearing dark glasses.'

'Why?'

'Why what?'

'Why will his be swathed in bandages?'

'Because that pot of boiling coffee apparently hit him full in the face and, apart from the pain of peeling flesh, his face can't be a very pretty sight.'

'Good God! Well I'll be blowed!' Reg sat thinking for a moment 'All I can say is, if it can't be proved he tried to kill her and that she acted in self-defence, though a bit extreme I do have to say, she could go down for a very long stretch for GBH you know, attempted murder even.'

'Reg, Reg, I know we're living in an age when people are suing each other left, right, and centre, more often than not for the most spurious of reasons, some patently screwy in fact but is a pot of coffee a dangerous weapon?'

'I would say so, yes, definitely, if it's boiling. I would most certainly class it as a dangerous weapon. Unusual I suppose, a bit out of the ordinary, unless there have been previous examples of its use in a domestic say which I suppose must have happened sometime or other, if not coffee then tea, or a saucepan, hopefully without sizzling fat in it. Housewives with a truly vicious temper temporarily losing control you know.'

'Reg, it was self-defence, believe me, this man is a killer, plain and simple.'

'Nothing is plain, nothing is simple.'

'Don't you start philosophising? Just start the ball rolling. Find out where this guy is and inform the Italian police or Interpol that you believe him to be a murderer, the killer of Joachim Caswell, more than likely a member of the Mafia then, if and when he returns to Rome, they could be waiting to take him in. You will be a hero all over again, Reg, just like you were with the Spitskaya affair.'

Thornton hated to mention the Spitskaya affair when Reg took all the kudos for solving a series of murders, the truth of the matter being it was he and Holly who did it all; but if Reg needed buttering up nothing was calculated to spread the butter softer, thicker and faster than mention of the Spitskaya affair.

'Yes, well...' he said, and rolled his tongue around his mouth while he was thinking, then pursed his lips. 'Thank you, Thornton; I'll certainly do as you say. Even if, and mind you I only say if, the man is actually not guilty of the murder in Rome, I'm sure the Italian police will be able to sort it out one way or another.' He frowned not being too sure whether any of that made sense but decided to continue nevertheless. 'In the meantime', he said, 'if Holly would like to come in and lodge a complaint, make a statement, it would make life a lot easier as far as an arrest and extradition is concerned.'

'That's not on the cards, Reg. No, I don't think Holly would be amenable to that.'

'Oh? Why not?' Now he was definitely suspicious; all his years of experience as a policeman coming to the fore.

'Well, think about it for a minute. What if the guy dies? She could be up on a murder charge.'

'Exactly.'

'Even if he doesn't die, like you said, it could be a case of grievous bodily harm at least. As it stands nobody but you, me, Holly and Luca know the details of what happened. Truthfully only Holly and Luca really know what happened because I was not an actual eye-witness but was standing outside the door to the flat, so strictly entre nous I think it would be better for all concerned to keep shtum about this.'

'Thornton, you can't possibly be serious! Do you know what

you're suggesting? You're asking me to break the law; withholding information from the police.'

'No one need know that.'

'True.' He pondered on it for a brief moment, lips pursed once more. 'All right, give me a description.' He looked around for a pad, pulled it towards him and picked up a ballpoint. He held it a little like an expectant lady waiting to cross off the numbers on her bingo card should she be lucky in hearing them called out.

'About six foot two or three, maybe even more...'

'A big lad.'

'...athletic looking, age somewhere between thirty and forty.'

Reg scribbled for a moment and then looked up. 'Is that it? Facial features.'

'Before or after the incident with the coffee? All right!' He held up two placating hands as he saw the look on Reg's face. 'Blue eyes, blonde hair, clean shaven, no distinguishing features, not that I noticed anyway.'

Reg looked up from his pad. 'A blonde, blue-eyed I-talian?'

'They do exist, Reg.'

'Sounds very dodgy to me, if you don't mind me saying so. If this I-talian guy is a dyed in the wool villain he could also have dyed his hair and be wearing contact lenses.'

'Take it from me, Reg, the hair and eye colours are genuine. I'm not that unobservant.'

Reg shrugged and went back to his pad.

'If you say so. Right then, I'll put out an APW and contact all the London hospitals. We'll soon have him bang to rights, never fear.' He looked at his watch. 'Care for a cuppa tea?'


I t wasn't too long afterwards that the phone rang in Thornton's office. He had tried ringing Holly earlier but there was no answer so he presumed she was at the studio busy being an efficient secretary and fending of the pawing American. He had a vision of what Mister Wagner looked like: short, paunchy, bald but wearing a badly fitting toupee, podgy hands, a false tan and constantly a bit under the weather and red of nose from too much imbibing of the hard stuff, probably *Kentucky Rye*. He had no doubt there would have been a certain amount of apprehension generated when Holly breezed in with a cheery greeting as though nothing at all had happened the previous evening and she had never set eyes on Luca Biancchi or he on her.

So who could be calling? Thornton wondered. It wouldn't be Esther and he didn't think it was Ernest J. unless he had more to tell him which somehow he doubted. Maybe it was an inquiry from a possible new client who would give him something to do and take his mind off the Breconfield affair. He lifted the receiver.

'Thornton King.'

'Thornton, old lad, Reg Venables.'

'Hello, Reg, this is a surprise. Got the bracelets handy? What can I do you for?'

'Ever the joker, Thornton, ever the joker. I just thought I would take the trouble to inform you that we have traced your I-talian.'

'That was quick.' Thornton sounded genuinely surprised.

'Not really. A general call to all the hospitals soon tracked him down. He was in the burns unit at Barts. After all there can't be too many people with facial burns of that magnitude, can there?'

'I suppose not, except maybe in a Hammer house of horror or unless they had been looking into an erupting volcano.'

'Quit the joking, Thornton, if you must know you have landed me in shit up to my Adam's apple and I am praying no one is going to make waves, not even ripples.'

'Oh, dear! How is that, Reg?'

'Because your I-talian is no longer in the burns unit and questions are being asked, that's how's that, questions that have to be answered and right at this moment I don't have the answers so what do you have to say to that then?'

Thornton looked at his watch. 'Let's meet on equidistant neutral territory, Reg. The pubs are still open and I can make *The White Horse* in about ten minutes. So can you so I will see you there. How does that grab you?'

'Ten minutes it is.'

Thornton carried two dimpled half pint mugs of warm brown ale from the bar to the table where Reg, fingers rapping nervously on the tabletop, was impatiently waiting. He hoped he wouldn't be too long. The lady wife had informed him she had a roast shoulder of New Zealand lamb in the oven and, next to salt-beef sandwiches Reg simply drooled at the thought of roast lamb with parsnips and roast potatoes.

'There you go', Thornton said as he sat down. It was almost closing time, the barman was busy starting to clear up, wiping down the counter, and the pub was nearly empty so they had plenty of space around them and could talk in confidence as long as they kept their conversation sotto voce. 'Cheers!'

'Your health.'

They raised their glasses, took their first sip of beer, put the glasses down and were ready for business.

'Right, Reg. Fire away. What seems to be the problem?'

'Leave it out, Thornton, you're joking again.'

'Never more serious, my man. You have a problem; maybe together we can sort it out. That's what we're here for.'

'The problem, dear boy…'

Thornton's mug stopped halfway to his mouth. Dear boy? Dear boy! Had he heard right? This really had to be serious.

'…is your I-talian.'

'Yes? What about my I-talian?'

'He's dead.'

Thornton, forgetting that he was about to take a sip of his beer, slammed down his mug slopping beer over the rim and stared at Reg who stared right back again and nodded.

'That's right. He's turned up his toes, Thornton, and there are a lot of very dodgy questions that have to be answered.'

'Such as what?'

'Like, first of all, how did I know him and why did I have an All Ports Warning put out for him in the first place? He had no identification on him, plenty of cash evidently, pounds and lira, so it was presumed by that that he was I-talian, but nothing to say who he was. Would I come in and identify him? No. I had never seen him before so how could I identify him? Then again, if I had never seen him before how did I know who he was? Could I explain why his clothes were coffee stained and why he had multiple burns to his face and neck? No I couldn't. Next question, if I had never seen him before why did I think he was a murderer, a member of the Mafia and that he had killed this writer fellow, someone else I had never met or heard of? And did I know how he had boiling hot coffee thrown all over him because it seems that's what caused the burns and whichever person was responsible was liable to a charge of murder, and if I don't tell them who it was, you know who, our mutual friend, no names no pack drill, I am withholding information and am in deep trouble. I tell you, Thornton, I am at my wit's end.' After that he needed a deep breath and a hearty swig of his beer and he took it.

'No need to be, Reg, no need at all. Let's just think this through logically. I know the old saying about deceiving and weaving tangled webs and all that but people are doing it all the time and getting away with it. I've listened to evidence being given in law courts and it's been so obviously a fit-up a child of five could see through it, but everyone takes it seriously and, like Nelson, turns a blind eye. The answer to your problem is really quite simple if you stick to the line I am about to feed you.'

Reg had taken his trusty comforting pipe from his jacket pocket and was now thumbing down tobacco preparatory to lighting it and inhaling its calming aroma.

'Go ahead,' he growled, 'but if it's crap you feed me I might have to arrest you for being an accessory before, during, and after the fact.'

'There is a quite common phenomenon you're actually well aware of, Reg, and that you've overlooked. Ever heard of the police getting a tip-off, Reg? Anonymously?'

'Well bugger me! Now why didn't I think of that?' From

sagging like a deflated balloon Reg suddenly sat upright and actually smiled.

'Because it was panic stations, Reg. Quite understandable I suppose, but after thirty illustrious years in the police force and having in your time given umpteen villains the third degree, I would have thought you should have been over it, panic I mean. As far as you know the informant could have been anyone of a number of snouts who would pass the info on for some reason or other, revenge perhaps? And I don't think anyone has ever died from multiple burns to the face, Reg, It would take a great deal more than that. He died from something else.'

'Yes, shock to the system maybe, heart failure, so it would amount to the same thing.'

'Well, before you think of going anywhere else with this, wait until the post mortem and then decide what to do. I won't pass the news on to Holly, it would only upset her despite the fact the bastard tried to kill her. Hopefully it was something else killed him and it wasn't down to her. In the meantime finish your beer and I'll get us another.'

'Y ou were right on every account, Thornton', Reg informed him with his next phone call. 'He was identified by the clothes he was wearing, a bespoke suit from a very well known tailor in Rome, a bloke called Armani I'm led to believe, evidently well known that is, and your man was murdered. The autopsy report says death by asphyxiation, obviously a pillow over the face while he lay helpless as a newborn babe.' Reg could be as much a drama queen as anyone else if he put his mind to it.

'That's number four,' Thornton said aloud after he had put down the phone, 'this really has opened a whole new can of worms. Who I wonder is going to be number five?'

# Chapter Sixteen

Ernest J. decided he had eaten enough shepherd's pie to last him a lifetime and would indulge in a leg of chicken though he was quite sure it would turn out to be as tough as the lamb. He took a quick surreptitious glance around and was gratified to see his quarry seated at a table alone, but he would have to make it quick if he wasn't to lose him as it seemed he was on the last mouthful of whatever it was he had had for his lunch. Ernest returned his attention to the queue ahead of him and silently cursed as he noted that wretched girl was still flirting with every man who hadn't arrived at pensionable age. His agitation grew at such an alarming rate he nearly dropped his bowl of spotted dick but, eventually, he made it to the cash register and she duly rang up the amount, took his money from a trembling hand, and he turned to head towards the previously ascertained table only to see it empty and William's lithe figure disappearing through the dining room door; and he lost it. With a crash a tray of chicken, chips, peas, brown gravy, spotted dick and custard hit the floor and the whole room turned in his direction. Heart thumping, Ernest J. blushed and stammered a sort of apology before hastily following his hero. There were no two ways about it; murderer or no murderer and whatever the consequences he would have to spill the beans, put William in the picture and warn him that Thornton was hot on his trail.

'Oy!' Colleen yelled, but Ernest J. took no notice. He was already almost at the door.

'Tch!' She clicked her tongue against her teeth, 'Some people,' she whined, 'I don't know. Who's going to clean it up then?'

She got some sympathetic reactions from the rest of the queue, those who weren't growing impatient as their food congealed on the plate, and they carefully avoided stepping in the mess until a cleaner armed with mop and bucket finally appeared.

The slip of paper from Holly, as secretary to Anton Wagner, inviting Thornton to Breconfield Studios to interview the great man duly arrived, so this was it. He was for the nonce the worldwide famous freelance journalist W. Simon Beale and in this guise was either going to get somewhere this time around or once more come away empty handed. If the latter proved to be the case he decided he would no longer pursue the matter. It had obviously become something of an obsession and obsessions can turn out to be highly dangerous phenomena especially when mixing with the likes of Luca Biancchi and no doubt more of his ilk. Apart from the fairly recent episode in the airport loo he'd experienced a brush with the Mafia in Italy once before, both in Milan and Rome and it was, to put it rather mildly, a pretty hair raising experience never to be repeated if it could be helped.

As a high flying freelance journalist he could hardly take the municipal bus to the studios or join another bunch of film crazy tourists guided by the redoubtable Marguerite who would more than likely be doubly vigilant after his previous escapade and would be seriously suspicious of his alias. No, to arrive in style he needed a car so there was only one thing for it, a visit to Harold Norris. He hadn't seen Harold for some time and Reg had recently brought him to mind anyway so he could kill two birds by making it both a business and a social call.

Thornton had long since given up any ideas of actually owning a car in London. He had decided it was not only extremely expensive both in running costs and insurance that went up in leaps and bounds every year, but there was the constant danger of having it stolen, wantonly vandalised, or broken into. Congestion was a nightmare and it was altogether a bloody great nuisance and bound to get worse as more and more vehicles hit the road and Harold Norris usually had a good selection of cars to choose from.

Thornton found him on the lot lovingly polishing the bonnet of a maroon Rover 3000 and that could very well be the car he needed to create an impression; huge, very butch, more like a tank, automatic drive and indicating money, considering the amount of petrol all that horse power was going to go through. Every penny would be worth it though if only he could get this whole affair out of his mind before it drove him out of his mind.

Harold gave no indication he was aware of Thornton's appearance. Even though he hadn't seen him for some time he just went on polishing the car's bonnet as though the newcomer wasn't even there; but that was Harold's way. He took in everything but pretended to notice nothing which is why Reg's spies and those of H.M. Revenue and Customs could never catch him out at anything even the slightest bit dodgy, and both sides were fully aware of the game being played; cat and mouse, hide and seek, sheriff's posse and outlaws.

'So what can I do for you this time, Thornton?' He asked without even turning around.

'How's business, Harold?'

'Business is good, yes, very good on my life, couldn't be better. You might say it's taken an up-turn, a refreshing change you might say, so just tell me what you want and, more importantly, how you are going to pay for it.'

'Nothing to worry about, Harold. Bank balance is extremely healthy at the moment and yes, I know, that makes a refreshing change as well. I'll write you out a cheque.'

'Cheques have been known to come from Malaysia and be made of a high grade rubber.'

'Do you want to see my bank statement? All right, you distrustful person, I'll cash a cheque and give you the cash. How does that suit you?'

'That suits me fine. Will you want a receipt?'

'Not if you give me a good deal.'

'Without a receipt, can do. No value added tax, know what I mean?' He tapped the side of his nose. 'What kind of car is it you want this time?'

'The one you're working on.'

'You have ideas above your station, Thornton, always have had. You think this car's going to cost peanuts?'

'No, but it is for a special reason...'

'Not a dangerous one I hope. No chance of any damage.'

'None whatsoever. Anyway, you're insured and as a valued customer I know you'll give me that nice discount just mentioned and if I really like the car I might buy it on the never never,' he teased.

Harold snorted, shook his head and, duster in one hand, Simonize can in the other, walked away. 'Come into the office and let's do the paperwork.'

Behind Harold's back Thornton gave the car's bonnet a couple of friendly taps and hastily rubbed off the finger marks with the sleeve of his jacket before quickly following.

'I hope you're not going to offer me a cup of tea while we're about it.'

'Never touch the stuff. What? All that tannin or whatever? Sheer poison. Rots the guts, strips the enamel off your gnashers. Mark my words, Thornton, stay well clear of it.'

Thornton loved the car, revelled in it in fact, though it didn't change his mind about actually owning one again. As an automatic it virtually drove itself. The engine was so silent he sometimes wondered if it was still turning. The day was balmy, just a few fleecy clouds scudding along, he could have wished the car was an open top but there you are, you can't have everything as the actress said and a saloon was probably more indicative of apposite status. He revelled in the capacious comfy leather seat, turned on the radio and admired the rich walnut dashboard.

He reached the studios, swung off the public highway and stopped in front of the barrier. The gate-man looked up from reading his paper and his eyes narrowed obviously with some suspicion as he took in the visitor. Thornton bright and breezy waved his piece of paper in Max's face.

'Appointment with Mister Wagner,' he said with a smile.

'Name?'

'Simon Beale.'

The man's eyes narrowed even further but he looked at his clipboard, made a tick and, with no further ado and without looking at the visitor again, raised the barrier and went back to his paper.

'Visitor parking behind B Block,' he growled and Thornton drove through thinking the man made it sound like a POW camp and he should be playing an SS officer in a wartime escape movie.

He had time before the appointment Holly had in fact dutifully arranged to quickly look up Ernest J. to find out if there had been any developments his end and so made his way back to the first office block.

Taking a quick look around in case he was being observed, and seeing no one who might be suspicious and who would ask him what he was doing, he opened the glass door and entered the corridor, made his way to the stairs, quickly climbed to the first floor and walked down the passage. The place appeared deserted. He thought he remembered which office on the left Ernest J. had been using and sure enough he found it with door wide open, only the room was empty. Obviously Ernest was where he should be, on the floor. If someone did question

Thornton's being there he could always make the excuse that he was looking for Wagner's office and got lost.

Disappointed in not seeing Ernest and not having the time to hang around, he was about to turn away when he noticed the pile of manuscript paper next to the typewriter and thought, curiosity killing the cat notwithstanding, that he would take a peek and see for himself what Ernest's writing was really like. Maybe Joachim had been a little too harsh in his criticism. On the other hand maybe not.

The manuscript was indeed Ernest's. The front page read

Hour of Agony
(Wokring Title)
A SCREENPLAY
By
ERNEST J. BLOOMBERG.

The script even boasted a copyright symbol. © He turned to page one.

(1) FADE IN ........................(1)
THEME MUSIC:   ROW ROW ROW YOUR BOAT, MERRILY DOWN THE STREAM, SUNG A CAPELLA, A MELANCHOLY SOUND.

CROSS FAED TO

"Wokring? Faed?" Whatever Ernest's writing was like he could do with a bit more practice typing wise.

(2) INT. KITCHEN. STUDIO. EST. SHOT. DAY. (2)
The room is squalid. There are dirty plates on the stained table; dirty dishes piled high in the sink. The windows are griny – (Thornton picked up a ballpoint and changed the N for an M)  - and it's obvious the place hasn't been cleaned for days if not weeks.

Cut to:

(3) M.C.U. ROBIN.  (3)

ROBIN, a good looking boy of about fifteen or sixteen is discovered seated at the table. He is dressed in school uniform and is studying a book. He closes it and is about to…

Thornton had taken a seat and been so engrossed in what he was reading, it would seem Ernest identified himself one hundred percent with the boy Robin, he didn't know anyone had entered the room until he heard the door close. He looked up from Ernest's misspelt masterpiece to see Max Dooley standing just inside the door and by the look on his face this spelt trouble. It was more than likely Thornton would now never know what the boy Robin was about to get up to.

'So, this is where you are, Mister Beale, Mister Snooper. I thought I knew your face. I had a suspicion you were up to no good. I wonder what it can be you're looking for.'

Thornton got up and raised two placating hands. The man was big, in fact he was enormous, not quite the size of a Sumo wrestler but in a fight his weight alone was distinctly to his advantage. Thornton noticed, belying his heavyweight appearance, he had rather delicate hands and small feet and, like so many of ample proportions he was no doubt pretty light and nimble on them. His eyes too were small made even smaller by his regarding the intruder with deep suspicion.

'Got me bang to rights, mate. Thornton made a pathetic boxing gesture with his right fist. I have to admit I was snooping. That's because I'm a friend of Mister Bloomberg's and I was interested in his new screenplay.' He indicated where it lay on the desk and took note at the same time of the heavy alabaster ashtray there, made even heavier by the addition of a carved eagle with claws and a mean looking beak. He leaned back, hands on the desktop either side of his buttocks. 'I had time before my appointment to look him up, Ernest I mean.'

'Friend?' Max laughed or made a noise that passed for a laugh. 'You're a friend of that little pansy?'

'Hey hey hey! That's a bit harsh isn't it?'

'If I ever get my hands on him, on his own where no one can interfere he'll wish he had never been born.'

'Oh? And why is that?'

'He ridiculed me. You know that? On the last picture he took the piss every time he saw me. Didn't matter who was around might hear. A right little smart arse isn't he? I couldn't get my hands on him then and I didn't like it and I said one day I would get back at him but he makes damn sure he keeps well out of my way or is always in company. He knows what's coming otherwise.'

'You're a big man, not an infant; couldn't you take a bit of ribbing from a kid? Who are you anyway?' as though he didn't know.

'You know who I am. I'm Max, Max Dooley. I was Cord Wainer's bodyguard. I was outside make-up the day he died and, even though no one accused me of failing in my duty, the studio kindly kept me on, gave me a job, made sure I was okay.'

Thornton thought about this for a moment. Something wasn't adding up here. The studio bosses would only have kept Max on if he was of use to them in some capacity other than a mere gate-man. Sympathy, consideration, generosity, these words were never in their vocabulary of the film world. Bodyguard? What else? Trouble shooter? What else? Hit man? What else? Obviously if the studio heads were cognizant of Cord's little peccadilloes and Max's involvement in them there was always the danger, now that the gravy train had rolled to a stop with the film star's death, Max could turn out to be a loose cannon. Much better to keep him close by, give him a job, pay him well over the odds and hope he doesn't get too greedy.

All this flashed across his mind but, 'Shouldn't you be on the gate?' He asked to gain a little time; but a little time from what? He didn't know. He just knew he was in a pickle and needed to find a way out of it.

'Mick, my sidekick's taken over, hasn't he?'

'Oh has he?'

'Yus. You don't think I'm the only one on the gate do you?'

'I suppose not. What else do you do for the studio? I mean, considering they're so kind to you.'

'None of your fucking business, mate!'

'Well actually I think it is, yes.'

'Is that right? And how do you make that out then?'

'You followed me here because you suspected I was snooping. Snooping to what purpose? What do you think I hoped to find? And now you're either going to march me to my car and see me off the premises or you're going to stand in front of that door and keep me here till you think of what to do with me. How will you explain my missing my appointment with Wagner when I don't turn up? That I didn't turn up at all?'

'No. That you're dead.'

There was another of those long silences that seemed to be forever plaguing the private investigator before he found his voice with, 'Well I never. I do believe you're not joking.' *Keep talking, Thornton, keep talking.* 'And how do you intend accomplishing that?'

'Easy. With this.' And, like a magician producing a rabbit from a shiny top hat or a pigeon from a silk handkerchief, his flick knife was suddenly in his hand and he was holding it out in Thornton's direction.

The P.I. being menaced had to admit he was not facing his latest contretemps without feeling an increased heartbeat and a decided cold snap in his lower regions and tension in the toes. For some reason, and at sight of the knife he knew why; Max really did mean business.

'Flick knives seem to be all the rage at the moment,' he casually offered, belying his beating heart and the tightness in his gut. 'Tell me why you want me dead.'

Though his intuition had already told him why, he thought he might as well get the answer from the horse's mouth as it were, then there would be no more doubting and his obsession would be over. Mind you, if the worst came to the worst, so might he be.

'To stop you snooping; what else?'

232

'Yes, but you still haven't told me what it is I'm trying to find.'

'The cove wot done in Preston, that's what you're hoping to find, Preston's killer!' His voice had risen almost to a shriek.

'Ye-es…And I do declare I have found him. Perhaps that is the very knife you used?'

'Maybe so, but knowing it won't do you any good because it stops right here.'

'Why did you do it, Max? Orders from above? From who?'

'That's none of your business Mister Snooper, none at all. I don't grass.' He made a couple of passes with the knife either preparatory Thornton surmised to the direct attack or just to show-off his expertise.

'Film making is a decidedly dodgy business, Max, don't you think? I know there have been murders in Hollywood, pretty ghastly ones at that, some of them, it would be entirely unnatural if there weren't, but it can't be too often murder is included in the making of a movie, or can it? What do you think?' He seemed to recall hearing about snuff movies but he'd rather not think about that.

What seemed to be idle chatter from Thornton might have put Max off his stroke but he was still very much on his guard as he tried to work out what the man might be playing at.

'Think of it, Max…' Still leaning back against the desk he groped behind him for the ashtray, hoping Max wouldn't notice. If Holly could save herself with a cona of boiling coffee he might at least stand something of a chance following her example with a heavy ashtray if it landed in the right place. It would be worth a try. Goodness only knows where Ernest got it as that large carved eagle made a very handy handle. Oh, it more then likely belonged to Joachim as this was his office. '…Was there ever a movie made without dire goings on?' Thornton continued, seemingly perfectly at ease. 'I don't mean trivial mishaps, you know, accidents that are bound to happen, but a thousand dramas and a thousand traumas: casting problems, stars throwing tantrums like five year olds, making impossible demands, writers and directors hired and fired, this person refusing to act with that person, jealousies, in-fighting, law suits flying in all directions, unions to keep pacified, super egos to mollycoddle, producers who think they know better than anybody else but in fact often know next to nothing, unhappy distributors. I suppose murder at some time or other could be a natural concomitant. Makes one wonder if it's all worthwhile, doesn't it? Until the final product if it turns out to be a winner. Take any film just as an example, any film at all. I was reading quite recently all about the making of *Breakfast at Tiffany's* and that movie went through all the trials and tribulations I've just mentioned. It was one of Hollywood's better products, won awards, but the man who started the ball rolling with the original book, Truman Capote, when asked what he thought of it, said it was crap, or words to that effect. And everyone concerned had all been through hell and high water in the making of it.'

Thornton wondered how long he could go on nattering or had Max already been put off balance? Not taking his intended victim by surprise and faced with this barrage of chat he seemed uncertain as to what to do. He suddenly frowned, obviously thinking hard, then he took a step forward, still menacing Thornton with the knife, the knife that Thornton now had no doubt killed Mel Preston.

'Did Preston kill Charmaine Carmichael?'

Max stopped. This was a new slant. He nodded.

'Why?'

'She learned a few things she shouldn't have learned and he caught her at it. That's what happens to nosey parkers.'

'And why did Preston have to die?'

'Same reason only more so. Because of what he knew he tried a spot of blackmail and the boys in charge weren't going to go along with that I can tell you.'

'No, I suppose not. Natural reaction, especially if he had something concrete to blackmail them with, which is why you were called in. What did he have on them, Max?'

'Don't ask.'

'But I am asking and as it looks as if I am going to die with the secret you might as well tell me.'

'More than my life's worth, mate. Preston tried to mix it with the Americans; I'm not so stupid as to try the same.'

'Seems to me this studio has been tied up one way or another with the Americans from the very beginning.'

'Dead to rights, mate. They reckon things are beginning to unravel and they've been leaning on Burrows, as if he didn't have enough troubles.'

'Such as what?'

'Well, for starters there's this little boy he's supposed not to have. Papers would have a field day with that if they knew, wouldn't they?'

'I wouldn't call it exactly a field day. After all it's not that uncommon is it?'

'Burrows would have seven pink kittens.'

'Now that *is* uncommon.'

'Especially as his mother was tucked away in an home to have him.'

'Yes.'

'It would be bad publicity if nothing else you got to admit; bad for the studio, bad for the film. A few people having their knuckles rapped. Nobody wants bad publicity, now do they? Know what I mean?'

'Oscar Wilde said the only bad publicity is no publicity.'

'Yeh, well he would, wouldn't he? And look wot happened to him. Bloody poofter.'

'That's great coming from you, considering your relationship with Mister Wainer.'

Max shrugged. 'Yeah, well that's something no one wants to talk about innit? Preston was a stupid git to think he could get away with it.'

'And you are stupid enough to think you can get away with this. You already have one murder on your hands.'

'I'm stupid am I? I'll...' It looked as though he was about to rush Thornton but again he stopped and the frown deepened even further. 'You're wired aren't you?'

Thornton said nothing merely smiled which goaded Max further. 'You bastard! You're wired! He gave vent to his feelings by calling Thornton every name he could think of which took quite a few seconds before he lurched forward and was only stopped when Thornton hurled the ashtray at him.

It missed.

Max had stepped back to one side to avoid it but the next second the door crashed open and Max went down, out for the count. He never knew what hit him and Thornton could hardly believe it. Standing in the doorway, grimacing and shaking his bruised knuckles, was William Harrowfield.

# Chapter Seventeen

'Are you wired?' William had picked up the ashtray and the fallen knife and handed them over, both of them being careful not to touch the knife's handle.

Thornton replaced the ashtray on the desk, closed the knife, wrapped it in his handkerchief, and shook his head in answer to William's question. He indicated the fallen Max. 'It would seem this one has also seen too many movies. How long have you been outside that door and just as important, why?' He slipped the knife in his jacket pocket.

'I saw you parking your car and followed you here.'

'Also, no doubt, to find out if I was snooping?'

'No, not really. I already knew that's what you would be doing. No, it was because I wanted to talk to you, to tell you that I never killed anyone. This…' He touched the still recumbent Max with his shoe '…has saved me the trouble.'

'Tell me, William…I may call you William?'

William nodded.

'There are a number of questions that puzzle me. Firstly, how did you know who I am?'

There was a groan and a stirring from the body on the floor.

'What do we do about him?' William asked.

'We don't do anything. Leave him where he is. If the big boys aren't as mad as rattlesnakes after this and if he doesn't end up as number five, callous as that might sound, he's going to have to face a murder charge. He might prefer prison to the first option though even locked up he wouldn't necessarily be safe. Either way I don't think we need worry too much about him.'

'Let's get out of here then before he really comes round.'

'First just answer my question. How did you know who I am?'

'Well, if you really want to know, your little information gatherer is hardly the most discreet person in the world, though he would make a first class witness. His description of you was bang on the nail.'

'That's because he's a born writer.'

'Really? Granddad had already told me about you going round to the pub asking questions and their first time I saw the boy detective was when he came and sat at my table when there were twenty others free and immediately started in on the questioning. I saw you park and would have followed you here straight away when I saw him follow you – he nudged the still recumbent Max with his shoe - but unfortunately a mate stopped to ask me something and it looks like two seconds later would have been too late.'

'Thanks. One second later would have been too late.'

They didn't bother to shut the door as they left.

'Thornton, not you again!' Reg gave a theatrical sigh. 'This is getting to be too much of a good thing if you ask me. People will start to talk. What is it now?'

Thornton took the chair opposite him, smiled and placed the flick-knife still wrapped in his handkerchief on the desk. Reg eyed it with some suspicion before looking back at his visitor.

'Well?'

'Your informant is about to make you hero of the hour, Reg. If this doesn't get you a gold star and send you to the head of the class nothing ever will. Careful how you open that, it's got a murderer's dabs all over it, possibly some blood stains tucked away as well.'

'Thornton, I am seriously of the opinion that this private eye thing has gone to your head. Nevertheless…' He carefully un-folded the handkerchief and sat looking at the knife. 'This is to do with Breconfield is it?'

'It is. Preston's murder in fact, the weapon that did him in. You can pass the info along to whichever division is handling it. Preston was killed by a man named Max Dooley. He was once Cord Wainer's bodyguard and since that one's unfortunate death has been employed in a position of security by the studio. I have no doubt getting rid of Preston was on orders from above. I know it in fact because Max informed me that Preston, rather stupidly when you come to think of it, was trying it on with a spot of blackmail which virtually sealed his death warrant.'

'And just how did you manage to recover this?' He waved a hand over the knife still lying on his desk.

'Well, if you really want to know…'

'I do. Oh yes I most certainly do.'

'I just happened to be in the studios…'

'Happened?'

'Happened, and Max decided to end my short and happy life with that.' He nodded towards the knife. 'Because he said I was snooping which of course I was. What else is a private eye paid to do? But you know who, up above the clouds, evidently doesn't want me for a sunbeam, not just yet.'

Reg shook his head in sadness. There was no hope for the man. As a good non-practising protestant himself he didn't believe religion was ever a subject for jocularity. He wasn't going to labour the point or get into an argument about it because religious arguments inevitably proved to be futile so he decided to continue.

'But why kill you? Killing you would appear to be a bit extreme wouldn't it?'

'He thought I might have discovered something I did'na

oughter. I hadn't in fact but he gave himself away and having done that had no alternative but to try and silence me for good. Got the picture?'

Reg nodded and reached for the knife to be stopped by a stentorian 'NO!' from Thornton which made him visibly start.

'Use my handkerchief until you can slip it into one of your little plastic bags.' He looked at his watch and got up to go. 'If I remember I'll call back for it some other time, the handkerchief I mean.'

'Hello, mum. Hello, dad.'

He had wiped his feet on the sisal mat that had "Welcome" dyed in it and stood there grinning from ear to ear as, totally speechless and with hearts thumping and trembling hands, they faced him standing at the open front door. He hadn't told them he was coming, knowing he would find them in and wanting it to be a surprise. They were hardly able to believe it was true, and soon came the hugs, even from Warren, the most undemonstrative of men, and the tears started to flow from all three.

A minute or so later they were seated still speechless in the front room. It was Eileen who found her voice first.

'Well…' was all she could say: and then, after a while, 'I'll make the tea. It will only take a minute. Kettle's already boiled.' And she hoisted herself out of her chair and waddled off to the kitchen to do that, leaving William alone with his foster dad who didn't know what to say either but kept looking at William as if he were a mirage or a dream who would disappear at any moment. He finally broke the silence.

'Well, son…'

'Dad?'

'It's been a long time.' His voice was hoarse with emotion and he had to cough to open up his throat.

'Yes, it has. I'm sorry.' He had left the house as a boy and now he had returned as a young man.

'You'll tell us all about it then.'

'Of course.'

'Wait till mother gets back then so we can both hear it.'

William smiled and nodded.

In the kitchen, Eileen, her hand on the kettle, hadn't even turned on the gas as she stood there in wonderment at the miracle, because that was what it was, a miracle. Eventually she pulled herself together, wiped an eye with the back of her hand and lit the gas.

'I must say you do look well.'

'I feel well.'

'Grown a bit.'

William couldn't help but smile.

'Working then?' Warren asked.

'Oh yes. I'm a qualified electrician, dad.'

'Well I never. Well I never, wait till mother hears that. An electrician on my word. So you've got yourself a good steady job then.'

'At Breconfield Studios.'

'Where would that be then?'

'It's a film studio in Bucks.'

'Oh, yes? Oh, wait a minute! Didn't I read in the papers there was a bit of a to-do there? A couple of nasty goings-on? It was on the television news as well I seem to recall.'

'That's right. A young secretary was murdered and a film producer.'

'Ah, here's mother with the tea.' He was obviously relieved to change the subject. He would need to think about William working in that kind of an environment, mixing with who knows what sort of people.

Eileen waddled back with a mug in each hand. Cups and saucers were for best, mugs were good enough for family. William didn't have to ask where Warren's was. He was familiar from childhood with a routine that never changed. She handed him his mug, smoothed her skirt beneath her with her free hand and sat.

'Just as you like it', she said, nodding towards the mug in his hand, 'two sugars and lots of milk, nursery tea we used to call it.' There was another short silence before she continued. 'I don't suppose you will be staying long then.'

'Mother...'

'No. 'Fraid not.' He smiled apologetically. 'I have to be back at work so it will be only for tonight, if you'll have me.'

'If we'll have you! Will you just listen to the lad? How could you say such a thing? As if we wouldn't.'

'Next time I promise to stay longer.'

William put down his mug on the little occasional table beside his chair, there was a coaster already in place, and got up. 'Excuse me. I left my case in the hall and I've got some presents for you.' He started to leave the room.

'Presents,' Warren said, 'well there's a surprise.'

'Oh, you shouldn't have,' Eileen added, 'there was no need.'

They waited patiently, Eileen taking a sip of her tea before putting down the mug on her occasional table, until William returned with a brightly wrapped parcel in each hand. He gave the first to Eileen and the second to Warren, went back to his seat and, smiling in anticipation, picked up his mug and took a sip of his nursery tea.

'Do we open them now?' Eileen asked. She sat with the parcel on her lap and both hands flat on top of it.

'Of course you do.' William laughed. 'Are you thinking of waiting till Christmas? Christmas is a long way off, mum, dad? Go on, open them.'

With great care they unwrapped their presents as William sat watching. Eileen's was the first to be unwrapped. She looked at the inner wrapping of protective cellophane and then looked at William.

'It's a table setting,' he said. 'Posh table cloth and napkins for when you have visitors and want to serve a dainty tea to impress or put it on the table for Christmas dinner maybe.'

'So it is, so it is.' She stroked the cellophane. 'I'll leave it like this till I want to use it. Thank you, William.'

'I got it from Debenham's in Oxford Street.'

'That was very thoughtful of you.' She started to fold the wrapping paper. There was a bag hanging behind the kitchen door in which paper and string were kept for future use.

William turned his attention to Warren who, his fingers no longer dexterous, was just producing his present from its wrapping.

'It's a genuine Fair Isle sweater, dad. Got it at the Scotch Shop so it has to be genuine. Pure Harris wool that is, comes from the Outer Hebrides so I am informed. Will help keep you nice and snug that will come the winter.'

'Thank you, William. But you shouldn't have spent your hard earned money on us.'

'Who would you like me to spend it on then? I owe you an awful lot, don't you think?'

'No, son.'

'You don't owe us a thing. We were well paid by the happiness you brought us when you were a child.' To be thoroughly Victorian it must be stated that at this point she smiled through her tears.

William could feel a lump in his throat and his own tears threatening and he wondered if this was some kind of implied criticism. No, in their eyes he could do little wrong. He knew he had hurt them badly by his disappearance and he knew they were dying to find out what it was all about. Should he take it slowly? Or should he start right in with explanations? He decided the latter course of action would be best; get it out of the way.

'I know you feel I behaved very badly and you are quite right to feel that way. I know I hurt you which was hardly the thanks you deserved after all you had done for me...' He saw Warren about to break in and raised his hand to stop him '... but I feel I ought now to try to.... to try and give you some idea of why it happened. You might find it difficult to understand but I will try.'

'You might have...'

'Yes, dad, I'm way ahead of you there. I might have, I could have, I should have but the fact is I didn't and nothing now can change that. I could have written, I could have telephoned, all these years and I was silent, not even greetings at Christmas when it would have been so easy to have sent a card, and now I regret that bitterly.' Again he had to raise his hand to stop Warren. 'Please believe me, I am not ungrateful for the loving home you gave me for so many years, I love you both and you are my family, but I… I…' He had to stop to control himself. Neither Warren nor Eileen moved.

William knew this was going to be an emotional moment but, having recovered somewhat, he carried on. 'I had to find out who I really am.' He looked hopefully from one to the other but their faces told him nothing. 'Can you understand that? Somewhere… somewhere…' He was searching for words now, the right way to put this. As he travelled down to them he had gone over a thousand times in his mind exactly what he was going to say but face to face it wasn't that easy. They had been hurt enough and he didn't want to hurt them anymore.

'Go ahead, son.' It was Warren who this time managed to interrupt without being stopped. 'Say what you want to say. We're listening. Aren't we, mother?'

Eileen nodded. Her hands were still flat on top of her present.

'You were… are… my foster parents and I could never have wished for better. My first experience as you know was pretty dreadful and I don't think I will ever forget it. It will be with me for life.' He shrugged and stopped, gathering thoughts as to what to say next. 'Believe me, mum, dad, you did nothing wrong except maybe you were too easy, too soft with me, I don't know, but there came a time just after I left school I suppose it was that I wanted, needed to find my real family, I mean my blood family. Can you understand that? It was such an urgent need like there was a great big hole in my life somewhere and it needed to be filled and I thought if I told you how I felt you would try and talk me out of it, save me a big disappointment perhaps or something like that. I'd saved up quite a bit from pocket money and that and my newspaper round and to my shame I sneaked away like a thief in the night.' He shook his head, thinking about it. 'Why didn't I leave a note even? Instead I've left you all these years wondering but I wanted to find my blood mother most of all. I wanted to see her, to be with her, to find out what she was like, to find out my background, why I had to be adopted.'

'And did you?' It was from Eileen this time.

William sighed and nodded his head. 'Yes, I found out.'

'And?'

'What did you find?'

It took a moment for him to gather his thoughts again before he continued. 'My mother is dead. She died some time ago, quite a while ago. Her name was Beryl Harrowfield and she was still Harrowfield when she died. She died in an institution and it was, through no fault of my own but as a result, it was me who put her there. No, that doesn't make sense. It was a man who had her put there, put her up the spout and left her and I was the result.'

'And your father?'

'What about him?'

'Did you find out who he is?'

'I did and, if you don't mind, let's just leave it at that.'

'But all this time,' it was Warren again, 'how did you live? Where did you live? Was there someone looked after you while you were being an apprentice?'

'Yes, my grandfather, Jimmy Harrowfield. He's a wonderful man. I hope one day you might meet him. I know you'll like him and I know he will like you. Sometimes he tried to talk me into getting in touch with you but for some reason I find hard to fathom, shame maybe for the way I had acted, I just couldn't bring myself to do it. Maybe I realised just how badly I had behaved. It wasn't that I didn't want to really, or that I ever stopped thinking of you but somehow... somehow... Ah well.' He managed another smile, if somewhat rueful. 'Here I am, the prodigal son, and I won't neglect you so much from now on in.'

245

'A short while back a very nice gentleman came looking for you.'

'Yes, Thornton King, and he found me which is why I am here, well, one of the reasons anyway. Am I still in my old room?'

'Of course you are. Its waiting for you, exactly as you left it.'

'Except of course she goes in there to clean it all the time, make sure everything's spick and span.' Warren smiled at his wife.

'Waiting for me to come back.'

'Waiting for you to come back.'

In the hall William picked up his suitcase and mounted the narrow carpeted stairs.

His room was as he had left it all those years before. He stood for a while taking it all in, everything so familiar and yet somehow belonging to a long lost past. It was almost as though he had walked into a film set, props carefully placed, the souvenirs of bygone years. He flopped onto the bed, lay back, gazing at the model Spitfire hanging from the ceiling, it had lost its propeller and one wing looked as though it might fall off at any moment, if there was any glue he would fix it, and within minutes he was asleep. If he had dreams, he would not remember his dreams when he woke up.

# Chapter Eighteen

Sunday had come around again and, after a breakfast of poached eggs on toast, the yolks covered with freshly ground black pepper, Thornton put the mill aside and in reflective mood went over the recent events.

He was just pleased that the puzzle had been solved. He supposed being threatened with death by two different flick knives in two different cities might be all in a private investigator's work but he sincerely hoped it would never happen again. He didn't know if his nerves could stand it. Maybe he should change his occupation. There must be something he could do that would (a) bring in a steady income and (b) not require him to put his life on the line. In fact when he first decided to be a private eye he never thought for a moment it would turn out to be so dangerous. It would be just run of the mill every day problems to solve though he supposed even a domestic could turn, and has been known only too frequently to turn decidedly nasty.

He decided he would have a lazy morning and then maybe pop into *The Green Man* for a spot of lunch. Yes, he thought, an excellent idea. He wanted to see Jimmy Harrowfield's face when he told him how he had discovered his grandson or, rather the other way around, how William had discovered him and, thanks to Ernest J. just as well that he did.

What *should* he say to Mister Bloomberg for giving the game away? He could call him up and pretend to give him a bollocking but it would be only pretence. After all, if it hadn't been for him, he, Thornton, might not be sitting where he was right at this moment but could be stone cold dead and stiff on a slab. He couldn't help wondering why Ernest had done it but no answer came to mind. The thought that the lad might have fallen in love being the reason for the indiscretion couldn't have been further from his calculations.

T he object of his musing meanwhile was sitting in his bedroom in Gunnersbury, typewriter clattering away as he imagined the object of his yearnings and himself in various situations. *Hour of Agony* was taking on a whole new dimension. He was quite sure that, if Caswell was still around and he showed it to him now, he would receive unstinted praise. Pausing in his typing, visions of the *Venice Film Festival* and *Golden Lions* possibly even Hollywood and the *Oscars* rose in his imagination before he resumed his writing. He wondered if he should give up for a while and have a quick session with the enlarger but decided his muse was well and truly with him and he should stick with her in case she deserted him. Though, with William in mind, he couldn't really envisage that happening. This thing was red-hot. His fingers just couldn't keep up with his inspiration as the mistakes in his typing witnessed. Did someone once not say genius is ten percent inspiration, ninety percent perspiration? Words to that effect anyway.

T hornton pushed open the door and strolled into *The Green Man.* On this occasion opening time was well past, there was a constant babble of voices, laughter, clouds of cigarette smoke, a game of darts in progress, and Reen at the bar was being rushed off her feet. The pot boy, almost into his eightieth year, was staggering from table to table collecting empties and dirty glasses. The Guv' was evidently around at the public and, no surprise to Thornton, there was a new barman this side – William Harrowfield who caught Thornton's eye and broke into a broad smile. Reen too, in the midst of serving a customer, saw him and nodded a greeting as he walked up to the bar and stood in a space just vacated.

'Hello, Thornton. This is a surprise. I'll be with you in a moment. Just let me finish what I'm doing.' William continued serving and only returned to Thornton once he had rung up the money in the old-fashioned cash register. 'Now, what can I get you?'

'A pint of half and half,' Reen said, grinning.

'Not today, Reen. Sundays I always go for the hard stuff.' He eyed the optics and pointed. 'I'll have a *Haig*.'

'*Haig* coming up.' William collected a glass and turned away to hold it under the optic for the measure of whisky. He brought it back and placed it on the bar in front of Thornton. 'Ice?' He reached for the small plastic and glass imitation barrel holding the ice.

Thornton shook his head.

'Hold on a moment, Thornton,' William said, 'while I tend to this customer.'

Thornton took his first sip of whisky and looked around the bar, wondering if there was anyone he might know. William returned.

'Actually,' Thornton said as he tried to hand over payment for the whisky which William refused to take, 'I was hoping for a bite to eat. Is that possible?'

'Nope, 'fraid not. We don't serve meals on a Sunday. Cook's not in. Hang on.' And he was off serving again. Thornton waited for him to come back.

'You were saying.'

'Oh, yes. Can offer you a nice arrowroot biscuit or a lump of good old Danish Blue if that takes your fancy. If it quietens down a bit, which I somehow doubt, I might be able to slip away for a minute and make you a ham sandwich. Hang on! I've got an idea. Why don't you stick around till closing time and you can have lunch with us upstairs? It'll just be cold meat and salad.'

'No, I don't want to put you to any trouble.'

'Hey! No trouble at all, and I'm sure Jimmy will be pleased to see you. Excuse me.' He dashed off to serve once more.

Thornton saw a couple getting up from a table to leave and he moved in quickly, seating himself on the settle a second before the other seats were taken. This created a problem. One scotch was not going to last till closing time but, if he got up for a renewal, he was sure to lose his seat and did he really feel like standing for the next hour and a bit? Maybe he should just sit tight. His tummy was beginning to rumble quite alarmingly and the thought of cold meat and salad was certainly appealing. There was nothing to assuage hunger back at the flat because he hadn't got around to doing a shop; the breakfast eggs were the last and, anyway, it would be good to talk to Jimmy again.

He was still debating with himself as to what to do when he noticed someone across the crowded bar staring at him; a man every inch as big as Max Dooley who, having got his attention, suddenly winked at him and Thornton's blood ran cold. Even though he thought he knew the man he couldn't think where from and it could have been the studios. Was this Max's sidekick at the studio gates and was he just as dangerous? Were they still intent on getting rid of him? Couldn't do much in a crowded bar but he could be followed on leaving. Good grief! The giant winked with the other eye and was now advancing on him. This wasn't a pick-up was it? Couldn't be; it wasn't that kind of pub but then these days you never could tell. There was still a spare seat at the table next to Thornton and the stranger was obviously heading for it.

With a broad smile the man placed his half empty pint mug on the table and his arse on the settle and said, 'Well, Mister King, fancy seeing you here an' all.'

'Do I know you?' A slightly startled Thornton asked.

'Course you do, course you do. You don't remember?'

Thornton shook his head. 'I'm afraid not. Sorry.'

'That's okay.' The man dropped his voice to a conspiratorial whisper which was actually loud enough to carry to a couple of tables away. 'Mickey Flynn,' he said, holding out an enormous hairy-knuckled paw which, when Thornton took it, completely engulfed his own hand but strangely, despite the firmness of the stranger's grip was also extremely gentle. Thornton eventually managed to retrieve his hand but still gave no sign of recognition. The man heaved a sigh, picked up his mug, and took a long draught that reduced the level in it to a quarter, after which he belched as loudly as his whisper and, dropping his voice even further and with another wink, if he winked much more he would develop a permanent tic, elbowed Thornton, friendly fashion in the ribs. It hurt.

'The Countess Cinelli,' he said, opening both eyes very wide as opposed to the wink. 'You know, I was her bodyguard when she was in London, the day she… you know…' He didn't actually wink again but he did look very serious.

'Oh, yes! Sorry Nicky…'

'Mickey…'

'Mickey, of course. Mickey. Sorry. I thought I knew you, knew the face that is, but I couldn't place you. Well, well. How have you been keeping?' Thornton's feelings of relief were palpable.

'Getting along, you know, getting along. How is the Countess? Seen her lately?'

'Yes, as a matter of fact. I was in Rome just recently. She's fine, just fine. As sprightly as ever.'

'I'm glad to hear it. Great lady. I'd have felt really bad you know if anything had happened to her but a man has to do what a man has to do…particularly to get him out of the shit, know what I mean?'

By this time the surrounding tables were all ears trying to pick up the dialogue above the general hubbub. Thornton looked around and immediately all the engrossed faces turned away.

'Sorry I had to do what I had to do, Thornton, but, well, you now how it is...'

'Sure. The gee-gees and the doggies made you do it.'

'Yeh, I guess you could say that.'

'I've just said it.'

'And if it hadn't been for Miss Day...' Mickey heaved a sigh and polished off his beer. 'How is Miss Day?'

'In top form.'

'Yes. I'm not surprised. Wonderful woman... No doubt about it, a wonderful woman.' There was a moment before he indicated Thornton's glass. 'Want another?'

'Let me.'

'No no, I hinsist.' He was already on his feet. 'Scotch was it?'

'It was.'

Mickey, glasses in hand, made his tortuous way to the bar leaving Thornton in deep thought. He had more than likely in discussions with Holly exhausted mutual acquaintances but there was always an outside chance it wasn't quite so, birds of a feather and all that, and maybe he would take a long shot so, when Mickey returned with the drinks and took his seat, he quite casually said, 'And how is Max?'

'Dooley you mean?'

Thornton nodded, lifted his glass. 'Cheers!'

'Cheers. Oh Max is fine. Crafty bugger. Living it up in sunny Spain last I heard.'

'Costa del Sol?'

'Costa da Packet.'

'Good for him.'

'Yes, lucky bastard, but then he can afford it, can't he?'

'Can he? How come?'

'Got well paid for what he did, didn't he?'

'Is that a fact?'

'Well, got to hand it to him, Mister King...'

'Thornton.'

'Thornton. It was high time he had a spot of real good luck come his way. When he was a kid his old man used to beat him rotten, not just with the belt but the buckle of the belt, a solid mass of bruises he was, and his old woman had religion till it was coming out her ears. It's no wonder he turned out the way he is.'

"Yes," Thornton thought, "there really is more than one side to every question."

'And what was it he did? To be well paid for it?'

But Mickey was not going to answer that; just tapped the side of his nose and gave Thornton another wink. Not to worry, it was another piece of information he could pass on to Reg Venables stacking up future favours. Reg, having been brought to mind, he said, 'Had any dealings with Reg Venables recently?'

'Reg Venables?' Mickey chuckled. 'He still a copper then? Thought he would have retired by now. Nah, haven't seen him for months.'

'Been on the straight and narrow have you?'

'Nah, just haven't been nabbed.' And Mickey laughed so loud and so long he brought the pub to a virtual standstill.

T he bar had been cleared, got ready for the evening opening and the doors locked. Reen had tottered home on weary legs and high heels to have a quick bite and put her feet up, she lived only a short distance away, so there was just the three of them. It might have been cold meat and salad but there was an assortment of meats: honey cured ham, ox tongue, cold chicken, fromage de tête. The English however have never really gone into salads in a big way and most times a salad means simply lettuce and tomato, maybe a few spring onions thrown in. Biscuits and cheese, the inevitable *Danish Blue* followed, and the meal, washed down as it was with a most potable Australian *Chardonnay*, was certainly enough to allay Thornton's tummy rumbles.

'Thornton', Jimmy cleared his throat. 'I apologise for being so devious on your last visit but I'm sure you will understand why.' He looked with such affection across the table at his grandson that there were immediate smiles all round. 'That really was an amazing sketch you had done considering it was an advance on a childhood photograph. Gave me quite a turn when you showed it me. Whoever did it, the man is a flaming genius. Of course I knew William was working at Breconfield and I have to admit I was scared for him. I didn't know what he was up to, how he would approach or react to his father, what was on his mind or what his intentions were. And, don't forget, while he was at the studio there had been two murders… That poor girl.' He stopped and shook his head. Thornton noticed there was no mention of "poor Mel." 'So, when you came here making enquiries about him, all I could do was plead ignorance. "No, never seen him before." Is that what I said? The problem is even now I don't know what's really on his mind.'

'You're still at the studios?' Thornton turned to face the younger Harrowfield.

William nodded as he buttered a biscuit. 'Filling in here at the pub is part time, weekends like to help out.'

'I take it, while you were doing your apprenticeship this is where you were living and Jimmy was…' He glanced in Jimmy's direction, 'I don't like the word keeping, should I say, sponsoring you?'

William nodded again. His mouth was full of cheese and biscuit. Obviously *Danish Blue* was a great favourite. He had only toyed with the meat and salad. 'The Petersons send you their best wishes by the way,' he finally said, having swallowed his mouthful and set to buttering another biscuit.

'Thornton, don't stand on ceremony. If you would like some more please help yourself.' Jimmy moved the plate of meat closer to his guest.

'Thank you, I'm fine for the moment.' He turned to William. 'I take it the Petersons are well?'

'They are.'

'Nice people,' Thornton said, 'such very nice people.'

'You don't have to tell me. Couldn't ask for better. I'm hoping they'll meet up with granddad soon. You'll like them, granpops, you really will.'

254

'I'm sure I shall. Thornton...' He was pouring Thornton another glass of wine, 'I was really very sorry to read about Caswell. Have you any idea what happened there? Sometimes I get the feeling there's a real jinx on that place. What was Caswell doing in Rome anyway? He was supposed to be working on the picture wasn't he? As you see, I do keep up with what's going on, well as much as I can. I don't know why. Nostalgia maybe. It's nothing to do with me anymore, hasn't been for a long time. Though I suppose now that William...' He trailed off once again.

'Caswell was murdered.'

'You don't tell me. Is that so? From what I heard he was pissed out of his mind, fell in the river and drowned.'

'No, that's what was put about but I can tell you he was definitely murdered and by his so-called friend, one Luca Biancchi. Ever heard of him?'

'Can't say that I have, no.' He toyed with the stem of his wine glass. 'Should I have done?'

'Not really. I believe he was Mafia. I also believe... well...'

'Go on, what were you going to say?'

'I believe someone in the studio ordered Joachim's killing.'

'Why?'

'Because he was about to make waves.'

'How? In what way?'

'He believed the film companies treated him very badly.'

'That's hardly either new or surprising. But how did they treat him, badly? Or shouldn't I ask?'

'Well, according to his contract, he should have been paid royalties for the television series he wrote for *Full Throttle* but in all these years he never received a penny; not a groat, not a rouble, not a cent, not a pfennig, not a mark, not a schilling, a lira, a yen, a drachma, a dinar, a peso, a krone, a rupee, a rand or a single solitary sou.'

'I presume by listing the various currencies you're telling me it has played all over the world.'

'It certainly has.'

'I watched *The Limey Gang are Here* when I was a kid,' William

255

said. 'Great stuff, loved it, couldn't wait for each episode. It's a hallmark of our generation.'

'Caswell told you all this did he?'

'Not only did he tell me, but he sent me a copy of his contract and I reckon he had a definite point. He was hoping I could recommend a lawyer who specialises in copyright who would take up his case for him but, alas, too late for that. By the time I got his letter he was already dead.'

'What happened to his killer? What's his name?'

'Luca Biancchi. He has also snuffed it.'

'Murdered?'

'I do believe so.'

'Good God! What is going on in that place?'

'There's more than one person would like an answer to that.'

Jimmy looked down at his glass as he toyed with it. 'This contract Caswell had, and I know something about contracts having virtually suffered a similar fate, who was it with?'

'It just says the producers.'

'No names?'

'Oh yes, of course, ah...' He stopped a moment to recollect. 'Ray... Ray... Timpson, that's it, Ray Timpson and Larry Grant.'

'Yes, I know them, though in the case of Timpson I should say I knew him. He's been dead almost seven years maybe even eight. Larry, I don't know what has happened to him, don't even know if he's still around in fact. Well, Caswell's dead so obviously no one is going to make waves.'

'Oh, yes, someone is. Me.'

Both Harrowfields stared at Thornton until finally Jimmy found his voice.

'You? Why?'

'You most probably don't know this but Caswell had a daughter.'

'I did know it. It was in his obituary.'

'Yes. Her name is Dora and she is handicapped from meningitis as a child. Joachim wanted that money for her, so that she could be looked after for the rest of her life. I would like to try and do it for him and for his ex-wife who I'm sure is finding it hard to cope.'

'She might have remarried,' William said.

'In which case my job will be even more difficult but I am sure not impossible, so in a way I hope not.'

'Hmn…' Jimmy was thinking. 'Well, you might very well stand a chance, Thornton.'

'Tell me how.'

'Again it's matter of international copyright. Who is supposed to be holding it at this moment?'

'*Centurion*, and they renewed it fairly recently.'

'Did they? Did they indeed? That's most interesting.'

'Why? Snap!' This was because William and Thornton asked the question simultaneously.

'Because, and I think I am right in this, the contract Caswell signed is no longer valid, hasn't been ever since the death of Ray Timpson. The original producers to whom he granted that copyright and *Full Throttle* in its original makeup are no longer, haven't been for some time and the copyright should have reverted to the writers. *Centurion* then has been selling a product it doesn't legally own. It's downright fraud in fact. Can you see why Caswell would have been a big fat fly in the ointment?' There was a moment's silence while Thornton digested this and then Jimmy continued. 'But you don't have to take my word for it. I can recommend a firm of lawyers who I am sure would be only too happy to take up the case.'

'No, leave the lawyers out of it. There simply isn't any money to start an action against a giant corporation like *Centurion*.'

'Yes, I'm sure that's what they rely on, and a couple of dozen high powered lawyers of their own both sides of the Atlantic to argue their way out of court or delay matters for so long their accusers grow tired of it all and give up or, like Caswell, die. Well, in this case, Thornton, you don't have to give up. If there's a fifty-one percent chance of winning this firm will take it up for you; no win, no fee. It won't cost apart from a small retainer.' Jimmy smiled and waited for Thornton's reaction.

'What's the name of this firm?'

*'Fletcher Bowman and Archer* of Lincoln's Inn.'

'Come again? You are kidding me of course.'

Jimmy chuckled. 'I know, it's quite outrageous really but a hundred to one chance it does happen. My dentists for example, are *Payne and Pullitt* and the lawyers believe it or not are Tom Fletcher, John Bowman and Jeremy Archer. Naturally they're always being ribbed, the usual one being have they hit the bull's-eye yet. Anyway, it won't do any harm to have a preliminary meeting with them, find out how the land lies and whether or not you have a chance and the best of luck to you. Have you had enough to eat?'

'An elephantine sufficiency thank you.'

# Chapter Nineteen

C *enturion's* London offices were located in Red Lion Square but Thornton didn't know with whom in the first instance he should make an appointment. Then he had his positively brilliant brainwave which to anybody else would have been perfectly obvious from the start. Holly could give him the information he needed. What was the point of having a mole burrowing away in the enemy camp if you didn't use her? She also gave him another piece of information to use as ammunition. It was being mooted in the studios that *The Limey Gang are Here* was about to be released on this new videotape.

So he discovered the person he needed to see was *Centurion's* formidable high powered lawyer by the name of Eileen Blenkinsop who seemingly nobody ever got to see or was even able to contact by telephone, being forever fobbed off with an excuse or a recorded message. Miss Blenkinsop obviously spoke only to those she wished to speak to and was therefore forever not available. There was however an intermediary, her assistant by the name of Sydney Holder, so it was he Thornton asked to speak to when the switchboard operator at *Centurion* after quite a delay eventually decided to answer his call.

'Centurion Films. Good afternoon, how may I help you?'

'I wish to speak to Mister Holder please.'

'Who shall I say is calling?'

'Thornton King.'

'Hold on please Mister King.'

Thornton held on. Eventually, after another long delay, the operator came back on the line.

'What did you wish to speak to Mister Holder about, sir?'

'I want to make an appointment to come in and see him.'

'Yes, but what is it you wish to see Mister Holder about, sir?'

'About a children's television series called *The Limey Gang are Here*.'

'In what connection do you wish…?'

Thornton lost it. 'Look! Will you or won't you put me through to Mister Holder?'

'Please don't shout at me, sir, I am only following instructions and doing my duty.'

'Get back to your Mister Holder please and tell him I will keep on trying until I do get to speak with him. Your switchboard will be red hot and my telephone bill will be astronomical but I don't care. Have you got that?'

'Hold the line, please, sir.' The voice was now very cold. It took a while but eventually Holder answered.

'Mister King?'

'Mister Holder. I presume it *is* Mister Holder I am speaking to.'

'It is. What can I do for you?'

'You can give me a day and time when you can see me in your office.'

'Oh. Is it… is it… what is it about? Is it terribly important?'

Thornton forbade saying he wouldn't be asking for an appointment if it wasn't important, instead of which he said, 'How about tomorrow morning, say eleven o'clock? How does that suit you?'

'Oh, no! Oh, dear me, no. I'm afraid I am completely booked up tomorrow. Yes, looking at my diary, hold on a moment, yes

I'm sorry but tomorrow is quite out of the question.'

'Very well, the day after. Same time. I look forward to seeing you then.'

'But… But…'

But Thornton had rung off.

T he day of the hoped for appointment, all spruced up and in his best bib and tucker and carrying a leather document case for effect, Thornton, determined to look as impressive as possible, duly called at Red Lion Square just before eleven o'clock. The girl behind the reception desk smiled a greeting.

'Good morning, sir. How may I help you?'

'I have an appointment with your Mister Holder.'

'Oh, I'm sorry, sir. Mister Holder isn't in today. He's off ill.'

'Oh dear. Not serious I hope.' The girl wondered why Thornton was smiling.

'A touch of the flu I'm told.'

'Never mind, I'll see Miss Blenkinsop then.'

'Very well, sir. Who shall I say it is?'

'Thornton King.'

He waited as the poor innocent, obviously not the girl he had previously spoken to on the phone and obviously not briefed, contacted the redoubtable Miss Blenkinsop while he fully expected an explosion at any second.

Eileen Blenkinsop eventually answered with a crisp bark. 'Yes?'

'There's a gentleman here to see you, Miss Blenkinsop, a Mister Thornton King.'

Did Thornton hear a gasp or an intake of breath at the other end? Maybe, maybe not, but he distinctly heard 'Oh!' After which there was a short delay before the disembodied voice continued with. 'Tell him to wait.'

'Miss Blenkinsop said for…'

'It's all right. I heard. Thank you.'

Thornton moved away from the reception desk to a black leather settee behind a long, glass-topped coffee table on which were a number of show biz magazines to keep him occupied while he waited and waiting he certainly had to do because it was almost twenty five minutes before the lift doors opened and an obviously extremely irate Eileen Blenkinsop appeared.

He put down the copy of *Variety* he was reading and looked up. But Miss Blenkinsop had arrived. She was much younger than he had expected as he got up to meet her. She was slim almost to the point of looking anorexic, her face which was hardly made up at all, a subtle touch of liner on the mouth, was grim, and the dress she wore was rather simple but obviously à la mode. A lady's gold watch adorned her left wrist. She advanced on Thornton but stopped before she could get close enough for a handshake.

'Well, Mister King… This is strictly not on you know. Not on at all. You come barging into this office without a by your leave…'

'If I may contradict you, Miss Blenkinsop, I didn't barge. In fact I never barge. I strolled in through that door as calm as you please.'

'Well now that you have strolled in as you put it what is it you want? I am an extremely busy woman you know.' She looked at her watch to make the point.

'Oh, yes I am well aware of that.'

'I beg your pardon?'

'I fully expect someone in your position to be an extremely busy person, which is why I hope I won't have to take up too much of your valuable time.'

'Well, you're taking up enough of it already so please just state your business and let's get this over and done with.' For emphases she looked at her wristwatch again as though she didn't know to the minute from the first examination what the time was.

'I wish to discuss *The Limey Gang are Here.*'

'I see. Well in that case I'm afraid you've wasted your time. As far as that series is concerned there can be absolutely nothing to discuss.'

'Oh, but I'm very much afraid there is.'

'Indeed? And what, if I may ask, is your connection? Are you a lawyer?'

'I'm a private investigator acting on behalf of someone who worked on the series.'

'I see.'

She suddenly noticed the receptionist was all ears so, instead of turning away to end the discussion, she hesitated. A good sign Thornton thought. 'Well we better have that meeting right now then and get it over and done with so come to the office.' With which she did turn away and made for the lift. Thornton followed.

The lift doors closed behind them and he was only too aware of her presence as they stood side by side both looking straight ahead. The lift doors opened at the third floor and they stepped out, Thornton dutifully following as they crossed a large open office with numerous cubicles in which bees were busy, busy, busy. He smiled at a couple in passing.

Blenkinsop's glassed-off, sound proof office with windows overlooking the square was in a far corner and, once inside, she closed the door, eliminating the clatter of typewriters and other office noises, seated herself behind her enormous executive desk and ordered Thornton to sit, pointing to a chair opposite, but he wasn't having it. Seated there he would have to face her from behind a pile of papers stacked high on her desk which would put him at a distinct disadvantage so he took a chair from the corner of the office and set it down where he could be on a level with her. Her eyes were narrowed almost to slits. He was obviously not going to be a pushover. He placed his document case on top of her pile of papers. She bridled visibly. There was a slight hiatus, each waiting for the other to start and then Thornton thought he had better get on with it before being accused once more of wasting the good lady's time.

'*The Limey Gang are Here...* I hear on the grapevine the series is about to be released on videotape.'

'Who told you that? Where did you get your information from? That isn't supposed to be public knowledge. It's not even in the trade press.'

'The good old grapevine. Can you stop rumours from spreading? Or maybe it isn't a rumour. You can put me right on the matter.' He was being rather pompous and he knew it. She thought, quite erroneously at this point, he was beginning to sound aggressive.

'Mister King! This is simply not on. I won't have it. You come into my office, in my opinion, itching for a fight…'

'On the contrary, Miss Blenkinsop, may I remind you I was invited into your office and a fight is the very last thing I want.'

'Look at the work I have…' She indicated the papers on her desk. 'A veritable mountain to get through. Do you honestly expect me to put all that aside because you bully me…?'

'Bully?'

'That's what I said. It's browbeating and tantamount to blackmail.'

'Bully, browbeat and blackmail, what alliteration.' Whoops! Said the wrong thing again. She was now almost white with rage.

'I think you had better leave, Mister King, right this minute. I do not have time to waste on jokers.'

'Why? I haven't said what I came to say.'

'I don't think I need or wish to hear it.'

'As a lawyer you should find it most interesting.'

This got to her. She looked at her watch again. 'Make it quick,' she snapped.

'The proposed videotape release of the series, who licensed it to the producing company?'

'We did of course, the corporation.'

'Of course. Then I think I ought to tell you I believe it to be a fraudulent act, totally illegal.'

For a long moment she stared at him and then broke into laughter. He waited for her to recover. After a while she pursed her lips, blew out hard and wiped an eye with a tissue she took from a box on the desk, gave her nostrils a quick wipe as well and discarded the tissue in the waste bin under her desk. She shook her head before she found herself able to speak. Thornton was happy to wait.

'Mister King, that is without any doubt the biggest load of rubbish. I think now I have heard everything. What on earth could have given you that totally preposterous idea?' She was still laughing slightly.

'Copyright.'

'What?' The laughter had disappeared.

'*Centurion* no longer holds the copyright and hasn't done for a number of years, ever since *Full Throttle* ceased to exist.'

'I said I thought I had heard everything but this simply gets better and better.' She leant back in her executive type swivel chair and clasped her hands behind her head, elbows out like a pair of wings. She obviously now felt totally secure. There wasn't even any need for her to give him the boot. In a few minutes he would simply run out of steam and slink off with his tail between his legs leaving her to get on with her busy busy day.

'Do carry on, Mister King. Elucidate. Put me in the picture. Give me the legal position. Tell me why we no longer hold the copyright. I'm all ears.'

'I have here...' he unzipped his document case... 'a copy of a writer's contract.'

'Are you a lawyer, Mister King?' At the mention of the word contract she had leaned forward again, no longer flying but elbows now on the desk, fingers steepled.

'No, but I am acting on behalf of one of the writers of the series, in fact the main writer who was also script editor, whose name is on every single script. I take it you know the name Joachim Caswell?'

'I do.' She raised an eyebrow. 'He's dead.'

'I should have said I am acting for Mister Caswell's heir.'

She said nothing; waited for him to continue.

'He had a daughter. She is now fifteen years old and handicapped. On her behalf I expect *Centurion* to pay a sum of money that will keep her for the rest of her life.'

'Really? And why should we do that?'

'Because in all the years since the series was made, *Centurion* has not paid Caswell a single penny in royalties and you owe him a not inconsiderable sum.'

'How do you make that out?'

Thornton had now removed from his document case a copy of Caswell's contract which he held out to her over the desk. She did not take it so he dropped it in front of her. It was a gesture almost of contempt and she did not like it. He was pleased. Once more he had got her rattled.

'If, and when you get around to reading that document, and I would advise you to do so, you will see it is made out between the producers of the series and the writer. The producers at the time were Ray Timpson and Larry Grant. Timpson died some years ago and the contract became no longer valid. The copyright returned to the writers. Is that not so? Do correct me if I am wrong.'

Still looking at him rather than at the papers in front of her she picked up the contract and only then transferred her gaze to it.

'Take particular note of clause five,' Thornton said. 'It couldn't be more straightforward. The company by not paying royalties due was in direct breach of contract and the death of Ray Timpson sealed it. *Centurion* has been trading illegally which is not good news for a major corporation wouldn't you say?'

'And I presume, if I should acquiesce to this, the other writers will come out of the woodwork with their begging bowls. What do I do about them?'

Thornton did not like that. Woodwork? Begging bowls? Is it begging to want what is owed you? It was his turn to narrow his eyes. His voice for the first time was hard and did hold a hint of menace.

'I hardly think what I am asking for can be described as begging. As for the other writers I have to admit here to being entirely selfish, having to leave them to their own devises. I am concerned only with Joachim Caswell's interest and believe me I intend to pursue the matter whether you like it or not.'

She looked up from the contract and smiled. 'Quite frankly, Mister King, I don't think you have a leg to stand on. If you don't believe me, go ahead and sue us.' With a gesture of disdain she pushed the contract to one side but Thornton noted she did not offer it back to him. He collected his case and got to his feet.

'I'll leave you to think things over, Miss Blenkinsop. You might like to discuss the matter with your high powered lawyers in Los Angeles before you come to any decision as to how to proceed. In the meantime here is my card for if and when you want to get in touch with me. So I'll bid you good-day.' He placed the card on the desk, she having no intention of taking it, and made for the door, opened it and turned back. 'I think I had better tell you that I am about to seek an injunction against the distribution of the videotape and there is one other thing you might care to consider. I don't think *Centurion* would appreciate the publicity when the world learns they are refusing to pay a handicapped child her just due, hmn?'

Again he turned as though to go, stopped and turned back. 'Oh, and one other thing, I have been in touch with my solicitors, *Fletcher Bowman and Archer* who seem quite eager to take on the case should we be unable to come to an agreement. Good morning, Miss Blenkinsop.' And this time he did leave, smiling his way out through the general office, down in the lift, through reception and out into the sunny square; but the smile disappeared when he realised he still hadn't a clue as to where the Caswells, mother and daughter were to be found.

# Chapter Twenty

Courtney Burrows, an anxious man with little to occupy himself, gazed out of his office window. It was raining heavily, visibility down to practically nothing, so no golf course was seductively beckoning though he could have spent time in the clubhouse he supposed but somehow he didn't feel like that. Would he anyway find convivial company there on a day like this? Only the diehard drinkers most of whom were died in the wool bores, especially one, Eric Smallpiece, who was bound to be there only too eager to bend his ears with inconsequential chatter about subjects which not only was he not interested in but which he knew nothing about.

Suddenly he seemed to find his vast office had miraculously shrunk and was giving him a distinct feeling of claustrophobia so he decided to call in on the set of *The return to Batani* and watch the filming for a while. It was high time he made his presence felt and who knows? There might be a new ingénue, a budding starlet he could pass the time of day with to momentarily forget his troubles. That bastard Wagner had been dropping unpleasant hints every time he had seen him and Courtney had the distinct feeling his time was running out. This was what you got when you mixed it with the Americans but was it really his fault or was he merely following in his father's footsteps?

Vlad the Impaler was infamous for the number of hopefuls who passed through his hands and between his sheets, the poor deluded mites hoping for better things to come, like a possible starring role in his next picture, little realising they didn't stand a cat's hope in hell but prepared nevertheless to give their all in great expectations. Some of them took part in somewhat risqué scenes being unaware they were filmed for his private collection. His nickname was a result of his priapic proclivities.

Scheduled for the day was a scene that started off with a drunken German officer dallying with a nubile young native girl while a couple of others hung around to dress the set in decorative fashion, so there was every chance there would be at least one to take Courtney's fancy. The scene would then continue with a captured Troy, strikingly handsome in his dirty dishevelled state, shirt virtually torn off in order to show that lithe muscular torso and sexy nipples, being brought roughly in by two brutish German soldiers, one of whom during rehearsal had been just a mite too familiar and had to be reprimanded by the first assistant, not so much verbally but with a cough and an admonishing finger. The officer would then not too gently push away his temporary inamorata in order to turn his attentions to Troy, possibly with a bit of subtle innuendo as to his true swinish Hun intentions, rather like the actor playing a soldier.

There was no red light showing above the heavy studio door so Courtney opened it and swaggered in to witness chaos as technicians went about their business and the assistant director was yelling to little effect for them to keep the noise down, there was supposed to be a rehearsal in progress.

Vlad didn't seem too perturbed but seated in the canvas chair with his name stencilled on the back was supposedly looking over his script. What he was actually doing was fantasising over a number of photographs submitted by nubile young actresses, or would-be actresses hoping for an interview or an audition.

Now and again he glanced up to note what was happening before looking down again, returning to his world of lascivious yearnings and readjusting himself.

Courtney moved up to him and coughed to attract his attention but due to the noise the cough was inaudible so he laid a hand on Vlad's shoulder, gave it a little squeeze and the director, after giving a distinct jump having been taken by surprise, looked up, indicated the vacant chair next to him and Courtney took it. This one had *Anton Wagner* stencilled on the back but Anton hadn't been near the set for days. He was far to busy doing other things. Holly, forever passing a pretty girl going into the office as she made her way out, had to be continually ordered not to return for a while so that he could possibly get on with important matters that didn't concern her. The man seemed insatiable: insatiable or impotent, one or the other, and it wasn't too long of course before the whole studio was joking about it including Ernest J. who joked to himself that maybe he ought to lend the man his pump. He was sorry there was no one he could share that particular joke with. What was it with these elderly randy leprechauns that they couldn't let a piece of skirt go by without wanting to rip it off?

At the moment, as the unit's temporary gopher, Ernest J. was on his way to make-up to call the film's star. Ernest's mind was as usual filled with two things, his screenplay and William Harrowfield. For once he wasn't dawdling but fairly skipping along, not wanting to be away from the set too long.

Since that day in Epping Forest Ernest, except for a brief meeting in the dining room during which he breathlessly gave William his warning, he had been denied any further sight of him but today, due to more absenteeism as there really did seem to be a positive flu epidemic going around, the object of his musings was working in the studio! He might not get much of a chance as far as any actual contact was concerned but at least now and again he could adore from a distance and maybe smoulder with a glance in return.

He had decided that by the end of his movie, the boy Robin

would have achieved adulthood and be a real man's man, possibly even go to war, to lie wounded and, as he lay dying would be comforted in the arms of his best friend, a bit of the Nelson touch. He wouldn't actually say "Kiss me, Robin" but it would get that close. He would do the rewrite this very evening.

'How's it going?' Courtney asked.

In reply Vlad lifted a thumb. He wasn't going to talk over the noise. The assistant was fast losing his voice as it was.

'On schedule are we?' He pronounced it the American way, 'skedule.'

Vlad raised his thumb again but, had he been Pinocchio, his nose would have grown by a good six inches. Courtney looked around, already growing bored and wondering why he had come and if he should stay.

The set consisted of three ramshackle walls painted to look like distressed wood and in one of which was an open doorway and a window frame with a jungle backdrop. Furniture and props were minimal consisting of a grubby camp bed with mosquito net, a shelf with a couple of books not to be looked at too closely, they were not only anachronistic but were in English, a wooden table and chairs, a bottle presumably of German beer vintage 1914 and what looked like a giant phallus but which was actually a sausage, and a knife with which to slice it. This was an essential prop which would aid Troy when escaping from capture. The elderly German officer, unshaven, fat and florid, sat on one of the chairs, his tunic off and slung over the back of the chair, shirt open and a girl on his lap. Make-up was busy spraying him with sweat, the heat of the studio obviously, despite the fat, not producing quite enough. The girl, avoiding the sweat spray was rehearsing the upcoming scene by being thoroughly coquettish. Soon she would be doing a proper love scene with the handsome young American star, Troy Tyler and she wanted to make sure she got it absolutely right, couldn't wait in fact, who knows to where it might lead? So in the meantime, despite finding him somewhat unattractive, she practised on her German officer who was getting quite horny from all the attention and was hoping they would start shooting soon before he did. He sent an appealing glance towards the camera but nobody around it seemed in the least bit interested in going forward as they stood around chatting among themselves and there was no one on the sound boom. And then Vlad suddenly came to life, his voice like a foghorn as he got to his feet and strode onto the floor.

'Right, what's the hold up? What's the problem? Come on! Come on!' He clapped his hands. 'Let's have some action here. You think you've got all day to swan around? QUIET!'

There was immediate hush. After the noise of so many voices, hammering, sawing, yelling instructions, the studio was as silent as a tomb. Nobody moved. They were as motionless as the buried figures of Pompeii. The quiet couldn't last long of course. The first assistant rediscovered his voice.

'Stand by, studio. We're going for a take.'

He looked like a pleading lapdog in Vlad's direction and the great man, satisfied discipline had been restored, nodded and returned to his seat, got up again to have a quiet word with his actors, after all he was supposed to be the director so he had better start doing a bit of directing, even if it was only a bit of meaningless flannel. Once again everyone stood by. The clapper boy, his board chalked up, was ready; focus puller and camera operator were on the job as was the sound boom operator and engineer, both with their head phones on.

'QUIET!'

'Stand by,'

'Roll camera.'

'Speed.'

'Sound.'

'Mark it.'

'Return to Batani, scene ninety three, take one.' It came out loud and clear. Clap went the board and the boy scurried out of shot.

'Action!'

The German officer stroked the girl's hair and pulled her towards him for a kiss.

'Mein liebling,' he drooled, before their rubbery lips actually met. This script was packed with meaningful dialogue.

Then there was silence.

'CUT!'

Vlad was out of his seat in a flash and in the middle of the floor looking around in wild exasperation. 'Shit! Where are the Germen soldiers? Where are the bloody soldiers? They're supposed to be bringing in Troy. What the fuck's going on here?'

Two sheepish German soldiers appeared at the door. 'He's not here,' the braver of the two said, not the one who had been slightly indiscreet with Troy who had responded with a sideways glance and a raised eyebrow.

'God damn it! Has he been called?' Vlad looked around, his glare lighting on Ernest. This had happened to Ernest before, in particular with that over-hyped cretin Cord Wainer. Why, oh why, can't these bloody stars do what's wanted of them? Why do they have to behave like... well, like stars? Fortunately, before Ernest could receive a right bollocking in front of the entire studio, Troy appeared, smiling his Colgate smile all around and apparently contrite and apologetic and was immediately forgiven, even by Ernest. After all, if it hadn't been for Troy's tardiness in arriving there would not have been that brief moment of intimacy with William Harrowfield when Ernest heaved a sigh of relief and, to his utter joy, spotted William looking at him. He pulled a "that was a narrow escape" type face and received a sympathetic smile in return that simply made his day.

'Right, stand by. We're going again.'

'Hold it! Hold it! What's the matter now?'

The girl had got off the officer's lap, swaying slightly on her little bare feet, and looking something the worse for wear. Obviously the heat and the sweat had got to her at last.

'I'm sorry... sorry... I don't feel very well. Could I have a glass of water please?'

'Somebody fetch her a glass of water and make it snappy.' Vlad was in no mood to be sympathetic with hysterical starlets. He picked up his script and pretended to be engrossed in it while they waited. He was in no mood to go back to the photographs.

Courtney decided, as far as he was concerned, that was enough filming for the day. He got up, gave Vlad another squeeze of the shoulder and set off to leave the studio. Then he changed his mind. Obviously as nothing was going to be happening for a while, not until the girl recovered anyway, he decided to take a walk behind the set and maybe chat up one of the decorative ones waiting there. It was then that he was brought up short in sudden shock as he thought he was seeing a ghost.

In front of him, not a yard away, was the face of the girl he had seduced and abandoned all those years ago. There could be no mistaking it, especially the eyes. They were her eyes, her beautiful Oriental eyes, but they were giving nothing away. For a long moment the two men stood facing each other. If Courtney could recover his power of speech what would he say? But, mouth open, he remained trembling and speechless. He could feel his heart racing. He wondered for a moment if he was going to faint. Then a disembodied voice called out.

'William! Where's that bloody pup?'

Courtney looked down and saw that the young man was carrying a small lamp.

'Coming right up!' William yelled back at the disembodied voice, looking up towards the grid as he did so. Then he looked back at Courtney. 'Excuse me, sir.' He said and, as Courtney dutifully stepped, or rather staggered aside, almost as though he had been physically pushed, William moved on to deliver the pup.

Courtney stood for a long moment where he was. He was trembling quite violently and had to lean against the studio wall before he recovered enough to shakily make his way out. All the way back to his office he was asking questions. Was it his son? Yes. Definitely. Definitely! He was the spitting image of his mother. Being called William endorsed it. His son was working in Breconfield Studios. Why? How long had he been there and what were his intentions? Was he there to make mischief? Blackmail maybe? Or something worse? There to avenge his mother for the way she had been treated? A picture of Jimmy Harrowfield flashed through his mind. Was it Jimmy who put him up to this, and why? He had to make sure the boy was who he believed him to be.

He paused at his secretary's desk in the outer office. 'Shirley, I want the names of all the electricians working in the studio. Get them for me please.'

Shirley Dorland looked up from her typewriter and reached for the phone. Of all the secretaries in the studio she was the eldest, having been there since her boss's father's time. She never queried any of the demands made on her; just carried them out.

In his office, with shaking hands, Courtney poured himself a stiff brandy before seating himself behind his desk. He lit a cigar. There would be a wait till the names came through. He would just have to be patient.

S eated once more in her mansion flat, Thornton was taking tea with Esther van Clef, Mrs Huntington, nee Fartfooker. He didn't know why he had been invited, his efforts on her behalf were over, done with, and the conversation was about ordinary everyday mundane things until she came to the point.

'Am I correct in believing you met Jimmy Harrowfield?' She asked.

'Yes.'

'How did you find him?'

'I looked for him and he was there.' He grinned. Esther was not amused. 'Sorry. It's a corny old gag anyway.' He accepted the cup and saucer his stony-faced hostess handed to him.

'Cake?' She demanded as if a refusal would be considered an insult or the height of bad manners.

'Yes please.' It was Battenberg again; obviously her favourite, or maybe she had bought a job lot at the local supermarket as their "best before" date approached.

She was still hatchet-faced so he thought he had better try and put things right without making another stupid crack.

'Jimmy seems to be in the pink and quite happy with his station in life. He doesn't appear to hanker after the good old days as it were.'

'I'm glad, very glad. And William?'

'William's terrific. No other words for it. As a son he would make any man proud. He saved my bacon you know.'

'So I heard.'

'Did you now? News certainly travels fast in the film business.' He wondered how she could have heard it. This time it certainly couldn't have been from Ernest J.

'I had tea with Holly at *Fortnum's*.'

'Ah.'

'And, at the same time, or just before William was saving your life, I believe you were assured by Mel's killer that it was indeed Mel Preston who killed Charmaine.'

'Yes. The police are now in full knowledge of the facts so you don't have to worry about twenty years slipping by.'

'Yes.' She sipped her tea.

He'd done it again. What was wrong with his tongue that it seemed to have a life of its own? He really must learn to control it.

'Why is William working at Breconfield?' She put down her cup.

Thornton shrugged. 'Why not? It's a job he's qualified for.'

'Hmn… He's not… he's not thinking of doing anything rash, is he? Stupid?'

'I wouldn't know about that. I don't think so, but if you really want to know you had better ask him yourself though I don't think, if he is intending to do anything rash, he would tell you.'

'Perhaps not. More tea?'

'Thank you, no.'

She lifted the cosy and preceded, fingers protected from the heat of course, to pour herself another cup.

'Is William working at the studios what you wanted to see me about?'

'You can surely understand, Thornton, why it would worry me. When you think of the history of the two families and how badly treated Jimmy has been what do you suppose will happen between William and his father? Will he do something awful that will break Jimmy's heart? The man has seen enough trouble from that direction.'

'Whatever reaction William might have with his father, Esther, there is nothing you and I can do about it.'

'You could have a word with him: pre-empt anything foolish.'

'I don't think so. Events must simply take their course. No amount of advice would make any difference. He would just resent the interference. Sorry. In the words of a popular song, what must be must be, che será será. Now I have a question you may be able to answer. Did you know Caswell had been married and there is a daughter? A handicapped daughter?'

'I knew about the wife. She was an actress before her marriage. I didn't know about the daughter until I read the obituaries. In what way is she handicapped?'

'I don't know. Evidently it's because of meningitis as a child.'

'Meningitis, yes. Very nasty, very nasty.' Esther shook her head in commiseration.

'I need to find them. They might not even be in London: could be living anywhere, John O'Groats for all I know.'

'Well I'm sorry but I cannot help you there. No, wait a moment. There is absolutely no reason why he should have done so of course but supposing Caswell told Charmaine about his wife and child, maybe she wrote something down somewhere. Yes, she kept an address book and a diary. I'll fetch them both. Strange man, Caswell, but then writers are all a bit weird don't you think? Not like normal people at all.'

'Like actors you mean.'

She gave him a wry look. 'In the meantime, Thornton, eat your cake like a good boy.'

Without a word Shirley laid the paper on the desk in front of her boss.

'Thank you,' he said but made no move to pick it up. 'Is there anything else?'

'Not at the moment, Shirley. Thank you.'

She left the room, wondering what it was all about as she settled back behind her typewriter and took a bite of her *Kit-Kat*.

It was a while before he could pick up the paper with hands still shaking and go through the list of names but there it was – Peterson, William. He remembered his visit to the orphanage all those years ago when he discovered the name of William's adoptive parents. He never followed it up but now it would seem his past had caught up with him at last. Everything was falling to pieces. What was the point of it all? What was the pointy of carrying on? Courtney was a broken man. There was nothing left for him. He had ordered Preston's murder, he was involved with mobsters. The only future he could foresee, if the likes of Wagner didn't do for him first, was a very long prison sentence. He remembered how his mother used to say, "Your sins will find you out." He got up and went to pour himself another stiff brandy.

Returning to his desk, he lifted his telephone and waited for her to answer. She had to wipe the chocolate off her fingers first.

'Yes, Mister Burrows?'

'Shirley, make an appointment for me to see my lawyers. Better still; ask Mister Jackson to come here and for him to bring my will.'

'Yes, sir.'

He had finished his cake, in fact had helped himself to another slice, before Esther returned with a book, a *Dataday Diary* in hand. She resumed her seat before she opened it and spoke.

'You're in luck, Thornton. Caswell did mention his wife to

Charmaine and she made a note of it in her diary. I was lucky enough to find it without having to go through pages and pages, the reason being that she had put her marker ribbon on that page. I wonder why.' She shrugged. 'Well, we will never know the reason for that, just curiosity on her part maybe, but all I can tell you is that Mrs Caswell lives, or did live, in Fulham. There's no other information.'

'Thank you, Esther. It's a start anyway.'

Max Dooley was languishing safely behind bars in a Spanish prison awaiting extradition. Reg Venables was in his office puffing contentedly on his pipe and basking in reflected glory. He was without doubt a policeman sans-pareil and the highest commendation would soon be coming his way. The station would dearly love to know who his informant was but, of course, Reg wasn't letting on. If he told them who it was, he argued, his contact might take fright, go to ground, do a quick disappearing act and he would lose a valuable source of information so best to keep shtum. This was generally accepted with a sage nodding of collective heads.

Roper thought he knew who it was but, just in case he was wrong, decided to keep his mouth shut as well though he discussed it with Blodwen while she fed the new baby.

Thornton found Mrs Caswell's number in the telephone directory but halfway through dialling it he put down the phone. After all he hadn't heard from Eileen Blenkinsop and he didn't want to raise false hopes. How much time should he give before he started to rattle the lady's cage? He was debating this with himself when the phone rang. There was no hesitation this time in lifting the receiver.

'Thornton king.'

'Ah, yes... Mister King... Eileen Blenkinsop here.'

Thornton who had been lounging rather sloppily in his chair,

279

suddenly sat bolt upright. "Speak of the devil," he thought.

'Miss Blenkinsop!' Obviously there was no need at the moment to do any rattling. 'How are you this very fine morning?'

'I'm quite well thank you.'

'To what do I owe the pleasure of this call?'

'I think we should have a meeting. How does tomorrow suit you?'

'Tomorrow suits me fine. Any particular time?'

'Shall we say the usual eleven o'clock?'

'Eleven o'clock it is.'

'Good. I will see you then.'

The phone went dead.

T hornton waltzed into reception at the offices of *Centurion* in Red Lion Square and greeted the receptionist with a big smile which was not returned. She was obviously the girl who had taken umbrage with his first phone call and he hadn't been forgiven for shouting at her so he sought to pour oil on the troubled waters. He stood at her desk.

'Thornton King to see Miss Blenkinsop.'

'Yes. Take a seat please, Mister King.' She couldn't have been more frigid if she tried.

Thornton half turned away, turned back. 'What's your name?' He asked beaming what he hoped was his sexiest smile. She blushed and for a moment sat glaring at him.

'Veronica,' she said.

'And your friends call you Ronnie I suppose.'

She nodded. 'I'll tell Miss Blenkinsop you're here.'

'Thank you so much.' He wandered back to the coffee table and its magazines but before he had time to sit down Veronica called him.

'Will you go up please, Mister King?'

Thornton nodded and made for the lift. He knew she was watching him all the way. As the lift doors opened he turned and gave her another smile. This time she smiled in return.

Ensconced once again in Eileen Blenkinsop's office, having pulled up his chair to face her, Thornton noticed the pile of papers on her desk had been considerably reduced.

She had stood to greet him and was now seated again. She indicated the coffee cup on her desk.

'Can I offer you some refreshment? Coffee? Tea? Something stronger maybe?'

'No thank you. I'm fine.'

'First of all, Mister King, please let me apologise for my behaviour last time you were in this office. I guess I was just so overloaded with work and anymore at that juncture could have constituted the last straw.'

'So I presume you haven't done anything about it then.'

'On the contrary, I have been in consultation with our lawyers in L.A. and they have agreed we may have a case to answer so they have authorised me to make you an offer on behalf of your client. Have you proceeded with the injunction?'

'Not yet.'

'Well, hopefully what I have to tell you may change your mind. We would like the video distribution to go ahead.'

She gave him her version of a friendly smile but he remained somewhat po-faced.

'So the lawyers in L.A. have suggested a sum of five thousand pounds as a buy-out.' Actually they had given her a figure in dollars but five thousand was the nearest equivalent in pounds. 'How does that sound to you?'

'Interesting but do go on.'

'You mean what is in the kitty for past royalty payments?'

Thornton nodded.

'The sum of compensation they reckon at fifty thousand... pounds. Would you consider that reasonable?'

'More or less, a little less than more,' and Thornton smiled. 'I take it this is also a one-off deal that will completely put a stop to any future payments.'

It was Eileen's turn to nod.

'In which case raise it slightly, include tax and it's a deal, providing of course that Mrs Caswell agrees and I don't really see any reason why she shouldn't. So shall we say fifty-five grand which together with the buy-out for the video comes to as nice a round figure as you could want and, let's face it, another five thousand to *Centurion* is small change but to Mrs Caswell and her daughter it means a great deal. Is it agreed or do you have to get confirmation?'

'No, it's agreed.' She opened a folder that lay before her and took out a document. 'This is a contract; it needs only the amounts inserted. Would you like me then to send it to your lawyers?'

'No, I can go over it myself.'

'Very well.' She returned the contract to the folder, got up and, taking it with her, headed for the door. 'I'll have it typed up right now and you can take it with you. It will just require Mrs Caswell's signature, witnessed, as you will see. Do you have her bank details?'

'I'm afraid not but I can soon get them.'

'Good, then the money can be transferred. I won't be but a moment.' She disappeared into the outer office. Thornton sat very still, hardly believing what he had achieved.

# Chapter Twenty One

Thornton and Holly were seated in Thornton's local; a pub Holly had never taken to, in fact was positively averse to. It was dingy, it was drab, it smelled of cigarette smoke and stale beer, she would not have gone to the toilet in a million years no matter how urgent the need, and it had a succession of young Irish barmen who never lasted more than a month and who always seemed to have dirty fingernails if they hadn't bitten them to the quick. Somehow after visiting it she invariably felt in need of a shower with lashings of shampoo, conditioner, gel and steaming hot water.

'I really cannot understand why you patronise this place', Holly grumbled yet again, looking around for the umpteenth time and shaking her head before transferring her gaze to the glass in her hand and examining it minutely for the slightest evidence of encrusted dirt.

'It's my local.'

'Your local what? Seems to me it's more like a social club for the local call girls.' She looked around again but could spy only two who could possibly be described as ladies of the night.

'Call them call girls if you wish but I know some very nice ones.'

'Do you?'

'Yes I do and one day I'm going to write a book about them.'

'Thornton, your head is in the stars do you know that? If it weren't for the fact that I am a lady of discretion I would say it's up your arse. Write a book! You can't even sign your name.'

'Neither could Shakespeare. Well, not properly anyway. What's got into you today, miss high and mighty? You're being most obstreperous do you know that?'

Holly laughed. 'Don't take it to heart, Thornton. Actually I am in a jolly good mood or I wouldn't have agreed to meet you in this dump of dumps. Cheers!'

'And what, if I may be so bold as to enquire, has put you in this jolly good mood?'

'I am no longer in the employment of Breconfield Studios.'

'Since when?'

'Since I walked out.' Having decided her glass was clean and she was not likely to pick up anything nasty, she sipped her drink.

'What happened?'

'Oh, a couple of things happened that might just be construed as accidental,' she put down her glass, 'but something deep down inside me said that was not the case and it was time to leave before there was another close shave, so I used Wagner as my excuse, threatening to sue them for sexual harassment and walked out. I didn't leave in my car just in case. Well you never know do you? I called a cab.'

'Did you get what you wanted?'

'I did. Thanks to my training in the ministry you will appreciate I got enough to put a number of dodgy gentlemen, including Mister Wagner, behind bars both here and in the states. It will take a little time though. You know with what snail like slithering the law goes about its business but, for me, it's back to Whitehall where my honour it would seem is quite safe. How about you? What have you been up to as you are no longer in the employ of the redoubtable Esther Fartfooker.' Holly laughed. 'I cannot believe that was her name, Thornton. You made it up.'

'Scouts' honour.'

'I'm not surprised she changed it.'

'She changed it when she married.'

'Oh, yes, of course.'

'This is what I have been up to.' He had his document case with him and now, having opened it, he produced the *Centurion* contract and handed it to her. Holly raised both eyebrows before looking up. She looked down again and up again before handing the document back to him. He slipped it into the case.

'Congratulations, Thornton. Oh yes indeed, many congratulations.'

'Thank you.'

'That really is a terrific piece of work. I take back every snide remark I've ever made and truly stand in awe of your capabilities.'

'I never know when to take you seriously, Holly Day.' There was the sound of an excited bark and a small dog by the name of Bijou entered followed by his mistress. 'Oh, look, there's my good friend Carlotta.' Thornton waved. 'Would you like to meet her?'

'Some other time, Thornton, some other time.'

T ownmead Road in Fulham winds its way more or less following the course of the river. It is a long road of small terraced houses down one side. On the opposite bank there looms a power station, enormous, brutal and ugly.

Thornton had telephoned to make an appointment with Mrs Caswell and his taxi dropped him off outside the house. She was already at the front door which opened almost onto the street waiting for him. She smiled tentatively as the taxi pulled away and Thornton made the three steps between the gate and the front door. They shook hands before she stepped aside and ushered him in with a gesture. He found himself in a small front room and the first words she spoke were, 'Can I offer you a cup of tea?'

"Good grief," Thornton thought, "I really ought to be in the tea business; next to politics, law, and banking, that's definitely where the money lies." Out loud he politely refused the offer, the next being for him to take a seat which he did in a rather shabby old wing chair. She took another.

'I'm sorry that chair's not more comfortable,' she apologised. 'It's so old. Desperately needs respringing and re-upholstering.'

'Then why don't you get it done? I know a very good man though, come to think of it, there are a few of them in the King's Road, aren't there? I passed their shops in the taxi on the way here.'

She didn't answer, but looked down at the fingers that were being nervously entwined on her lap. Thornton noticed she still wore a plain gold wedding band. She was a woman of medium height with a slightly bulky figure but she could only be described as *jolie laide,* not that she was unattractive.

The girl he had worked hard for was seated in the corner of the room. Unlike her mother she was very slender and, if it hadn't been for the ravages of her childhood illness that left her with a slight squint and it seemed an ever open mouth, she would have been beautiful. It was no wonder Caswell thought her a gift. She was rocking with slight movements: too and fro, too and fro, too and fro.

'What, Mister King, do you think an upholsterer would charge for doing up a chair like that and, more important, no matter what he charged how would it be paid for?'

She had thought him extremely insensitive to have made that remark when he must surely be aware of her situation.

'*Centurion* will pay for it.'

'I beg your pardon?'

'Mrs Caswell, I didn't explain fully on the telephone what this visit is all about.' He was playing Father Christmas, the Easter Bunny and the Good Fairy all in one and enjoying it. 'Please take a look at this. I know I said I had something important to tell you but this will explain it all.' He had once again taken the contract from his document case and stretched out to hand it

286

to her. She took it with trembling hands, got up and reached for her glasses on the mantelpiece, put them on and sat silently reading it through before she took off her glasses and looked up at him.

'Does this mean what it says it means?'

'It does, once you put your signature to it and it is witnessed.'

She was crying silently and unable to say anything more.

'So you see, you can get this very uncomfortable chair done, or, if the fancy takes you, even get yourself a new one. And if I may be so presumptuous as to give you a word of advice: that might seem like a great deal of money at this moment, in fact it is a great deal but there is no guarantee it will last as long as needed and I suggest you take some sound financial guidance. I have a very good friend whose father is a banker and I am sure he will be happy to take that on. I'll get Holly to speak to him and to open an account and the money can be transferred direct. When it's safely stowed away I suggest you take Dora to the seaside for a much deserved holiday before you think of anything else.'

'Thank you, Mister King.' It came out in a whisper and then much stronger when she turned to her daughter. 'Dora, say thank you to Mister King.'

'Yak hew,' Dora said.

Thornton smiled. 'There's no need for thanks, Mrs Caswell, I've enjoyed myself. And now I wouldn't say no to that cup of tea.'

# Chapter Twenty Two

I t must surely be lunchtime Thornton thought and looked at his watch. Yes, it most definitely was. He had got absolutely nowhere with the crossword puzzle so tossed the paper aside and got up to leave the office. He thought a big helping of cod in crispy batter, chips, and maybe a helping of mushy peas plus thinly sliced white bread and butter as only a chippy could serve would go down a treat.

He clattered down the stairs, paused to look in his mailbox, it was empty, and moved on out into the street. He would get the first edition of *The Evening Standard* to read while he was eating. Maybe *Grey of Fallodin* was running again and he would back her this time but she had been in good form lately and the odds would be considerably shortened.

For the second time he was brought up with a shock when he saw on the billboard in large letters the ominous headline –

STRANGE DEATH AT FILM STUDIOS.

His first thoughts were for William and he took a copy of the paper, stopping to read where he stood. Thank God, it wasn't William… It was his father! This was immediately followed by the thought that William could have had a hand in it. He literally scuttled along to the chippy, ordered his meal and sat at a table to read.

*Late Thursday night a fire was discovered in an office at the Breconfield Film Studios. It was located in the office of the Chief Executive Officer, Mister Courtney Burrows II and the office had no smoke alarm so the fire was blazing fiercely when discovered and took some considerable time to be extinguished. Three fire crews were sent to the studios and, when finally able to enter the office, they discovered the body of Mister Burrows at his desk. It would appear he had been drinking quite heavily and must have fallen asleep or passed out. He was smoking a cigar at the time which it is believed fell into the waste paper basket beneath his desk so starting the blaze. The police say there is no evidence of foul play although at this stage they are keeping an open mind and will await the results of a post mortem.*

*It would appear there is a positive jinx on the studios as there have been three murders committed on the premises, firstly the murder of the gate keeper and a young secretary, Charmaine Carmichael, granddaughter of the famous film star Spring van Clef who told our interviewer she was deeply distressed by Mister Burrows' untimely death, followed so soon after the death of the producer Mel Preston… Everyone at the studios is understandably in deep shock.*

*Mister Burrows leaves a wife but no children.*

Indeed they would be in shock, Thornton thought as his plate of cod and chips was set down steaming in front of him and he put the paper aside, and the papers haven't twigged about William but then why should they unless they troubled themselves with some deep investigative journalism? He noted that neither Esther nor Jimmy had been interviewed but that would probably come later. What really happened in that office he wondered as he salted his chips but before he could cogitate any further he was greeted by –

'Mister King,' and he looked up to find an anxious looking William standing by the table. He slipped into a seat opposite.

'Talk of the devil. I was just thinking about you. You're like a Jack in the box, William, popping up when least expected. How did you know where to find me?'

'I went to your office and you weren't there of course but when I came out I saw a lady in the street. She was walking a little dog.'

'Ah, yes, Bijou.'

'She gave me the usual spiel, you know, about having a good time and that,' he grinned, 'and when I said no she asked was I looking for someone and told me this is where you might be, either here or in your local.'

'Help yourself to a chip.'

'Thank you.' He did so, dipping it in ketchup.

'I'm sorry to read about your father.' He tapped the paper with his middle finger.

'Yes. Is that why you were thinking of me? That's what I wanted to talk to you about; I can't really say I'm sorry. So he was my father but we never knew each other, so what I… well I wanted you to know, if there is anything fishy about his death, Mister King, it wasn't me.'

'You came into town to tell me that?'

'I suspected you would immediately jump to that conclusion but, believe me, Mister King, parricide is not in my nature. This is no modern Oedipus you see sitting here though at times in the past I have to, in all honesty, admit I did think of it. But I assure you violence of any kind is not for me and I bumped into him recently at the studio and thought he looked a very sad man.'

'The chickens will eventually come home to roost as they say. How is your grand-dad?'

'He hasn't said anything but I think he might feel the wheel has come full circle and that it was somehow, as you've just said, inevitable.' He shrugged. 'He'll just get on with the rest of his life.'

'He's a good man.'

'Yes, he is. Another reason why I wanted to talk to you is,

strange as this might seem, I had a visitor from a firm of lawyers and it seems my father has left half his estate to me in his will...'

'Congratulations.'

'The other half goes to his wife of course. Now I knew nothing about this. It has come as a complete surprise but, should there be any suspicion of... of...'

'Murder.'

'Yes... well... would I be a suspect because of it?'

'I shouldn't think so. Have you an alibi? Where were you the night of the fire?'

'I was with a girl.'

'Will she testify to that?'

'I don't think so.' He bit his lip. 'She's a married woman.'

Thornton shook his head. He wanted to say like father like son but instead all he said was, 'Fancy some fish and chips?'

William nodded.

'Good. Well then, I suppose that's a wrap... wouldn't you say?'

www.ingramcontent.com/pod-product-compliance
Lightning Source LLC
Chambersburg PA
CBHW030032180626
46810CB00001B/327